THE EXAMINER

Also from Janice Hallett and Atria Books

The Appeal

The Twyford Code

The Mysterious Case of the Alperton Angels

The Christmas Appeal

THE
EXAMINER

Janice Hallett

ATRIA BOOKS

NEW YORK   LONDON   TORONTO   SYDNEY   NEW DELHI

ATRIA
BOOKS

An Imprint of Simon & Schuster, LLC
1230 Avenue of the Americas
New York, NY 10020

First Atria Books hardcover edition September 2024

Simon & Schuster: Celebrating 100 Years of Publishing in 2024

For information about special discounts for bulk purchases, please contact Simon & Schuster Special Sales at 1-866-506-1949 or business@simonandschuster.com.

The Simon & Schuster Speakers Bureau can bring authors to your live event. For more information or to book an event, contact the Simon & Schuster Speakers Bureau at 1-866-248-3049 or visit our website at www.simonspeakers.com.

Manufactured in the United States of America

1 3 5 7 9 10 8 6 4 2

Library of Congress Cataloging-in-Publication Data

Names: Hallett, Janice, author.
Title: The examiner / Janice Hallett.
Description: New York : Atria Books, 2024.
Identifiers: LCCN 2024009443 (print) | LCCN 2024009444 (ebook) |
ISBN 9781668023426 (hardcover) | ISBN 9781668023433 (paperback) |
ISBN 9781668023440 (ebook)
Subjects: LCGFT: Detective and mystery fiction. | Novels.
Classification: LCC PR6108.A4955 E93 2024 (print) |
LCC PR6108.A4955 (ebook) | DDC 823/.92--dc23/eng/20240308
LC record available at https://lccn.loc.gov/2024009443
LC ebook record available at https://lccn.loc.gov/2024009444

ISBN 978-1-6680-2342-6
ISBN 978-1-6680-2344-0 (ebook)

For Alison and Samantha,
my oldest and wisest friends

THE
EXAMINER

Dear reader,

I need to oversee the final grades for a master's degree at a prestigious university. Despite access to all the documents I require and some I wouldn't normally expect to see, I find myself unable to grade the submissions. In fact I can't quite work out what happened on that course at all. It was either something so disturbing I can't even bring myself to write it down, or, as the police seem to think, it was nothing.

I'd appreciate your help. Please read the enclosed and let me know. For context, it includes an academic year calendar marked with key dates, the official guidelines that govern our marking process, and my correspondence with the college admins.

Be aware that if my worst fears are true, then one of the students on this course is dead.

Thank you,
The Examiner

Janice Hallett

Royal Hastings Academic Year 2023–24

Assignment 2 deadline

SEPTEMBER

SUN	MON	TUE	WED	THU	FRI	SAT
					1	2
3	4	5	6	7	8	9
10	11	12	13	14	15	16
17	18	19	20	21	22	23
24	25	(26)	27	28	29	30

First day of autumn term   *Pitch prep meeting*

OCTOBER

SUN	MON	TUE	WED	THU	FRI	SAT
1	2	3	4	5	6	7
8	9	10	11	12	13	14
15	16	17	18	(19)	20	21
22	23	24	25	26	27	28
29	30	31				

Deadline assignment 1

NOVEMBER

SUN	MON	TUE	WED	THU	FRI	SAT
			1	2	(3)	4
5	6	7	8	9	10	11
12	13	14	15	16	(17)	18
19	20	21	22	23	24	25
26	27	28	29	30		

Assignment 3 deadline

DECEMBER

SUN	MON	TUE	WED	THU	FRI	SAT
					1	2
3	4	5	(6)	7	8	9
10	11	(12)	13	14	(15)	16
17	18	19	20	21	22	23
24	25	26	27	28	29	30
31						

Pitch meeting at RD8   *Last day of term*

JANUARY

SUN	MON	TUE	WED	THU	FRI	SAT
	1	2	3	4	5	6
7	(8)	9	10	11	12	13
14	15	(16)	(17)	18	19	20
21	22	23	24	25	26	27
28	29	30	31			

1st day of spring term   *Easter Monday*   *Trip to Somerset*

FEBRUARY

SUN	MON	TUE	WED	THU	FRI	SAT
				1	2	3
4	5	6	7	8	9	10
11	12	13	14	15	16	17
18	19	20	21	(22)	23	24
25	26	27	28	29		

Assignment deadline

MARCH

SUN	MON	TUE	WED	THU	FRI	SAT
					1	2
3	4	5	6	7	8	9
10	11	12	13	14	15	16
17	18	19	20	21	(22)	23
24	25	26	27	28	(29)	30
31						

Last day of term   *Good Friday*

APRIL

SUN	MON	TUE	WED	THU	FRI	SAT
	(1)	2	3	4	5	6
7	8	9	10	11	12	13
14	(15)	16	17	18	(19)	20
21	22	23	24	(25)	26	27
28	29	30				

1st day of summer term   *Assignment 5 deadline*   *RD8 visit studio*

MAY

SUN	MON	TUE	WED	THU	FRI	SAT
			1	2	3	4
5	6	7	8	9	10	11
12	13	14	15	16	(17)	18
19	20	21	22	23	24	25
26	27	28	(29)	(30)	31	

Long essay deadline   *Assignment 6 deadline*

Big RD8 launch event!! and final day of MMAMs course

JUNE

SUN	MON	TUE	WED	THU	FRI	SAT
						1
2	3	4	5	6	(7)	8
9	10	11	12	13	14	15
16	17	18	19	20	21	22
23	24	25	26	27	28	29
30						

Last day of summer term

To: Matilda Ricci
From: Ben Sketcher
Date: May 30, 2024
Subject: As discussed

Tilda,

I've gathered together everything I think is relevant. This includes the coursework, final essays, and tutor reports I downloaded from Central, plus everything I could get hold of from the Doodle message board, email cache, diaries, and chat groups.

After our first message exchange today, I've placed everything in chronological order from when they started the course last year.

Ben

Message group: 2024 Examiners, May 30, 2024

Ben Sketcher

Anyone else read the Multimedia Art MA submissions yet?

Tilda Ricci

Hello Ben. Who are you?

Ben Sketcher

Sorry, should introduce myself. I'm from Central. Your external examiner.

Karen Carpenter

Ooh-er! Sounds rude!

Ben Sketcher

External examiners are appointed from a separate college, Karen—in my case, Goldcrofts—to oversee the grading of courses otherwise marked internally. This verifies that no over- or under-marking has taken place.

Karen Carpenter

I know. Just being mad ol' me!

Tilda Ricci

No, I haven't read the submissions yet, but sounds joyous. Will probably read tomorrow.

Ben Sketcher

Couldn't sleep, so went through these submissions last night. The whole thing is odd.

Tilda Ricci

It's a revamped MA. We've had to overhaul our art courses and qualifications, make them workplace-relevant, employer-friendly, etc.

Karen Carpenter

Not so airy-fairy.

Tilda Ricci

Promote logical problem-solving as well as creative solutions. The department has been drastically reduced and all our Fine Art MAs have been discontinued. Of course there'll be hiccups during the transition, but Gela will soon knock any corners off!

Ben Sketcher

The tutor, Gela Nathaniel. Do you know her?

Tilda Ricci

Oh yes, she's a stalwart of Royal Hastings. She's devised and taught our postgrad art degrees for many years.

Ben Sketcher

I asked the tech department to retrieve what they could from Doodle. I'm sending you the group's messages so you know what they were discussing behind Gela's back.

Tilda Ricci

I'm sure everything's fine.

Ben Sketcher

Nonetheless, please give me a shout when you've read. I don't want to sound alarmist. I may be mistaken. But I can't help thinking something awful has happened.

Ben Sketcher

Let me clarify that. Something awful *may* have happened, and if it did, then everyone else is covering it up.

Royal Hastings, University of London
Multimedia Art MA (Full-Time Program) 2023/4

Notes for External Examiners

This course is designed to bridge the gap between creative-arts education and the workplace.

It is examined on a **portfolio** of coursework, both practical and written. This **must** include a **long essay** on the **final project**. Coursework should demonstrate a clear progression, improvement, and application of learning.

For the **final project** students are commissioned by an industry sponsor to devise and produce a bespoke art installation, with multimedia elements, to a precise brief and budget. Students must collaborate to research and create a work that best meets the sponsor's brief within practical limitations and the timescale given. This process is intended to emulate the roles played and the challenges faced by real-world creative professionals.

The "long essay" is a **separate** work documenting and exploring the project from an **individual** point of view. Students are encouraged to be creative in their execution of the long essay, but not at the expense of a full and clear account. Given the collaborative nature of the course, this is each student's opportunity to demonstrate their **personal** approach to the brief and to evaluate their experience working as part of the team. They are encouraged to identify where the project succeeded and failed, and to detail any learnings that can be taken forward into the workplace.

Students are marked first on the progression they make during the course as a whole. Second, on their problem-solving skills and approach to change within a dynamic environment. And, finally, on their understanding of and adaptation to the opportunities and limitations of **teamwork**.

Royal Hastings, University of London
New Student Info: Using Doodle

Doodle is the intranet and messaging system used by Royal Hastings' students and staff. All new students must register in the week **before** their course starts. You will need your email address, mobile-phone number, and unique Student Reference Code to set up a Doodle profile. You are welcome to get Doodling with your coursemates as soon as you register on the site. Doodle keeps all digital communications within the remit of the college and protects all parties in the event of a dispute. If necessary, admin staff will help you set up your free account via the Doodle app on your phone and laptop or desktop computer.

Doodle may be used for the following:

Message boards:
There is a main message board for your course and year. All students and staff may post or start new threads at any time. Check Doodle every day to see notices and discussion topics from your tutor, admin staff, or fellow students.

Private messages and emails:
Contact staff and students directly or set up private chat groups.

Diary:
The diary and calendar function helps you manage your coursework deadlines. In addition, you may keep a private record of your thoughts each day. Many students find this helps with their mental health, as it is a record of how you feel over a period of time. Each diary entry may only be amended on the day. After midnight, the previous day's entry is locked and cannot be altered.

Coursework submission:
Written coursework may be submitted via Doodle, with the exception of some final essays and practical work that must be handed in at the admin office.

Royal Hastings does not tolerate bullying or discrimination on its campus, nor will it do so on Doodle. Users are encouraged to report antisocial behavior to their tutor or admin staff.

Doodle is designed to be fully accessible to all students, but if there is anything we can do to improve it, please use the "suggestions" button on the home page.

Happy Doodling.

Doodle message group MMAM(FTP), September 21, 2023:

Jem Badhuri
Hello! Great to meet everyone. There's six on the course, right?

Jonathan Danners
Hi Jem. Yes, there were six names on Gela's email, plus Hannah, the administrator.

Patrick Bright
Hello all.

Jem Badhuri
I'm so excited for this course! I've just done a BA in FA at West Middlesex. Anyone else straight from their first degree?

Patrick Bright
This is my first degree—assuming I get to the end of it.

Jem Badhuri
Aw, don't say that, Patrick. Can we call you Pat?

Patrick Bright
That's fine, Jem.

Jonathan Danners
My first degree too. Know how you feel, Patrick!

Ludya Parak
Hey. Excited to meet you all next week.

Jem Badhuri
Hi Ludya! How do we pronounce your name?

Ludya Parak
Exactly how it looks.

Patrick Bright
Gela is pronounced with a hard G, even though it's short for Angela, which has a soft G.

Alyson Lang
Can anyone near Guildford give me a lift in on Tuesday?

Jem Badhuri
Hi Alyson with a Y. Sorry. My dad's driving me from North London every day. Well, the days we have to be in. He can't believe we only do Tuesdays, Wednesdays, and Thursdays!

Ludya Parak
Anyone else vegan?

Jem Badhuri
I am. Well, I eat cheese.

Alyson Lang
About access to the MM studio on the days we aren't officially "in." This is a coursework degree. It's essential we can come and go whenever we want, yet Hannah says keys aren't issued to students. We have to ask a technician to unlock it and they aren't there 24/7. Anyone else pissed off?

Patrick Bright
It does seem a bit inflexible.

Alyson Lang
It's unacceptable. I make my best work at night. When I did a 3D module at Portsmouth they had a keypad with a code. We could access the room whenever.

Jonathan Danners
Might be worth mentioning.

Alyson Lang
If we all go to Hannah together on day one and lodge the complaint, Gela will *have* to ask for at least one set of extra keys.

Jem Badhuri
I won't need to access the studio out-of-hours. My dad said he'll drive me in on any Monday or Friday if I need extra time.

September 25, 2023:

Jem Badhuri
Can't wait to meet you all tomorrow. Did you get Hannah's email about picking up a welcome pack at the admin office before we go to the Media Arts building? There's one student who hasn't replied on this thread yet. Cameron Wesley. Hope she hasn't dropped out already.

Cameron Wesley
He.

To: MMAM(FTP)
From: Gela Nathaniel
Date: September 26, 2023
Subject: Assignment One

Dear all,
I hope you enjoyed your first day of MMAM(FTP) as much as I did. What a pleasure it was getting to know you all outside of the interview process. Thank you to Hannah for organizing our welcome buffet lunch.

It's going to be a year of as much fun as hard work and, at the end of it, you'll have a real-world project to look back on and feel proud of. As I explained in our introductory class, this is a valuable opportunity to explore the ups and downs of a creative career, with the support and guidance of staff and peers.

I was delighted to hear you've all read your welcome pack and registered on Royal Hastings' Doodle Board. Keep an eye on our section, as I'll post or email anything you need to know there. You can socialize on other media, public and private, of course, but as this is a collaborative degree, we ask that you discuss college matters and coursework on Doodle only. This protects everyone, in the unlikely event of a dispute.

Regarding the request to issue keys to the multimedia studio: it seems one or two of you feel passionate about access to the room at times that suit the way you work. I've spoken to the department and it's a no, I'm afraid. The safety of all students and the security of the site are paramount. Also, the department feels that adapting your natural creative process to the demands of a more regular work environment is a positive exercise within the remit of this course.

Now to your first assignment! This is a broad, liberal task to establish the coursework segment of your final grade. In short:

Assignment One
Devise the logo for a fictional start-up company. This should take the form of a 2D illustration or a 3D model, plus one _short_ multimedia (film/sound/animation/graphics) promotional presentation suitable for playing on a screen in a company's foyer. Deadline: October 19, 2023.

The studio and its equipment are at your disposal, likewise the technicians, who can help and advise you. I'll be available myself for the rest of this week as we are onboarding the BA group next door. If you have any questions, just ask.

Best wishes,
Gela

Doodle message group [Private] Patrick and Gela, September 26, 2023:

Patrick Bright
I don't have to do the multimedia presentation, do I?

Gela Nathaniel
You do. It's 50% of the assignment.

Patrick Bright
But we said I'd concentrate on sketching and watercolor.

Gela Nathaniel
The MA is in Multimedia Art. That means digital and animation. You've got the software.

Patrick Bright
My laptop says "Not enough space to open FlowHand 11." I don't have any other programs on it. Not even Internet Explorer. I thought we said I could stick with traditional art?

Gela Nathaniel

Sorry. I can't seem to favor one student over the others. Please try to come up with something. Your shop assistants seem to be tech-savvy. Could they help?

Patrick Bright

I'll ask Joy. She usually sorts out my phone.

Gela Nathaniel

Phones—argh! Thank you, Patrick, you've just reminded me.

Doodle message group MMAM(FTP), September 26, 2023:

Gela Nathaniel

Typical! I forgot something crucial, and the technicians will take a dim view if I don't make you aware. Today was an exception, but from now on, no mobile phones are allowed in the studio. The reason is twofold. First, the room poses all sorts of dangers to expensive electronic devices—paint, varnish, glue, chemicals, and so on. Second, thanks to the volatile materials all around, the art studio is particularly vulnerable to fire. Mobile phones are considered an elevated risk to life and property and must be left in the metal tray by the door. The building is secure and the door is covered by CCTV. You may visit your phone in the tray as often as you like, within reason, during the day. Thank you for your cooperation and understanding.

Ludya Parak

I've got two kids. My phone stays with me. I'll apply for special consideration.

Doodle message group [Private] Hannah and Gela, September 26, 2023:

Hannah O'Donnell

Quick reminder: diversity forms for the MMAM(FTP) group. We haven't received any yet.

Gela Nathaniel
Yes, yes, will sort!

Doodle message group MMAM(FTP), September 26, 2023:

Alyson Lang
Gela didn't ask anyone about the studio keys.

Jem Badhuri
To be fair, what she says about security makes sense.

Jonathan Danners
Great to meet you all in person. Like I said over lunch, I haven't done any "real" art since my A-levels, thirteen years ago. It's daunting even being in a studio again.

Patrick Bright
Jonathan, you and I are similar in that we've worked in the art world, but not created work ourselves. I don't know how we'll compete with Alyson. A proper artist.

Jem Badhuri
I'm a proper artist!

Patrick Bright
Sure, but Alyson is already a name. Confess to googling you, Ali. Very well done.

Alyson Lang
It was just an Emerging Talent Award ten years ago. Still trying to emerge. It's a tough business, folks.

Patrick Bright
You can still be proud, however long ago it was—and of losing all that weight since. Must've been at least forty pounds. Any tips for me?

Alyson Lang
Swimming, tennis, and no carbs after 5 p.m.

Jem Badhuri
I thought you'd all be recent graduates. I'm the youngest by at least ten years.

Patrick Bright
Gela said she likes a mix of people. Diversity is always good.

Jonathan Danners
We're certainly all different, but we're all in the same place on the same journey, so let's support each other along the way.

Patrick Bright
Hear! Hear! And learn from each other. All for one and . . .

Ludya Parak
I can't make tomorrow, for personal reasons.

Cameron Wesley
This hellish Doodle thing. A '90s dot-com start-up wants its message board back. Why no page-visit counter?

Jonathan Danners
. . . one for all!

Alyson Lang
I'm writing a formal letter to the department head about fitting a keypad. Keys are so last century. It's meant to be a state-of-the-art studio, FFS.

Doodle message group [Private] Jem and Jonathan, September 26, 2023:

Jem Badhuri
Hi Jonathan! Like I said in the Aviator at lunchtime, I'm more than happy to give you an intro to working with clay. It's a (literally) hands-on medium that takes you anywhere you want to go. I can come in early any day and we'll go through the basics together.

Jonathan Danners
Hi Jem. Thanks for the offer. Perhaps a bit later on, when I've found my feet with the coursework.

Jem Badhuri
No problem. Let's chat later in the week.

Jonathan Danners
Good idea.

To: MMAM(FTP)
From: Gela Nathaniel
Date: October 9, 2023
Subject: The studio

Dear all,
It has been brought to my attention that someone from our course—I won't say who—has been less than polite and courteous to a particular member of studio staff.

May I remind you that the art technicians are knowledgeable professionals who work hard, under pressure, to keep our studio and workspaces clean and ensure we have supplies of whatever materials we need. They are to be treated with the utmost respect.

The person concerned has apologized, and Griff has accepted that apology. I'll say no more at this stage. But if I hear of any further incidents, I shall be less than pleased.

I look forward to receiving your first assignments on or before the given deadline.
Gela

Doodle message group MMAM(FTP), October 9, 2023:

Ludya Parak
Wasn't me.

Jem Badhuri

What happened? Does anyone know? Must've been after I left on Thursday. I'm trying not to bother the technicians.

Patrick Bright

Gela implies one of us has been rude. I find Griff very gruff, but hope I haven't said anything that's been taken the wrong way.

Jonathan Danners

Gela says they apologized, so I think you're in the clear, Pat.

Patrick Bright

Ah, didn't see that bit. Must have a guilty conscience.

Jem Badhuri

Tony is so slow. Rita is always helpful, but she's only part-time. Who would have complained about us?

Ludya Parak

I wasn't even in past 4 p.m. last week.

Jem Badhuri

Jonathan, Alyson, and Cameron—do you know what Gela's talking about?

Jonathan Danners

No idea.

Cameron Wesley

Clueless.

Alyson Lang

OK, so this is what happened. Last Wednesday, Tony let me stay overnight. On Thursday evening Griff said I had to leave at six. I wasn't rude, just pointed out the inconsistency in studio policy. One night I can stay, the next I can't. That's *all* it was. He clearly has a problem with strong women. I said I was sorry, but if it happens again, I *will* lodge a complaint.

Doodle message group [Private] Jem and Patrick, October 9, 2023:

Jem Badhuri
Thought we'd chat in private. Shall I invite Jonathan too?

Patrick Bright
I'm honored, Jem. Jonathan? Yes, do. He's grand.

Jonathan Danners *has been added to this group.*

Jem Badhuri
Oh. My. God. I guessed it was Alyson. How embarrassing for Gela, and the rest of us.

Patrick Bright
Poor gruff Griff!

Jem Badhuri
While I appreciate her point about accessing the studio when she can be most creative, there's no excuse for being rude to tech staff. They work really hard.

Patrick Bright
They're all characters, no?

Jem Badhuri
Jonathan, did you know Gela meant Alyson in that email?

Jonathan Danners
I've been concentrating on my assignment.

Patrick Bright
You and me both. How's it going?

Jonathan Danners
I could've used photography as my main medium—it's what I'm most familiar with—but I'm here to expand my skills, so I tried a simple resin design and basic stop-motion. Learned a lot, but it's not come across in the work. It looks naïve and amateur next to everyone else's.

Patrick Bright
Gela knows your circumstances. We're not competing with each other—we're building our skill sets. What you've done sounds ambitious.

Jem Badhuri
Has anyone seen Alyson's assignment yet?

Patrick Bright
Yes. She showed me today. It's out of this world.

Jem Badhuri
Have you seen it, Jonathan?

Jonathan Danners
I have. Patrick's right.

Jem Badhuri
Well, it's no wonder. She's been a professional artist for years. Why is she even on this course?

Patrick Bright
Ah, there's always something new to learn.

Jem Badhuri
If you ask me, she's rude, disruptive, arrogant, and is only here to take advantage of the facilities, which she wants to access at night, alone, so no one can see how much stuff she's using. I'm going to mention it to Gela.

Patrick Bright
Gela is Alyson's biggest fan.

Jem Badhuri
That's what I find so unfair. Gela acts as if Alyson is the best artist here and expects us to worship her too.

Jonathan Danners
Need to get back to my assignment.

Jem Badhuri
I'm going to say something. Just not sure when yet.

Jonathan Danners *has left the group.*

Jem Badhuri

Did you notice he wouldn't say anything negative about her?

Patrick Bright

Have you finished your assignment, Jem?

Jem Badhuri

All except the final touches. Can't wait to hear what Gela thinks of it.

Patrick Bright

Wish I had your confidence!

Jem Badhuri

If you hear anything more about Griff-gate, let me know.

Doodle message group [Private] Jem and Cameron, October 10, 2023:

Jem Badhuri

Great session in the studio today! Thought I'd start a private chat because we haven't connected yet. You're always speaking to Alyson and never post on Doodle. Do you struggle with technology, like Pat?

Cameron Wesley

Ha! I don't even like the word "intranet," let alone this Arial hellscape hammering my retinas.

Cameron Wesley

Apols. Inappropriate rant. Still working on myself.

Jem Badhuri

I'm thrilled with how my assignment has turned out. Have you seen my sculpture waiting by the kiln?

Cameron Wesley

Nope. Can't take eyes off Ali's work. Girl leaves the rest of us clinging to the perch.

Cameron Wesley *has left the group.*

Jem Badhuri
Really? Well, not for long.

Doodle message group [Private] Jem and Patrick, October 16, 2023:

Jem Badhuri
Thanks for your help, Patrick. Who'd have thought working in art supplies would qualify you as a detective?

Patrick Bright
Indeed! Although you're the detective, Ms. Badhuri. Remember what I said. Don't go in all guns blazing. There might be a perfectly innocent explanation for the discrepancies.

To: Gela Nathaniel
From: Jemisha Badhuri
Date: October 16, 2023
Subject: Alyson is stealing

Hi Gela,

I've been conducting an investigation into another MMAM(FTP) student and my findings are below.

As you know, I like to maximize my hours on each assignment and have no suitable facilities at home—unlike Alyson—so I've familiarized myself with the whole area, the studio, stockroom, and storage cupboards, so I don't have to keep buzzing for a technician. This means I know exactly what's been taken out, or not, on any given day.

I had my suspicions, but needed proof before I came to you with them. For the last week Patrick and I have been making a note of which stock items have been signed out and when, plus what's missing, without a formal paper trail.

You must know Alyson sneaks into the studio overnight whenever Tony is on lates. That's a matter in itself, but it's not the subject of my investigation. The sad fact is, items are going missing from the storeroom, overnight, whenever Alyson is here by herself. This is everything that "walked out" over one night alone. Tuesday last week:

Material	Quantity	Trade price	Total
Acrylic paints	500ml pots x 11 assorted colors	£3.33	£36.63
Plaster mix, white	10kg bags x 3	£6.15	£18.45
Resin	1liter bottles x 4	£14.03	£56.12
Triple canvas packs	3	£4.87	£14.61
			£125.81

You'll notice these are all trade prices. This is thanks to Patrick, who knows the costs exactly, thanks to his art-supplies shop. We weren't sure if Royal Hastings pays trade or retail prices. So, the above loss to the department is a conservative calculation.

It could be that Alyson is using these materials for her assignment, but eleven pots of acrylic paint? Three whole bags of plaster? Patrick says that's enough to make an installation for the foyer of the Tate Modern. We aren't meant to be working on canvas for this, so why the canvases?

I suspect Alyson is stocking her personal studio at home with whatever she can get her hands on from the cupboards here. Working overnight gives her the best opportunity to do so. As Patrick says, she can park behind the sheds and move larger items quickly. The true extent of her thieving is difficult to work out, as more obscure items could have gone missing without me noticing.

I'm happy to continue monitoring the stocks if you require more evidence before calling the police. Patrick will back me up.
Jem

Doodle message group [Private] Gela and Patrick, October 16, 2023:

Gela Nathaniel
You've been helping Jem "investigate" items missing from the studio?

Patrick Bright
I'm sorry, Gela. How could I say no? She was so fired up and indignant on behalf of the department.

Gela Nathaniel
Perhaps let me know next time, so I can address it *before* she gets fired up.

Patrick Bright
I feel sorry for her. She's so young. There's no one remotely her age on the course.

Gela Nathaniel
She's old enough to accuse someone of theft. Now I have to go through the formal channels and at least appear to investigate it.

Patrick Bright
And that's not what we want. I know.

Doodle message group [Private] Gela and Jem, October 16, 2023:

Gela Nathaniel
Can I have a quick word with you before tomorrow's session?

Jem Badhuri
Of course. I'll get my dad to drop me off early.

Doodle message group [Private] Jem and Patrick, October 17, 2023:

Jem Badhuri
I've spoken to Gela. Let's just say a certain someone won't be stealing for much longer.

Patrick Bright
"Excellent," I cried. "Elementary," said she!

Jem Badhuri
Who? Gela? Well, no one will worship Alyson anymore, knowing she's a thief.

To: MMAM(FTP)
From: Gela Nathaniel
Date: October 18, 2023
Subject: Assignment One

Dear all,

This is your final reminder that completed Assignment One materials must be sent to Hannah (or, in the case of 3D items, left with Rita) by close of play tomorrow (Thursday).

On Tuesday we'll spend some time going through each project as a group. Be prepared to chat, informally but in detail, about your idea and how you achieved it. Also be prepared to critique each other's work. Learning to give and accept criticism to a high level is a key part of this course.

Good luck to those of you in the final stages.

See you Tuesday.

Gela

Doodle message group [Private] Hannah and Jem, October 18, 2023:

Hannah O'Donnell
Hello Jemisha. This is to open up a dialogue about how you're getting along on the course. You're the youngest and we are all keen for you to know you're supported at every stage. If you need anything, please do not hesitate to ask me, Gela, or anyone else in the department.

Jem Badhuri

Thanks, Hannah! I'm getting along just fine. I was a tiny bit disappointed to find everyone was so much older. Patrick is in his fifties! Almost as old as my mom and dad. But this MA is only a year and I'm looking forward to all it holds.

Doodle message group MMAM(FTP), October 20, 2023:

Gela Nathaniel

The deadline for submitting your first assignment is now passed. Thank you everyone. I'll see you at 10 a.m. in the studio on Tuesday. Enjoy your weekends.

Jem Badhuri

Thanks, Gela! I've loved working on this project. Enjoy your weekend too!

Ludya Parak

I'll be late on Tuesday.

Doodle message group [Private] Jem and Jonathan, October 23, 2023:

Jem Badhuri

Hi Jonathan! If you fancy an intro to clay in the downtime between assignments, I'll be in the studio tomorrow morning, as usual.

Jonathan Danners

Won't be in early tomorrow. Giving Alyson a lift.

Doodle message group [Private] Jem and Patrick, October 23, 2023:

Jem Badhuri

Do you know if Gela has confronted Alyson about her thieving yet?

Patrick Bright
Steady on. We don't know for sure she's stolen anything.

Jem Badhuri
We do! We've done the math.

Patrick Bright
Gela will sort it. Hopefully she'll have a quiet word, and if Alyson is doing anything she shouldn't, she'll stop.

Jem Badhuri
She should be kicked off the course. Gela should thank us personally for rooting out a thief.

Patrick Bright
It's out of our hands now. You've done a great job, Jem. Now concentrate on getting that MA.

Jem Badhuri
I hate to think the department is being drained of its resources, which we know are scarce enough, by one selfish person.

To: Gela Nathaniel
From: Jemisha Badhuri
Date: October 23, 2023
Subject: Re: Alyson is stealing

Hi Gela,
Have you spoken to Alyson about her stealing from the storeroom? I'm happy to give a statement to the police, and I know Patrick will be too.
  Jem

To: Jemisha Badhuri
From: Gela Nathaniel
Date: October 23, 2023
Subject: Re: Alyson

Jem, no one is stealing from the storeroom. We aren't the only group to use this space. The technicians move items around frequently between both studios, depending on what each group is doing. The BAs were working in clay and resin when you noticed a shortage of those. They also needed canvases and acrylics, and you discovered those missing. Please do not spread rumors about anyone in our MA group—it reflects badly on us all. You are doing well and (I hope) enjoying the course, which you are now free to concentrate on exclusively.

Gela

To: Gela Nathaniel
From: Jem Badhuri
Date: October 23, 2023
Subject: Re: Alyson

Hi Gela,

Thanks for looking into it. I just want to assure you I have nothing against Alyson, but I have a very good sense when it comes to people, and something about her pings my radar. But not to worry. Like you say, I'm doing well on the course and intend that to continue. See you tomorrow.

Jem

Doodle message group [Private] Jem and Patrick, October 23, 2023:

Jem Badhuri
Gela is covering up Alyson's thieving.

Patrick Bright
Ah now, I don't think she'd do that.

Jem Badhuri
Royal Hastings' art department has dropped most of its master's courses already. This is one of the few left. It looks bad if anyone, least of all the golden girl, has to leave under a cloud and so soon.

Patrick Bright
Let's look forward to tomorrow's session. Excited to see everyone's work for the first time.

Doodle message group MMAM(FTP), October 24, 2023:

Ludya Parak
Please tell me at least one other MMAM has been up all night and feels like shit this morning.

Patrick Bright
You said it. Lying awake worrying about the assessment today.

Jonathan Danners
Ditto. When I finally got to sleep, I dreamed Gela was staring in disgust at my model.

Ludya Parak
You guys were awake all night. I was editing my promo. ALL NIGHT. Finally sent it at 4:30 a.m.

Patrick Bright
You didn't hand it in Thursday?

Ludya Parak
Gela gave me an extension. Personal stuff.

Jem Badhuri
I'm so excited!

Alyson Lang
I got an extension to this morning as well. At the studio now, if anyone fancies a pre-assessment smoke.

Jem Badhuri
Smoking isn't allowed in the studio. Or outside.

Alyson Lang
There's a neat little unofficial hang-out space beyond the rear double-doors to the parking lot.

Jem Badhuri
I don't smoke.

Jonathan Danners
I might start today.

Patrick Bright
See you there.

Ludya Parak
Like I said. Gonna be late. Family reasons.

Cameron Wesley
I'll join you for a puff, Ali.

Doodle message group [Private] Jem and Patrick, October 24, 2023:

Jem Badhuri
I've noticed something about Cameron. If he's not on his phone in the corridor, he's flirting with Alyson in the studio.

Patrick Bright
Oh Jem! You're a sharp one, but I don't think he flirts with Alyson. They just get along.

Jem Badhuri
He has the loudest, clearest voice of the whole group, but when he's on his phone he whispers.

Patrick Bright
I suspect he's still doing his regular job, even though he was supposed to step back to make time for this course. He's on his laptop in the bar every lunchtime.

Jem Badhuri
How can he focus on his MA? Gela will have something to say about that. I have to put my phone in the tray now, but I'll make sure she knows.

Patrick Bright
Nearly at the studio myself. Let's get through this first assessment!

Doodle message group [Private] Gela and Cameron, October 24, 2023:

Gela Nathaniel
I don't know if your phone had anything to do with events in the studio today, but in the future, switch it completely OFF when you leave it in the tray.

Cameron Wesley
Apols.

Gela Nathaniel
What was that anyway? I've never heard a shriek like it. Not from a phone.

Cameron Wesley
Because your phone belongs in a museum, Gela. If you had the latest model—or even one from the last decade—you might have facial recognition that, set to the highest security level, would alert you when it detected a stranger's face looking at the screen.

Gela Nathaniel
Well, why the panic?

Cameron Wesley
I deal with top clients and corporations. That phone is jam-packed with sensitive strategy plans and embargoed info. When the alarm goes off, it alerts the office. They instantly assume it's either been stolen or my security compromised. I had to get straight on to them or they'd call the cops.

Gela Nathaniel
No one at Royal Hastings is going to compromise your company's data, I can assure you.

Cameron Wesley
Well, *someone* picked up my phone and looked at it while I was distracted in the studio.

Gela Nathaniel

If it's a top model, then someone was possibly curious. It doesn't mean they tried to hack into it.

Cameron Wesley

Benefit of the doubt, sure. But it stays in my pocket from now on. Anyway I'm surprised you—or anyone—remembers that, quite frankly, insignificant episode, after what happened next, FFS.

MMAM(FTP)
Coursework Module: Assignment One
Tutor's Report, October 24, 2023

Brief: Devise the logo for a fictional start-up company. This should take the form of a 2D graphic or a 3D model, plus one short multimedia (film/sound/animation/graphics) promotional presentation suitable for playing on a screen in the company's foyer.

Overview: For their first assignment I devised a brief that would allow students to utilize familiar materials, while extending their diverse skill sets into unfamiliar mediums. All approached it with unbridled enthusiasm and submitted well within the deadline. For their 2D logo, oil or acrylic on canvas was discouraged in favor of mediums popular in today's commercial world. Photography, computer graphics, and illustration were all used.

Jemisha Badhuri
Jem devised a logo for a charity that clears litter from shorelines, especially plastic detritus that can entrap sea animals. She submitted an 18-inch foyer ornament of her logo in clay, which she textured by hand. It combined human hands with waves from the sea. The impression was of humanity embracing the animals and ecosystems of the oceans. For the multimedia part, Jem devised an innovative soundscape, also intended for use in the charity's reception area. This she made using audio clips of ocean noises, inventively mixed to create a soothing, calming air, all the more impressive because sound was not part of Jem's BA. Apparently she took a course in sound electronics over the summer. Her commitment and enthusiasm paid off. Grade: B+

Patrick Bright
This is Patrick's first experience of formal art education. His logo was for his own art-supplies shop, which currently doesn't have one, beyond its name in block capitals. He used pencil on paper for his

2D design and sketched a hand holding a pencil and sketching another hand on paper. It was competently drawn. While this felt too detailed for a logo, during group discussion a "sketch of a hand sketching a hand" proved a hot topic and evoked the circular nature of life and art. Patrick spoke about the similarly circular nature of selling art materials—to people who will sell what they make with them. His CGI clip was less successful and froze at the same place every time, until we gave up. Patrick explained that his shop assistant, Joy, hasn't mastered FlowHand 11 yet. Grade: C

Jonathan Danners
Jonathan achieved a B grade in his Art A-level, thirteen years ago. This was his last experience of creating work for himself, and I'm afraid it showed. His logo, for an engineering start-up, was a red 3D model of a disjointed cube, constructed, origami-style, from strong card and mounted on a metal rod, set in a black resin base. His intention was that as the model turned, the perspective would also change and include one angle that showed the disparate elements as a perfect cube. His stop-motion clip sought to demonstrate this. Unfortunately, at no angle does this happen. In discussion with the group, Jonathan was forced to admit that what he planned for the piece had not been realized. I considered awarding this work an E, the lowest grade short of a fail, however, I wanted to reflect the courage and ambition showed in tackling this deceptively simple design. Grade: D

Alyson Lang
What can I say about Alyson Lang that wasn't said at the ART Emerging Talent Awards in 2013? The fact that she has chosen our course to improve her skills and build her business is a testimony to our reputation as an industry-focused art-education provider. Her logo was for a sustainable fast-food retailer. It blended images of a burger and a globe—but she had applied color by mixing acrylic paint with specialist solvent to attain a smooth, professional finish. Her animated clip was equally outstanding, and featured endangered animals handing a sustainable vegan burger to the viewer. Grade: A

Ludya Parak

Ludya works freelance as a graphic designer. However, her attendance so far has been patchy. This assignment was accompanied by a special-consideration form, to indicate that personal matters have prevented her from fulfilling the project to the best of her abilities. Her 3D logo for a paddleboarding company was achieved using a simple piece of wood in the approximate shape of a paddleboard, topped by a stylized figure in dynamic pose, with an oar. It transpired that these items had not been made but salvaged from her sons' toy box. Her social-media promo clip blended still shots of paddleboarders enjoying the sport. Her clip lacked imagination. However, it presented the company's product accurately and was aspirational. Grade: C

Cameron Wesley

Cameron is taking this MA to help balance the stress of his full-time job in financial marketing, which he says he's doing part-time now. For his assignment he used FlowHand 11 to devise a 2D logo for a financial-services company aimed at young graduates. It looks more like a restaurant logo, but in discussion with the group he explained that this disconnect was entirely deliberate. The logo is pitched for a generation uninterested in the products offered by financial-service providers. For his social-media promo he adapted comedy footage obtained from the archives of a company he worked for, which, although entertaining, was not in the spirit of the assignment or the course. Grade: C–

Doodle message group MMAM(FTP), October 24, 2023:

Jem Badhuri
Phew! Apart from the fire, that went really well.

Cameron Wesley
Alyson, if you want a job in advertising, call me. We need disruptors.

Ludya Parak
Alyson, you are brutal. But I love you.

Alyson Lang
Hate constructive-criticism bullshit. It's just shit. I only did what the piece inspired me to do.

Cameron Wesley
Literally setting someone's work alight. Go, girl!

Patrick Bright
Jonathan, are you OK?

Jonathan Danners
Fast work with the extinguisher, Patrick.

Patrick Bright
Could see the whole place going up.

Jem Badhuri
I wouldn't know how to put a fire out.

Patrick Bright
That's thirty years surrounded by paper, aerosols, and flammable liquids in the shop.

Jem Badhuri
If Jonathan makes his model again, he could improve his grade.

Patrick Bright
Good point. It's worth asking Gela.

Jem Badhuri

Ludya, did I hear right—you used your little boy's broken cricket bat and doll for your 3D logo?

Ludya Parak

Yep, and pics from his paddleboard class on Saturday. Stoked to get a C.

Jem Badhuri

Is that allowed? We're meant to make our artwork, surely?

Ludya Parak

Salvage is carbon-neutral and takes waste out of the environment. Gela should be encouraging us to recycle and reuse *way* more than we are.

Alyson Lang

Agreed. Anyone else struggling to work in the space given to us in that studio? I propose those of us who work in 3D should move into the cutting room. Might start a petition.

Doodle message group [Private] Jem and Jonathan, October 24, 2023:

Jem Badhuri

Hi Jonathan. You must be smoldering as madly as the remains of your model. It happened so fast I didn't realize until it was over. I've tried to warn Gela there's something off about Alyson. Most artists have a sensitivity about them. She just doesn't. I can't explain any better than that. Still, what you were saying about science, engineering, and art being very close to each other could potentially be interesting. It's a shame you didn't remotely realize your idea. If nothing else, it proves you were right not to take a course in engineering! If you ask Gela about resubmitting your assignment, please can you let me know? By the way, my offer of a tutorial in working with clay still stands.

Doodle message group [Private] Jem and Patrick, October 24, 2023:

Jem Badhuri

If Jonathan gets to improve his grade, then we all should.

Patrick Bright

But Alyson setting fire to Jonathan's paper model—right there in the studio. And those terrible things she said about it. Outrageous.

Jem Badhuri

Well, from what Gela implied, she only gave him a D because he at least had an idea, even if he couldn't actually create it. Reading between the lines, she thought his piece was a straight E.

Patrick Bright

We're supposed to support each other, surely.

Jem Badhuri

I can't believe Alyson got an A. No one gets an A on their first assignment.

Patrick Bright

To be fair, her idea was a tricky one to pull off and the result was brilliant.

Jem Badhuri

My opinion: Gela thinks Alyson's presence is a good advertisement for the course. That woman could get away with murder.

To: Gela Nathaniel
From: Griff Technician (Maintenance)
Date: October 25, 2023
Subject: Fire damage

Dear Mrs. Nathaniel,

It has been brought to my attention that a fire occurred in the MA studio yesterday.

Apparently, a wastepaper bin full of ash sludge and extinguishant had been left for the technicians to discover and dispose of. On further investigation, we saw that a fire extinguisher had been deployed but placed back on its stand as if nothing had happened. There were no

Incident Forms waiting for me this morning, so I would appreciate if you could complete one, explaining in detail the exact circumstances of how the fire came to start and be put out. I take it no one was injured and the alarms were not triggered.

Griff

To: Griff Technician (Maintenance)
From: Gela Nathaniel
Date: October 25, 2023
Subject: Re: Fire damage

Sorry, Griff! Yes, we had a small fire during the MMAM(FTP) session. One of our students made a cardboard model and, as part of his presentation, used a lighter to illuminate it. Before I could stop him, the inevitable happened.

Luckily, another of our students was quick to grab the nearest fire extinguisher and it was all over in seconds. The fire was tiny. No one was injured and it didn't even trip the smoke detectors, as you noticed. I'll complete an Incident Form, and, rest assured, it won't happen again. Thank you for clearing away the detritus.

Gela

To: Gela Nathaniel
From: Griff Technician (Maintenance)
Date: October 25, 2023
Subject: Re: Fire damage

I know the model you mean as I helped the gentleman with his resin base. I also saw the bin post-conflagration—it was swimming with ash. The fire must've destroyed far more than just that little paper cube on a stick. I am pleased to say that, thanks to our fast work, a new fire extinguisher has been installed to replace the spent one.

Attached is a copy of the studio regulations. If you could circulate this to your group, no one will be in any doubt that naked flames are not allowed anywhere near the art studio at any time. I look forward to receiving your Incident Form today.

Griff

To: Gela Nathaniel
From: Jemisha Badhuri
Date: October 25, 2023
Subject: Grades

Dear Gela,

About our grades. Has Jonathan asked to resubmit Assignment One? If so, and you agree, will he be re-marked and his grade potentially changed?

I was given a B+. I understand early grades are deliberately low, so we are inspired to work harder. However, I too would like the opportunity to resubmit my project with a view to improving my grade and therefore my potential for a higher final result.

If Jonathan has that chance, then it's only fair the rest of us do.

Jem

Doodle message group [Private] Jem and Patrick, October 25, 2023:

Jem Badhuri

In all the excitement of the fire, I forgot to ask you about Cameron. I heard you chatting to him—what's he like?

Patrick Bright

Oh, nice enough. Suited and booted, in a corporate way. Maybe not who you'd expect on a course like this. He hinted at having problems and being advised by his therapist to pursue a hobby to help him relax. I didn't want to say, but signing up to a full-time master's degree perhaps wasn't what that therapist had in mind.

Jem Badhuri

What sort of problems?

Patrick Bright

Oh, well it would be rude to ask.

Jem Badhuri

Not to worry. I'll send him a private message.

Patrick Bright
No, Jem, please don't. He told me in confidence and it's personal information.

To: MMAM(FTP)
From: Gela Nathaniel
Date: October 25, 2023
Subject: Assignments Two and Three

Dear all,

Further to the fire incident yesterday, Griff has asked me to circulate the studio policy document, attached. As I said in our very first session, giving and receiving criticism is a vital part of this course. Assignment One was as much about how you responded to others' work as it was about your own creative vision. This brings me to your second assignment.

Assignment Two
Your portfolio will sell your work, but <u>you</u> must sell <u>you</u>. Write an introduction to you, both as an artist and as a person. Imagine they are the first few paragraphs of a speculative email to a prospective employer (300–450 words). Deadline: November 3, 2023.

This assignment comprises the brief essay above PLUS an interview-style presentation on Tuesday, November 7, during which the rest of the group will form the panel. Convince us <u>you</u> are the person to hire.

Please send your completed essays to my email address by the end of next week. As this assignment does not require practical work, it will run alongside Assignment Three, due in three weeks.

<u>Assignment Three</u>
Use digital software to devise a multimedia campaign of posters, print advertising, and social media. The brand or product may be that from Assignment One, a different fictional brand, or an existing popular brand. Create <u>two</u> elements for submission. Deadline: November 17, 2023.

The studio and its equipment are at your disposal, likewise the technicians, who can help and advise you. If you have any questions or queries, just ask.

Best wishes,
Gela

Doodle message group MMAM(FTP), October 25, 2023:

Ludya Parak
Shit! Writing assignment.

Cameron Wesley
Total 'mare.

Patrick Bright
There goes the weekend!

Jem Badhuri
And I'm at a wedding too.

Ludya Parak
Has anyone got a spare user log-in for FlowHand 11? Pretty please.

Jem Badhuri
Gela said we need to buy our own.

Ludya Parak
It's £385

Patrick Bright
I can't make head or tail of it.

Ludya Parak
You can log in with the same activation code on two devices at once. Is anyone using theirs on one device? I can log in on my laptop. It won't make any difference to you.

Patrick Bright
Oh, in that case no problem. What's an activation code?

Jem Badhuri

It's tricky at first, but well worth the money, IMHO. FlowHand is *the* design software. Gela said we must have our own copy of the latest version if we want to be taken seriously as professionals.

Ludya Parak

That's a pile of poop. I'm already a design professional, FFS. I work on ProDrawX all the time. But they changed the accessibility protocols. Gela won't be able to open my files in FH11.

Patrick Bright

Might ask you for a few lessons, Jem.

Cameron Wesley

Our designers use it at work. I'll get you a code.

Ludya Parak

Cheers, Cameron. Owe you a drink.

Jem Badhuri

We should all have our own legitimate copy for the course.

Doodle message group [Private] Patrick and Ludya, October 25, 2023:

Patrick Bright

I know Jem can be a bit much, but she doesn't mean any harm. She's a lovely girl who probably spends too much time with her parents. Let's make allowances and not snap at her.

Ludya Parak

If everyone puts up with her, how will she learn?

Doodle message group [Private] Patrick and Jem, October 25, 2023:

Patrick Bright

Hope Ludya didn't upset you, Jem. She can be a bit short with everyone. It's her personal style. She doesn't mean it.

Jem Badhuri

Thanks, Patrick! I don't let other people upset me. Can I tell you something in confidence?

Patrick Bright

Go on.

Jem Badhuri

Something strange happened this morning. Dad had a meeting, so he dropped me off early. When I tried the studio door it was unlocked. That usually means Alyson has been there overnight and is clearing up, but I didn't hear her music. She always has her phone blasting out old tunes. I was making a cup of tea when there was a noise from the stockroom corridor. Someone moving, but secretly, like they didn't want me to hear. It wasn't Alyson—she always thunders out to say hello. This was someone else.

Patrick Bright

One of the technicians?

Jem Badhuri

I shouted hi and popped my head in, but there was no one there. The room was empty. I know they didn't come past me, so they must've slipped out of the rear door and escaped before I arrived.

Patrick Bright

Very strange!

Jem Badhuri

The weird thing is, Alyson breezed in half an hour later. She said she'd been talking to the department head about fitting a keypad. I said I'd heard someone else in the studio and she said it was probably her leaving for the meeting.

Patrick Bright

There you go. Mystery solved!

Jem Badhuri

No, Patrick. Mystery deepens. It wasn't Alyson I heard. She leaves a smell of cigarettes behind her wherever she goes. The person I almost caught left behind a smell of alcohol.

Doodle message group [Private] Hannah and Jem, October 31, 2023:

Hannah O'Donnell

Hi Jem, Gela has asked me to contact you about the time you arrive at the studio now. You seem to be getting earlier and earlier? We'd rather you arrived at 9:30 a.m. with everyone else, as whichever technician is on the early rotation has to work across both studios and can't keep an eye out for you. Students shouldn't really work alone in the media-arts building, least of all a young woman.

Jem Badhuri

My dad drops me off early if he has meetings in London. There's no other way I can get here. Anyway I like to sort out my little corner before everyone else arrives. Alyson's a woman and she stays in the studio all night on her own. Although she isn't exactly young.

Hannah O'Donnell

The department feels a greater responsibility to you as you are so much younger than the rest of the group. You can wait in the Aviator café or the memorial garden?

Doodle message group MMAM(FTP), November 2, 2023:

Jonathan Danners

How is everyone dividing their time between the two assignments? When I'm trying to work on one, I find myself worrying about the other.

Jem Badhuri

I know what you mean. I wrote my personal essay first, as it has to be in first. Now I can concentrate on the multimedia campaign.

Ludya Parak

Haven't started either.

Jem Badhuri

But the essay is due in tomorrow.

Ludya Parak
I'll do it this evening. So long as I get it in by midnight, that's "before tomorrow" right?

Patrick Bright
Finished my personal introduction. So cringey writing about myself!

Jonathan Danners
How personal do you get? On the one hand, it's a job interview; on the other, well, my life experiences are why I'm pursuing this career change.

Patrick Bright
Get personal. I have.

Cameron Wesley
Business is all about who you know—and who knows you. Show them *you.*

Alyson Lang
Not doing the essay. I have anxiety over writing things.

Alyson Lang
And before anyone asks, Gela is fine with that.

MMAM(FTP)
Coursework Module: Assignment Two
Tutor's Report, November 7, 2023

Brief: Write an introduction to you, both as an artist and as a person. Imagine your essay as the first few paragraphs of a speculative email to a prospective employer (300–450 words).

Overview: For Assignment Two I gave the MA group a short writing task designed to mimic the type of brief email pitch they will send out frequently in the real world. Many of the students are unused to expressing themselves in words, and in some cases this showed. However, we discussed the shortcomings of each during our role-play exercise, where we created an interview-style panel for each student in turn. The upshot was a lively and productive learning environment that saw everyone grow in confidence and ability.

Jemisha Badhuri

My name is Jemisha Badhuri. I am twenty-one years old. I achieved a BA with first-class honors in Fine Art from West Middlesex. Unlike everyone else on this course, I have a career ahead of me. Not behind me, like Patrick. And I'm not taking it because my design business is on the rocks, like Ludya, or because it's cheaper to ~~steal~~ use college art materials than buy my own, like Patrick says Alyson does. I'm also conscientious and engaged, unlike Cameron, who is combining this course with another job and probably doing neither very well.

I plan to work as a commercial sculptor and soundscape producer. The moment I touched a piece of clay, in primary school at the age of five, I knew it! This is my medium. No doubt, as my brothers like to tell me, it's a power trip. You can bend and shape clay any way you want. Say there are things you can't control in other areas of your life—and if you've got four older brothers, believe me, this is a real possibility—then at least you are master of that piece of clay. Once you've manipulated and fired it, good or bad, it will be that way forever.

I discovered the potential of sound more recently. My BA course didn't teach it and I've sent a long letter to the head of department there explaining why it should be included in the curriculum. Having said that, because so few artists realize sound is even a thing, I'll have an advantage when I start my new business. I'll make sculptures for corporate organizations and complement them with soundscapes. It's the best of all worlds: clay can be anything you want it to be—sound is everything you could possibly imagine.

If you decide to employ me for the commission that I'm pretending exists for this essay, you will get a hard-working and creative 3D artist who thinks outside the box. But I also think *inside* the box, if that's what you want. Because I know being a commercial sculptor means bending and shaping your artistic vision to your clients' needs. For the duration of our time working together I will bend and shape my substantial creative powers to you. In short, I am the best person for this job.

Tutor's Report

Initially I rejected this essay because it contained an unsubstantiated accusation against another student. Ms. Badhuri subsequently changed the word "steal" to "use" and resubmitted the work. While I appreciate the student's willingness and ability to apply her skills to her client's needs, I felt the essay was a missed opportunity to examine more deeply her inspirations and motivations, which would help a potential employer understand and engage with her artistic direction. Jem was made aware of the pitfalls of negative marketing when I asked her to read out her essay to the class. While one sells oneself in an interview, it should never be at the expense of other candidates. Such comments reflect far worse on the person making them. Grade: C

Patrick Bright

How difficult is this? I haven't written proper sentences and paragraphs for years. I'll introduce myself and why I applied for this course. I was born in Schull, which is on the southwest coast of Ireland and it's pronounced "skull," as in cranium. It's a beautiful place, but I joined a friend who was going to work in London—this is in the late '80s. I got a job at an art-supplies shop and I'm still there. When the owner retired, I used my inheritance and bought him out. It's in an old parade of shops dating back to the Middle Ages in a back street by Leicester Square. It's called Modern Art. Terrible name, but it was opened in the '60s and its reputation is so strong, why change? I've always sketched and painted on the side, but at my age it's now or never. A few things happened and they made me think about what I should do for the rest of my life. I realized I want to give up the shop and become an artist, for a few years before I retire. Just to have done it, you know?

Gela was an occasional customer. It was ages before I realized she was a tutor at Royal Hastings. During one of our chats I mentioned my dream of working for myself, going back to Schull, living by the sea. She suggested I apply for this MA. It sounded good. I wanted to approach my art from a commercial angle, simply to sustain it. The commitment is only a year, and with the two good shop girls I've got now, I can run the store alongside the coursework.

Tutor's Report
Patrick introduced himself well, but failed to sell his artistic skills or his approach to work. It would be hard to see why a potential client would choose him over a candidate with greater insight into their own professional offering and greater marketing skills. Grade: C–

Jonathan Danners
I like to think I would have studied for a BA in Fine Art at the usual time, but it wasn't to be. So I've come back to education relatively late in life. I'm thirty-one and the last decade has been challenging. My mother was seriously ill during my A-levels, so I gave up a uni place to look after her while my father ran the family art gallery. It's a small place in Gloucestershire, but it has a good reputation. My mother passed away ten years ago, even though she had overcome the cancer, so the doctors said, but her immune system was weakened and she contracted pneumonia.

My father was devastated because they'd always run the place together and he was convinced she'd recover. Unfortunately, that wasn't the last tragedy. My sister had very complex health needs from birth. She was always part of the family, even though from her early teens she lived in residential care. Whether it was connected to my mother passing away we'll never know, but my sister had a sudden decline and after a couple of months she too passed away.

By this time I was running the gallery with Dad, and strangely enough, it was a very successful time, despite all that went on behind the scenes. We launched several local artists and hosted some exhibitions straight from London. I started to look at BA courses, but had to put that aside again when my father was diagnosed with a heart and lung condition.

He took a backseat during his treatment, while I ran the gallery full-time. It was years before he was well enough to come back. I'm cautiously happy to say that, for the time being anyway, his condition is improved and he's feeling better than ever. I know it played on his mind that I'd missed out on my uni years, and he was very keen for me to go back and complete my education. That determination got him through some of the darker times.

When I came to apply for a course I was more than a decade older than most BA students, and rather than study with people from another generation, I decided to opt for a more commercial program. That's why I chose the Multimedia MA.

Tutor's Report
Jonathan's essay was certainly very personal. However, it did little to sell his work to a prospective employer. In our group exercise Jonathan was encouraged to use his experiences as a springboard, but to avoid coming across as maudlin or appearing to play the sympathy card. Grade: C

Alyson Lang
See the special-consideration form I sent to Hannah.

Tutor's Report
Alyson detailed her personal reasons for not completing this

assignment. Her grade is based on the quality of her previous work. Grade: B

Ludya Parak

I'm a fast, creative graphic designer with fifteen years' experience in many diverse organizations and for a wide range of products and services. I started my career in the design department of a film distribution company, working on posters and DVD covers for world markets.

I went freelance in 2010 and focused my skills on UK-based FMCG. Brands I've worked with include Persil, KitKat, Nivea, and Heinz. My integrated social-media push for Night-Night Nappies won Best Online in *Vision* magazine's Advertising Awards 2018. The brand generated a 72% uptick in consolidated sales for the duration of the campaign.

What I will bring to your product or service is my unique brand of original thinking and many years' experience working with new media to deliver your brand message directly to your future customers. I am now studying for an MA in Multimedia Art. This is to build on my skills and help usher in a new personal era of creativity and inspiration. There is no better person to hire for your next award-winning campaign, and no better time to hire me.

Tutor's Report

Despite being shorter than the required word count, Ludya's essay proved to be a lesson in effective, succinct personal marketing. She was also an outstanding interview candidate. Her experience of pitching herself and her work in the real world showed. Grade: A–

Cameron Wesley

Cameron Wesley studied marketing and promotions at Greenwich Institute of Marketing. Cameron Wesley has vast experience in team management. Cameron Wesley can motivate people to maximize sales and operations in a progressive lean environment. Cameron Wesley is equally exceptional as a team member and as a leader.

Cameron Wesley has acknowledged and addressed some personal shortcomings in his current role and, rather than fight them, has decided to take positive steps and move his career sideways from team management to creative. Cameron Wesley recognizes that, in the long term, this route provides greater personal fulfilment and financial returns. That's why I'm doing this course.

Tutor's Report

Not only is Cameron's essay too short, but it fails to deliver the task set by the assignment and displays an overreliance on business-speak, with a complete absence of personal communication. More than this, it is lifted directly from the archived personnel page of a company he worked for six years ago and has been poorly edited—he deleted the bullet points but failed to remove the repetitions of his full name. While Cameron was an excellent interview candidate with boundless confidence, his style is more suited to middle management than to freelance presentation of artistic work. His grade reflects his noncompletion of the essay. Grade: Ungraded

Doodle message group [Private] Hannah and Cameron, November 7, 2023:

Hannah O'Donnell
Hi Cameron. Just to let you know, the work you submitted for Assignment Two is set to be ungraded. What we do in this situation is give you the opportunity to rewrite and resubmit that work. It's nothing to worry about, but we need to organize it as soon as possible, so you don't fall behind the group.

Cameron Wesley
When's the deadline?

Hannah O'Donnell
This Friday.

Cameron Wesley
No can do. Can the mark stay?

Hannah O'Donnell
Well, yes. But coursework is half your final grade, and most students like to maximize their grades as they go along.

Cameron Wesley
Balls! Just let it stay.

Doodle message group [Private] Jem and Patrick, November 7, 2023:

Patrick Bright
Well done, Jem. Great work!

Jem Badhuri
Thanks, Pat! You too. I really enjoyed the role-play.

Patrick Bright
I wish you hadn't mentioned me in relation to all that business about Alyson and the stock cupboard. I only helped you with some prices, that's all.

Jem Badhuri

OMG Cameron! His essay was terrible, and his interview so evasive. Yet when he talks, everyone listens. He's like a politician.

Patrick Bright

Surely underneath it all he's as insecure as the rest of us.

Jem Badhuri

I'm not insecure. But I'm not like Cameron, either.

Patrick Bright

Did anything strike you as odd during the role-play? Alyson said she studied at Gonville, then quickly corrected herself to St. Martins. She and Gela laughed, like it was an in-joke.

Jem Badhuri

Alyson didn't even write anything for this assignment. Well, I managed to slip a couple of remarks into my essay. Do you think anyone noticed?

Doodle message group MMAM(FTP), November 7, 2023:

Alyson Lang

For the record, Patrick, I don't work overnight here just to use materials and equipment. I'm a night owl. It's how I work.

Patrick Bright

Jem was joking, weren't you, Jem? Very funny!

Jem Badhuri

Phew! I really enjoyed the role-play, but I was more nervous than I thought. Gela was a tough interviewer. Thought I did well, especially as I'm the youngest. Ludya was amazing, but then she's been promoting herself for years, so it was hardly a stretch for her.

Ludya Parak

Thanks.

Jonathan Danners

Glad that's over. Big shout-out to Alyson, Cameron, and Ludya. All three of you are ace at interviews. I felt embarrassed the whole time. Ridiculous really. I've interviewed so many people myself.

Jem Badhuri

Your story is so tragic people might employ you out of sympathy.

Patrick Bright

Jonathan did great. Useful exercise, no? We got to make mistakes in a safe space. You're right, Jonathan. It made me think of all the girls I've interviewed for the shop. Hope I wasn't too fearsome.

Doodle message group [Private] Jem and Ludya, November 7, 2023:

Jem Badhuri

Hi Ludya! Do you fancy going for lunch or a coffee in the Aviator? On me.

Ludya Parak

Why?

Jem Badhuri

We haven't spoken much on the course and it would be great to know each other better.

Ludya Parak

Maybe.

Jem Badhuri

And Assignment Three requires work in 2D, which is not my forte, to say the least. I have a few questions.

Doodle message group MMAM(FTP), November 13, 2023:

Alyson Lang

My portfolio has gone. I left it on the shelf under my studio table on Thursday. It wasn't there when I got in this morning. It's a black leather case with a metallic sticker of a skull on one corner. Please tell me one of you has picked it up and kept it for me.

Jem Badhuri

I'd never leave anything in the studio overnight, personally.

Alyson Lang

I didn't leave it there, I forgot to pick it up when I went home. It has my sketchbook and other personal items.

Patrick Bright

Sorry, no. Have you asked Hannah? It may have been handed in. Or the technicians? They might have put it safely aside somewhere.

Doodle message group [Private] Alyson and Hannah, November 13, 2023:

Alyson Lang

Has anyone handed in a large black portfolio bag? Metallic skull sticker on one corner. Left in the MA studio. I asked the technicians. They haven't seen it.

Hannah O'Donnell

Nothing yet, but I've only just got in. Was there anything valuable in it?

Alyson Lang

Yes! My sketchbook. And various personal items.

Hannah O'Donnell

We don't recommend leaving anything of value in the studio. Fingers crossed it turns up.

Doodle message group [Private] Gela and Alyson, November 13, 2023:

Gela Nathaniel
Hannah says you've lost something?

Alyson Lang
My portfolio, FFS. It was on the shelf under my table. I never leave anything in the studio and the one time I do, it fucking disappears!

Gela Nathaniel
What was in it?

Alyson Lang
What do you think? Work.

Gela Nathaniel
If an outsider were to come across it, would that be a huge problem?

Alyson Lang
It would depend who they were. Yes, probably.

Gela Nathaniel
There's no point panicking. Sit tight. Carry on as normal.

Message group: 2024 Examiners, May 30, 2024

Tilda Ricci
Ben, I've read pages and pages of this. Can you tell me briefly what the problem is?

Ben Sketcher
This is just how the course started. Tensions fester, grow, and come to a head during the final project.

Tilda Ricci
Yes, the "real" commission, funded by a local company.

Ben Sketcher
They constructed an interactive sculpture, an artistic "installation" for a corporate function.

Karen Carpenter
That's it! I had the details, now where did I put them?

Ben Sketcher
If possible, I want to attend that event.

Karen Carpenter
It's too posh for the likes of us!

Tilda Ricci
That's above and beyond. You only need to check the grades aren't too high or low.

Karen Carpenter
Found it! But it's a private function, Ben. Sorry. It says "Invitation only."

Tilda Ricci
When is it?

Karen Carpenter
May 30.

Ben Sketcher
That's right. Tonight.

Doodle message group MMAM(FTP), November 14, 2023:

Alyson Lang
Panic over. Portfolio turned up unscathed. Thanks, Gela.

Gela Nathaniel
Everyone, please take care of your personal things while in the studio. Alyson was lucky a BA student found it and brought it to the staff room.

Doodle message group [Private] Jem and Patrick, November 14, 2023:

Jem Badhuri
Have you noticed something?

Patrick Bright
Are you gossiping, Ms. Badhuri?

Jem Badhuri
Yes. About Jonathan and Alyson.

Patrick Bright
Ah, you mean when they refused to wine and dine the industry guest? Gela didn't like that at all. I've not seen her so worked up.

Jem Badhuri
The funny thing is they *both* objected to taking the guest out and snapped at Gela. Last night, when I was waiting for Dad, they were together in the studio. From my little spot by the door I could hear them discussing Assignment Three. They were really friendly and chatty. What do you make of that?

Patrick Bright
I don't know.

Jem Badhuri
A few weeks ago they spoke to each other in single words, if at all. If they could avoid each other, they did. It's been like that since Alyson set fire to his assignment. But TBH he should've thanked her—he resubmitted

and got a C, when Gela point-blank refused to let anyone else improve their grade that way. Jonathan seems to have forgotten that now.

Patrick Bright
What did you think of the industry guest then? Nice old fellow?

Jem Badhuri
He has a gallery, but then so does Jonathan, and he's the least talented student on this course.

Patrick Bright
Ah, now that's not so.

Jem Badhuri
That's what Gela thinks. You can hear the awkwardness in her voice when she talks about his work.

Patrick Bright
He's one of the least experienced. He'll catch up.

Jem Badhuri
How did he get on this course? Gela selected me. She came to my degree show. A hundred students were exhibiting their work, but it was *me* she noticed and invited to apply.

Patrick Bright
That's nice. I imagine Gela has to balance things. The designers who want to improve their art and the artists who want to commercialize their work. That's before you get to the clashes of personality!

Jem Badhuri
Clashes of personality? OMG! What have you noticed?

Patrick Bright
Oh, just big characters, lots of talent and ambition. But everything will shake down for the final project, I'm sure. It's a group effort, so we'll have to get along for that.

To: MMAM(FTP)
From: Gela Nathaniel
Date: November 14, 2023
Subject: Final project

Dear all,

I trust you're approaching the closing stages of Assignment Three. Before Christmas we'll work together on a collective pitch for the final project. This is the main, collaborative assignment that accounts for 50% of your final grade. You'll work on a real-world professional installation, then write your own personal account of the project—a document we call "the long essay."

I'm delighted to say that a local company, RD8 Systems Ltd., which delivers cloud-based solutions, has agreed to hear our pitch for their launch of a new technology next spring. From now until the end of term we'll work on and rehearse our pitch, ready for a group presentation in front of their panel on Tuesday, December 12. Please ensure this date is in your Doodle Diary and every other calendar you have. Exciting times!

Gela

Doodle message group MMAM(FTP), November 14, 2023:

Jem Badhuri
What's a cloud-based solution? Rain?

Patrick Bright
Ha-ha! It's gobbledygook!

Jem Badhuri
What's gobble dy gook? A "solution"? Must be some sort of liquid.

Patrick Bright
Gobbledygook means nonsense talk.

Cameron Wesley
RD8 develops systems that integrate radio-frequency identification and wireless-communication technology with internet applications to optimize security and mobility.

Patrick Bright
Sounds like you know all about this, Cameron.

Jonathan Danners
He's copied and pasted from the company website. Basically, they combine old (radio) and new (internet) technologies so that things like credit-card payments work on-the-move.

Jem Badhuri
Radio? That's awesome. I LOVE radio. My whole family too. I've been listening to the radio all my life.

Alyson Lang
What's Gela thinking? Could she have found a duller company in a more obscure industry?

Ludya Parak
Dream job. Geeks and nerds don't know a single damn thing about design. Give them any old shit and they're happy.

Alyson Lang
Because they don't appreciate aesthetics. What's the ecological profile of this company? Are they committed to human rights?

Patrick Bright
Wikipedia says they developed early weapons systems, back in the day.

Alyson Lang
Exactly. I'd rather spend my time helping an ambitious start-up, a charity, or a company with a genuine altruistic vision. At the very least, an organization that appreciates the hard work and talent that goes into a creative project.

Ludya Parak
I'd rather work with a company that has the MONEY.

Jem Badhuri
Do we get paid?

Cameron Wesley
It's a sponsorship deal. I've worked with colleges before. Big enthusiasm, small invoices, juicy tax breaks. Happy days!

Jem Badhuri
If this is a real job, shouldn't we get the money for it, not the department? What do you think, Alyson? It's only fair.

Patrick Bright
I imagine there are legal restrictions on that, Jem.

Jem Badhuri
Still, it's really exciting. Wait till I tell my dad!

Doodle message group [Private] Patrick and Jem, November 15, 2023:

Patrick Bright
How are you getting along with Assignment Three? Need a shoulder to cry on?

Jem Badhuri
No. I'm almost done.

Patrick Bright
I badly need a hand with that software. It's quite the mystery.

Jem Badhuri
If you need help, just ask.

Patrick Bright
How kind of you, young Jem! Thank you.

Jem Badhuri
Not me. Tony the technician. I heard Jonathan say how good he is with FlowHand. I'm too busy with my own assignment.

To: Gela Nathaniel
From: Griff Technician (Maintenance)
Date: November 16, 2023
Subject: Studio policy

Dear Mrs. Nathaniel,

Your MA student Alyson was talking to a lady in the studio this morning. This lady left out of the rear doors as I arrived. She wasn't from our department and the snippet of conversation I overheard was of a personal nature. May I draw your attention to the regulations that stipulate no one outside the department—staff, students, and registered guests—is allowed onto college property. This includes the studios, all outbuildings, and storage facilities.

I assume this unofficial guest gained access via the overflow parking lot, where there is a gap in the fence. Please can you impress upon your students that college property is not a suitable venue for an all-night drinking session.

The empty wine bottles have been recycled.

Griff

To: Griff Technician (Maintenance)
From: Gela Nathaniel
Date: November 16, 2023
Subject: Re: Studio policy

I'm so sorry Griff. Alyson barely drinks at all, so who this mysterious guest was, I don't know. As you say, it's not allowed and I'll make sure she and the other MA students are fully aware of college rules.

Gela

Doodle message group [Private] Gela and Alyson, November 16, 2023:

Gela Nathaniel
You had someone in the studio overnight. Who was it?

Alyson Lang
It doesn't matter.

Gela Nathaniel

Unregistered guests are expressly not allowed on college premises. It's a particular problem when maintenance staff have to clear away wine bottles. What were you doing?

Alyson Lang

It won't happen again.

Gela Nathaniel

Please ensure that is the case.

Doodle message group [Private] Jonathan and Gela, November 17, 2023:

Jonathan Danners

Gela, I think you should know something about Assignment Three.

Gela Nathaniel

If you want to tell me, go on.

Jonathan Danners

I don't want it getting back to me and causing trouble. It's just when I see something that's wrong on every level, I want to put it right.

Gela Nathaniel

You have my word.

Jonathan Danners

Basically, Jem is a 3D artist, clay and sound are her comfort zones, while 2D isn't her bag. She knows she's going to get a mediocre grade . . . I'm afraid she's paid Ludya to do the 2D part of her assignment.

Gela Nathaniel

How much?

Jonathan Danners

I don't know. It must've been a couple of hundred, surely? Else it wouldn't have been worth Ludya's time and risk.

Gela Nathaniel

Did they work together? Did Jem tell Ludya what she wanted and Ludya created it?

Jonathan Danners

Well, to an extent. But the vision and skill set are Ludya's, not Jem's. I wouldn't say anything if I didn't think it was detrimental to the group and against the spirit of the MMAM course.

Gela Nathaniel

Thank you for telling me, Jonathan. You did the right thing.

Doodle message group [Private] Gela and Ludya, November 17, 2023:

Gela Nathaniel

How much did Jem pay you to do half her assignment? Don't deny it. I know she did.

Ludya Parak

Who told you?

Gela Nathaniel

Never mind that. How much did you get?

Ludya Parak

Three hundred eighty-five dollars. Her dad paid it, obvs. I'm a professional. I don't turn work down. Kids need to eat and I need my own FlowHand 11. The code Cameron gave me for the online version is years out of date. Anyway, it's much less than I'd usually charge. Mates' rates and all that.

Gela Nathaniel

Cash?

Ludya Parak

Yes, cash. What of it? What are you going to say, Gela? Nothing.

MMAM(FTP)
Coursework Module: Assignment Three
Tutor's Report, November 21, 2023

Brief: Use digital software to devise a fully integrated multimedia campaign to encompass posters, print advertising, and social media. The brand or product may be that from Assignment One, a different fictional brand, or an existing popular brand. Create two elements for submission.

Overview: The group know each other better now and are familiar with each other's working styles and abilities. The third assignment demonstrated a significant step forward in their relationships and, as a result, an improvement in the quality of work produced, with group members helping and advising each other. Thanks to this, we now have six projects that I am proud to display on the screens in the foyer of the Media Arts building before Christmas break. The object of our first three assignments has been to integrate the group into a supportive, productive team. I am happy to report there is now a solid foundation on which to build as we move into the final project phase.

Jemisha Badhuri

Jem chose to create an integrated campaign for her ocean animal charity from Assignment One. She devised a prototype well-being app that allows the user to play calming ocean sounds whenever they feel stressed or anxious. Its monthly subscription fee would benefit the charity. She also devised an e-poster for train stations, airports, and escalators, which incorporated waves washing over multiple screens. Jem's app was well conceived and executed, but her 2D screen campaign was outstanding and showed a particularly professional hand, especially surprising given that she has no experience in this area and so far has only worked in familiar mediums on this course. The success of her design demonstrates a willingness to venture out of her comfort zones of clay and sound and try her hand at something different. Grade: A–

Patrick Bright

Patrick again chose to work on a campaign for his shop. His first element was an extensive e-billboard ad campaign, designed to be displayed alongside major roads. His second element was a social-media reel that incorporated a quotations game, with quotes relevant to art supplies. While a trade-based supplies company would probably never require either of these, the simple design of pencils and paintbrushes falling like rain was eye-catching enough and showed that he has at least started to work with FlowHand 11. His quotations game revealed that Patrick is unfamiliar with the sort of content likely to go viral on social media. However, inadvertently he managed to create something that potentially could. As "The pen is mightier than the sword" scrolled across the screen, it froze on "pen is." Grade: B–

Jonathan Danners

Jonathan devised a multimedia campaign for his family art gallery. It comprised a print ad and e-poster for local bus stops and roads, intended to drive footfall to a new (fictional) exhibition. It was entitled "The Beauty of Fraud," a quirky event featuring artworks known to be clever fakes, such as an image of the *Mona Lisa* melting into an inflatable Halloween skeleton with an alarming decomposed skull, to demonstrate that one never knows what is lurking beneath the surface. Jonathan's campaign was a clever idea but never quite delivered, thanks to his basic lack of technical ability. While collaboration is encouraged on MMAM, Jonathan would also do better if he concentrated on his own work and not that of others. Grade: C–

Alyson Lang

Alyson once again delivered an ad campaign as good as, if not better than, any devised by a top agency. She also showed her confidence and courage in that she chose a completely new project. Her print and poster ads were part of a (fictional) recruitment campaign for Royal Hastings, advertising for a senior tutor on this very course. Her poster depicted an unhappy woman in a suit gradually becoming less conventional in her dress until she was relaxed and happy in her new role. She set herself a difficult task and not only achieved her aim, but excelled. Grade: A+

Ludya Parak

Ludya continued her ad campaign for the paddleboarding school of her first assignment. Unfortunately, she came unstuck early in its execution, because beyond a reel of her personal snaps of children paddleboarding, there wasn't much else to work with. Most of the pictures included Ludya herself, revealing that she wasn't even the main photographer for this piece. Ludya submitted her work five minutes before the deadline, alongside a special-consideration form citing "personal reasons" preventing her from completing the task to the best of her abilities. She has submitted a special-consideration form with every assignment so far. Her design feels rushed and not up to her usual standard of solid competence. She needs to balance her time effectively between this course and her paid work. Grade: D–

Cameron Wesley

Cameron submitted a solid campaign of e-posters and print ads for a well-known brand of tampons and sanitary towels. It was designed to highlight the company's ecological credentials and sustainable, biodegradable materials in the face of competition from reusable products. A quick google took me straight to a trade-paper article about the campaign, which ran six years ago, was nominated for an industry award, and was devised by the company Cameron worked for at the time. He is not even named as a creative on it. I cannot grade Cameron for work that is clearly not his. He has been contacted and a meeting requested to discuss his future on the course. Grade: Ungraded

Doodle message group [Private] Hannah and Cameron, November 21, 2023:

Hannah O'Donnell
Your assignment is ungraded again. Can you meet with me and Gela this week?

Cameron Wesley
Bit busy. I'll submit something else.

Hannah O'Donnell
Nonetheless, we'd like to discuss how best to support you in completing this course.

Cameron Wesley
Gela knows why I'm not as productive as the others. I'll try and send something by the end of the week.

Doodle message group MMAM(FTP), November 21, 2023:

Jem Badhuri
Cameron, did you not submit anything at all?

Patrick Bright
He hasn't been on Doodle for ages, Jem.

Jem Badhuri
I think he's going to leave the course. Gela will have more time for the rest of us.

Patrick Bright
I hope not. One less team member to muck in on the final project.

Jem Badhuri
I'm stoked about my grade for Assignment Three. 2D is a nightmare for me. I find the software easy enough to use, but I know my strengths and weaknesses. I think and work in three dimensions.

Jonathan Danners

You seem to have mastered 2D for this assignment.

Jem Badhuri

Yes, phew! I hope we get to do some proper construction for the final project. I'd love to explore salvaged materials.

Alyson Lang

Gela says a keypad will be in place when we get back from the Christmas break. It'd better be.

Jem Badhuri

Interesting what Gela was saying about building a team, so we each have different responsibilities for the final project. Can we choose what we do?

Patrick Bright

Was wondering this myself. Don't want to be landed with tasks I'm not able to perform and letting the whole team down. But I spoke to Gela and she assured me she'll give us each a role that suits our skill sets, but also stretches us, so we learn.

Ludya Parak

I can't commit huge chunks of time. Personal reasons.

Jem Badhuri

Gela decides? OK. Thanks, Patrick.

To: Gela Nathaniel
From: Jemisha Badhuri
Date: November 21, 2023
Subject: The final project

Hi Gela,

Patrick said you choose who gets to do what for the final project.

I would like to put myself forward for the role of project manager. I may be the youngest, but I've been an artist for longer than either Jonathan or Patrick and my youthful outlook means I can connect with a younger audience, which is usually what advertisers want, according to Cameron.

I approach obstacles with a can-do attitude and I get on with every-one. The final project is for a company that makes parts for radios, which I've been listening to my whole life. I am very aware of the other personalities on this course and what their limitations are. Ludya is chaotic and lazy, unless she's being paid. Alyson is good, but she knows it. Jonathan really should have chosen a beginners' course. Patrick is a nice man, but lacks energy and direction. Cameron is probably going to leave the course anyway.

My dad is very generous. He helped fund the degree show at West Middlesex, where you saw my work for the first time and asked if I wanted to apply for this MA. Seems so long ago now! I know he'll want to donate something to Royal Hastings' art department too.

Happy to chat after tomorrow's session.

Jem

To: Jemisha Badhuri
From: Gela Nathaniel
Date: November 22, 2023
Subject: Re: The final project

Dear Jem,
Thank you for your email and kind offer to lead the final project. Further to our chat today, I'll be outlining RD8's brief next week and appointing roles for the pitch meeting and the project itself.

Let's just say every student will get the role that best suits their experience, skill set, personality, and scope for improvement. All will be revealed in due course.

Gela

Doodle message group [Private] Jem and Patrick, November 22, 2023:

Jem Badhuri
So excited! Gela is going to ask me to lead the final project.

Patrick Bright
Well, congratulations.

Jem Badhuri
She hasn't said so in as many words, but I can read between the lines.

Patrick Bright
To be honest, I feel very uncomfortable.

Jem Badhuri
Oh no, poor you. Why?

Patrick Badhuri
If I tell you, you must promise not to breathe a word to anyone.

Jem Badhuri
I promise.

Patrick Bright
It's Alyson and Jonathan. To put it delicately, I think they're having an affair.

Jem Badhuri
OMG! But she's married.

Patrick Bright
Quite. She's mentioned the husband giving her a lift in several times.

Jem Badhuri
I noticed a change in the way they spoke to each other, but have you seen anything conclusive?

Patrick Bright
You know I drove in yesterday, well, after the session I got all the way to the car, only to realize my phone was still in the studio tray. By the time I'd trudged back, everyone had gone and the front door was locked. I nipped to the rear doors. From there I saw Alyson and Jonathan at the sink in the cutting room, just chatting, close together, but nothing untoward. I was about to clear my throat when he gave her a peck on the cheek and moved away to the cupboard.

Jem Badhuri
Is there a rule against students having affairs? Should Gela be told?

Patrick Bright
I don't think there is such a rule. It's not our business. It's simply that I find it very awkward.

Jem Badhuri
But how can Jonathan even *like* a woman who set fire to his Assignment One model?

Patrick Bright
Attraction is complicated. Some people like to be dominated. I think.

Jem Badhuri
Her husband, though! He deserves to know.

Patrick Bright
Not at all. Ignorance is bliss. Anyway, he may already be aware. Relationships can be strange.

To: MMAM(FTP)
From: Gela Nathaniel
Date: November 30, 2023
Subject: Final project—the pitch

Dear all,

Further to our session today, here are the details you'll need as we prepare for our pitch to RD8 on December 12. You will each have a part to play in the meeting, with clearly defined discussion points relating to the roles you've been assigned. Please spend the time between now and then working on what you'll say to the panel. Please also research the industry of cloud-based communications systems and the company RD8. But most of all: ideas! In our preparation sessions I expect each of you to contribute at least three creative ideas for the company's big event next summer.

Remember, this project will be 50% of your final grade. You will work on it together, then write a long essay from your personal point of view. In this you will analyze where it went right and (hopefully not too badly) wrong, and what you learned from the experience. In the meantime, here is the team list:

Jonathan Danners	project manager
Alyson Lang	creative director
Ludya Parak	time manager
Patrick Bright	resource coordinator
Jem Badhuri	financial manager
Cameron Wesley	teamworker

The project manager will assign other roles as and when they arise. These titles form the structural foundation of the team, but you will all help to shape the creative vision and take a hands-on approach to constructing the installation to the client's brief.

I hope you're all looking forward to this exciting adventure!
Gela

Doodle message group MMAM(FTP), November 30, 2023:

Alyson Lang
I've just heard some good news. Guess what it is.

Jonathan Danners
Cameron, I'd like you to take notes at the meeting on Tuesday.

Patrick Bright
He's left Doodle, Jonathan.

Jonathan Danners
Does anyone know his phone number?

Patrick Bright
I'll take notes, I don't mind.

Jonathan Danners
Thank you, Patrick. I'll take over when it's your turn to speak.

Ludya Parak
I don't bother preparing for meets. Prefer to wing it. All this buildup creates nerves and a lack of flow in the presentation. Plus I've got stuff this weekend.

Jem Badhuri
Personal stuff?

Jonathan Danners
If Cameron was still in this group, he'd confirm that in the real world there would be competition for a contract like this. We'd be fighting for it, so we'd have to prepare. Luckily Gela has already done the difficult bit of winning the commission.

Ludya Parak
Yes, personal stuff, as it happens.

Jem Badhuri
I'm going to ask Gela to change my role. Numbers aren't my thing.

Alyson Lang
She must've been impressed with your calculations when you were trying to get me kicked off the course for stealing.

Jem Badhuri
I don't know what you're talking about.

Alyson Lang
Apparently you had a spreadsheet and everything.

Jem Badhuri
Stuff went missing whenever you stayed overnight—anyone would be suspicious.

Ludya Parak
You actually did that, Jem? Wow. That is devious.

Patrick Bright
Now, now, Jem only saw something she thought was awry and didn't want the whole department to suffer. In any case, it was weeks ago. Water under the bridge.

Alyson Lang
I don't want to work with Jem.

Jem Badhuri

I don't want to work with Alyson. Or Jonathan, but fat chance of that, seeing as Gela put him in charge. At least Cameron has gone, because he'd be a nightmare. Patrick is the only nice person on this course.

Ludya Parak

Settles down with snacks to watch the entertainment.

Jem Badhuri

I don't want to work with Ludya, either. I'd end up doing everything. I know her type.

Jonathan Danners

I'd be careful about throwing accusations around, Jem. When you point the finger at someone, there are three fingers pointing back at you.

Ludya Parak

OK, so by "my type" you mean . . . ?

Alyson Lang

We don't have to like each other. We just have to work together.

Jem Badhuri

The team list is a joke. Ludya in charge of time management? She can't manage her own time, let alone everyone else's.

Jonathan Danners

Gela has appointed roles that challenge us.

Ludya Parak

I haven't been a professional in this industry for fifteen years without being a good time manager. If I was sitting on my ass all day with nothing else to do, I'd submit my projects on time. I'm not. Anyway, I submitted your assignment on time, didn't I?

Patrick Bright

What do you mean, Ludya?

Ludya Parak

Jem commissioned me to do her 2D assignment. I'm a PROFESSIONAL, so of course I accepted the job. She got a B+.

Alyson Lang

I could tell it was your work from a mile away. Gela knows too, btw.

Ludya Parak

I know she knows. What I don't know is who told her? Did you, Alyson?

Jonathan Danners

Team, let's chill out. We know each other better now. We've got our main project coming up. We can look forward to working together in a spirit of collective creativity. We all want to learn the art of turning our skills and talents into professional employment. It's what we signed up for when we applied for this course and I, for one, am here for it.

Jem Badhuri

You, for one, are the least professional person on this course. Ask Patrick. He saw you and Alyson kissing in the cutting room. He was disgusted.

Ludya Parak

Whoa! This group is getting wilder by the minute.

Patrick Bright

Now I told you that in confidence, Jem. That's not our, or anyone else's, business.

Jonathan Danners

Team members' personal lives have no relevance to the project.

Jem Badhuri

Not even when one of them is married? What would Alyson's husband say if someone felt he deserved to know and told him?

Alyson Lang

Is that a threat, Jem?

Jem Badhuri *has left the group.*
Cameron Wesley *has joined the group.*

Cameron Wesley

OK, so Gela says I have to rejoin this Doodle nonsense for the final project. Any news?

Jonathan Danners
You've got the role of teamworker, Cameron.

Cameron Wesley
Too vague. I respond best to positive, forward-thinking job titles.

Ludya Parak
Teamwanker.

Ludya Parak *has left the group.*

Cameron Wesley
Team leader or management consultant. I'll speak to Gela. She knows I lose interest if I'm not in charge.

Patrick Bright
Team MMAM. We've cleared the air and I'm now leaving the group—temporarily—to concentrate on my research. I'll see you all bright and early Tuesday, ready to refine our pitch to RD8.

Patrick Bright *has left the group.*

Alyson Lang
Anyway the keypad will be fitted on Friday.

To: MMAM(FTP)
From: Hannah O'Donnell
Date: December 1, 2023
Subject: Final project brief

Dear all,
I'm delighted to include below your brief for the final project.

Brief: RD8 is planning to launch a new system that blends radio waves with cloud technology for a new generation of mobile payment systems. The MMAM team has been commissioned to create a multimedia installation in the foyer of RD8's headquarters for the launch event. It is to be an eye-catching, interactive, showstopping feature, experienced by guests at a summer-evening champagne reception. It should inspire, entertain, and educate, alongside the company's own speeches and presentations.

Students are encouraged to minimize the risk of controversy and bear in mind RD8's commitment to inclusivity, regardless of gender identity, race, ability-status, age, or religion.

Deadline: May 30, 2024
Approved by: Angela Nathaniel, course tutor

Doodle message group [Private] Hannah and Gela, December 4, 2023:

Hannah O'Donnell
I still don't have the diversity forms for the MMAM(FTP) class.

Gela Nathaniel
You know what it's like in the studio. Always messy with paint, clay, glue, etc. I'm waiting for a clean day to hand them out. Bear with.

Hannah O'Donnell
Thanks, Gela.

Message group: 2024 Examiners, May 30, 2024

Ben Sketcher

Hi Karen, just wondered, do you have contact details for Hannah O'Donnell? She is/was admin for the MMAM(FTP) course.

Karen Carpenter

Let me finish eating this cake.

Tilda Ricci

Is there a problem with your access to the Doodle archives, Ben?

Ben Sketcher

I'm interested in Hannah's opinion on the group. To put it politely, some members didn't get along, and it isn't always clear—even with access to their Doodle messages—how far they were prepared to take that hostility.

Karen Carpenter

Well, I see she's still in her role at RH. Can I give her your details?

Ben Sketcher

Thanks, Karen. She may be a witness to something.

Tilda Ricci

A witness? I've been reading the messages and I have to agree the atmosphere was not particularly harmonious. But you think someone had a hidden agenda?

Ben Sketcher

Something like that.

Karen Carpenter

I've noticed something funny, Ben! You're an external examiner for an *art* course—and your name is "Sketcher!"

Karen Carpenter

Ha-ha-ha!

Ben Sketcher

Actually it's an occupational surname, like yours, Karen. Sketcher comes from the Yiddish word "Shekhter." It means "ritual slaughterer" or "butcher."

To: MMAM(FTP)
From: Gela Nathaniel
Date: December 4, 2023
Subject: Agenda

Dear all,

As promised, here is our agenda for the important MMAM(FTP) meeting so that we can spend this week preparing our pitch for the big day. Remember your participation in, and contribution to, these meetings will be marked as part of your final grade. The very straightforward agenda is below.

1. Discussion of roles
2. Research into RD8 and cloud solutions
3. Ideas! Ideas! Ideas!

If you have your own agendas, please post on Doodle and I'll log in before the session to make sure we discuss everything.

    Gela

Doodle message group [Private] Jem and Gela, December 4, 2023:

Jem Badhuri

Gela, can I speak to you in confidence? Certain students are bullying me. I need to know you're on my side.

Gela Nathaniel

That's awful. I'm sorry to hear that, Jem. Royal Hastings has protocols in place for this. Would you like me to lodge the complaint for you? In the first instance you will be asked to describe the bullying to an impartial member of admin staff—that is, someone who isn't involved with our course.

Jem Badhuri

No need for that. Let's keep it between us. You can help improve the situation quite easily if you agree with me more often in the studio. That would really help me get my voice heard.

Gela Nathaniel
May I ask who it is that bullies you, and how?

Jem Badhuri
Alyson and Ludya. Cameron probably would, if he ever spoke to me; and since Jonathan forgot what happened to his Assignment One model, and started an affair with the woman who set fire to it, he's been talking down to me too. Patrick is the only one who doesn't.

Gela Nathaniel
OK, well, I'll see what I can do.

Doodle message group [Private] Gela, Jonathan, Alyson, and Ludya, December 4, 2023:

Gela Nathaniel
Please, everyone, make allowances for Jem. Despite everything, she's a fireball of ambition, notices the smallest nuance of behavior, and could very easily become the troublemaker who disrupts this whole thing, if we're not careful.

Doodle message group [Private] Gela and Ludya, December 5, 2023:

Gela Nathaniel
Alyson and Jonathan are getting less discreet.

Ludya Parak
It shouldn't affect anything.

Gela Nathaniel
Jem and Patrick don't like it.

Ludya Parak
It's none of their business. Or anyone else's on the course.

Gela Nathaniel
I think Jem may have been a little sweet on Jonathan at the start. She's always seen Alyson as a rival, now this too. I'll stamp on any complaints that come my way, but please be careful how you speak to her.

Ludya Parak
Sorry, I've got a lot going on with the kids. OK, I'll see if I can get them to tone it down or deflect.

Gela Nathaniel
Something that doesn't involve setting fire to the studio again, please.

Doodle message group [Private] Gela and Alyson, December 5, 2023:

Gela Nathaniel
Do you know what you're playing with?

Alyson Lang
What do you mean?

Gela Nathaniel
You and J. It disrupts the other students.

Alyson Lang
We're two adults who met and fell in love. Happens all the time.

Gela Nathaniel
It adds an unnecessary layer of risk.

Alyson Lang
While they're gossiping about our steamy affair they're not noticing anything else, are they?

Doodle message group [Private] Gela and Jonathan, December 5, 2023:

Gela Nathaniel
Just a quick word. I hope you and Alyson can be more discreet in the future. An obvious relationship can disrupt the harmony of a group.

Jonathan Danners
I'm sorry. We should have been more careful.

Doodle message group [Private] Cameron and Gela, December 5, 2023:

Cameron Wesley
Can't make the course days this week. Something's come up at the office. I'll be there on the 12th. Wouldn't miss that for the world.

Gela Nathaniel
OK, thanks for letting me know.

Cameron Wesley
Kiss-kiss.

Gela Nathaniel
Kiss-kiss.

To: MMAM(FTP)
From: Gela Nathaniel
Date: December 5, 2023
Subject: New entry system

Hello all,
Some of you will already have noticed the studio door now has an electronic keypad. This means only people with the code can enter the studio. The door is opened from the inside by pressing the green button on the left, although I'm assured that, in the event of a fire, throwing yourself against it will do the trick.

The code is F3919A. Of course it is confidential and not to be shared with anyone outside our group. See you later for our exciting pitch preparation session in the studio.

Gela

Doodle message group [Private] Jem and Gela, December 5, 2023:

Jem Badhuri
Dad's been helping me research RD8 and you'll never guess what they pioneered a few years ago: binaural sound! I know all about this from my sound course. It's super-innovative. I think you should consider reappointing the roles so that our project leader has some knowledge and experience of the client's key tech.

Gela Nathaniel
Thanks for letting me know, Jem. I don't think their new system incorporates binaural sound, but perhaps Mae and her team can confirm either way. If so, then I'm sure your expertise will be beneficial to the team, and to Jonathan as project leader.

Doodle message group [Private] Hannah and Gela, December 6, 2023:

Hannah O'Donnell
Your MMAM diversity forms?

Gela Nathaniel
Sorry, sorry! Soon, I promise. Only our first session preparing for the client pitch is about to start. I'm literally going in now.

Hannah O'Donnell
OK. As soon as you can.

Doodle message group [Private] Gela, Ludya, Jonathan, and Alyson, December 6, 2023:

Gela Nathaniel
Are you OK, Ludya?

Ludya Parak
Yep. Thanks for asking.

Doodle message group [Private] Patrick and Gela, December 6, 2023:

Patrick Bright
Do you want me to write the meeting report as if everything went smoothly?

Gela Nathaniel
Yes, please. And thank you for stepping in.

MMAM(FTP)
Meeting on December 6, 2023, to discuss the pitch to RD8

Present: Gela Nathaniel, Jonathan Danners,
                              Alyson Lang, Ludya Parak, Jem Badhuri,
                              Patrick Bright
Apologies for absence: Cameron Wesley
Notes taken by: Patrick Bright
Agenda: Discussion of roles
                              Research into RD8 and cloud solutions
                              Ideas! Ideas! Ideas!

- Gela began by assuring everyone the roles she's given us will not be changed and that when we're out of our comfort zone it's an opportunity for learning and growth. If we think we've been given the wrong role, it's something we can bring up in our long essay.
- Gela asked us to present our research. Jem volunteered to go first. She spoke at length about another area of RD8's business: binaural sound, which she studied on a course recently. Apparently it's a complex mix of sound waves that are so precise and intense they can make you *feel* things—a science called ASMR (I looked it up and it stands for "autonomous sensory meridian response"). Jem played us some YouTube videos, so it's a proper thing. Binaural sound is recorded using a microphone shaped like an eyeless human head on a stick. Downright creepy, if you ask me! Young Jem had more to say, but Gela suggested we move on to the actual project.
- We spoke about "cloud solutions" and what it actually means— put simply, computerized things that happen automatically, not on your laptop or phone, but in the atmosphere. There are locations for the storage, but it uses old-fashioned radio waves too. I have to admit I really am none the wiser, even after it was explained several times. My technological know-how extends only to whether a button I press works or not. All credit to the others, who grasped it immediately. I think the younger generation is just more attuned to this sort of thing.

- RD8 have been around since the Second World War and developed technology for walkie-talkies, guided missiles, pagers, and microwave ovens. However, in recent years they moved into secure payment transactions. So when you tap your card to pay for a meal, you can bet RD8 had a hand in whatever device the waiter is holding.
- Gela then tried to explain how RD8 have made further advances in security that mean businesses all over the world can exchange money over the cloud. This technology will be launched by the company to its clients at an event in May. That event is what we are creating an installation for. Luckily we'll hear all this from the horses' mouths when we do our pitch.
- Next we threw around some ideas relating to technology things. Jem suggested binaural experiences for the guests, with a blackout room where they could immerse themselves in sound alone, delivered through special headphones where ASMR recordings could be played to them. Alyson felt we could move away from technology completely. Her idea was that we half-paint a large canvas with our designs, then give each guest an apron, a paintbrush, and some paints, so that every one of them has a hand in completing the picture. I should have said before, the company's brochure is entitled "Completing the Picture." Ludya said we could leave the wall blank and the guests can *start* the picture as well. I suggested a one-handed game. This got some laughs, until I explained: everyone will have a champagne glass in one hand, so we could make an electronic game they can play with the other. RD8 make remote controls and the like, so I would hope they'd have a game somewhere people could play. Jonathan mentioned an exhibition that came to his gallery, where each frame was empty and artwork was projected onto it. The art was created by a computer, out of every painting that had been fed into it. Gela said that as it had already been done, we didn't really want to go there. Ludya said she was at an Albanian wedding where they had a tunnel that the guests walked through to get to the ballroom. We could have a tunnel leading into the room where the event will be held, so guests feel they

are walking into "RD8 land." Jonathan suggested a chronological journey, starting with abstract designs of radios, planes, and missiles, then moving on to credit cards, as if the guest is being drawn through the history of the company to the present day.

- Finally, Gela said that was exactly what she hoped we'd do. Use everyone's ideas to create an exciting presentation for the client, which we will spend the rest of this week rehearsing and refining.

We ended by discussing what we'd wear to the pitch—whether creatives are expected to don suits and ties or something more relaxed. Gela suggested wearing what reflects our personality but also makes the client feel confident that we are on the same page as they are. She said appearances are crucial, and that reflecting your client can mean they choose you over someone they see as less like them.

The meeting ended at about twelve thirty.

Doodle message group [Private] Jem and Patrick, December 6, 2023:

Jem Badhuri
You didn't put anything in your notes about the argument.

Patrick Bright
I messaged Gela and asked if I should. She said no.

Jem Badhuri
But if her behavior isn't documented, then she can't be judged on it. No one should get a better grade just because Gela doesn't want anyone to fail the course.

Patrick Bright
It's exciting, no? The project. Designing something for a real event. I feel buoyant about it. We all had something to contribute. I hope they don't use anything I said—it was the ramblings of a dullard in comparison!

Jem Badhuri
What did *you* think of my ASMR idea?

Patrick Bright
It was ace, Jem! I've never heard of ASMR or binaural recording, but it "sounds" amazing. You never know, perhaps RD8 would like to see it in the installation. You can always ask at the pitch meeting.

Jem Badhuri
I have every intention of asking at the pitch meeting.

Doodle message group MMAM(FTP), December 11, 2023:

Hannah O'Donnell
Hello MMAMs! Just to say good luck for your pitch tomorrow. Has everyone got transport to RD8? Gela asked me to post a reminder to share cars and travel together, where possible.

Jem Badhuri
Patrick is driving me. Hannah, can I fix a meeting with you about something personal? It's about another member of the group.

Hannah O'Donnell
Of course. Send me an email at the admin address, please, Jem.

Doodle message group [Private] Alyson, Ludya, Jonathan, and Gela, December 11, 2023:

Ludya Parak
Jem has asked Hannah for a meeting "about another member of the group."

Gela Nathaniel
I've briefed Hannah on what happened yesterday. She'll deal with it.

Ludya Parak
Could I get dumped from the course, when I'm the victim?

Gela Nathaniel
That won't happen. Jem is on a learning curve. She's not used to working as part of a team. Her family life is all about her. Her BA degree was all about her. We all learn at some point that we're not the center of the universe, she's just learning a bit later than usual.

Alyson Lang
Gen Zs—love 'em, full of sass. Jem's fine, she has the skin of a rhino.

Ludya Parak
She'll be fine? What about me, FFS?

Gela Nathaniel
Her idea was totally in line with the company's business and her skill set.

Alyson Lang
I thought it was good.

Jonathan Danners
Me too. Better than my idea and Patrick's put together.

Ludya Parak

RD8 are in the business of connections, communication. They are all about bringing people together. The immersive installation at their launch party should be a collective experience that unites the audience. That's why they've chosen a group of ARTISTS on an ART course to devise and construct it. Jem's idea was EXCLUSIVE. The exact opposite. Headphones, blindfold, an internal experience . . . it meant sending people away into their own worlds. Alone. I don't care how amazing binaural ASMR is, it doesn't bring people together.

Jonathan Danners

I get it, but is that the hill you want to die on? Arguing with Jem?

Ludya Parak

Argh! No. Just so tired!

Gela Nathaniel

The RD8 panel will decide. If they don't like our main idea, then we can pitch the others.

Ludya Parak

True. Clients go gaga over the very thing you only mentioned to fill up time.

Jonathan Danners

What are the RD8 people like, Gela?

Gela Nathaniel

As you'd expect. Straight. Corporate. Unreadable.

To: Hannah O'Donnell
From: Jem Badhuri
Date: December 11, 2023
Subject: Ludya

Dear Hannah,

As you suggested, I'm putting my complaint in writing. It's about the way my work and I are dismissed. Ludya in particular was scathing about my ideas in the pitch prep meeting. She got very heated—far in excess of the situation. Patrick didn't include in his notes everything that happened.

My ideas are excellent and they incorporate leading-edge technology of the future, but it's so difficult to be heard on this course. It's as if what I say counts for nothing. I'd like to submit a formal complaint about it now, in case this sad situation continues and I have to escalate things beyond MMAM to Central admin.

Best wishes,

Jem

Doodle message group [Private] Gela and Hannah, December 11, 2023:

Hannah O'Donnell
As you said, Jem has put her complaint in writing.

Gela Nathaniel
What exactly is her complaint?

Hannah O'Donnell
As far as I can tell, her voice not being heard by the rest of the group.

Gela Nathaniel
Did she mention that she threw a chunk of clay and hit Ludya square between the eyes?

Hannah O'Donnell
No. Are you serious? That's unbelievable.

Gela Nathaniel
Ludya had a clay stain, in a perfect circle, slap-bang in the middle of her forehead.

Hannah O'Donnell
That's classed as physical assault, I'm afraid. Was Ludya hurt? Shall I oversee her complaint?

Gela Nathaniel

She won't be making a complaint. Luckily, it was soft and unfired. Jem was just making a point. We had a chat. Ludya doesn't want the aggravation, and I don't blame her.

Hannah O'Donnell

OK, well, best of luck for your big client meeting. Hope nothing like that happens there.

Gela Nathaniel

Don't even joke about it.

To: Gela Nathaniel
From: Mae Blackwell, RD8 Systems Ltd.
Date: December 12, 2023
Subject: Thank you

Dear Gela and the MMAM team,

It was a pleasure to meet with you today and discuss the launch of our new Integrated Cloud Exchange System (ICES) scheduled for next summer. Listening to the ideas that we have sparked in your students was delightful. We are very happy for you to focus on our company heritage, provided there is equal emphasis on the future, where this product will essentially be positioned.

Your entire team impressed us with their vision for the fabric time-tunnel that will lead our visitors through the company history. However, we were especially taken with Jemisha Badhuri. Her idea for the ASMR experience and interactive sculpture of a binaural microphone demonstrated a perfect blend of past, present, and future. The sensory aspect—to unite sight, sound, and touch—is absolutely what we, as rather dull computing specialists, particularly enjoy! If only smell and taste could be incorporated too, but we will rely on our wonderful catering contractor for that!

While Jem explained her vision, we noted the reluctance of the rest of the team to commit to it within budget. We have since made some inquiries and I'm happy to report there's a solution. Our company has an archive storage facility in rural Somerset called Thorney Coffin, which, despite the name, is in a very beautiful location. They store documents, prototypes, plans, research, etc., but also collect, restore, and curate a great many examples of historical communications equipment in a fascinating private museum. I can make a few phone calls and book your sourcing group an appointment. At the very least it will provide information and inspiration for the historical aspects of your design, and I'll ask if they have any authentic items that you might like to incorporate in the installation.

We understand you'll start work after the Christmas break, so we look forward to liaising with you from then on.

With thanks and best wishes,

Mae Blackwell

Doodle message group [Private] Jonathan, Gela, Alyson, and Ludya, December 12, 2023:

Jonathan Danners
So much for Jem toeing the party line.

Alyson Lang
I admire her. Can't help it.

Ludya Parak
She'd better not change the entire direction of the project, Gela.

Gela Nathaniel
She won't. It's annoying, but Mae and I get along. I'll have a quiet word.

Doodle message group MMAM(FTP), December 12, 2023:

Gela Nathaniel
Well done, everyone! You were all fantastic. I've had hugely positive feedback from Mae that includes an invite to the company's private museum! Now it's the holidays: rest, relax, and recharge your batteries ready for an exciting spring term, when you'll have the chance to

explore unfamiliar mediums on an individual basis as we work on the final project together. I'll see you all on January 9. In the meantime, Happy Christmas to those who do . . . happy holidays to those who don't. Gela x

Jem Badhuri
Thanks, Gela. Just want to thank the group for supporting me in presenting my vision to RD8.

Patrick Bright
They loved your idea to the moon and back, Jem. Well done.

Alyson Lang
Well done.

Jonathan Danners
Great, congrats.

Ludya Parak
See you all January 9.

Cameron Wesley
RD8 store old shit purely for the tax benefits they get as curators of national heritage. Ditto supporting educational establishments—i.e., us. Merry Crimbo.

Message group: 2024 Examiners, May 30, 2024

Ben Sketcher
Did all the students submit their final essay in person?

Tilda Ricci
They did. It's a requirement of the course—of any course here—that final-grade written work is submitted both online and in hard copy at the admin office. They have to sign a disclaimer that the work is theirs. Practical work is submitted via the technicians.

Ben Sketcher
And if their circumstances mean they can't be there in person?

Tilda Ricci
They can apply for special consideration, either in advance or in retrospect, if, for example, they have a car accident on the way.

Ben Sketcher
When they handed their long essays in, did you see each and every one of the MMAM students yourself?

Tilda Ricci
No, Gela did. She did the relevant paperwork in the admin office. Why?

Ben Sketcher
There are bizarre discrepancies between what the students say on Doodle and what they write in their final essays. I've broken up and inserted sections of these essays, so you can see what I mean.

Tilda Ricci
I wouldn't expect the essays to be identical on every point. People are so very different. Not to mention the fact they know they are being graded.

Ben Sketcher
Sure. But you wouldn't expect accounts to differ on whether one of the students disappears or not, would you?

Tilda Ricci
No. Indeed.

Royal Hastings, University of London
Multimedia Art MA
Final Project

Candidate name: Jemisha Badhuri
Candidate number: 0883479

Introduction:
For the introduction to my long essay, I'll tell you about me.

I grew up listening to an actual radio. Not DAB. Not online. A solid-state Murphy with two giant tuners. AM and shortwave. Cracked glass dials. A scratchy fabric speaker that smelled of dust and dried ginger. It came here with my grandparents; they thought it would pick up their favorite stations wherever it was in the world, but realized too late radio doesn't work that way. When they heard I was studying art, they said they might as well have stayed in Kharagpur, where they could at least tune in to Bangladesh Betar every day. They were only placated when Dad explained this is a multimedia art course with a strong business angle. Seriously, I'm a trailblazer in my family and I have to be, because my four older brothers never once stood up to them.

So as soon as I knew what our final project was going to be, I told Gela how perfect I'd be for project leader. Sound is my thing. I've listened to radios my whole life. Music stations. Talking stations. I've tuned in to places on the other side of the world. The whole thing fascinates me. Just this summer I took a course in sound electronics that meant I had to go to Stevenage every day for a week. That's how committed I am.

And it's not even the only reason I was the best person to lead this project. I know myself. I'm a racehorse: I function best at the front. I can give instructions, solve problems, motivate people, lead by example. I'm a perfect storm of confidence, talent, and ability. Whatever it is, I know I can do it. The feeling is more than the words I know to describe it. I'm young, I'm here, and I want it all. Everything it's possible to get out of life—the most, the max, everything.

So Gela gives me the role of "financial manager." If I didn't know

98

better, I'd swear both my grandparents had been whispering in her ear, in my grandfather's case from beyond the grave (he died in August). I played every card I had, but "Jonathan is the lead and nothing will change my mind" is all Gela would say. I mean, I guess I'm basically second-in-command. I still get hands-on experience making the actual installation, but I won't lie: it smarts to this day.

So, as the conclusion to my introduction, I'll say this: in the execution of this project, if anything happened that shouldn't have—if something went wrong, and if every last one of us seems to hold a different opinion about what that was—remember: there wouldn't have been any problems at all if I had been project manager.

Doodle message group MMAM(FTP), January 8, 2024:

Gela Nathaniel

Happy New Year, MMAMs! Hope everyone enjoyed the break. RD8 were as good as their word. I've arrived at my desk to find an email from their museum. What's more, they can GIVE us bags of old components they were getting rid of anyway. Some of you have mentioned how keen you are to work with salvage, for environmental reasons. Let's discuss the visit tomorrow!

Alyson Lang

FYI, the code on the studio keypad has been changed to F4815A.

Gela Nathaniel

Are you there now?

Alyson Lang

Yes.

Gela Nathaniel

Everything OK?

Alyson Lang

Yes, fine thanks, Gela.

Doodle message group [Private] Hannah and Gela, January 8, 2024:

Hannah O'Donnell

Happy New Year! The Admissions Office has nudged me. They still haven't received diversity forms from your MMAM group.

Gela Nathaniel

Sorry! You've been chasing since September. It's been frantic here, with the final project and—if you remember—some discord between students.

Hannah O'Donnell

It's just a few boxes to tick and a signature. If they were set up to complete online I'd message on Doodle, but technology hasn't caught up with this part of the admissions process.

Gela Nathaniel

I know. So sorry. We've got to organize a trip to Somerset.

Hannah O'Donnell

Our inclusion policy is under scrutiny, and they need to know who attended which school, etc., for the next prospectus.

Gela Nathaniel

Some of our students are in their forties and fifties. Does it really matter which schools they went to?

Hannah O'Donnell

It does to the university's demographic profile.

Gela Nathaniel

You only have to look at us to see how diverse we are. That's what matters.

Hannah O'Donnell

Perhaps hand out the forms today and get them filled in on the spot? I've left them in your pigeonhole.

Doodle message group MMAM(FTP), January 8, 2024:

Jem Badhuri

Happy New Year, everyone! Hope you all enjoyed the holidays. I've been listening to an amazing book about three pioneering female artists. Have any of you ever wondered if biographers will get all the facts right about you, after you're dead?

Patrick Bright

Oh Jem! It's never even crossed my mind. The book sounds interesting, though.

Jem Badhuri

It is. You'd love it, Pat. And you, Jonathan. I'll play it in the car on the way to Somerset.

Jonathan Danners

The sourcing team hasn't been finalized yet. I'll be there, and Pat, because he's resource coordinator, but not everyone can come. I need to chat with Gela before I make the announcement.

Doodle message group [Private] Jem and Gela, January 8, 2024:

Jem Badhuri

Gela, can you confirm I'll be on the sourcing team? It makes sense. I'm responsible for the sound aspect of the installation—radio is my thing, I can monitor the group's spending, and I've never been to Somerset before.

Doodle message group [Private] Gela and Jonathan, January 10, 2024:

Gela Nathaniel

Cameron must be part of the sourcing team. He can be your relief driver. We can't expect Ludya to do all the driving just because it's her vehicle.

Jonathan Danners

Really? I'll put him on the list, but can he spare the time? He's driving to his office every day after class. Clearly still doing his job full-time.

Gela Nathaniel

If we create an obligation to the team, it might spur him into taking a more active role and prevent him being kicked off the course. I don't want any dropouts, for any reason.

Jonathan Danners

Hope you're right. While we're on the subject, Jem is still talking as if she's coming with us. Please convince her it's best she doesn't. I expect we'll go out in the evening and there'll be alcohol. She's not streetwise and I don't want to be liable for her—or give that onerous responsibility to anyone else.

Gela Nathaniel
I understand. Leave it with me. I have an idea.

Doodle message group [Private] Gela and Patrick, January 10, 2024:

Gela Nathaniel
I'd like your help on a sensitive matter. Jem can't go to Somerset. There's no room in Ludya's car. Could you help me spin the argument that her role is best fulfilled back here in the studio with me?

Patrick Bright
I have an even better idea. She can take my place. I don't need to go and I hate long car journeys.

Gela Nathaniel
You most certainly do need to go, Patrick. You're resource coordinator! It's not merely the space issue. Jem's never been anywhere without family hovering over her. She'd be an additional responsibility for everyone else.

Patrick Bright
She's looking forward to it. She'll be quite upset.

Gela Nathaniel
This is how I'll frame it: RD8 want her large clay-head sculpture, so we must start work on it ASAP. While you're all away, she and I will collaborate on the wire base. It's in the shape of a binaural microphone, and Jem knows better than anyone what that is. Can you promote that idea to her? Back me up?

Patrick Bright
I don't know.

Gela Nathaniel
Thank you so, so much. I owe you.

Doodle message group [Private] Gela and Cameron, January 10, 2024:

Gela Nathaniel
Please set aside January 16 and 17 for the sourcing trip to Somerset.

Cameron Wesley
Kiss-kiss.

Gela Nathaniel
Kiss-kiss.

Doodle message group [Private] Cameron and Jonathan, January 10, 2024:

Cameron Wesley
Gela says I'm in the sourcing team and I have to go.

Jonathan Danners
Great idea. We really need you, because none of us like driving long distances—if Ludya gets tired, you can take the wheel.

Cameron Wesley
Great to know I'm valued for my comprehensive insurance.

Doodle message group [Private] Gela and Jem, January 11, 2024:

Gela Nathaniel
Jem, I've been wrangling the logistics. RD8 loved your idea of the large clay replica of a binaural microphone, but as it wasn't in our original plan, we need to crack on with the groundwork for this additional piece *ASAP.*

Jem Badhuri
When we come back from Somerset?

Gela Nathaniel

You and I aren't going to Somerset. The needs of the team are best met if we stay in the studio and focus on the project.

Jem Badhuri

But the team will be given salvage materials. I need to be there to examine them.

Gela Nathaniel

A bag of discarded components can easily be sorted here. I've got a two-day schedule for us. We'll have breakfast in the Aviator, then spend the first morning constructing a framework to hold the sculpture and protect it in the studio. I'll take you for lunch at the Orangery—you won't have been there, it's the formal academic dining room—and in the afternoon we'll concentrate on starting the wire base.

Doodle message group [Private] Jem and Patrick, January 11, 2024:

Jem Badhuri

Gela says I can't go to Somerset with the rest of you. She wants me to work on the installation with her.

Patrick Bright

Well, she must value your skills, to want you there at ground level. I don't blame her, Jem—your work in clay so far has been exceptional, and the giant head-shaped thing is all your creative vision.

Jem Badhuri

That giant head-shaped thing is a replica binaural microphone in clay. You're right, no other artist on this course has my passion for sculpture. Gela said she'll take me for lunch at the Orangery. If she orders wine, I might get some gossip out of her.

Patrick Bright

The Orangery? Students can only eat there if invited by a member of academic staff. That's more than an honor, Jem. And yes, you find out the gossip from Gela, and I'll report back on the trip—we can have a full debriefing session afterward!

Jem Badhuri

Excellent idea! Thank you, Patrick—that's a date!

Doodle message group [Private] Jem and Gela, January 11, 2024:

Jem Badhuri

It'll just be you and me?

Gela Nathaniel

Yes. And on the second day, when the team is on its way home, we'll have brunch together and clear some space ready for the fabric tunnel. It should be a productive and pleasant couple of days.

Jem Badhuri

That's a date!

To: MMAM(FTP)
From: Gela Nathaniel
Date: January 12, 2024
Subject: Sourcing trip to Somerset

Dear all,

Before it gets old, I'll say Happy New Year for the last time. Now, work on our final project truly begins!

I'd like to reiterate the importance of collaboration and sharing ideas, skills, time, and expertise. As project leader, Jonathan is responsible for assembling sub-teams to complete tasks as and when they arise. The sourcing team consists of Jonathan, Patrick, Ludya, Alyson, and Cameron. The team will drive to Thorney Coffin on January 16, visit the company's collection of vintage radios for design inspiration, and pick up the salvage items the staff have set aside for us. They will stay overnight at a Travel Inn and return home the following day, delivering the items to Royal Hastings on Thursday. Ludya has already submitted her receipt for a rapid charge for her EV.

Meanwhile, Jem and I will start the structural centerpiece of the installation. While the event takes place in May and this is January, I must remind you that RD8 will need to see and approve our work well in advance of the launch date, and it is their prerogative to request changes and amendments as we go.

I expect you to keep detailed records—ideally a diary—of your work for the final project. This will remind you of what happened and when, so you're not lost for detail when you write your long essay. Doodle has a diary function: please use it. I cannot recommend strongly enough that you do this work as you go along.

Good luck to the sourcing team. We'll see you on Thursday!

Gela

Doodle message group MMAM(FTP), January 15, 2024:

Jonathan Danners

Hello, team. This is to finalize plans for our sourcing trip to RD8's facility in Somerset tomorrow. Ludya has kindly volunteered to drive Alyson, Patrick, Cameron, and me. She has a very comfortable electric minivan that will easily seat all five of us.

Ludya Parak

I'll need a hand getting the child seats out. And, Jem, that invoice must be paid ASAP or my kids starve.

Jonathan Danners

We're booked into the Yeovil Travel Inn overnight. Thanks to Patrick and Jem for sorting accommodation near to where Ludya can charge the minivan overnight.

Jem Badhuri

I've got your invoice, Ludya. Dad will help me do the bank transfer tonight.

Patrick Bright
It's not quite the Ritz, but there's a garage across the way and Tripadvisor says it has a Costa Coffee vending machine and a pastry shelf. I'm thinking of breakfast.

Jonathan Danners
Alyson has spoken to Polly—Mae's PA at RD8—who, in turn, is liaising with the Somerset facility.

Alyson Lang
She said even though they're very busy, short-staffed, and usually closed on Tuesdays, they'll give up their own time and open especially for us.

Patrick Bright
That's nice.

Alyson Lang
That's classic passive-aggression.

Jonathan Danners
Finally, Cameron is our relief driver, if and when required. See you all, 9 a.m. sharp. Let's do this.

Jem Badhuri
Good luck to the sourcing team. Can't wait to examine the goodies you bring back.

Patrick Bright
Thank you, Jem. We'll keep the home team up to speed with our progress every step of the way.

Jonathan Danners
We won't have time to keep anyone in the loop. See you Thursday.

Ludya Parak
You three: when I arrive at Tooting Broadway Station, get ready for a running jump. There's no parking.

Alyson Lang
Sweet-talked the OH into dropping me off.

Jem Badhuri
By "OH," do you mean your husband, Alyson?

Alyson Lang
Yes.

Jonathan Danners
I'll be there. Patrick?

Patrick Bright
Think I might have a cold starting. If it gets worse, I'll cry off. Will text Ludya.

Jem Badhuri
Oh no! Pat, hope you're OK. I've got my fingers crossed you're better in the morning.

Cameron Wesley
I'll need extra luggage space. Bringing two laptops. There'd better be 5G in that neck of the woods.

Doodle message group [Private] Jem and Patrick, January 15, 2024:

Jem Badhuri
Hope you're not ill tomorrow, Pat. I want all the gossip from the trip.

Patrick Bright
Thought I'd mention it, in case.

Jem Badhuri
Alyson's husband is dropping her off for a night away with Jonathan. Do you think he suspects anything?

Patrick Bright
I have absolutely no idea, Jem. That pair is a mystery to me.

Doodle message group [Private] Jem and Patrick, January 16, 2024:

Jem Badhuri
Morning, Pat! Are you awake? Hope you're feeling better. Are you still going?

Patrick Bright
Morning, Jem. Yes, I'm going. Don't be too disappointed to miss it. I'm sure it'll be dull as dishwater.

Jem Badhuri
Aw, thanks, but I'm not disappointed. It's only overnight. Gela and I can get to know each other. Anyway, my dad hates me being away from home.

Patrick Bright
Thank goodness Ludya and Cameron are designated drivers. It's a long haul down to Somerset and back.

Jem Badhuri
Is it? I've never been. But there are no prizes for guessing why Ludya volunteered to drive. Dad says she must've charged up a truck, from the size of receipt she handed in.

Patrick Bright
Well, she has one of those electric minivans. And I thought she was short of cash!

Jem Badhuri
Do you think she lied about her income to get her course fees paid?

Patrick Bright
Has Jonathan spoken to you about a roll of fabric for the tunnel? Apparently it should be delivered to the studio today. He probably mentioned it to Gela.

Jem Badhuri
I have no idea. Even though I'm financial manager, he always speaks to Gela, not me.

Royal Hastings, University of London
Multimedia Art MA
Final Project

Candidate name: Jonathan Danners
Candidate number: 0883482

Introduction:
I don't like to speak for other people, but it's my educated ob-
servation that students who apply for a course like this anticipate
learning how to build and maintain a career in the art world.
Those drawn to this industry tend to be sensitive, thoughtful, freethinking individuals and don't expect a pressure-cooker environment of ruthless competition. They certainly do not expect that
toxic atmosphere to be fueled, fanned, and stoked by staff.

The project for RD8 was executed under the most difficult
and trying conditions. Whatever the client thinks of the outcome,
it is a tribute to the clash of personalities, hidden agendas, and
career sabotage that only escalated as the course progressed. My
mother and sister both died while my father was gravely ill, but I
can honestly say this MA has been the most traumatic and stressful
year of my life.

It is tempting to think everything went wrong during that
disastrous trip to Somerset. On paper, perhaps it did, but the rot
had already set in. It's hard now to say when exactly the downward spiral began. Was it the day I met Gela? When we fell into
step and got talking, just to pass the time. Devising a new MA, she
was looking for students with management experience. Thinking
about it now, I should have just walked away.

Doodle message group MMAM(FTP), January 16, 2024:

Jonathan Danners
Are you nearly here, Ludya? It's past nine and we're all outside the station.

Patrick Bright
Hi Ludya, we've called and messaged. Cameron suggested also Doodling, as you might have Apple Watch notifications for that. If you have an Apple Watch, that is. Anyway, we're wondering if you're nearly here?

Alyson Lang
It's nine fifteen, Luds.

Ludya Parak
Voice Siri driving at the lights by the big Lidl.

Patrick Bright
Which Lidl? Is it nearby? Alyson says the museum has to close at three.

Ludya Parak
Fluff ucks ache am on my way.

Royal Hastings, University of London
Multimedia Art MA
Final Project

Candidate name: Ludya Parak
Candidate number: 0883481

Introduction:
If I told you the truth, you wouldn't believe it.

My backstory:
I was born in London, but my parents are Albanian. Yes, like Dua Lipa. No, I don't know her. Went to school in Dulwich. Did a foundation course in Wimbledon, then studied design in Warwickshire. I'm a graphic designer and met Gela through a networking event in Dalston last summer. She sold MMAM to me and suggested I apply. I told her I'm a single parent and some things are in short supply. Like money and time. But she said she'd help out with both. She organized a grant for the fee and said I could choose my hours. I'm grateful for the grant, but none of the other students on the course have young kids and they couldn't accept I wouldn't be in the studio 24/7. I can't lie, I'm glad it's all over.

Doodle message group [Private] Jem and Patrick, January 16, 2024:

Jem Badhuri
Where are you? Has anything gone wrong yet?

Patrick Bright
We're on the highway. All good.

* * *

Jem Badhuri
Where are you now?

Patrick Bright
Nearly at Yeovil. I'll let you know how we get on.

* * *

Jem Badhuri
Did you get there OK? What was Ludya's driving like? Are Alyson and Jonathan behaving themselves?

Patrick Bright
All good, Jem. Very interesting place. A bit weird. But they gave us lots of bits and pieces. You'll be delighted.

Jem Badhuri
Let Jonathan know the roll of fabric he didn't tell me about has arrived. We don't need it yet, so Gela and I stashed it out of the way.

Patrick Bright
We're stopping off to eat, then crash at the motel.

Jem Badhuri
There's no budget for food. You'll have to pay for yourselves.

* * *

Patrick Bright
Jem, we're at the Travel Inn. There's a problem. I remember booking five of the cheap rooms, but the receptionist says the booking is for one room only.

Jem Badhuri
Yes, a super family room. It sleeps up to six. There's only five of you.

Patrick Bright
It sleeps six, but it's one double bed and two sets of children's bunks.

Jem Badhuri
Yes, great value. So much cheaper than five separate rooms. Because I amended the order within twenty-four hours, the lovely lady on the phone refunded the difference. I was only thinking of the budget, especially after logging such a hefty receipt from Ludya. If anyone doesn't like it, they can pay for their own room.

Patrick Bright
They can't. The place is fully booked. The receptionist says it was booked out yesterday by people attending a funeral.

Jem Badhuri
There must be lots of other hotels.

Patrick Bright
We rang around a few, but they were fully booked too, and even if they hadn't been, the car is so low on charge it has to be plugged in all night. I don't know what we're going to do. We can't all bunk up together in one room.

Jem Badhuri
Have Jonathan and Alyson bagged the double bed? OMG, I bet they're fuming!

Patrick Bright
I may have to sleep in the minivan.

Doodle message group [Private] Ludya and Jem, January 16, 2024:

Ludya Parak
Why? Because no one wanted you to come with us?

Jem
I'm financial manager and I'm maximizing our budget. Don't know what the problem is.

Royal Hastings, University of London
Multimedia Art MA
Final Project

Candidate name: Patrick Bright
Candidate number: 0883480

Introduction:
This is the thing. Where do you begin with something like this? Because I'm certain it started long before the first day of the course. So long before I don't even know when or how.

Perhaps I should introduce myself and why I applied. Even that, I can't be sure about now. I know I had nothing to lose. Or so I thought.

Why I'm here:
We had a nasty break-in at the shop. It was early morning and I wouldn't normally have been there, but I was doing inventory out the back. The two girls were in front. I heard someone crash through the front door, two men in hoods and masks with crowbars. There was shouting and screaming. I peered through the door and saw one of them smash the till. First thing in the morning there's nothing in there, and most payments are cashless now anyway.

The girls were crouched on the floor while the two hoods rummaged for whatever they could find. They were no *Ocean's Eleven*. I squeezed myself into the little meter cupboard, pulled the door to, and held my breath. One fella was shouting at the girls, asking where the safe was, where we kept the money.

I was shaking like a leaf. They came into the storeroom and started throwing bottles of chemicals around but didn't know what they were looking for, so went back out front, grabbed jewelry, purses, and phones from the girls and took off.

I heard their car rev away and crept out. They'd hit the poor girls across their faces. I called 999, the police came and went, then we cleaned up. But I didn't get over it. The girls went back to work—

they're made of stronger stuff than I am. I feel stupid saying I've got PTSD when they had it so much worse.

Anyway, my thoughts turned to Schull and my pipe dream about retiring there. That's when Gela got chatting to me about her new art course.

The process:

Right from the start things were not right, by a long shot. It felt like there were tensions and histories between people, even though as far as I was aware we were all strangers who met that first day. Only young and I Jem seemed—and I use the word reluctantly—normal. She's the youngest on the course and I'm the oldest, but we gelled. Let's face it, everyone in between was just mad crazy. And I include Gela in that.

Take that first project, for example. We had to imagine a start-up company and produce a logo for them. Simple. OK, so we all come up with something and Gela gets us to critique each other's work. Alarm bells. Art is subjective. Surely no one wants to be nasty. I didn't see the benefit of the exercise, but anyway.

I don't know if it was a statement about how Gela was trying to set us against each other or what it was, but it's my opinion now that Jonathan and Alyson cooked up and staged what I can only describe as a reckless melodrama. Alyson stalked over to Jonathan's 3D paper model, insulted it and him, in the nastiest terms, and honest to God, she set fire to it right there in a room full of paper, wood, and accelerant. My heart nearly stopped on the spot. When I think of the fire regs we adhere to in the shop—grown adults playing a trick like that. Jonathan and Alyson. That pair were thick as thieves from the get-go, and Gela was . . . even I don't know what I'm getting at here. She was powerless against them.

Doodle message group [Private] Gela and Cameron, January 16, 2024:

Gela Nathaniel
Did you just call? Everything OK?

Cameron Wesley
Freaking Jem has booked us all in one room!

Gela Nathaniel
Are there enough beds?

Cameron Wesley
Yes, but four of them are five-foot bunks. She might be a youngster happy to bed down wherever, but the rest of us like our own personal space—and toilet!

Gela Nathaniel
I'm sure she was only thinking of the budget. Drive back tonight instead of staying?

Cameron Wesley
We might have to. Things are getting heated, and now the boss is calling. Kiss-kiss.

Gela Nathaniel
Kiss-kiss.

Royal Hastings, University of London
Multimedia Art MA
Final Project

Candidate name: Cameron Wesley
Candidate number: 0883483

Introduction:
Jem says our brains listen to our heartbeat all the time, even while we're sleeping, so we're naturally tuned in to sound and rhythm. It's why a gentle, regular beat is soothing. If the beat slows, our heart slows too, because it instinctively matches the rhythm and flow of other hearts. I was excited for our project, but unprepared for how this team would change me. Our heartbeats merged, and in the process, we were all reshaped and twisted.

The team:
Teamwork is the essence of humanity, is it not? Many hands make light work. You can't break a stick in a bundle. Groupthink. I come from a business background and that means putting aside your feelings to make difficult decisions. Say someone in the team messes up. They make a humdinger of a boo-boo and there's no going back. Doesn't matter how much you like them, how good they are at their job—they have to go. If you make excuses to let them stay, you will regret it. The decision will haunt *you*, it will be used against *you*, and it will destroy *you*.

Doodle message group [Private] Patrick and Jem, January 17, 2024:

Patrick Bright
There's been a big row over the room. I'm happy to sleep in the car, but Cameron isn't. Ludya's desperate to get home, but there's not enough charge in the minivan. She's so tired she burst into tears. We've all been drinking, so will have to wait till one of us sobers up enough to drive. Cameron has only just tested under the limit, but we don't want to risk him getting behind the wheel too soon, so we're giving it a bit longer. Can't message anymore. Things are very strained.

Jem Badhuri
That's hilarious! OMG, what a disaster! See you tomorrow—well, today now.

Doodle message group [Private] Jem and Gela, January 17, 2024:

Jem Badhuri
Hi Gela, lovely to work with you yesterday. I much prefer one-to-one interactions, and this construction project is totally my thing. I've had a lot of art tutors in my time, but you are by far the most inspiring.

Gela Nathaniel
Good. I enjoyed working with you too. Best get some sleep, though, we've got another busy day tomorrow.

Jem Badhuri
I've heard from Patrick and apparently the trip to Somerset is turning into a disaster. There was a big mix-up over the room, followed by an even bigger row, and now Cameron has to drive them all home as Ludya is so upset.

Gela Nathaniel
If the sourcing team visited the museum and collected the material as planned, then it was a successful excursion.

Doodle message group [Private] Gela and Cameron, January 17, 2024:

Gela Nathaniel
You're coming back tonight now?

Gela Nathaniel
Of course you're driving, so can't answer.

Cameron Wesley
Yes. Driving back. Will drop the loot off at RH shortly.

Gela Nathaniel
But it's nearly 2 a.m. What happened? What was the row about?

Cameron Wesley
Will bring you up to speed soon.

Doodle message group MMAM(FTP), January 17, 2024:

Jem Badhuri
A big welcome home to the sourcing team. Hope you had a lovely trip.

Jonathan Danners
We did. Thank you for messaging so early, Jem.

Jem Badhuri
Can't wait to get my hands on all those old radio components. When will you bring them to the studio?

Jonathan Danners
They're already there. We had to pass RH on the way back. Otherwise Ludya would have to drive back in again tomorrow.

Ludya Parak
And that ain't happening.

Cameron Wesley
It's all nasty rubbish they were throwing out anyway.

Jem Badhuri
Isn't the college locked at night?

Jonathan Danners
The overnight security staff all know Alyson. We explained, they were fine. The bags are piled up under the stairs if you feel like a rummage when you get in, Jem.

Jem Badhuri's Doodle Diary, January 17, 2024:

Gela says keeping a diary will help with the long essay, so here I am. Well, what a day! We unpacked four sacks of goodies the sourcing team collected from Somerset. The general consensus was that RD8 had taken this opportunity to get rid of every piece of junk they had—but I don't see things like other people.

These old components will transform our fabric tunnel, and to complement them, I suggested we make papier-mâché replicas of the more interesting pieces and embed them in the walls to create depth and fill space, because even though we have a lot to upcycle, it won't be enough for what we're planning. Also it means we can play with texture, especially if we use resin—I'm full of ideas.

I was excited to show the sourcing team the wire base that Gela and I worked on while they were away. Gela said they wouldn't be as impressed as we both are. I showed them anyway. She was right. They were so tired they hardly spoke to me all day.

When the rest of the class went to lunch together, I stayed in the studio to eat my sandwiches and scroll through social media, as usual. But I was still buzzing, so thought I'd explore the cupboards and storeroom for more inspiration. The tunnel needs as many surface contrasts as possible. Imagine walking down it, stretching both hands out to either side, above you even, and feeling that texture as you go, stopping to examine anything that feels particularly interesting. Papier-mâché, resin, clay— what else can we use? I rummaged around to see what might be hiding at the backs of shelves and cupboards.

Then, stuffed behind a box of books on the very bottom shelf, my fingers touched something that hadn't been there before: an old radio. Dials, speaker, tuner, like the old Murphy from my childhood. I can't explain it, but some things are so old they have an aura around them. When I was monitoring Alyson's use of art supplies, I knew every item in this cupboard, and that old radio wasn't there then. It wasn't there yesterday, when Gela and I were searching for the rolls of modeling mesh Griff hid away (we eventually tracked them down to the top of the tall cupboard). No, this radio may be old, but it's new to us.

The bags from RD8 are full of bits and pieces. If the sourcing team got a whole radio, why didn't they mention it? But more than that: does it work? Authentic sound from a genuine old wireless set would make my soundscape complete.

My imagination was racing ahead when I heard Patrick asking if I was OK. He was probably wondering what I was doing on the floor of the cupboard. When I showed him what I found, he was silent for ages.

Patrick Bright's Doodle Diary, January 17, 2024:

Logged on to this diary part of Doodle. Maybe it'll help. Why did I go to Somerset? It never felt right. Must've had a premonition.

We spent the first bit of the journey chatting about the course and all that's wrong with it. Then we fell silent, as everyone but Ludya dropped off. We were woken up by her swearing the minivan through a flock of sheep, then a leafy gauntlet of winding country lanes that got ever narrower, with passing-points of frozen mud and terrifying blind corners. No signs and nothing that looked like the RD8 facility. Finally we rounded a bend and there it was, perfectly disguised by the landscape. A gray, oblong building. No windows.

We knocked on the only door and waited. It was quiet as the grave. Like there weren't even any birds around. Finally there was movement behind the door and a woman unlocked it, as if she was reluctantly letting us in on a secret. She was friendly enough, but as soon as I got inside, it felt strange. It was muffled and quiet, a controlled atmosphere.

"So you're art students?" The woman looked us up and down. "Only, you seem quite old." Jonathan explained it's a master's course, so we're mature students. The woman smiled as if thinking: "You can say that again."

We followed her through several locked doors that she opened with keypads. The corridors were dark and silent, the air perfectly still and cool. Then she opened another door and ushered us into the darkness. A click and the lights flickered on.

It was set up like a museum, but utterly spotless, not a speck of dust, and no other visitors. A dark cavern, lined up and down with old radios from the earliest days of the technology. Some were sitting on tables and others were sealed in glass cabinets, with gauges and dials monitoring the air. No light and a low temperature, as if they were trying to freeze time.

"Do you never show anyone this?" I asked. "Is it secret?"

The woman laughed. "No," she scoffed, "it's not secret. Professor Brian Cox came here a couple of years ago to film a program for BBC Four. We often invite corporate guests and host internal away-days for the London and Humberside offices. People who work in the communications industry *love* this place. Feel free to look around, but don't touch *anything*. The materials are very old, and the oils in your skin will degrade them. When you're ready, come back to reception and I'll have some refreshments for you—we can't let you eat or drink in here. I'll make sure the items for your sculpture are ready when you leave."

With that, she was gone, and we all fanned out around the room to look at the exhibits. Very impressive. I was captivated by a beautiful wooden radio: a Marconiphone Tombstone from 1933, according to the label. I sensed Alyson behind me. "The old and new," I said. "See the digital temperature gauge?" A square of little red numbers glowed in the relative darkness.

"That's a hygrothermograph," she said. "It measures humidity, not temperature." Well, that told me.

I wandered around, fascinated by the displays. The others did the same. But just as I was at the far end of the room, about to turn around and make my way down the other side, there was a commotion by the door. Shouting, the clattering of shoes on a polished floor. More voices. I set off to see what it was, but as soon as it started, it was over and silence resumed. The voices sounded like Ludya and Jonathan, so when

I came across Cameron scowling over his phone, I asked him what had happened.

"Oh, Ludya kicked off about something. I wouldn't worry about it. You got a signal, Pat?"

It was only Cameron and me in the museum now and it was quieter than ever. The door we had come in through was propped open by a rubber wedge, the only other door firmly closed and locked by a key-pad. Ludya, Alyson, and Jonathan must have all gone out. I crept a little closer to the door and looked through the crack. Ludya was pacing to and fro, also looking at her phone. Then she glanced up and down the corridor. There was a look on her face I'd never seen before. Focused. Determined. Calm. Usually she's either bored to the point of couldn't-care-less or on the brink of emotional meltdown.

"Seen this, Pat? My cousins had one. Who'd have thought a lurid brick of plastic shit would ever end up in a museum?" Cameron was looking at a 1987 Philips Roller. But I felt jittery and not sure why, so I wandered back out to the corridor.

"Everything all right, Ludya?"

"Yeah, me and Jonathan just had a . . ." She trailed off as if something along the corridor had distracted her. I glanced up there myself, tried to see what she was looking at—nothing. "But it's OK now."

I made my way back to reception and found Jonathan and Alyson already there, waiting.

"Is Ludya OK?" I asked. "Thought I heard shouting—"

"Jonathan surprised her, accidentally, and she made it clear that anyone approaching her personal space should announce it, in writing, days in advance." Alyson had her cigarettes and matches gripped in her hand. Her face, lips, and knuckles were white.

"Ah, she's got a lot on her plate, and it must be difficult leaving the kiddies."

"I don't see why," Alyson sniffed. "Her mum is looking after them."

There was an awkward silence until the woman appeared and led us to a kitchenette, where we found a little spread of sandwiches and cake.

"Thanks for leaving me alone in Spookyville, *mates*," Cameron boomed. Until then I hadn't thought the place spooky, but once he said it, a shiver lodged in my spine.

Ludya joined us and I sidled over to give a few words of support.

"Suffer with anxiety myself, Luds. I've jumped a mile in the air when someone's come up behind me, and the first emotion that floods in after that is anger. I'm sure Jonathan didn't mean anything."

She just stared at me, and none of them spoke much the rest of the time we were there.

On our way out we were given not one but *four* huge bags of old radio components that weighed a ton. Ludya's minivan groaned under the weight. I commented how excited Jem would be, but no one replied. Then Cameron mumbled that it was probably all junk. No one replied.

With the vehicle loaded up, off we went to a pub for dinner, and things gradually returned to normal. Until we arrived at the Travel Inn and the nightmare began. It was only the next day, when Jem found something in the cupboard, that I put the pieces together. Well, some of them.

Jem Badhuri's Doodle Diary, January 17, 2024:

Eventually, Pat said Alyson and Jonathan got the radio from RD8.

"Then why hide it?"

He didn't have an answer. "Jem, you're a good girl, with a very fierce sense of right and wrong, but let's not say we found it."

"But, Patrick," I said, "it's perfect for the installation. Let's see if it works."

Royal Hastings, University of London
Multimedia Art MA
Final Project

Candidate name: Jonathan Danners
Candidate number: 0883482

Sourcing materials:
What RD8's regional base in Somerset lacks in size, it makes up for in intrigue. We were struck by its remoteness. The stark, industrial gray block of a building. The lack of a workforce. No one else noticed, but while we were maneuvering down tiny country lanes, our eyes peeled for signs of civilization, we passed through a set of steel gates, fully open and strangely blended into the undergrowth. I take it our approach had been seen from miles away and our imminent arrival expected.

There were just three parking spaces in front of the building, two occupied by instantly forgettable cars. Ludya parked in the third, and so began a pleasant visit that would end in chaos.

History in the making:
This is where RD8 not only maintain their own company records and data going back decades but also curate a private collection of vintage radios and other communications equipment—their own and that of manufacturers from around the world. It's set up like a museum, one that almost no one visits, despite the curator's claim.

We were shown into a darkened room. Low lighting protects the old materials from UV degradation, while temperature and humidity are closely controlled and monitored. It's a level of protection most museums and galleries can only dream of.

We were assured that bags of salvaged materials would be waiting for us to take away. Then we were left alone to explore the museum. In the entire history of twentieth-century communications there cannot be a type of radio or transmitter that RD8 haven't collected, restored, and displayed in that huge room. Stunning.

Conflict and compromise:

From there we found a pub for dinner, where we stayed drinking and chatting until after 9 p.m. After that, things stopped running smoothly. We arrived at the Travel Inn to find Jem had canceled our rooms and booked us all into one family room. There were no other hotel rooms for miles around. A couple of us wanted to drive home there and then, but Ludya didn't, and it's her car. The rest of us had had too much to drink.

There was a reasonable tide of opinion that Cameron shouldn't have had any alcohol, knowing he was the relief driver. He explained that he didn't realize he'd have to drive that night, as the room issue hadn't yet arisen. Things got very heated. Ludya was crying because she felt pressured into driving home.

In the end, she drove us all to the nearest gas station. I bought a pack of home Breathalyzer tests and we all drove back to wait in the family room for one of us to test safe for driving. Finally, at five to midnight, Cameron tested safe. After waiting for a bit longer to account for a potential margin of error in the test, we all got into the minivan and he drove back.

To: Gela Nathaniel
From: Mae Blackwell
Date: January 18, 2024
Subject: Somerset

Dear Gela,

I've heard from the Thorney Coffin site. Your MA group descended on them as planned. Hopefully the inspiration gained and materials collected will be worth the trip.

I feel you should know—just in case the students don't tell you themselves—that apparently there was a small scuffle and our staff had to break it up. I'm sure it's nothing more than fuses running short after a long journey, but some of the exhibits are very delicate, so the students involved were escorted to reception to calm down.

They were both very apologetic afterward, so we allowed them to continue their visit, but I feel you should be aware, in case the disagreement finds its way back to Royal Hastings.

Thank you again for working with us on our big launch. We can't wait to see what your class comes up with for the installation!

Yours sincerely,
Mae Blackwell

To: Mae Blackwell
From: Gela Nathaniel
Date: January 18, 2024
Subject: Re: Somerset

Dear Mae,

I am so sorry to hear my students were brawling in the museum—and after you were kind enough to invite them. The news hadn't reached me. It seems they decided to keep that aspect of the trip under the radar. All I can do is apologize. The group is full of strong personalities with lots of creative ideas, so emotions can run high. I'll have a word with them and ensure there will be no repeat of such behavior.

Yours,
Gela

Doodle message group [Private] Gela and Cameron, January 18, 2024:

Gela Nathaniel
I've heard from Mae. There was a "scuffle" at the museum. What happened, and why haven't you mentioned it?

Cameron Wesley
Didn't think it was relevant.

Gela Nathaniel
Of course it's relevant!

Cameron Wesley
Look, it was nothing. Over in seconds, they apologized and patched things up. I'm not telling tales.

Gela Nathaniel
It's your job to tell tales. Kiss-kiss.

Cameron Wesley
Kiss-kiss.

Patrick Bright's Doodle Diary, January 18, 2024:

I wondered at the time what secret they were keeping. Is this all it was? An old radio stolen from our client's private museum? I can't help thinking it was pure devilment. The excitement. Did Ludya kick off when she saw Alyson sneak a radio under her coat? Or did Alyson dare Jonathan to steal something and he did it to please her? That relationship is a strange one.

One thing's certain: there's no hiding anything from Jem. She found the radio and now wants us to try and get a sound out of it while everyone else is in the bar at lunchtimes. She's usually on her own in the studio then, and I can't help but wonder if she wants the company. It can't hurt, can it? Their liquid lunch gets longer every day, so today, as soon as we were alone, we dragged the radio out and had a good look at it.

Jem said it's even older than her grandparents' radio that came from

India in the '70s. We switched it on, but all we got was white noise. The dials and tuner window were blank, so we had no idea what wavelength it was on. Time ran out and we shoved it back in the cupboard. I told Jem not to breathe a word about it, in case Gela found out and objected—at the back of my mind was the suspicion that we shouldn't have it here at all.

Conscious one of the others might wonder, I wrote a note on it: "Jem and I are trying to get this to work, with a view to including it in the installation. Only white noise at mo, but haven't tried properly yet. Hope that's OK."

Doodle message group [Private] Jonathan and Ludya, January 19, 2024:

Jonathan Danners
Shit shit shit!

Ludya Parak
WTF now?

Jonathan Danners
I'm in the studio sorting stuff out. Pat and Jem found the unit.

Ludya Parak
How, FFS? I hid it on the bottom shelf at the very back of the darkest cupboard. You can't see shit in there, and Patrick has at least one plastic knee.

Jonathan Danners
I guess Jem found it. They want to use it in the installation.

Ludya Parak
Can't deal with this. I have enough to worry about right now.

Jonathan Danners
You need to come in ASAP. Leave the kids with a neighbor or something, but get here.

To: Gela Nathaniel
From: Griff Technician (Maintenance)
Date: January 19, 2024
Subject: Mess

What are your MA students up to in that studio? The devastation when I came in this morning was beyond the pale. Again, despite my email after last time, something has been burned. There was ash in the sink and melted plastic stuck to the drainer in the cutting room. We had all better hope that comes off.

Outside, another shocking mess awaited me, with that nice fabric you bought for your installation torn up and stuffed in one of the big bins. It arrived only a couple of days ago, yet must've been in there a while, judging by the rubbish on top of it. I started to drag it out, but saw it was smeared with either brown paint or dried blood, so left it for you to deal with. I still remember the dead-pig incident of 2008.

If throwing out that fabric was a mistake, someone had better retrieve it before tomorrow morning (early), because that's when the trash men come. I've instructed Tony and Rita to leave well alone.

Griff

To: Griff (Technician)
From: Gela Nathaniel
Date: January 19, 2024
Subject: Re: Mess

What? That fabric cost a fortune. I will most certainly be retrieving it today, Griff. I don't care what tragedy befell it—we need every inch of it for the installation. Thank you for letting me know, and please rest assured I will be confronting the sourcing team over this.

Gela

Doodle message group [Private] Gela, Alyson, and Jonathan, January 19, 2024:

Gela Nathaniel

What happened?

Gela Nathaniel

Why is our tunnel fabric in a bin, and in such a condition it reminded Griff of the time a student brought in a dead pig?

Gela Nathaniel

If I don't know what happened I can't cover it up, can I?

Jonathan Danners

We'll meet you in the parking lot before class on Tuesday. Not the studio—Jem will already be there.

Doodle message group MMAM(FTP), January 23, 2024:

Gela Nathaniel

I have some bad news. It seems someone has vandalized the tunnel fabric and stuffed it in one of the big bins outside. I've retrieved it, but, sad to say, it's in a terrible state. I'm at the dry cleaner in town negotiating a decent price to have it washed and mended.

Jem Badhuri

Oh no! Who would do something like that? Did someone break in? Have you called the police?

Gela Nathaniel

No. Just to update everyone: the fabric arrived while you were all in Somerset. Jem and I stored it in the alcove by the rear doors, thinking it would be safe until we needed it. There was no reason for anyone to check on it, so we don't know what happened or when. Luckily Griff spotted it in the bin outside. No one's noticed any signs of a break-in and nothing's been stolen, so we should keep the whole incident to ourselves.

Jem Badhuri

That's the danger of having a keypad and not a key. Anyone can pass the code to anyone else.

Ludya Parak

Anyone can have a new key cut. Sorry, Gela, that's rubbish.

Alyson Lang

Shame I haven't been in the studio for a while. I could have scared them off.

Patrick Bright

Thank goodness you weren't, Alyson. They might have been violent. Let's be grateful things are no worse.

Gela Nathaniel

This dry cleaner says he can repair it—but it's too big even for his largest washing machine. I may have to cut it in half.

Alyson Lang

That's fine—we can hide the join in the design. Tell them yes.

Jem Badhuri

But how much do they charge? Our budget is tight at the moment. If we cut it into smaller pieces, we can each take one and wash it at home.

Gela Nathaniel

Good idea, but the dry cleaner is so accommodating I don't want to take the job away now.

Gela Nathaniel

Attaching scan of his receipt here for you, Jem.

RECEIPT SUPERSUDS DRY CLEANERS

Clean and Mend
2 x large sheets for art project

Tears x 3
Stains, incl. mud, vomit, and blood (from dead pig)

£70.00 plus VAT

Doodle message group [Private] Jem and Patrick, January 23, 2024:

Jem Badhuri
Who do you think did it, Pat?

Patrick Bright
Did what?

Jem Badhuri
Vandalized the fabric. The sourcing team were at RH the night after the fabric arrived. You drove back, remember, and dropped off the old radio components.

Patrick Bright
We only popped in and shoved the bags where you found them. After the night we'd had, we couldn't get home quickly enough. Gela said the fabric was by the rear doors. We didn't go near it.

Jem Badhuri
I bet you left the door open and vandals got in. Who was last out? Was it Alyson?

Patrick Bright
I don't think we did. It's just one of those things, Jem.

Doodle message group [Private] Jem and Patrick, January 25, 2024:

Jem Badhuri
LOVE that radio!

Patrick Bright
At least the power source is stabilized.

Jem Badhuri
The electric shock wasn't too bad, was it?

Patrick Bright
No, no, I'm fine.

Doodle message group MMAM(FTP), January 29, 2024:

Gela Nathaniel
I've collected the fabric and it looks OK—you can barely see the stitching. We can cover up any imperfections with paint and clever lighting.

Jonathan Danners
Good. Thank you.

Doodle message group [Private] Cameron and Gela, January 29, 2024:

Gela Nathaniel
You haven't been in, and now you're not picking up?

Cameron Wesley
Sorry. Busy. Look, I have to withdraw from the MA. Just say Somerset made me realize it isn't for me.

Gela Nathaniel
And the RD8 project?

Cameron Wesley
The others can do it.

Gela Nathaniel
I mean kiss-kiss.

Cameron Wesley
Everything's changed. You can get me out of it.

Gela Nathaniel
You've completed nearly half the course and *may* have built up just enough grades for a pass—I'll check with admin—it seems a shame to give up now. Do what you can, when you can. I can grade you on that.

Cameron Wesley
Can't guarantee doing anything.

Gela Nathaniel
Leave it with me. Kiss-kiss.

Cameron Wesley
Kiss-kiss.

Doodle message group [Private] Hannah and Gela, January 29, 2024:

Hannah O'Donnell
I've checked and Cameron doesn't have enough credits. In any case, the examiner's notes specifically mention the final project as being 50% of the mark. He could qualify for a discretionary pass if he submits a special-consideration form that cites mitigating circumstances as to why he couldn't complete the course. What's the reason?

Gela Nathaniel
I don't want a withdrawal, especially not at this stage, it reflects so badly on the course. Cameron is my corporate poster boy. I need this MA to work—the department has shrunk, all my other courses are gone. My hours aren't viable without this.

Hannah O'Donnell
I mean, what's *his* reason for not taking part in the final project?

Gela Nathaniel
He's very ill. And doesn't know from one day to the next whether he'll feel well enough. Only he's a private man and doesn't want anyone to know.

Hannah O'Donnell
Then definitely get him to submit a special-consideration form. It's confidential.

Gela Nathaniel
I will. Thank you, Hannah. Thinking about it, I'm sure he'll be able to complete the essay, if nothing else.

Doodle message group [Private] Gela and Cameron, January 29, 2024:

Gela Nathaniel
OK, I've spoken to Hannah and here's the deal. You don't have to do any further work, because you're unwell. The exact illness is unspecified because you're a very private man. However, you will have to submit something for the long essay. Tricky, as you won't have built the installation, but you attended the pitch meeting and the trip to Somerset, so you can get a few thousand words out of that, I'm sure. We'll think of something by then.

Gela Nathaniel
Cameron?

Cameron Wesley
Yes, yes. Fine. OK. If you can make it work, so can I. Can't always respond immediately—too much going on here. Thanks for that, Gela. Kiss-kiss.

Gela Nathaniel
Kiss-kiss.

To: MMAM(FTP)
From: Gela Nathaniel
Date: January 29, 2024
Subject: More news

Dear all,

Well, as if the damage to our materials wasn't bad news enough, I have more. Cameron is unwell and will be unable to help out much with the final project, so Jonathan will redistribute his tasks. Luckily, Cameron's built up enough credits to continue with the course and will still submit a final essay; it's just the practical work he'll be unable to complete. I have no doubt you'll take this in your stride. After all, people come and go from real-world situations all the time, and everyone else must accommodate that.

Onward and upward! On this course you are expected to explore diverse materials and venture out of your comfort zones. So Assignment Four is to run alongside the final project:

Assignment Four
Choose a medium you have not worked in before and demonstrate any aspect that inspires you about the final project. Seek help and advice from those group members who favor that medium, and in turn help others to explore your favorite medium for the first time. Deadline: February 22, 2024.

I've given you freedom to express yourselves, so here's looking forward to seeing some extraordinary work!

    Gela

Doodle message group [Private] Jem and Patrick, January 29, 2024:

Jem Badhuri
Do you think he's in rehab? I never found out who it was that smelled of alcohol in the studio that morning.

Patrick Bright
We shouldn't speculate, and we'll soon be so busy we'll forget Cameron was ever here.

Jem Badhuri
Cameron who?

Patrick Bright
I see what you did there—very funny!

Doodle message group MMAM(FTP), January 30, 2024:

Jem Badhuri
I didn't realize we'd have other assignments alongside the final project. Oh well, photography is my least-explored medium. Jonathan, will you show me the ropes?

Jonathan Danners

Of course. I can lend you a camera if you want good-quality prints, or we can see what your phone's like—if you'd rather do a digital collage.

Jem Badhuri

Whoosh! I'm hurtling out of my comfort zone. Can we chat about it in the studio tomorrow?

Jonathan Danners

We can, and perhaps you can introduce me to the art of sound?

Jem Badhuri

That's a date!

Alyson Lang

What a stupid assignment. I'm forty-four. I'm familiar with every medium.

Ludya Parak

Way out of my lane in clay. Jem, are you up for a chat tomorrow?

Jem Badhuri

I'm helping Jonathan.

Ludya Parak

So that's a "No, I won't help you?"

Patrick Bright

You'll have time for both, I'm sure, Jem.

Alyson Lang

I'll help you, Ludya. I'll focus on stop-motion and we can help each other.

Ludya Parak

Thanks, Ali. You're a professional.

Jem Badhuri

What will you do, Pat? There are so many mediums you haven't worked in, you're spoiled for choice.

Patrick Bright
Resin. I like the end results, but the chemical process scares me. You need a technician present and I hate bothering them, but it's my least-explored medium, so they can't complain, surely.

Jem Badhuri
If you need any advice, just ask.

Patrick Bright
That's nice of you, Jem, thank you.

Jem Badhuri
I mean ask Griff—he's really good with resin.

Doodle message group [Private] Jem and Cameron, January 30, 2024:

Jem Badhuri
Hi Cameron. We haven't spoken much, but I'm still sorry to hear you're not well. At least you got in a trip to Somerset before your decline. Get well soon.

Cameron Wesley
Thanks, Jem. Appreciate the sentiment. Good luck with the final project.

Doodle message group [Private] Jem and Jonathan, February 1, 2024:

Jem Badhuri
Thanks for the photography master class, Jonathan. I'm going to smash this assignment.

Jonathan Danners
Thanks for the lesson in sound. Let's hope Rita recovers, after being alarmed by our screaming!

Jem Badhuri
You won't believe the lengths I've gone to for a great soundscape. It's all part of the fun! How is Alyson getting on with Ludya? She hasn't been in for days.

Jonathan Danners

Who?

Jem Badhuri

Alyson.

Jonathan Danners

She has. You must've missed her.

Doodle message group [Private] Patrick and Jem, February 8, 2024:

Patrick Bright

You're right about the technicians, Jem. Rita and Griff have both helped. I'm making resin paperweights with items suspended inside them. Corporate gifts.

Jem Badhuri

When can we show the others our radio? That white noise will be very useful to my soundscape. The fact it comes through a vintage unit is exactly the merging of past, present, and future that the client wants. Plus, if the tunnel fabric is less than perfect, we'll need a big statement to make up for it.

Patrick Bright

I've seen the fabric; if you don't look too closely you'd not know anything had happened. White noise is fascinating, isn't it? Electrical activity in the upper atmosphere. Storms, lightning, flashes of energy. A whole lot of turbulence is going on up there over our heads while we tinker about on earth, oblivious.

Jem Badhuri

Please can we show them on Tuesday? Dad has to pick me up an hour late after his meeting.

Patrick Bright

Be prepared for Jonathan to veto the idea of including it in the installation. I'm still not sure how we came to have that radio in the cupboard. Promise, now.

Jem Badhuri

Pat, you're a dear, but also a spoilsport. OK then.

To: Gela Nathaniel
From: Griff Technician (Maintenance)
Date: February 9, 2024
Subject: MA group

You asked me to keep you informed about how the MA group are tackling their next assignment. This is where they work in unfamiliar mediums and help each other, yes? Well, Jonathan is teaching Jem about photography, although it strikes me she's telling him more than he's telling her. In turn, she's showing him how to work with sound. For this they hogged the media room for the whole of Tuesday. They almost gave Rita a heart attack when Jem screamed as if she was being murdered. It transpired this was for a soundscape.

You said Alyson is showing Ludya how to use a potter's wheel and Ludya's giving Alyson a master class in stop-motion, but they haven't been doing it here, so I can't say how they've been getting on. You have an odd number of students, then asked them to pair up, so there's bound to be one left on their own and it's Patrick. He seems adrift. It's a shame your other fellow left. Anyway, Patrick's decided to learn about epoxy resin, and it's been me and Rita who've talked him through it and kept an eye while he makes all the rookie mistakes. On this note, teaching is not in our contracts, and despite Patrick being polite and enthusiastic, the technicians have enough work to do without babysitting a novice.

You asked how they're fitting in this assignment between their work on the final project. In short, they aren't. I haven't seen any progress made on the tunnel material or the clay head all week. Having said that, Jem plays with a hissing and squawking old radio whenever she's alone in the studio and thinks no one is watching.

Griff

To: Griff Technician (Maintenance)
From: Gela Nathaniel
Date: February 9, 2024
Subject: Re: MA group

Thank you, Griff. I'm so sorry you've all had extra work, with Patrick being left on his own. I didn't specify that this was a pairing-up task, but I should have realized they would naturally end up doing so. Alyson and Ludya have been meeting in Alyson's studio to work on their pieces—that's why we haven't seen them. Not sure what Jem is doing with an old radio, but she'll tell me soon enough. I'm glad to hear they're all working hard. I knew they would neglect the final project. It's all part of their learning curve. Thank you, Griff, and apologies again for the extra pressure on your team.

    Gela

Doodle message group [Private] Jem, Patrick, Jonathan, Alyson, and Ludya, February 13, 2024:

Patrick Bright

I've set this group up for the five of us because obviously Cameron isn't around now and we want to show you guys before we tell Gela. But Jem and I have a surprise for you all. Can we gather in the studio at 5 p.m. tomorrow—after Gela leaves, and before Jem's dad picks her up?

Jem Badhuri

We have to start the tunnel structure tomorrow, so everyone has to come in anyway.

Ludya Parak

Might be in tomorrow, might not. And before anyone asks, I've already left my assignment with Rita.

Alyson Lang

See you there.

Jem Badhuri

I've been bursting to tell you all for days, haven't I, Patrick? It's very exciting!

Doodle message group [Private] Jonathan, Alyson, and Ludya, February 13, 2024:

Alyson Lang
Should've burned that unit along with everything else.

Jonathan Danners
It's keeping Jem and Pat busy. We should message Cameron to say get well soon. *All* of us.

Ludya Parak
Gela's determined he'll finish the course from his sickbed.

Jonathan Danners
Up to you, but it's only polite. I'm going to.

Doodle message group [Private] Jonathan and Cameron, February 13, 2024:

Jonathan Danners
Sorry to hear you're under the weather, Cam. Hope you're better soon.

Cameron Wesley
Cheers, mate. Good luck with the course.

Doodle message group [Private] Ludya and Cameron, February 13, 2024:

Ludya Parak
Thanks for driving back from Somerset. Sorry to hear you're ill.

Cameron Wesley
No worries. Cheers.

Doodle message group [Private] Cameron and Alyson, February 13, 2024:

Cameron Wesley
I've said it before and I'll say it again—if you ever want to work in advertising or marketing, give me a call. Let's stay in touch.

Alyson Lang
Thanks, Cameron. Appreciate the offer. Get well soon.

Royal Hastings, University of London
Multimedia Art MA
Final Project

Candidate name: Jemisha Badhuri
Candidate number: 0883479

The aims of the project:
I'd like to say it all started last year, when we went to RD8 to "pitch our brief." Four of their people sat on the opposite side of a big table and told us about the market for wireless communications. Their voices bounced off the partitions in that cavernous meeting room as we all sat nervously in a row. One by one the others stammered out their prepared speeches. Apart from Cameron, who blustered through his.

Of course it didn't start then, really. Gela had been speaking to RD8 for months. They'd already agreed to commission the work from us. And so much for it being a discussion. I knew how this meeting would unfold. They'd talk, we'd listen. We'd squeak our speeches, they'd shuffle politely in their seats.

I'd prepared a breakdown of costings to assure them a time-tunnel installation could be achieved within their budget. That was *supposed* to be all I said. Now, if I'm given a limitation, I push beyond it. That's just me. So I presented my own idea to RD8.

The most breathtaking ASMR sound is recorded binaurally—in three-dimensions. It feels like the source is a moving, living entity that plays with your sense of space, time, and self. You think someone is whispering in your ear, breathing down your neck, and what they say cuts right to your core. It picks up the rhythm of your heartbeat, the flow of blood in your veins. It permeates your entire life system. Binaural recording isn't simply a nice way to experience music, or a gimmick for horror films. It's a technology that literally hacks into your brain. It is the future.

But to appreciate ASMR, you need headphones, and apparently Gela agreed with Ludya that headphones were not in the spirit of the installation. She said that RD8 wanted to reflect the ability of their technology to bring people together and that head-phones would do the opposite.

I disagreed.

So I explained to RD8 how the tunnel would reflect the history the company is so proud of, while my idea—a binaural ASMR soundscape, playing literally in their ears—would ensure they *felt* that connection. That link between the earth, the body, humanity, and the unseeable mysteries of space and time that radio waves are . . . Then once RD8's guests emerge from the tunnel they arrive in the future, as our centerpiece reveals itself to be a human head, a showstopping replica (in clay) of a binaural microphone. Science finally meets and melds with humanity. I finished my pitch and waited for the response.

Everyone in the room was silent. Gela exhaled. Jonathan cleared his throat. Then one of the marketing ladies spoke. She said what a great idea, but could we do it within budget? I said yes. With clay, papier-mâché and any salvaged hardware we laid hands on, we could create my idea cheaply and easily. I'd costed it out and it was more than doable.

Did we achieve our aims?
The whole project would've been different if I'd gone to Somerset. What went on there? All I know is that something came back with them and haunted us all from that moment on. Was it the radio? What we heard that afternoon in the studio? Even now, I'm not sure. But it started long before that meeting. It began the moment we arrived in the Media Arts Department in September. And if I manage to submit this exam paper safely, then it's going on even as you, the examiner, read this essay.

WhatsApp chat between Hannah O'Donnell and Ben Sketcher on May 30, 2024:

Ben
Is this Hannah O'Donnell, who works in admin for the Media Arts Department?

Hannah
Who is this?

Ben
Ben Sketcher. External Examiner for the MA in Multimedia Art.

Hannah
I can only apologize. How on earth did she get your number?

Ben
Sorry, who?

Hannah
Jemisha Badhuri. Has she contacted you about her grade? I know she wants to.

Ben
She hasn't, but send me her number and I'll be sure not to answer if she calls.

Hannah
Good idea. I'll forward it. Is there anything I can help you with?

Ben
I have a question about the Multimedia Art MA. Did anything strange happen on that course?

Ben
Hannah?

Hannah
I'm glad you asked. There is something.

Ben
You can tell me in confidence.

Hannah

Have any of the essays mentioned a voice?

Ben

Yes. What do you know about it?

Hannah

I heard it myself. Overheard it.

Ben

What did it sound like? What did it say?

Hannah

It asked for help. Said it was trapped.

Ben

Could it have been a part of the installation? A recording made by the students?

Hannah

It may have been. Only their panic was real. It affected them all in different ways.

Ben

Hannah, can we meet?

Hannah

Absolutely not.

To: Gela Nathaniel
From: Griff Technician (Maintenance)
Date: February 13, 2024
Subject: The MA group

There's nothing in our health-and-safety guidelines about messing with building electricity. But those guidelines can always be rewritten. Gela, please tell your MA group it's dangerous and has to stop.
   Griff

To: Griff Technician (Maintenance)
From: Gela Nathaniel
Date: February 13, 2024
Subject: Re: The MA group

I'm sorry, Griff. You're right. They are so keen and inventive there's no holding them back. But of course this must stop. I'll have a word with them.
   Gela

Doodle message group [Private] Gela, Ludya, Alyson, and Jonathan, February 14, 2024:

Gela Nathaniel
Please be careful using building electricity. The technicians are across everything that happens in that studio.

Jonathan Danners
It isn't us. Patrick is helping Jem experiment with radio circuits. We're staying late tonight to hear some noise they picked up.

Ludya Parak
Shit, is that all it is?

Gela Nathaniel
So it's nothing to do with you?

Jonathan Danners
No.

Doodle message group [Private] Jem, Patrick, Jonathan, Alyson, and Ludya, February 14, 2024:

Jem Badhuri

Don't forget the surprise Pat and I have been working on. The big reveal is 5 p.m. tonight! Don't be late—my dad is due around then and he doesn't like waiting.

Patrick Bright

I'm sure everyone will be there.

Patrick Bright's Doodle Diary, February 14, 2024:

We've got a mystery here. Jem wanted to see if that old radio worked, but I didn't want her playing with the electrics on her own, so I've been helping. Sure enough, once I wired a plug to it, we got a hissing, squawking, and crackling—the atmospherics. Young Jem was thrilled because she could use it in her soundscape. It was more like white noise to me, but I was pulled along by her sheer enthusiasm, and we arranged to show the others once Gela has left for the day.

But something happened as we all sat around that radio in the studio. The white noise came through sure enough, but suddenly it dropped away to complete silence, as if a radio station had started broadcasting—and into that silence came a voice.

"I'm trapped. I don't know where I am, but I'm alone here. If you can hear me, send help." Something like that. It had a strange timbre. You couldn't tell if it was a man or a woman. It felt live, like through a walkie-talkie. Spine-chilling. My blood ran stone-cold. Who was it?

Then the atmospherics kicked back in, as if the broadcast was switched off as suddenly as it had been switched on. Jem was frozen to the spot, so I leapt to the dial, tried to get back to the same frequency, but I was all fingers and thumbs and there are no markings on that thing. We all stood around and looked at one another. I have to say that for a group with a lot of issues, we were united in our shock at that voice.

We jumped out of our skins again when Hannah leaned in at the door. She had Jem's dad with her, a kindly old man who clearly thinks the world of his little girl. When she wasn't in her usual pickup spot, he'd gone straight to admin in a panic. Jem, who is never short of things to say, quickly got her bags together and left with barely a word. Hannah glanced around at us and said to make sure we switched everything off. She had a look on her face. Had she heard it too?

Jonathan and I played with the dials but couldn't find that broadcast again, and by the time we were ready to leave I think we'd all decided it was nothing. Only now, when I'm alone in the dark myself, I can't help thinking about that poor, trapped person, pleading for help over the airwaves.

Doodle message group [Private] Jem and Patrick, February 14, 2024:

Jem Badhuri
OMG!

Jem Badhuri
I've been listening to the radio all my life and never heard anything like that.

Patrick Bright
Feel a bit shaky.

Jem Badhuri
If only the dial had wavelengths, we could find it again. Wish I'd recorded it.

Doodle message group [Private] Patrick, Jonathan, Alyson, and Ludya, February 14, 2024:

Patrick Bright
Guys, Jem is beside herself about the weird radio station. She's talking about recording it. If she puts that in the RD8 soundscape, we'd better have a paramedic with a defibrillator on standby at the event.

Jonathan Danners
Managing Jem's enthusiasm is a key part of my role.

Patrick Bright
Had you better come clean?

Jonathan Danners
Don't start this again.

Patrick Bright
About that radio, I mean.

Doodle message group [Private] Gela and Cameron, February 14, 2024:

Gela Nathaniel
Kiss-kiss.

Cameron Wesley
Kiss-kiss to you too.

Gela Nathaniel
When are you back? We could meet up for a drink.

Cameron Wesley
A work drink?

Gela Nathaniel
Have you seen the date? A not-work drink.

Royal Hastings, University of London
Multimedia Art MA
Final Project

Candidate name: Ludya Parak
Candidate number: 0883481

The project:

It started weird and stayed weird. I'm not averse to strangeness. Strangeness is just life, right? Doesn't mean anything is wrong, simply that people are people. Our group was diverse, as you'd expect. Only we're drawn to others like ourselves. The clique factor. This course is what happens when everyone is really, really different.

We went in to pitch our ideas to RD8, a company of engineer geeks and tech nerds who love codes, computer languages, and programming. I'd never get a client this big in real life, but I've worked for many tiny start-ups who aim to be like them. Gela was smart getting them on board. They know nothing about art, so we were free to explore and experiment. Best of all, they have the money. Not that they paid anything near market value for the work we did. Still, when Jem went off script and pitched her own idea, of course they liked it. I thought the ASMR headphone experience didn't belong in an installation designed to connect people, but what could I say after that?

It's OK. I signed up to this course to explore 3D design and learn skills that complement my screen-graphics work and that's what I got to do. Only, when we all went down to Somerset, shit got real. It's like before that we were playing at this. It wasn't quite real life. I should never have agreed to drive. It makes me tired and when I'm tired I get angry, and I do and say things I shouldn't. I'm not the only one. Jem canceling our motel booking! Holy shit, the girl has so much to answer for. Although it's not her fault, or mine. Whose was it? Alyson, Jonathan, Cameron, and Patrick.

Mysterious sounds:

So you'll know by now, a radio was "borrowed" from the RD8 museum in Somerset, a place called Thorney Coffin. You couldn't make it up. The thing was dead, but Patrick and Jem performed some sort of miracle and it picked up a signal. Jem was totally stoked for the noises that unit made. I could tell the consensus was: well, if it keeps her occupied she won't notice anything else—and remember if Jem's not happy, she will make trouble until things go her way again. I learned that the day she threw a piece of clay at me.

Then came the voice.

"I'm trapped in the dark. Please help me."

Doodle message group [Private] Jonathan, Alyson, Jem, Patrick, and Ludya, February 15, 2024:

Jem Badhuri
I've got my dad to pick me up an hour later again tonight. Let's get the radio out and try to find that station again. Who can stay?

Ludya Parak
Not me. Kid stuff.

Jonathan Danners
OK. Yep. Good idea.

Doodle message group [Private] Jem and Patrick, February 15, 2024:

Jem Badhuri
It came through at exactly the same time as last night, but said something different.

Patrick Bright
"I'm trapped. Floating in the dark. Please help me." If it's a recording, then it's not the same recording as yesterday. It sounds live to me, Jem.

Jem Badhuri
"Floating in the dark" sounds like he's on a boat. Shall we tell Jonathan to call the Coast Guard?

Patrick Bright
Let's not involve outsiders.

Jem Badhuri
We could ask RD8 what the radio is? They might be able to help.

Patrick Bright
Let's not bother the client. Jonathan's heard it two nights in a row now. He's project manager, so it's up to him what—if anything—we do with that wireless.

Doodle message group [Private] Jonathan, Alyson, Jem, Patrick, and Ludya, February 15, 2024:

Jonathan Danners
Right, this is important. The old radio is distracting us from our coursework and final project. From here on in, it's out of bounds. No one is to touch it. Jem and Patrick—do I have your word?

Patrick Bright
Absolutely. I get the heebie-jeebies just thinking about it.

Jem Badhuri
If Doodle had emojis, I'd put a really sad face here.

Jonathan Danners
Jem, do I have your word?

Jem Badhuri
OK then.

Jonathan Danners' Doodle Diary, February 20, 2024:

"The sounds I am listening to every night at first appear to be human voices conversing back and forth in a language I cannot understand. I find it difficult to imagine I am actually hearing real voices from people not of this planet. There must be a more simple explanation that has so far eluded me." Nikola Tesla, 1918

"I have been at work for some time building an apparatus to see if it is possible for personalities which have left this earth to communicate with us." Thomas Edison in an interview in the October 1920 issue of *The American Magazine*

Both were working just after the First World War—a time when millions of young men had died and a generation was living with irreparable grief. At the same time technological, scientific, and industrial progress were rapid.

On February 14, 2024, we heard this:

"I'm trapped in a dark place. Please help me."

On February 15, 2024, we heard this:

"I'm trapped. Floating in the dark. Please save me."

It was the same voice. But not the same words. As if the voice has one opportunity every day to broadcast its plea for help. Or perhaps it's speaking all the time, but the atmospheric conditions are only conducive to broadcast for a minute or so per day. He sounds like he's clutching at straws—and so are we.

Doodle message group MMAM(FTP), February 20, 2024:

Gela Nathaniel
I see you're all busy with the salvaged components in the studio. We'll have a catch-up meeting this morning to check everyone is happy with their tasks and discuss your long essays. Like I said, you can keep a full diary, or you can NOT keep a diary and have more work to do later in this process when you'll also have practical work as well. The choice is yours.

Patrick Bright
Thanks, Gela. I'm firmly in the "keeping a diary" camp!

Ludya Parak
Guess which camp I'm in.

Jem Badhuri
Thanks, Gela. I'm keeping a diary too.

Doodle message group [Private] Jonathan, Alyson, Jem, Patrick, and Ludya,
February 20, 2024:

Patrick Bright

Should we tell Gela about the radio and the voice, or not?

Alyson Lang

It's not relevant to the project.

Jonathan Danners

Please, let's just forget the radio—and no one mention it to Gela.

Jem Badhuri

The man sounds trapped. He needs help. Should we call the police?

Alyson Lang

It's recorded. I looked it up. It's a "numbers station"—a radio broadcast
for spies. They aren't even used anymore.

Jem Badhuri

How do you know what we heard, Alyson? You weren't here.

Alyson Lang

I was there. I heard the voice.

Jem Badhuri

You weren't in on either day I stayed late.

Jonathan Danners

Ali was in on the first day, for sure.

Patrick Bright

Yes, she was here, Jem, but you were so excited, it's no wonder you don't
remember. Now I googled numbers stations. They broadcast numbers
or music. Nowhere does it mention a voice that claims to be held
prisoner.

Ludya Parak

I mean, people who are trapped tend not to be trapped with broadcasting
equipment? Right?

Jem Badhuri
He could be stuck on a mountain. In a cave. In a forest. On a boat out at sea. He'd have a radio then.

Patrick Bright
We heard it at exactly the same time two nights in a row, but the voice said something different each time.

Jem Badhuri
You could ask RD8.

Jonathan Danners
We MUST NOT involve the client.

Jem Badhuri
But they gave us the radio, didn't they?

Patrick Bright
The sourcing team weren't given that radio.

Jonathan Danners
Alyson is right; it's most likely an old government radio channel. They keep them open, in case other forms of communication are compromised. Recorded messages like these help them check the channel is working. Now, please, can we forget the voice and the radio and concentrate on the course?

Ludya Parak
Assignment Four is due this Thursday. If you need a link to the special-consideration form, just ask.

Doodle message group [Private] Jem and Patrick, February 20, 2024:

Jem Badhuri
Patrick, when you said the sourcing team wasn't given that radio, what did you mean?

Patrick Bright

Oh, it's probably not relevant, but I've a feeling it might be in our possession unofficially. It's only a feeling, though.

Jem Badhuri

I don't understand.

Patrick Bright

I was wandering about, looking at all the old tech. I don't know exactly what happened, but Jonathan and Ludya started arguing about something. Nothing physical; she was screeching, he was telling her to calm down. But the RD8 lady came and asked them to step outside. Minutes later they were skulking in the corridor. I didn't see where Alyson was because Cameron was chatting to me.

Doodle message group [Private] Jonathan, Alyson, and Ludya, February 22, 2024:

Jonathan Danners

FFS, all their messages say the unit shouldn't work at all. What is that voice?

Ludya Parak

It's weird, but it's the least of our problems right now. Just get rid of it? The radio, I mean.

Message group: 2024 Examiners, May 30, 2024

Tilda Ricci

OK, what is going on, Ben?

Ben Sketcher

Good, you've got to the radio bit.

Tilda Ricci

Cameron submitted a final essay and is scheduled for a discretionary pass, on the basis of his ill health. Unfortunately, I fear Gela made that up to keep him on the course in name only. You think there might be a relationship between them? A conflict of interest?

Ben Sketcher

I think there's more than that. I've been looking into the group and the admissions procedure. This is a new course. It was never advertised and doesn't appear in this year's prospectus.

Tilda Ricci

MMAM was devised after our prospectus was published and long after the usual admissions process was underway. Gela wanted to assemble a class of good, experienced artists as her inaugural year. She could take what she learned from them and adapt the course for a more generalized intake going forward. She'd seen some promising candidates. I remember this crossing my desk about a year ago—it was completely transparent. All fees were paid up front.

Ben Sketcher

Gela chose each and every one of those students by hand. But they weren't all experienced artists. Patrick and Jonathan were acquaintances who had shown a passing interest in getting into art. She personally sought out the others to join the course.

Tilda Ricci

I'd say that showed initiative on the part of the tutor. The department is under pressure to make its courses relevant to the job market. All Gela's MAs have been cut, and the BA course is fully staffed. This one is her idea and she has to make it work.

Ben Sketcher

The university has admissions criteria. Demographics they must adhere to.

Tilda Ricci

They're a very diverse group. Gela is a woman of color herself and has been active in opening opportunities to students from underrepresented groups. Personally, I think she's done an excellent job. Whatever problems you've picked up on, Ben, I am confident the tutor is entirely innocent.

Ben Sketcher

Gela brings the group together. She arranges for them to pitch an idea for an art project to a local manufacturer. In sourcing material for it, they discover a strange voice broadcasting from a mysterious radio. Then someone disappears. Or at least one of the students seems to think so.

To: MMAM(FTP)
From: Gela Nathaniel
Date: February 23, 2024
Subject: Assignment Four

Dear all,

Thank you for submitting your Assignment Four projects in good time. I gave you freedom of expression, with the only stipulation that you must work in your least-explored medium and create something inspired by the final project. When we're all back in the studio next week we'll view and critique the work. It should prove light relief from construction of the head and the tunnel.

Enjoy your weekends.

Gela

Doodle message group [Private] Jem and Gela, February 23, 2024:

Jem Badhuri

Is Alyson still coming to the studio or is she working from home?

Gela Nathaniel

That's a strange question, Jem. Of course she's coming in, although mainly at night.

Jem Badhuri

Have you seen her lately?

Gela Nathaniel

Yes. I'm sure I have.

To: Gela Nathaniel
From: Griff Technician (Maintenance)
Date: February 23, 2024
Subject: Your MA students

Some of your group are hanging around the studio after hours fiddling with an old radio they keep hidden at the back of the cupboard (behind the old frames). Heaven knows what they're trying to do, but they wait until all us technicians are gone before they start. If their activities mean our department encounters extra cleanup work, then you will be hearing from me.

Griff

To: Griff Technician (Maintenance)
From: Gela Nathaniel
Date: February 23, 2024
Subject: Re: Your MA students

Bless! They're so keen on their final project. I'm sure they won't cause any trouble, but thanks for letting me know.

Gela

Doodle message group [Private] Patrick and Ludya, February 24, 2024:

Patrick Bright
I've tried talking to Jonathan. It's hopeless. That poor voice. We've got to tell someone, so he can be rescued.

Ludya Parak
They never say where they are, so what can we do?

Patrick Bright
What do you think it is?

Ludya Parak
An old radio drama? An actor's voice? Whatever, it's Jonathan's problem. We shouldn't have that radio, you shouldn't have got it working. It wasn't in our plan. It's distracting everyone and wasting our time.

Patrick Bright
Jonathan said something very strange. In that museum, materials don't age. He said this radio could be a prototype from any time within the last hundred years and, if it is, then that's the exact time Tesla and Edison were working on machines to contact the dead.

Ludya Parak *has left the group.*

Patrick Bright
The dark place our man wants to escape from. He could be in limbo, either unaware he's passed away or, for some reason, unable to reach the Other Side.

Doodle message group [Private] Gela and Cameron, February 26, 2024:

Cameron Wesley
Long story short, the sourcing team have a radio they should never have taken from the museum. If the boss gets it back, no questions will be asked.

Gela Nathaniel
Griff mentioned this. It's in the studio cupboard.

Cameron Wesley
Tell them it's dangerous and has to go back.

Gela Nathaniel
How could it be dangerous?

Cameron Wesley
You're a creative powerhouse, Gela, you'll think of something. Leave it at the rear doors tonight and I'll collect early tomorrow morning. Kiss-kiss.

Gela Nathaniel
Kiss-kiss.

To: MMAM(FTP)
From: Gela Nathaniel
Date: February 26, 2024
Subject: Tomorrow

Hello all,
Bad news about the old radio some of you have been experimenting with. The technicians were clearing up and noticed it had woodworm, which caused quite a panic in the studio. All the benches are wood, plus

the floorboards and the tables. Griff has taken the offending article and quarantined it in a plastic bag.

Luckily you've got plenty of other components to help you construct the installation, and in any case, the priority now is to devise and program the multimedia elements of the display. Remember we have until the middle of April to create something to show the client for their top-line feedback.

See you in the studio tomorrow.
Gela

To: Gela Nathaniel
From: Griff Technician (Maintenance)
Date: February 26, 2024
Subject: Question

This old radio in a bag by the back door: sure you want it scrapped? Jem said something about using it in your installation.

To: Griff Technician (Maintenance)
From: Gela Nathaniel
Date: February 26, 2024
Subject: Re: Question

Please leave it there. Someone will run in tomorrow morning and grab it. Please don't tell the students I said that, just tell them it has woodworm. I need to return it somewhere with minimum fuss and bother. This group has been enough trouble, I don't want any more. Please, Griff, can you do that for me?
Gela

MMAM(FTP)
Final Project—First Phase
Tutor's Report, February 27, 2024

Brief: Create a multimedia installation in the foyer of RD8's headquarters for the company's in-house event. The company is launching a new generation of mobile-payment systems that blend radio waves with cloud-based technology.

Overview: The students prepared for a pitch meeting with their client by researching the company and the wider world of wireless payment systems. We rehearsed our pitch in the studio and divided the presentation between all six group members. The result was a perfectly crafted talk that suitably impressed Mae and her team at RD8. There followed a sourcing trip to the company's facility in Somerset and thus began our construction of the experiential tunnel, clay sculpture, and immersive sound experience for the installation.

Jemisha Badhuri
As financial manager, Jem delivered a report into how much the installation would cost the client and why it was so expensive. Always enthusiastic, Jem delivered her proposed speech and then suggested a few further ideas of her own. Jem was selected for this course because her creative flair in more unusual mediums—sound and 3D—is outstanding. Given her relative youth, one might expect her to be a rather more reticent and self-effacing character than she is.

Patrick Bright
Patrick is resource coordinator for this project, a role I gave him to counteract his habit of shrinking behind some of the more dominant members of the group. If it's possible for someone to be too nice, Patrick is that. In this role he proved quite unable to assert himself, leaving Jonathan to take up the slack. Even a simple matter of booking hotel rooms was whisked out of his hands by Jem, who

had another agenda entirely. Patrick should work on his confidence in taking the initiative.

Jonathan Danners

I chose Jonathan as project leader because I felt he deserved to have power restored to him after what happened with Alyson and his first project. He and Alyson have established a personal relationship quite at odds with how she treated him that day. Still, I could not have chosen anyone better to lead this group of creatives. Jonathan is calm, decisive, and fair.

Alyson Lang

Alyson is the best creative director this project could have. She thinks inside and outside the box simultaneously. Despite this, she is also mindful of how important it is to keep other students happy, and will adapt her work to ensure the client's needs are met, as well as those of the group.

Ludya Parak

So far Ludya has managed her time, and that of the group, effectively, although it is fair to say that deadlines have not loomed over us yet, so "time" will tell if she can keep up the good work. Ludya was selected for this course because professional design expertise will bestow credibility on it. So far she has not disappointed.

Cameron Wesley

It is with great sadness that Cameron has had to step back from the practical side of this course. Seeing as he attended the sourcing trip and will write a long essay, there is no reason he should not be able to scrape a grade. As a high-earning professional looking to build his creative skills, he is a valuable member of the team and it would be a shame to lose him completely.

Doodle message group [Private] Gela and Cameron, February 27, 2024:

Gela Nathaniel
Have you got it?

Cameron Wesley
Yes, it's safe. But I can't keep messaging you. It's too risky.

Gela Nathaniel
I understand. Kiss-kiss.

Cameron Wesley
Kiss-kiss.

Doodle message group [Private] Jem, Patrick, Jonathan, Ludya, and Alyson, February 27, 2024:

Jem Badhuri
The radio is gone. Sob! Is woodworm that bad?

Patrick Bright
Woodworm is that bad. I hadn't noticed it, though. Did anyone else?

Ludya Parak
Gross. No.

Doodle message group [Private] Jonathan and Gela, February 27, 2024:

Jonathan Danners
You're not picking up. I've called three times.

Gela Nathaniel
I'm driving. Don't message me on Doodle.

Doodle message group [Private] Jem and Patrick, February 28, 2024:

Jem Badhuri
Where's Alyson?

Patrick Bright
How do you mean?

Jem Badhuri
She wasn't in the studio this morning.

Patrick Bright
She was, I spoke to her in the foyer about my resin mold. She went straight next door to work with the potter's wheel. You're right, she didn't come back after that. Probably smoking with the undergrads.

Jem Badhuri
Jonathan seemed a bit down. He came in with Gela this morning. Far earlier than usual.

Patrick Bright
You're very observant, Ms. Badhuri—anything else I should know?

Jem Badhuri
You'd be surprised what I notice, Pat! I wonder if there's trouble between J and A. They were glued together before Somerset. Now Jonathan is super-quiet and it seems Alyson is hardly ever here.

Royal Hastings, University of London
Multimedia Art MA
Final Project

Candidate name: Patrick Bright
Candidate number: 0883480

Finding my style:
I'm a sketcher, I draw from life. The human body is especially fascinating. I've done the odd life-drawing class, but it's faces that inspire me. I don't know, I was hoping this final project would involve human subjects, but instead I found myself working with machines and parts of machines. The nearest we got to a human body was the giant head that Gela and Jem made as a showstopper centerpiece. It doesn't even have eyes or ears.

Because I'd never studied art I was keen to find my style, as they say. That's what I got talking to Gela about, over the months she was coming into the shop. She told me about her fine-art courses and I thought, yes, that's exactly what I want to be doing. Exploring different drawing styles, working out where my skills are most suited. I'd like nothing more than to escape somewhere and watch people, sketch them, and perhaps paint in oils any scenes or figures that spoke to me. That's always been my dream. An MA would give me that chance. I'm sure that's how the conversations went. So how did I end up on this course? Struggling to operate software and thinking about ad campaigns and marketing? It was Gela. She's some smooth-talking salesperson, that's for sure. I can see why she wanted Alyson, Jem, Jonathan, Ludya, and even Cameron. But why did she want me?

So instead of finding my sketching style I learned to work with various media, and despite my misgivings, it did prove a revelation. I learned how to create computer animations and tried out epoxy resin. That's the clear stuff used to make solid ornaments. You mix liquid resin with a hardener, pour it into a mold, leave it a couple of days and you've got a solid transparent block in whatever shape your mold was. But more interesting than that, you can suspend things in the resin, so you've got jewelry or a little ornament at the end. People suspend egg timers, glitter, trinkets, action figures, or watch parts. I remember seeing shamrocks in resin at the tourist shops when I was a child. I've sold the raw materials for years, but never used them.

Now I intend to go back to Schull to paint and sketch for a few years, but I'll need to support myself before I can get by selling paintings. When Rita showed me how to use the resin, I was struck by an idea. That area of southwest Ireland is a very popular location for weddings. Imagine you're just married, you're about to throw your bouquet, but it has some wonderful blooms in it—say, a rose—and you want to keep that as a symbol that your love will never die. So you pluck it out, throw the bouquet and give that single flower to me.

Now resin is strange stuff. You can seal anything inside it—so long as that thing is dry. A fresh flower will rot from the inside, so you have to dry it first. I'd take your wedding rose and submerge it in silica powder for a few days before I arranged the dehydrated bloom in resin. There you have your wedding flower and happy memories, perfectly preserved in an ornament that will last forever.

It's a simple business. I know where to buy all the materials at the lowest prices and it would take the pressure off selling paintings before I've found my style. The idea grew and grew, but I didn't tell anyone else on the course. Not Gela and not even Jem, who I get along with fine. Why not? It's hard to say, even now.

Looking back on this course, perhaps it wasn't so much about me finding my style as finding my voice.

MMAM(FTP) WhatsApp group started by Patrick Bright. Added to the group are Alyson Lang, Ludya Parak, Cameron Wesley, Jonathan Danners, and Jem Badhuri, February 28, 2024:

Patrick
How does everyone feel?

Jem
We're not meant to talk on WhatsApp. Gela won't like it.

Patrick
It's Gela I want to talk about.

Jem
We can do that in a private Doodle group. No one reads them. It's just that RH need access to our convos in case of online bullying. It was the same at West Mids.

Jonathan
What are you getting at, Patrick?

Patrick
Gela said the radio has woodworm. I know what woodworm looks like and that radio didn't have it. What else is she lying about?

Ludya
Whatever. I wouldn't worry about it.

Patrick
I got in early this morning and that radio was outside the rear doors, wrapped in a carrier bag. You'd think it was being thrown out, only it had a card on top, blank except for two lipstick kisses in Gela's shade of pink.

Royal Hastings, University of London
Multimedia Art MA
Final Project

Candidate name: Jemisha Badhuri
Candidate number: 0883479

Moments of change:
A couple of years ago my brother Adi thought he wanted to be a
life coach. He took me to a personal-development seminar in an old
church on Piccadilly, where the ceiling was so high and the place so
busy that a cacophony of voices swirled and echoed right up to the
roof and back. When everyone fell silent to hear the speaker, it was
as if those voices were still up there, trapped above us, talking and
whispering.

The speaker said life is about change. That's how we grow and
develop, but to change we have to let go of the past. Most of us,
she said, are bad at this, especially when a situation that *was* good
turns bad. We cling to the past and deny the need for change, telling ourselves everything is as fine as it ever was, when it isn't. Well,
I couldn't understand why everyone around us was nodding and
murmuring as if the speaker was delivering a universal truth. I stuck
my hand in the air. Adi hissed, "No, Jem, not now," but his words
flew up to the roof. "I don't think that's true," I shouted, and I could
tell the speaker wasn't happy at her speech being interrupted. "It's
not true of everyone. I love change. When something that was good
turns bad, I don't hesitate to move on. The trick is recognizing that
moment when it happens, because it might be something very small
that gives the game away. Most people aren't listening hard enough
to notice." My words chased each other upward and swirled in the
air over our heads.

The speaker's steps clip-clopped down the aisle. She stopped at
our row. "Ah," she said, "you're right. We need to be alert to those
moments that trigger a realization. A very good point."

In the end, Adi stayed on his accountancy course.

I stand by what I said that day: I'm much better than most people

176

at initiating change and coming to terms with it. There's a reason that episode comes to mind at this point in my essay, because it might seem as if I didn't put that skill into practice on the MA. It wasn't because I had no idea anything was wrong, it was because I wanted the rest of the group to think I didn't realize. Even now I can't say for sure exactly when Alyson stopped coming in. Gela said Cameron left, but it was Alyson who disappeared. I don't think she came back after Somerset.

Perhaps her leaving the course could've been explained away with any number of excuses, but it wasn't. This is the strange thing. Everyone else pretended she was still here, but somewhere just out of sight.

Was that speaker right, after all? Were they in denial that she'd gone and tried to fill an Alyson-shaped hole in the group with talk about where she was and what she was doing?

I told that speaker I was happy to walk away when things turned bad, but on this occasion I stayed. I wanted to know what had happened, and staying on the course was my best chance of finding out.

MMAM(FTP)
Coursework Module: Assignment Four
Tutor's Report, February 29, 2024

Brief: Choose a medium you have not worked in before and demonstrate any aspect that inspires you about the final project. Seek help and advice from those group members who favor that medium, and in turn help others to explore your favorite medium.

Overview: This assignment is designed to give the MA students a taste of multitasking. Creative professionals often work on several projects simultaneously, and this is where time management, discipline, and application all come into play. While they are busy with their tasks for the final project, Assignment Four is a free brief with a stipulation that they help others on the course. Supporting fellow professionals while under pressure themselves will test their patience and generosity, not to mention how willing they are to work as a team.

Jemisha Badhuri

Jem is a 3D and sound specialist, so she chose to explore the 2D world of photography, while helping Jonathan work in sound for the first time. She submitted a series of photographs in a harsh tonal black and white, taken in and around the studio. She titled the series "Work in Progress." Most of the photographs were of Alyson's bench, which, while not the tidiest, wasn't the most representative, either. On the whole I feel Jem hasn't gone far enough, literally and creatively, to produce this piece. While she worked with Jonathan to create her photographs, and helped him with his assignment, I understand that she refused to help others who approached her for assistance. This is not in the spirit of the course. Grade: C+

Patrick Bright

Patrick worked with Griff and Rita to explore the tricky medium of epoxy resin. Unfortunately, no other member of the course came forward to help him, which both surprised and disappointed me. It has to be said, though, that none of them count resin art among their specialties. I was impressed with Patrick's newfound enthusiasm for this medium, which is far removed from his key subject of freehand drawing. He made seven cuboid paperweights, each containing a dead scorpion suspended in transparent resin. Five were posed to appear at rest, one was poised with its sting ready to strike, and one was curled up in death. He gave a paperweight to each of us. While all were well made, I remain unsure how they relate to the final project. Grade: D–

Jonathan Danners

Jonathan worked with Jem to learn the basics of sound. Sound does not, necessarily, need to be technically advanced to be effective, but to create something truly captivating and inspiring requires an ear for the medium. Jonathan's three-minute soundscape was of a man screaming. As the scream went on and on, the distortion was adjusted to reveal that the screaming was actually a woman (Jem). This effect requires a higher level of technical ability and equipment, which makes me wonder whether Jem had a greater hand in its creation than might be assumed. Jonathan can be commended on his work helping Jem with her photography. Grade: B–

Alyson Lang

Alyson has mastered most artistic mediums, but stop-motion film is her least explored. For this she worked with Ludya at Alyson's home studio, thereby neglecting their work on the installation. This is the perfect example of failure to multitask that could set a bigger project behind schedule. Ludya, who is in charge of time management, should have had more foresight. Alyson, however, managed to captivate everyone who watched her short film. She borrowed radio components from the salvage bags and created a stop-motion clip whereby six components inside a radio each "ate" one another until only one was left. That piece was so sad in its lonely prison, it threw itself onto an electrode and burst into flames. A very moving and poignant film. Grade: A–

Ludya Parak

Ludya is an accomplished stop-motion artist and clearly had a strong hand in Alyson's film. She chose to work in clay for her own project, and for once submitted it on time and without a special-consideration form. She fired her statuette in Alyson's kiln, then painted and glazed it herself. It was striking in its simplicity and, under normal circumstances, would earn her a decent grade. However, I wonder how a face melting into the ground, its mouth set in a hopeless yawn and eyes pleading heavenward is inspired by the final project, which so far has run smoothly and is firmly on course? Strangely, both Ludya and Jonathan created an artwork around a scream; one could almost say Jonathan's soundscape accompanies Ludya's sculpture. Grade: C–

Cameron Wesley

Cameron Wesley did not submit any work for Assignment Four, having partially withdrawn from the course. However, he remains in touch with his team and engaged with the final project. Grade: Ungraded

Doodle message group [Private] Jem and Patrick, February 29, 2024:

Jem Badhuri
What did you think of Alyson's film?

Patrick Bright
It was fine. I mean, you can tell she worked with Ludya. It's Ludya's style.

Jem Badhuri
Gela loved it. Shame Alyson wasn't there to get her grade and see what everyone else had done.

Patrick Bright
She popped in earlier. Apparently she had a hospital appointment.

Jem Badhuri
That's what everyone said. I wonder what's wrong with her.

Patrick Bright
You can't ask, in case it's something "down below."

Jem Badhuri
Is that why no one asks? Anyway, thank you for my paperweight, Pat. I'll treasure it as a memento of the MA.

Patrick Bright
You're welcome, Jem. The scorpion will guard your papers and stop them blowing away. I made seven, so thought I might as well hand them out. I was going to let Griff have Cameron's, but Gela spotted it and said she'd keep it for him.

Jem Badhuri
I feel like giving away my photographs, as they didn't get me a good grade—but my dad likes to display any work I do, so I'll take them home.

Patrick Bright
Here's a thing: I thought your grade was unfairly low. Your photographs were more clearly inspired by the final project than anything the rest of us came up with.

Jem Badhuri

Thanks, Pat. I agree. Where did you get the scorpions? Aren't they from hot countries?

Patrick Bright

They are, but there's an artist I know through the shop. She mounts dried insects in frames, even dries them herself. I begged some specimens from her.

Jem Badhuri

Why would anyone do that? Scritchy-scratchy things! Yuck!

Patrick Bright

Not at all. Insects are grand. Perfect miniature machines with exquisite detail and symmetry. Flowers are nature's artwork, but insects are nature's engineering.

Jem Badhuri

I'll take your word for it, Pat.

Doodle message group [Private] Jem and Jonathan, February 29, 2024:

Jem Badhuri

Congratulations! You only got a B– but that's high for you.

Jonathan Danners

Thanks. And for your help.

Jem Badhuri

Alyson must be delighted with an A– in her least favorite medium. Gela said her film is easily as good as anything Ludya would make.

Jonathan Danners

There's no point complaining to Gela.

Jonathan Danners

What I mean is, she knows the two of them worked together. *We* worked together, after all. It was part of the brief.

Jem Badhuri

I don't always pick up on these things, so have to ask or risk saying something that triggers someone. But out of interest, are you and Alyson still an item? Or has she gone back to her husband?

Jonathan Danners

One: what makes you think she ever left him? Two: if you don't want to trigger someone, don't say anything.

Doodle message group [Private] Jem and Jonathan, March 5, 2024:

Jem

Is Alyson OK? She hasn't been in the studio for weeks.

Jonathan

She has, you've just not bumped into her. She has work to do.

Jem

Did her husband find out about her affair with you?

Jonathan *has left the group.*

Doodle message group [Private] Jem and Alyson, March 5, 2024:

Jem Badhuri

Hi Alyson! Sorry not to have bumped into you recently in the studio. Hope nothing's wrong.

Alyson Lang

I'm busy with a big commission, so can only come in now and again. There's nothing wrong, Jem, don't worry.

Doodle message group [Private] Gela and Cameron, March 5, 2024:

Gela Nathaniel
Patrick made paperweights for Assignment Four and gave one to each of us. He left yours with me. Do you want it?

Cameron Wesley
It's 2024. Who uses paper? Keep it. My loss is your gain, Gela!

Gela Nathaniel
It's a scorpion in resin and I've already got one myself. Your boss has gone quiet, is she happy?

Cameron Wesley
Spoke to her this morning. The unit is back where it belongs. She said something about owing you something, and that she had to sort it? I could tell she felt she'd said too much, so I didn't ask.

Gela Nathaniel
I know what she means. Tell her thanks from me. Missing you. I spend as little time in that viper's nest of moaning, whining, back-stabbing sociopaths as humanly possible.

Cameron Wesley
Bit harsh, darling. Not young Jem, surely!

Gela Nathaniel
Jem the velociraptor? You never felt the full force of her ruthless ambition. And since when was I your darling?

Cameron Wesley
Sorry, old habits and all that. Send me an HR chit about my attitude and I'll take the learnings forward.

Gela Nathaniel
Can you send me what you've done of your essay?

Cameron Wesley
Thought you could help me there.

Gela Nathaniel

You told me you'd already written something about burning out of the corporate world to pursue a different career, as it's not that far from what actually happened.

Cameron Wesley

You're right. Just found it in my files. It's attached. Funny how writing about yourself brings out the truth, no matter how much you want to hide it.

Gela Nathaniel

What do you mean?

Cameron Wesley

Got the sinner's urge to confess and said a bit too much.

Gela Nathaniel

That's fine. I'll delete anything inappropriate; fill in the gaps and you can scrape a discretionary.

Cameron Wesley

Should we discuss all this on here? The consensus is that Doodle can be accessed and read.

Gela Nathaniel

Urban myth. Theoretically, yes, but in practice that's a legal path no one has ever gone down, in my experience. As soon as the course ends, everything is permanently deleted. Literally someone will have to die before this is accessed.

Cameron Wesley

Interesting. Thanks for that. Kiss-kiss.

Gela Nathaniel

Kiss-kiss.

Royal Hastings, University of London
Multimedia Art MA
Final Project

Candidate name: Cameron Wesley
Candidate number: 0883483

A bit about me:

Mentioning no names, lest I spontaneously combust with unresolved anger, but I once worked for a big ad agency. We handled all the top global brands, Fortune 500 companies, some high net-worth individuals on a PR basis, and many myriad organizations. Lost interest in working for other people, left with a colleague to set up our own agency. Won't say it was the worst thing we could've done, but it never went right, that's for damn sure. Thought a major client was coming with us—they pulled out at the last minute and stayed with the old company. Then our second client, much smaller but important to us, was bought out and their business went to the buyer's agency. OK, we can generate our own business—we'd done that for years already. Only outside the big-name bubble, the garden ain't so rosy. The place was full of bears with their bums in the honey. They gas about thinking outside the box, but risk is something they take with other people's money, right?

Suddenly my director gets pregnant and moves to France with her partner. Pulls out completely. I was stranded. I looked up old friends, but none wanted to move. Advertised and recruited. Got stung by a stream of liars and bullshitters. They say it takes one to know one: well, I couldn't spot them. My wife left. Her call, but crap for me. I was done. Was that burnout or plain disillusion in my fellow human? I sought help for my mental health. As they say. First of all with a good mate called Jack Daniel's, and then with a colorful bunch of his other friends at a posh loony bin called the Sanctuary.

There they said, among other things, that when you get stuck or find you're not challenged anymore, make a change. Well, I'd done that and it had failed right out of the sky in a trail of flames. So

I avoided group therapy by haunting every class, from chocolate-tossing to candle-bothering. One of them was an introduction to art. Well, the teacher was the finest-looking woman in the place. She got me feeling inspired again for the first time in forever. You know, chucking clay around and slapping paint on paper is big fun! That's why, a while later, when I was back on my feet with a new company in a whole new sector, I decided to take this job myself, rather than leave it to one of the other private investigators.

WhatsApp chat between Ben Sketcher and Hannah O'Donnell, May 30, 2024:

Hannah
Cameron has a company of private investigators. He specializes in financial fraud, corporate security, and industrial disputes. He didn't want the other group members to know. Gela took me aside before the course began. She was worried I might accidentally say something.

Ben
After trying to run a company and complete an MA, he soon realized he couldn't do both. I wonder . . . was he at Royal Hastings to help with burnout or to investigate something?

Hannah
I don't know if it's connected, but Alyson's attendance dwindled at about the same time. I mean, she stopped coming in to Royal Hastings but was still messaging on Doodle.

Ben
She and Ludya worked together on Assignment Four.

Hannah
Well, they each completed assignments, but was Ludya responsible for both? The affair between Alyson and Jonathan. I've wondered if it was going on *before* the course started?

Ben
Do you know her husband's name?

Hannah
No. No one ever mentioned him to me.

Ben
What if he can afford to pay a PI to enroll on an MA course and keep an eye on his wife? It sounds to me as if Gela was in on the whole thing and even seems to know Cameron's "boss." If she means his client—Alyson's husband—perhaps she's been "enticed" to collude.

Hannah
Gela wouldn't risk her whole career for a few pounds.

Ben
Who says it's a few pounds? It could be enough to make it worth risking your career, especially if you're close to retirement and that career is hanging in the balance. Cameron may have left the course when he'd gathered enough evidence for his client. But nonetheless he has a particularly close relationship with Gela.

Hannah
You think so too?

Ben
They say "kiss-kiss." Is that an affair between them, or the name of his investigation into Alyson's behavior?

Hannah
Gela is a well-respected academic. I've known her for years. She's lovely and very professional.

Ben
And yet she's doing everything she can to ensure Cameron scrapes a pass, when he left the course in January. Hannah, you say the students panicked when they heard the voice. Only I've read a lot of their correspondence now, and panic doesn't seem to be a factor.

Hannah
Exactly. You'd think all they were worried about was their coursework and final project, but underneath I think there was a lot more going on.

Ben
What could possibly have gone wrong on an art course?

To: MMAM(FTP); cc: Gela Nathaniel
From: Jonathan Danners
Date: March 19, 2024
Subject: Final project update

Dear Team,

As the Easter holiday is coming up, Gela has asked me to send this update so we all know where the final project is. I've broken the installation into three parts:

The Tunnel	wood and wire, covered with fabric; papier-mâché, resin and clay embellishments, painted components
The Head	wire and papier-mâché, textured with clay
The Tech	lighting, music, and soundscape, plus headphone technology

The base of the head-shaped sculpture is almost complete, thanks to Gela and Jem. I've heard some positive remarks from the undergrads and am confident this will be a striking centerpiece to the installation. We should all bear in mind these large sections will need to be moved from RH and reassembled at RD8. Any extra weight will make that trickier and, importantly, more expensive. If you can make something hollow, please make it hollow. If papier-mâché would work as well as clay or resin, please use papier-mâché.

The tunnel is still in its early stages and requires a *lot* more decoration. The embellishments that represent RD8's technological advancements over the last hundred years are very small, and we need lots to make it look and feel as interesting as we promised the client. In the next couple of weeks, I'd like everyone—whatever their other roles—to commit to making at least ten items a day for the tunnel.

This brings me to the tech. Jem has so far not played us her soundscape. Ludya has not told us what music she wants, if any. As for the lighting, we will have the services of an electrician on the day, but not before. We must devise a lighting plan in advance and adapt it there and then. Not ideal, but we need to mold our creative work to the limitations of our client, so it will have to do.

That's where we're at. Any questions, just ask.

Jonathan

Doodle message group MMAM(FTP), March 19, 2024:

Jem Badhuri
Why is Ludya doing music for the final project? Music will clash with my soundscape.

Jonathan Danners
Your soundscape is delivered through headphones. We need music to enhance the guests' journey through the tunnel.

Jem Badhuri
No, my soundscape will hook them in and draw them through the tunnel. That and the headphone experience are all part of the same thing. We don't need music.

Ludya Parak
I was only going to set up a Spotify playlist of chill-out tracks, but I'm not bothered. It's one less thing to do.

Jem Badhuri
You're hardly doing anything anyway.

Ludya Parak
I'm flat out making fiddly little shit for the tunnel. I've got no nails or fingerprints left.

Patrick Bright
And very good you are at it, Ludya. I don't know why Jonathan mentioned music. It hasn't been discussed before. I've not even thought about it.

Jonathan Danners
You haven't had to think about the music, Patrick, because that's not your remit. You've been focusing on sourcing and construction, as per your role. I'm thinking ahead to the practicalities of the installation. That's what being project manager is all about.

Alyson Lang

We can have a chill vibe in the champagne reception area. The guests are supposed to enjoy themselves—as well as listening to Jem's soundscape.

Jem Badhuri

My soundscape will be a dramatic journey, but ultimately uplifting.

Jonathan Danners

I'd like to hear what you've done so far, Jem. As project manager, I need to be across all the tasks.

Patrick Bright

Me too! Go on, Jem, will you play what you've done so far?

Jem Badhuri

I can't play what I've done so far because sound doesn't work like that. It's layered. You'll have to trust me.

Doodle message group [Private] Jonathan and Jem, March 19, 2024:

Jonathan Danners

Promise you haven't used the radio voice in your soundscape.

Jem Badhuri

Would it be a problem if I had?

Jonathan Danners

I'm concerned about copyright. We don't want our client slapped with a lawsuit by whoever wrote the film or radio show it comes from.

Jem Badhuri

Gela got rid of the radio before I had the chance to record it. Is Alyson still using the studio at night?

Jonathan Danners

Yes, she's most productive that way, and she's on quota with components too.

Jem Badhuri

I might stay late one day this week and catch up with her before she starts. What time does she arrive?

Jonathan Danners

Tricky. She doesn't have a routine. Alyson is a butterfly. You can't predict her next move.

Doodle message group [Private] Jem and Patrick, March 19, 2024:

Jem Badhuri

Hi Pat! Here's a funny thing. Jonathan says Alyson's been in the studio at night. Apparently, that's when she's been casting her quota of tunnel components.

Patrick Bright

She's always been a night owl.

Jem Badhuri

I know every inch of her workstation and I keep track of everything in and out of the store cupboard. She hasn't been in at all. There are always finished components in her out-basket for you to collect, but they aren't made here. I suspect Ludya is making them for her.

Patrick Bright

It's a nice conspiracy theory, but I think you're wrong, Jem. Ludya makes three little nuts and bolts, then huffs and puffs around the studio as if the rest of us are sitting on our asses strumming lutes. If she's making Alyson's quota too, we'd hear about it.

Jem Badhuri

The photographs I took of Alyson's workstation for Assignment Four weren't just to show the arduous process of creation, like I told everyone. I took pictures over five days, to prove Alyson hadn't been in, should I ever need to. I take one every morning now.

Patrick Bright

I'm confused. Why would you need to prove something like that?

Jem Badhuri
It's my insurance policy. So if she gets a high grade, I can challenge it.

Patrick Bright
You'd do that?

Jem Badhuri
Of course. But only if I get a lower grade. If I get a high grade too, I won't rock the boat. So we'll see.

To: MMAM(FTP)
From: Gela Nathaniel
Date: March 20, 2024
Subject: Final project and Assignment Five

Dear all,

Thank you, Jonathan, for that concise and helpful update. This is our last week before the Easter break, so it's a good time to take stock. The Media Arts building will remain open, and you are welcome to take advantage of that to meet your construction deadlines.

I would reiterate the need to prioritize those embellishments for the tunnel wall, and with each one that you make, please alter the number on the quota list pinned to the noticeboard, so we end up with the appropriate numbers of each design to mark the historical progression of the journey.

In the real world, creative professionals need to work extra hours at home, or during holidays, to meet company deadlines. So while you're all busy re-creating things from the past, here's Assignment Five:

Think of something in your own past that is now gone, lost, or over, and re-create that for an abstract or impressionistic piece. This is a free assignment designed to keep you thinking creatively while engaged in the more mundane tasks of construction and manufacture. Deadline: April 19, 2024.

Any questions, please ask!
Gela

Doodle message group MMAM(FTP), March 20, 2024:

Ludya Parak

I'm not coming in over Easter, FFS. How can she expect us to do a whole new assignment?

Jem Badhuri

I can't wait! It's so frustrating not having a studio at home.

Alyson Lang

If the studio isn't accessible over the bank holiday, I'm lodging a complaint.

Patrick Bright

We can work at home, no?

Ludya Parak

Yeah, right.

Royal Hastings, University of London
Multimedia Art MA
Final Project

Candidate name: Ludya Parak

Candidate number: 0883481

Where things went right:
Are you kidding me? In hindsight, not much went right, but a lot went wrong while we were frantically trying to make it right. Every solution had a hidden disaster. It was like climbing a ladder, where each rung got you that bit closer to the top, but threw up its own unique problem that nothing on previous rungs prepared you for. We're supposed to be artists and think outside the box. Jonathan and Patrick supposedly had management experience—they didn't use it. But at least they stayed the distance.

As you can tell, I'm scratching around to find ways in which this whole thing went right, and all I can say is: the MMAM(FTP) course is designed to give individual artists experience of creative teamwork. After Somerset, we had to work together and we had to get creative, so yes to that.

Where things went wrong:
We made components like a production line. It's the kind of task proper artists get assistants and interns to do. We couldn't mass-produce them in multiple molds because we'd promised the client a tunnel that took us through history, and we'd need too many different molds to be cost-effective. Each one had to be made and finished by hand. If ever there was fuel for OCD, that was it. But as the days went on, I got into it more and more. Mum came down so that I could zone out from the kids. I stayed overnight. Surprising how little sleep you get by on when you have to.

I think because our plans worked at that point, it felt like they would continue to work. But I should've seen the bigger picture. If only the voice wasn't there, hanging over us. That's what paralyzed us, stopped us moving on. I sunk every misgiving I had into a repetitive routine. Alyson did the same. Patrick floated around being quietly useless, but Jonathan . . . he became obsessed. Not with making the components—that would've been too useful—no, instead, he focused on the voice.

Doodle message group [Private] Jem and Patrick, March 30, 2024:

Jem Badhuri
Happy Easter for tomorrow! We don't celebrate it, except to eat chocolate and cake.

Patrick Bright
Well, I'm in Currys looking for a new freezer before they close for the holiday, so you could say I don't celebrate it, either. The shop girls gave me a lovely egg and I'll certainly be eating that later.

Jem Badhuri
Aw, that's nice. Good luck with your assignment!

To: Gela Nathaniel
From: Griff Technician (Maintenance)
Date: April 10, 2024
Subject: Your MA group

You wanted me to report on their usage of the studio over the three-week break. As follows:

Jem	one or two days per week
Patrick	three days per week, Tuesday to Thursday, much as normal
Jonathan	two days per week
Ludya	two days per week
Alyson	zero
Cameron	zero

Royal Hastings, University of London
Multimedia Art MA
Final Project

Candidate name: Jonathan Danners
Candidate number: 0883482

The voice:
All that security at RD8 isn't solely to keep curious cattle out.
Or in other words: it is, in a way. The company develops technology far more interesting than secure wireless payments. The
sheer dullness of that switches people off. I often wonder if that's
the idea. How did they get to Gela? There are only four ways:
money, ideology, coercion, and ego. MICE. Four reasons people
get caught in a trap.

What has everyone else said about the voice? I'll say this . . . that
unit wasn't what we thought it was or needed it to be. But sometimes a project changes shape. We have to be flexible and adapt. I'm
sure that's in the course notes somewhere. The voice—a man with
an English accent—came through at the same time every day, but
every time he said something different. That he was trapped, being
held prisoner in a dark place. He asked to be rescued, but didn't say
where he was or who was keeping him captive.

Since the Second World War RD8 have led communications
technology for the security agencies. That contract must dwarf any
commercial work they do for the retail industry, but they need their
credit card and banking software as a smoke screen. In days gone
by, undercover agents could tune in to radio wavelengths to pick
up coded messages that only they could decipher. The "numbers
stations," as they're called, remained a Cold War curio for decades.
Most world powers operated them and some still do. Just in case the
world's digital and electronic systems break down or are sabotaged.
Radio waves will always be there.

That unit was alone in the center of a small, dark room, quite
separate from the museum. A rectangular box no bigger than a
house brick, on its own plinth. The place was temperature- and

humidity-regulated by a state-of-the-art system, plus a backup with its own power source. One thing was certain: they did not want anything corroding or degrading whatever was inside. It was strangely timeless. Could have been preserved for a hundred years or made last week. With no visible power source of its own, it seemed to be dead and we would soon find out why. Then Jem and Patrick started playing with it. It kept them busy, so we let them.

Until the voice came through. Sense told me it was a recording. Yet it sounded live. It sounded as if that man was actually broadcasting his sad, plaintive message every night. It's what Patrick thought as soon as he heard it. But the wavelength remained obscure and the internal workings didn't give anything away. It was the key, but we didn't know how to turn it. Or where the lock was. It may not have been what we had hoped for. But it isn't what they told Cameron it was, either.

Doodle message group [Private] Gela and Cameron, April 15, 2024:

Gela Nathaniel
Term starts tomorrow. Can you come in and show your face around the studio? Just let Hannah, Griff, and Jem see how hard you're trying to contribute to the final project, despite sickness, etc.

Cameron Wesley
I'm on another job. It's at that tricky stage. Can't simply leave.

Gela Nathaniel
I need photographs for the prospectus—should this course be approved. Ideally a bright, enthusiastic, diverse cohort looking busy in the studio, everyone smiling and happy.

Cameron Wesley
You want everyone looking happy? Are you serious?

Gela Nathaniel
Informal bribery. I'll take that key picture on the day I give them their—highly inflated—grades for Assignment Five.

Cameron Wesley
Good luck with that. Kiss-kiss.

Gela Nathaniel
Kiss-kiss.

Doodle message group MMAM(FTP), April 15, 2024:

Jem Badhuri
What's everyone done for Assignment Five? I'm not as old as the rest of you, so haven't lost as much. I'm still racking my brain.

Patrick Bright
I'm spoiled for choice.

Jonathan Danners
Do we really have to go to a dark emotional place for this? I've got too much to think about.

Patrick Bright
Lost car keys perhaps, Jonathan?

Jonathan Danners
Whatever I do, it'll be a photography project on PowerPoint. I'm done with unfamiliar mediums.

Ludya Parak
I've got an idea. It's a tribute to lost innocence.

Jem Badhuri
A video of your children falling off their paddleboards?

Ludya Parak
No.

Jem Badhuri
What are you doing, Alyson?

Cameron Wesley
Good luck all. Hope it goes well.

Alyson Lang
Photography probably.

Jem Badhuri
I mean, what have you lost?

Alyson Lang
Don't know yet.

Gela Nathaniel
Popped on here to say I'll be taking pictures in the studio over the next week or so. They are for the new prospectus and will entice students on to next year's course—should it be approved. I'll try to avoid faces, but if you're recognizable, then I'll clear their use with you. Good luck with Assignment Five.

Doodle message group [Private] Jem and Patrick, April 15, 2024:

Jem Badhuri
Wouldn't it be funny if Alyson made a tribute to her husband?

Patrick Bright
She hasn't lost him, I don't think.

Jem Badhuri
If he's found out about her affair, he could have filed for divorce. Have you noticed anything interesting?

Patrick Bright
I haven't, but I'm not as sharp as you.

Jem Badhuri
When was the last time you saw Alyson?

Patrick Bright
A couple of days ago.

Jem Badhuri
Where was she? Did she speak to you?

Patrick Bright
In the foyer of the Media Arts building. She was talking to someone from the BA course. A youngish guy with long hair. I took it she'd been in the studio all night and was on her way home.

Jem Badhuri
And yet I've taken a photograph of her workstation every morning since the middle of last term and it's not changed at all. Mum and Dad compared all the pictures and that's what they say.

Patrick Bright
She's quite tidy, though. It's possible she's working here at night, but has another commission she's doing at home during the day. It doesn't surprise me if she's outgrown the course. She was always strides ahead of us.

Jem Badhuri

If you ask me, Gela only loves Alyson because she's good publicity for the MA.

Patrick Bright

No one is asking you, Jem. NO ONE. People cut you too much slack, but you'd do well to mind your own fucking business.

Jem Badhuri's Doodle Diary, April 15, 2024:

When someone is very nice—I mean super-friendly and helpful—it can be because they're people-pleasers. They don't really want to help you but feel they should and will avoid confrontation at all costs. I'm sure it eats away at them until they're driven to a breaking point and snap. They care more about being liked than they do about their own health and well-being. I'm not a people-pleaser.

The trouble with people-pleasers is you never know what they're really thinking and feeling, because half the time they don't know themselves. I've always got along with Patrick, but in the six months we've been on this course I haven't learned a single personal thing about him. He has an art shop, wants to retire back to his roots in Ireland and realize his dream of being an artist. That's it. I've asked him plenty of questions over the months. I've asked if he's married; or has any children, brothers, and sisters; whether his parents are alive. He's replied every time but, thinking about it, he's never actually answered any of those questions.

He's a lovely, gentle man who's a pleasure to work alongside, but he's a people-pleaser and he'll do anything to avoid the truth, if the truth is unpalatable or ugly.

I feel quite proud I got him to snap at me on Doodle. Where did that come from? Anger, exasperation, or fear? I know one thing for sure now—I can't confide in Patrick anymore. This may be a course that helps develop teamwork skills, but as far as my suspicions about Alyson's disappearance are concerned, I'm on my own.

Patrick Bright's Doodle Diary, April 15, 2024:

Jonathan is getting to me. He's off his rocker. This is the very time we need to pull together and he's jeopardizing it for everyone. We all have our roles to play and our jobs to do, and obsessing over that voice is not helpful to anyone. He tunes in every day. Records it, writes it down, pores over the words. Ludya is in no position to help him and I won't even ask her. I've snapped at Jem on Doodle and feel rotten. She has a ruthless streak and I don't want her plotting against me. She may be young and naïve, but shit sticks if you throw it.

To: Gela Nathaniel
From: Griff Technician (Maintenance)
Date: April 16, 2024
Subject: Resin use

Dear Mrs. Nathaniel,
Rita went to get resin for the BA group and discovered your MAs have used it all. They must have taken it home, because they all know a technician must be present to oversee resin work and none of us have seen this much used all term. I don't want to place chemical products under lock and key, but if we suspect they are being used recklessly, I will have to.
    Griff

To: Griff Technician (Maintenance)
From: Gela Nathaniel
Date: April 16, 2024
Subject: Re: Resin use

Dear Griff,
I am so sorry. The MA group need resin to create texture on their installation. You'll see they've made molds to scale up radio components and are turning them out at a rate of knots. Patrick is especially good at working in this medium now. You'll see it gives them more control over color, as otherwise the genuine components are all gray and black. I'll ask Jonathan to factor this into his budget and we'll restock the cupboard as soon as possible. Thank you for bringing this to my attention.
    Gela

Doodle message group MMAM(FTP), April 16, 2024:

Gela Nathaniel
Griff has noticed how much of his supplies we're using up for the resin components. Please can we restock the cupboard and buy our own resin and hardener from now on.

Jem Badhuri
The budget is almost used up.

Jonathan Danners
I don't think we factored in quite how many components it would take to cover that tunnel wall. Papier-mâché is more cost-effective, even if resin gives us a better finish.

Ludya Parak
Papier-mâché is so tedious. It's doing my head in.

Jem Badhuri
Get your kids to do some.

Ludya Parak
Um, no. Because rented apartment, kids, and glue . . .

Patrick Bright
We need resin components to cover larger areas. I can work on shallower molds. It also gives us a professional finish. Papier-mâché tends to look like a school project.

Alyson Lang
It *is* a school project.

To: Gela Nathaniel
From: Mae Blackwell, RD8 Systems Ltd.
Date: April 19, 2024
Subject: Thank you

Dear Gela,
I hope you are well. It's been so long since we met, I wonder how the

students' installation for ICES is coming along? May we organize a visit to Royal Hastings to log its progress and perhaps submit some feedback, so that anything we don't like can be altered in good time?

Best wishes,

Mae Blackwell

To: MMAM(FTP)

From: Gela Nathaniel

Date: April 19, 2024

Subject: A visit from RD8

Dear all,

Mae and her team from RD8 are scheduled to visit our studio at Royal Hastings next Thursday, April 25. They will inspect our progress and highlight anything that gives them cause for concern. This will be a useful exercise in receiving, processing, and responding to real-world client feedback. As those of you who have worked professionally know, this can be an important and sometimes frustrating part of the job. However, this space is a relatively safe one to explore and overcome the feelings that criticism can invoke.

Attendance in the studio on the day of RD8's visit is mandatory. Please, everyone, try to keep the studio tidy for that event.

Best wishes,

Gela

Doodle message group [Private] Gela and Cameron, April 19, 2024:

Gela Nathaniel

I need you to come in next Thursday.

Cameron Wesley

I told you, I'm on this job.

Gela Nathaniel

Not 24/7.

Cameron Wesley
YES.

Gela Nathaniel
Come on, this wasn't part of the deal. I need MMAM to work for marketing professionals. You're my poster boy and Alyson my poster girl. Neither of you has graced the studio in heaven knows how long!

Cameron Wesley
I didn't realize everything would be sorted so soon. The boss terminated my contract after Somerset.

Gela Nathaniel
You're the boss.

Cameron Wesley
I mean the client. I'm on something completely different now. Things change. That's the nature of the business.

Gela Nathaniel
But where does that leave me?

Cameron Wesley
Exactly where you were before.

Doodle message group [Private] Gela and Alyson, April 19, 2024:

Gela Nathaniel
Please can you come in next Thursday? Meet and greet RD8, show them around the studio and what we've done so far. You're a key member of the team and they're looking forward to meeting you.

Alyson Lang
The others will get by fine.

Gela Nathaniel
Jem is already suspicious you're not coming in.

Alyson Lang
Just chill, FFS.

Gela Nathaniel
Chill? You said you'd do the course. Throw yourself into it. Please!

Alyson Lang
No promises.

Doodle message group [Private] Cameron and Jonathan, April 19, 2024:

Cameron Wesley
FYI, chat with Mae, below.

> **Mae**
> We're concerned about kiss-kiss.
>
> **Cameron**
> I've told you. It's safe.
>
> **Mae**
> Then let's arrange for you to return it.
>
> **Cameron**
> Bit awkward. Put it somewhere safe, and now I'm on another job.
>
> **Mae**
> Do you want money? Is that it? Because if that's the case, then I will have no hesitation in escalating my concerns.
>
> **Cameron**
> Don't want money. There are things I can't say at the moment, but it's nothing for you to worry about.
>
> **Mae**
> Don't fucking patronize me, Cam.
>
> **Cameron**
> I'm not. It's safe and I'll return it soon. Can't talk.

Jonathan Danners
FFS, delete this from Doodle!

[Thread deleted]

Doodle message group MMAM(FTP), April 19, 2024:

Jem Badhuri
Can't wait to see what Gela says about my Assignment Five. I've imagined losing something and feel really sad now. I didn't realize how much it meant to me. Anyone else felt like that?

Jem Badhuri
Was tempted to throw something in clay as well, but pretty sure Gela will be happy with just a soundscape. What's everyone else doing?

Jem Badhuri
Hello, klaxon! Calling all the MMAMs. Jem to MMAMs. Where is everyone?

Jem Badhuri
Oh well, if you want to ignore me online as well as in the studio, that's fine.

Jem Badhuri's Doodle Diary, April 20, 2024:

As soon as Dad mentioned he had to visit a client in Gloucester an idea popped into my head. I'd never have suggested I go with him on such a boring trip otherwise. He's in the restaurant now, selling the owner as much catering equipment as he can, while I'm in the car dictating this diary into my phone. I've already looked up our next destination: the Danners Gallery. It has a four-and-a-half-star rating on Tripadvisor. Visitors like its homely feel and range of exhibits. It has a children's art room and hosts a local photographic competition every year.

It's just a visit to a friend's family business. One I've heard a lot about over the last few months. It won't seem strange that, being in the area,

I asked Dad to drive us there. He never willingly goes to any art gallery, but when I impressed upon him how vital this visit is for my MA course, he agreed. Anyway he's glad of the company on such a long drive.

That left the slight problem of my quota of components for the installation—we all took a bag home to work on over the weekend. After some gentle persuasion, Mum and Nani said they'd make them.

What do I expect to find when I get to Jonathan's art gallery? I don't know. Maybe it's something in his voice, or maybe it's me and my suspicious mind. Whatever reason, I didn't mention my visit to him—or anyone on the course. Here's Dad now, and he's whistling! They must've bought a lot of cookers.

Doodle message group [Private]: Jem and Gela, April 21, 2024

Jem Badhuri
Can you send me the photographs you took in the studio?

Gela Nathaniel
Why?

Jem Badhuri
To show Mum and Nani. They'd love to see us all beavering away. Especially famous artist Alyson Lang, busy making her art.

Gela Nathaniel
I can't let you have images of other students. Privacy issues, etc.

Jem Badhuri
I thought they were for the prospectus and don't include faces?

Gela Nathaniel
OK, well, I'll forward a selection.

MMAM(FTP)
Coursework Module: Assignment Five
Tutor's Report, April 22, 2024

Brief: Think of something in your own past that is now gone, lost, or over, and explore it with an abstract or impressionistic piece. This is a free assignment designed to keep you thinking creatively while engaged in the more mundane tasks of construction and manufacture.

Overview: In the students' work for Assignment Five I hope to see their emotional engagement with themes of loss, memory, and nostalgia while they are superficially preoccupied with the dry, mechanical tasks at hand. They are free to work in any medium, so I expect all will revert to their favored patterns. I will be looking for, and marking them on, the *heart* of whatever piece they devise.

Jemisha Badhuri
For her lost item, Jem chose her father. He is in fact very much alive, but she imagined he had passed away and the result was most extraordinary. For someone who has so far skirted around deep emotions, Jem went the extra mile for this assignment. In her introduction she said, "I usually love my imagination and the awesome places it can take me, but when it conjures up feelings of my dad dying, I wish I could just switch it off. Because that place is worse than hollow and empty. It feels like I've had my own heart torn away." Her soundscape was beautiful and haunting. She had recorded a series of domestic sounds, a soft male voice, talking and chuckling. It very much evoked a sense of family, warmth, and home. This faded to a lonely silence, something Jem has created in her soundscapes before. Not silence exactly, but a quiet, contemplative void edged with tiny personal sounds: breathing, sighing, the scratch of a pen on paper, the tap of fingers on a smartphone. Jem is a master of sound. Grade: A

Patrick Bright

Choosing to create a pencil sketch on paper, Patrick introduced his piece as a general expression of loss that he's experienced during his life. It's the most detailed work I've ever seen from him. A male figure with its head bowed is strongly drawn on its left side, but the pencil strokes become fainter and the image fragmented as it stretches across the paper, giving the impression that with each loss something of one's inner strength and resilience is eroded, the spirit is worn thin and floats away from the core being. As if what Patrick grieves for most is his loss of self. Strangely, one could place the sketch alongside Jem's soundscape for a very effective installation. Grade: A

Jonathan Danners

Jonathan's photography project, mounted on PowerPoint, depicted a series of images designed to represent the women he has lost in his life. His mother and sister have both passed away. Photographs include discarded flowers, smashed wineglasses, and smeared lipstick. It made for uncomfortable viewing, but more because the images seemed to mourn the loss of a romantic relationship rather than the heart of a family. Still his presentation, which included a musical score, was entertaining and demonstrated how far Jonathan has come since his first disastrous assignment when his paper cube on a stick met a fiery end. Grade: A–

Alyson Lang

Working in digital animation for Assignment Four must have fired Alyson's enthusiasm for this medium, because she chose it to illustrate the loss of a beloved pet dog. The simple cartoon followed a stick-figure person and their stick-figure dog, from puppyhood through to old age, when the owner becomes the now-paralyzed-dog's carer. Strangely, when the dog dies, the owner has the animal stuffed and placed at their feet by the fire, in a macabre re-creation of their relationship. A bittersweet happiness is restored, and the film ends on a note of beautiful ambiguity as the bereaved owner settles into a state of denial that his or her faithful companion has gone. Much food for thought. Grade: A

Ludya Parak

Ludya also chose a simple animation, very similar to Alyson's. Her focus was on the loss of self after motherhood. A mother bird has a nest of chicks. As soon as they hatch, her mate flies away, leaving her with a demanding brood who eventually pluck her feathers out to keep themselves warm, but still scream at her to find food. Unable to fly, she is obliged to hunt in the undergrowth, where she is killed by a fox. The fox is scared away by the fledglings, who all fly down and feast on their mother's body. A grim story, but evocative and I'm sure many will identify with it. Grade: A

Cameron Wesley

Despite his long-term illness, Cameron worked hard to complete Assignment Five. He delivered a watercolor on canvas that showed a road winding and stretching into the distance. While Cameron was feeling too poorly to attend the assessment class and introduce his work to the group, in an email he explained that this road demonstrates the soul's journey after loss—not the soul left on earth, but the soul who has died. Cameron imagines that they too feel the anguish of separation and must face their continued existence without their loved ones on earth. He has not thus far submitted anything in his favored medium of paint, so it was a pleasure and privilege to see this interesting and emotional piece. Grade: A

Doodle message group MMAM(FTP), April 23, 2024:

Jem Badhuri
I'm a "master of sound"! I can't believe we've all got A grades.

Patrick Bright
Your soundscape and presentation were the best work you've done,
Jem. If ever a top garde was thoroughly deserved, it was that.

Jem Badhuri
I know, but not everyone's was as good, and they still got A's. Gela
must be thinking strategically. She wants to encourage us, so we're not
downhearted when RD8 visit the mess that will be their installation.

Jonathan Danners
The installation is not a mess. This is simply a tricky phase. All projects
hit these moments. It feels as if we'll never achieve the showstopping
effect in our imaginations, but we will. We merely have to keep putting
one foot in front of the other.

Patrick Bright
I don't agree, Jem. Your head sculpture is very impressive and that's the
centerpiece. You're the master of sound and you're our soundscape
artist. Jonathan's right: we're doing fine. Our Assignment Five projects
were all brilliant.

Ludya Parak
We've been on the course six months. We've all learned a lot, right? So
Gela's telling us we've improved. Let's just get through the rest.

Jem Badhuri's Doodle Diary, April 23, 2024:

Jem Badhuri, master of sound. That's my new—as in doesn't exist yet—
company making relaxing soundscapes for foyers, shopping centers,
and communal spaces. Once I get my MA Distinction, I'll get my brother
Adi to create a website.

I can see exactly what Gela was doing. Giving us all a boost when everyone is flagging and anxious about RD8 seeing the installation in a less-than-perfect state. Gela says they'll understand it's only half-done, but can a client who is not creative imagine the finished article? It might be like me trying to explain abstract sculpture to my dad.

Ludya made Alyson's film. Alyson still hasn't been in. Knowing Ludya, she's being paid to do Alyson's coursework. Gela is happy to pretend the golden girl is still here and loving the course. It's not right or fair, but knowing it is useful ammunition, should I need it.

The big surprise of Assignment Five was Cameron's painting, the first practical assignment he's completed properly. Everyone said how moving it was, and Gela gave him an A like the rest of us. I'm no expert in 2D, so I'll take their word for it. Only, a few months ago copying and pasting from his company website was the extent of his artistic skills. I know Gela majored in watercolor earlier in her career. Am I implying a connection there? Yes.

She asked us to send her our enthusiastic quotes about how brilliant the course is for the new prospectus. She's thinking positively and preparing all the materials she'll need for *when* the course is approved—not *if*. So that's another reason we've all got A's. When I'm Gela's age, I hope I'm not as transparent as she is.

But do you know the funniest thing of all? Gela took pictures of us working in the studio. I asked her to send me some, for Mum and Nani, and she did. Only, when we all settled down at home to look through them, we all agreed: there are only four students there: me, Jonathan, Patrick, and Ludya. Cameron's already left, of course, but there were no pictures of the golden girl at all.

Message group: 2024 Examiners, May 30, 2024

Tilda Ricci
I see now what you're concerned about, Ben. Gela was so determined the MA would be approved that she did whatever it took to make it succeed.

Ben Sketcher
That's certainly part of it.

Tilda Ricci
It's possible she completed Cameron's assignment herself, so he had just enough coursework to scrape a pass. She turns a blind eye to Jem paying Ludya, and later does the same when Alyson apparently leaves the course. My only concern is that this correspondence doesn't constitute solid evidence.

Ben Sketcher
Well, what would?

Tilda Ricci
It's a tough one. We know this sort of thing goes on, but given the time, energy, and legal fees that go into investigating it—with no guarantee we'll win a case, even if we're right—it's better to mark down where you see foul play and let the grades do the talking.

Ben Sketcher
Even in a case of fraud?

Karen Carpenter
Aw, come on. It's not fraud if no money was stolen.

Tilda Ricci
No one wants to compromise Royal Hastings' reputation with accusations that cast shadows over its academic rigor. All for the sake of an *art* course?

Karen Carpenter

Isn't this MA about finding creative solutions to business problems? I'd say paying a professional to do your coursework falls into that category. Ha-ha!

Ben Sketcher

You should read on, Tilda. There's another layer entirely to this story, and it's only thanks to Jem Badhuri that we know.

Tilda Ricci

The young girl?

Ben Sketcher

It's thanks to her willingness to blow the whistle that we may still be able to stop tonight's event.

Tilda Ricci

It's a college project for an altruistic local company. Possibly their vision for it exceeded their resources and abilities, but why would we need to stop it?

Ben Sketcher

I'm driving there now. I might have to call the police.

Jonathan Danners' Doodle Diary, April 24, 2024:

"No light. Please help me. I'm trapped."

Every day, at the same time, always a version of the above.

Who is it and where are they? How to communicate with them? What do we say?

The unit is impenetrable in its simplicity. It had its own room, its own display case. Why would it have been so isolated, so revered. What technology is this? When Edison and Tesla worked on machines to contact the dead, both stopped. Because they failed? Or because they succeeded . . .?

Is this a place between worlds where souls get stuck? What if Mum and Sophia are stuck in a place like this? Calling out on a frequency only this unit can hear, day after day.

To: MMAM(FTP)
From: Gela Nathaniel
Date: April 24, 2024
Subject: RD8 visit tomorrow

Dear all,

Thank you, everyone, for your support last week. I have some fabulous shots for the prospectus. Please send me your positive quotes about the course as soon as possible. Perhaps focus on how useful it will be for your careers and for building your business, if you have one.

Now RD8 are visiting tomorrow, so let's take today to prepare. We want them to feel valued, so I expect you to tidy up, provide light refreshments, and present the work-so-far in its best light. You should also organize who will speak about which aspect of the project, and decide how you'll gather the client's feedback in the most productive way. I'll take a backseat to allow our project leader to optimize his role, but of course I'll be watching and listening to everything!

See you tomorrow,
Gela

Doodle message group MMAM(FTP), April 24, 2024:

Jonathan Danners
So that there are no surprises in our meeting tomorrow, I'm going to suggest that I lead the RD8 delegation around the studio and allow you each to come in with pre-agreed info at opportune times. Jem, can you play them what you have of the soundscape?

Jem Badhuri
I haven't layered it yet. It'll sound like rubbish. I can talk them through where I'm at.

Jonathan Danners
Good. Ludya, if you can demonstrate the work we're doing on the components and how time-consuming it is—to explain why we haven't covered as much of the tunnel wall as they might expect.

Ludya Parak
Sure.

Jonathan Danners
Patrick, can you show them the head?

Jem Badhuri
I should talk about the head. It was my idea.

Patrick Bright
Absolutely. It's Jem's baby.

Jonathan Danners
Jem is talking about the soundscape and I want us all to have something meaty to speak about. Pat can say how we've left the interior of the head hollow so that, on the day, their electronic guys can integrate the headphone technology ready for guests to experience Jem's soundscape.

Patrick Bright
Of course. Jem, don't worry, I'll tell them it's your part of the project.

Ludya Parak

We don't have individual parts of the project. It's collective. That's the whole point.

Jonathan Danners

We'll all support each other. Confidence and enthusiasm go a long way.

Ludya Parak

I'll have to think of something that I'm confident and enthusiastic about to get me through. I'm joking. See you all tomorrow.

Jem Badhuri

What's Alyson doing?

Jonathan Danners

Alyson can't make the visit.

Alyson Lang

I might. I'll try.

Jonathan Danners

Really? Well, in that case you can explain how we're creating the tunnel. If you don't make it, I'll do that bit.

Doodle message group [Private] Patrick and Jem, April 24, 2024:

Patrick Bright

I have no intention of taking the credit for your head sculpture, Jem. Of course I need to speak for a bit about something, and the head makes sense. I'll make sure the client knows it's all yours.

Jem Badhuri

Thanks.

Patrick Bright

We're OK now, are we?

Jem Badhuri

Yes.

Doodle message group [Private] Gela and Hannah, April 25, 2024:

Hannah O'Donnell
I'm still missing your diversity forms.

Gela Nathaniel
I know, I know! Sorry. In the meantime, here are some quotes and photographs from MMAM students for the prospectus.

Hannah O'Donnell
Has the course been approved for next year then?

Gela Nathaniel
Not yet, but nearly. I'm sure. You'll have all you need for when it is.

Hannah O'Donnell
OK, but I need the forms as a matter of urgency.

Gela Nathaniel
"The MMAM(FTP) has kick-started my creative inspiration and given me vital business-building tools. I can't think of a better way to combine art study with the needs of the workplace."

Gela Nathaniel
"I wanted to move my marketing career to the creative side but lacked experience and confidence. MMAM(FTP) has given me every tool I need to combine art and business."

Gela Nathaniel
"The MMAM(FTP) course really opened my eyes to what can be achieved while creating artistic solutions to workplace problems. I know employers will value this qualification."

Hannah O'Donnell
Which students provided which quote?

Gela Nathaniel
Does it matter? We don't name them in the prospectus.

Hannah O'Donnell
No, but for my records.

Gela Nathaniel

Alyson, Cameron, and Jonathan respectively. I'll send the others as I get them.

Hannah O'Donnell

And the diversity forms?

Gela Nathaniel

Yes, yes, yes. Those too. Sorry, Hannah, it's a big day today and I need to sort things out here.

To: Gela Nathaniel
From: Mae Blackwell
Date: April 25, 2024
Subject: We've arrived

Gela, I called you, but it went straight to voice. We're stuck at the front gate. Security say they have my name and that I'd be with just two guests. Only everyone is so excited to see the installation, I've brought the technical, marketing, and development teams. Unfortunately, they won't let us in.

I hope you can sort this quickly.

Mae

WhatsApp chat between Gela Nathaniel and Mae Blackwell, April 25, 2024:

Gela

Apologies for this mix-up, Mae. I'm on my way to the front gate. Can I ask how many there are?

Mae

Including me: fourteen.

Doodle message group MMAM(FTP), April 25, 2024:

Gela Nathaniel
There are fourteen people from RD8. They're at the gate now.

Jonathan Danners
Fourteen? Someone get more mugs.

Jem Badhuri
Griff, Rita, and Tony are collecting and washing mugs from other kitchens.

Ludya Parak
We're clearing space in the studio. Give them a tour of the Quaker Building. That'll buy us time.

Jonathan Danners
How? I don't know a thing about it.

Patrick Bright
Take them the long way around. Under the arch, through the quad, beside the water feature.

Ludya Parak
Built in 1866 by Quakers as a schoolhouse, it was sold to philanthropist Robert Hastings, who rebuilt it as a hospital for women.

Jem Badhuri
Take them to the garden outside the Aviator. Those flowers smell gorgeous.

Ludya Parak
In WWI it was a hospital for wounded troops, then a convalescent home for TB survivors. Is that enough?

Gela Nathaniel
Where are the chairs with backs?

Jonathan Danners
One of the tech guys has a question: why are the lower windows round and the upper windows arched?

Ludya Parak
Are you asking me? Don't know. I'm copying and pasting from Wiki.

Patrick Bright
This is as much space as we'll get in the studio. We dare not move the tunnel or the head. Neither is stable.

Gela Nathaniel
Bring the guests in now, Jonathan. It looks fine. It's a working studio. They'll understand that.

Jem Badhuri
It would be useful if Alyson were here.

Alyson Lang
I came in during the weekend. My quota of components is on my table. Good luck, everyone.

To: MMAM(FTP); cc: Gela Nathaniel
From: Jonathan Danners
Date: April 25, 2024
Subject: Project Manager's report on RD8's visit

Dear Team,
Gela has asked me to write a report on today's visit by our client and to log their initial feedback, so those team members who were not part of the hosting party—Alyson and Cameron—are brought up to speed on this crucial milestone.

At first we thought the team from RD8 was late, but it transpired Mae had brought considerably more people with her than security was expecting. I collected them from the gate, while Gela, Ludya, Jem, and Patrick hastily cleared space in the studio and found more mugs and cookies. While it was a small point in the grand scheme, it turned into a major stress factor, precisely when we should have been relaxed.

We can take several learnings from this experience. The main one being: next time, establish how many clients are coming. Something as basic as not having enough teabags can derail an otherwise carefully organized event. In hindsight, I would have made it clear to the client in advance exactly how many of them could visit.

I felt at times the presentation we'd prepared was disrupted by clients wandering where they shouldn't, touching things, and wanting to "have a go" with items in the studio completely unconnected to their project. Some were clearly from the more scientific end of the spectrum, whose attention was not held by our speeches on the progress of the installation. Herding cats came to mind.

However, it must be said Ludya spoke well about the tunnel, Jem did a great job explaining her soundscape, and Patrick was very eloquent and interesting when he took us all through the evolution of our centerpiece, the clay head. Unfortunately, one of the delegation tried to lift it up, and it was only Gela's quick thinking and fast action that saved it from toppling off its plinth. Mae Blackwell, who we all remember from the pitch meeting, was a very engaged visitor, and luckily so, as she is *the* person to impress.

That brings me to her topline feedback. She said, and I quote: "Wouldn't it be better if the soundscape is piped into the tunnel, to avoid excess tech and allow us to focus on the artistic vision?" She also mentioned something about the tunnel being more visibly branded with the company logo and specific radio components that broke new ground in their time, plus some other things—their names escape me—that she would like to see prominently among the "decorations" on the tunnel walls. We can expect written feedback in a day or two.

After corralling the rest of them back into the studio, we made tea and coffee, then showed them the door. In the nicest possible way. In our debriefing session afterward we all felt a mixture of relief that the visit was over and disappointment that our work hadn't elicited the unbridled delight we'd hoped for. We all decided to tidy up, and not act on Mae's feedback until we have her official response, as she'll tie together the thoughts of all the others.

Finally, I'd like to thank the entire team for their hard work and for being flexible, positive, and good-natured throughout the client visit.

Jonathan Danners
Project Manager

Doodle message group MMAM(FTP), April 25, 2024:

Jem Badhuri
We should have let them throw some clay on the potter's wheel.

Patrick Bright
That's a very good idea. If we'd made the visit into more of a corporate day out, like on *The Apprentice,* they'd have been less fidgety.

Jem Badhuri
They'd realize how difficult it is and appreciate how hard we worked. Then they wouldn't make stupid comments.

Ludya Parak
Clients are clients. We could fly them to the moon and still get pages of feedback.

Jem Badhuri
They're in the business of radio communications—in other words: SOUND. Yet they have no idea how ASMR works. You NEED a binaural microphone and headphones.

Patrick Bright
I think you made that quite clear, Jem.

Jem Badhuri
Well, I had to say something. The head Gela and I have been working on is a replica of a *binaural* microphone. If we ditch the headphones, we can't have a truly *binaural* soundscape, this won't be a *binaural* installation, which means the centerpiece of our whole structure doesn't flow.

Jonathan Danners
They liked the head sculpture.

Jem Badhuri
But without the binaural soundscape it won't make sense!

Cameron Wesley

Clients make dodgy decisions the whole time. But they're paying. I vote we do what they say.

Jem Badhuri

I vote you keep your oar out of a project you haven't done anything for. Don't even know why you're still in this message group.

Ludya Parak

If they don't want binaural sound, they don't want it. Way back, I said a collective sound experience is more appropriate to their brief, not an individual one.

Jem Badhuri's Doodle Diary, April 25, 2024:

I'm fuming and it's affecting my judgment. I've been working on that head for weeks, and now Mae says she doesn't want the binaural soundscape. To them it doesn't matter. To me, it does. Shape matters. It's shaped like a very specific piece of equipment, and it won't make any sense if we don't use that equipment in our installation. No one else cares. Grrrr!

I must calm down, but of course Ludya is delighted. I could hear in her voice how pleased she was. I hadn't planned to lose my temper, but sometimes it's necessary for other people to see how much you care. Anyway, after I'd told Mae exactly what I thought of her feedback, I headed for the storeroom to recover. I like the storeroom. The smell of the art materials, paint, resin, varnish, paper, wood. Very calming.

As I got to the door I stopped dead in the corridor. Someone was in there. You just know, don't you? I froze instinctively, but I wasn't afraid. I wanted to listen . . . Who was it? Had one of them snuck away to the storeroom to rummage through the shelves while their colleagues crawled all over our installation with their stupid ideas and tone-deaf opinions? Or was it Griff, Tony, or Rita? A BA student looking for supplies?

I edged around the corner. They were at the far end and must have had their back to me, because they didn't stop searching. It was a girl from the development team. Jessica. I was introduced to her in quick succession with all the others and got a whiff of her fruity perfume. As she moved past me to shake Jonathan's hand, somewhere I registered that her shoes didn't make any sound as she walked. Was she intending to sneak off and look for something? The old radio that the sourcing team had brought back from Somerset? Gela said it had woodworm and was disposed of, but what if that wasn't true?

I slipped back out of the room and down the corridor, stood by the water cooler, and gathered my thoughts. Is that why so many of them came today? So we wouldn't be able to keep track of them? Who are they all anyway?

I'm going to write this here, because no one else will see it. I'm not going to mention it in my final essay, that's for sure. I'm here to get an MA, and that's what I intend to walk out of this place with. However, a few things have got me thinking about the people on this course. Chief among them: what I discovered during my visit to the Danners Gallery that I haven't dared write down until now.

Doodle message group [Private] Jem and Jonathan, April 25, 2024:

Jem Badhuri
Hi Jonathan. I want to apologize.

Jonathan Danners
OK. Well, we all feel passionately about our work. Mae will understand that, I'm sure. The key is to move forward, fulfill our creative ambitions, but also meet the client's needs and expectations.

Jem Badhuri
I mean, I'm sorry I didn't mention something sooner. When I left the studio to calm down, I found someone snooping around the storeroom.

Jonathan Danners
Rita or a student from one of the other studios?

Jem Badhuri
It was Jessica from the RD8 development team. Could she have been looking for the radio? The one Gela said had woodworm?

Jonathan Danners
The radio was returned to RD8. Gela mentioned it.

Jem Badhuri
But people lie. They lie about all sorts of strange things.

Jem Badhuri's Doodle Diary, April 25, 2024:

Dad and I wandered innocently into the foyer and I was struck by the acoustics. There was a muffled feel to it. The sort of atmosphere that would make a good background space for a sharp, crisp soundscape. I must mention that to Jonathan when I get the chance—the Danners Gallery could be my first-ever paying client.

Dad was in a good mood after his meeting, but taking him to an art gallery is like taking a dog shopping. It will follow you, walk when you walk, stop when you stop, but it has no interest in its surroundings. He paces after me, making acidic comments about the pieces on display. "I could do that if I had paper and paint, but I wouldn't bother" is a favorite of his. "*Your* work is better than that" is a favorite of mine, although I wish he wouldn't have that tone when he says it, as if *even* Jem, of all people, can do better.

I wondered whether Jonathan's dad would be there, given his age and health, but when I heard the unmistakable raspy drone of an elderly man speaking about a planned extension to the main building, I knew it was him. I wanted to follow the voice down a corridor off the foyer, but "Barbara," who turned out to be the assistant manager, stood in our path and asked if we wanted to be shown around the exhibition.

I said yes. Dad sighed. But this was my chance to find out if everything Jonathan has told us about himself is true. I'll just have to make something up to keep Dad happy later. So Barbara leads us through the rooms, which have a crisper, cleaner feel than the foyer. Any soundscape here would need to be softer and less intrusive, perhaps water or distant birds, although my plan would be to switch up the soundscape relative to the exhibition. This one is by local artists over the age of sixty, so I'd loop some gentle boomer music into the mix. Barbara tries to take us around every exhibit, explaining each nuance in detail, until I tell her I'm only really interested in sculpture. Dad sighs again, but this time with relief, because there are far fewer of those than of paintings.

That's when Barbara got *really* excited because they have some "amazing" 3D work she can show me, and she was right. I was blown away by a series of clay death masks—not real ones, she was quick to say—but imagined death masks of the five senses: touch, hearing, smell, taste, and sight. Each was subtly nuanced, *very* well conceived and executed. Then there was a towering piece, as tall as I am, shaped like a Grecian urn, she said, but tapering at the top and fired to such a cold, smooth finish that when my fingertips touched it a freezing shiver went right through me. We have a long chat about texture, and, luckily, Barbara starts to warm up. I'm waiting for the right moment.

Meanwhile Dad's footsteps scrape behind me like he's being taken to the vet. But he never moves far away, so I have to be careful how I phrase my key questions. Finally I manage to say, casually, "How is Mr. Danners senior? I heard he was unwell."

He doesn't have to speak: I can tell Dad is wondering how I know anything at all about a stranger in a town I've never been to in my life.

"He's much better—more so than ever," the lady chirps. "Do you know Goff then? He's in today."

"No, please don't bother him." The last thing I want is Jonathan hearing from his dad that a Bengali girl dropped by with her dad—he'd know immediately it was me. "I read about the gallery in a blog. Apparently his son took over for a few years."

There is something about the way she pauses. "Jonathan? Well, he was around a *bit* more," the woman says, an edge of frostiness in her tone as a cold stew of office politics stirs under her words, "but *I* took over management and curating. I've been here seventeen years, so it was the most seamless way."

"Oh, I'm sorry," I say, "I thought Jonathan did, seeing as his mother and sister had already died." It felt clumsy, even to me . . .

"Yes, it's been a very sad time." She sighed. "But Goff didn't want this place to be Jonathan's responsibility, not when there's a team of us to keep it running."

So at least that part of Jonathan's sob story is true, even if he exaggerated his role in managing this place. I was deflated. But what had I expected? Something that might explain things. Lies to stop us asking questions. There were times I thought there might be no Danners Gallery in Gloucester, until a quick google revealed there was. Then I wondered if Jonathan had made up a past because he'd been in prison perhaps, or was an addict, into drugs or gambling. It'd all gone through my head to try and explain why the more I got to know him, the less I trusted him. Why, after that trip to Somerset, Alyson never came back to Royal Hastings.

We arrived at another sculpture, this one a cube covered in fine spikes. I ran my fingers over the bristly bits. Barbara ran her fingers over the bristles too and giggled as they pinged.

Ding! Dad gets a text and moves away to check his phone. This is my last chance to shake the tree, as Nani says whenever I question why she does something trite and pointless.

"But Jonathan wants to be an artist. I'd have thought running his own gallery is a good place to be, if you want to make and show your own work."

Barbara's fingers stop mid-bristle. She removes her hands from the sculpture and inhales sharply.

"Jonathan isn't an artist."

"He's not particularly skilled, but he's doing an MA in multimedia at Royal Hastings, seeing as he missed out on doing a bachelor's at the usual time."

"Well, he must be changing career then. I've known the family longer than that and he's never been remotely interested in art or the gallery." She stops herself, as if she doesn't want to trash-talk her boss's son, and starts to walk away.

I followed her to the next sculpture. "He had to look after it, in the ten years since his mom and sister died. Perhaps he got a taste for it over time."

"Which blog did you read all this in?" Barbara hesitates and lowers her voice. "Margaret and Sophia died two years ago. Jonathan didn't miss out on college. He did his bachelor's at Imperial, well over a decade ago. That's where he met Suzie . . ."

"Suzie?"

"His wife, Suzie. They've been married, oh, at least ten years."

I didn't have to fake my surprise. "I'm sorry," I said. "You can't trust what you read on the internet. What job does he do then?"

"I don't know. Something ecological." There's a note of suspicion in her voice by now—she firmly changes the subject to the next sculpture, a cage with a football inside it. You reach in and try to move the ball around. She told me who the artist was, but my mind was racing so fast I instantly forgot it.

"Something ecological."

Royal Hastings, University of London
Multimedia Art MA
Final Project

Candidate name: Patrick Bright
Candidate number: 0883480

Where it went right:
When the delegation from RD8 descended on us in the studio it was like a murder of crows alighting on a newly sown field. They were everywhere. Picking things up, touching things, opening doors and drawers. But their reaction to the installation was something I wasn't prepared for. And bear in mind at this point it looked in a sorry state. The tunnel was merely a length of fabric stretched across the room, folded and splayed out for us to glue the components on, while the head was a large wire frame only just starting to take shape with clay on a papier-mâché base. Yet you could tell these nerdy types were captivated. Impressed by a world they knew nothing about (because if they had known, they wouldn't have been impressed at all). Still, I felt proud of the work.

There were moments like that during the course. Fleeting times when I felt buoyed by a good grade or a positive comment from Gela. I only wish I could get that feeling from *me* and not have to rely on other people to approve of what I do. That's the key to success, I'm sure. So long as I know what I've done is good or right, that should be enough.

Where it went wrong:
As I've said before, certain things were off from the get-go. But the few weeks we were all working flat out, heads down, making components to cover the tunnel, that was a more peaceful time. You see, there were four types of component: resin replicas we could make in the studio, but limited due to cost; papier-mâché replicas we could make off-site; original components from the bags of junk that RD8 supplied, painted and varnished (we could take those home too); and clay replicas—again we needed the studio for those.

At first it was hard to concentrate, but after a while I lost myself in the task. It helped me forget. I've mainly worked with people, staff, customers, suppliers, and have sketched in my spare time. But this was different. I could forget everything while I was making those items. Layering paper into molds, gluing, painting, and waiting—it's repetitive enough that your mind moves into an automatic state. It stopped me thinking. Then I resented it when someone spoke and expected an answer. As soon as I was dragged out of that stupor, the thoughts came crashing back. Fear. Disbelief. Horror. Had certain things really happened, or were they all part of the art?

I thought about artists who were famously crazy. Were they mad to begin with or sent mad by painting so much sky above the battle-ships? Or pressing clay onto the endless legs of a giant statue? You can see why the big names employ assistants. I know, I've had those assistants in the shop. It's an unspoken fact. Makes you think about attribution. The fact is that we made that tunnel without Alyson or Cameron. The head is supposed to be Jem's project, but Gela is putting just as much into it. Yet the installation will be credited to the six of us equally. And if we're all responsible, who is guilty?

I can't help wondering what everyone else has put in their es-say about where it all went wrong. Because I blame Cameron, and Cameron alone. Then, God help me, I tried to put it right.

Doodle message group MMAM(FTP), April 29, 2024:

Gela Nathaniel
I'm in possession of RD8's extensive feedback. Forwarding Mae's email to you all. My advice is to read, breathe, and keep calm.

To: Gela Nathaniel
From: Mae Blackwell, RD8 Systems Ltd.
Date: April 29, 2024
Subject: Thank you

Dear Gela and the MMAM team,
Firstly, may I say how much we all enjoyed our visit. It was an honor and a privilege to see our installation taking shape.

We've now had the chance to discuss where we want the project to go from here. I have collated those thoughts into a dossier of notes covering all aspects of the work, under a series of twelve general headings, followed by a page of references and a mood board to accompany the section on "color and ambience" (compiled by the marketing team). However, I can summarize as follows:

1. Can we ensure the tunnel is of a sufficient size that people of all heights can walk upright through it with ease? If there is not enough material for this, perhaps think about turning it into a wall frieze?

2. We know binaural sound is central to the "experience" you intend to give our guests, but on reflection we'd prefer a more open and inclusive soundscape. I understand you feel headphones are important to your vision, but we would like you to rethink this and will pay an additional £500 to cover extra costs incurred by this change.

3. We'd like to see more specific references to our historical importance. Wary that the organization of components on the tunnel walls might look like a jumble, pieces of white card with text explaining our history would be helpful.

4. Could we rethink the use of color in the tunnel? Perhaps a

cooler, more muted feel? Some components are painted in garish shades.

I'm sure these changes won't take you long. If there are any further questions arising from this feedback, please do not hesitate to contact me.

Best wishes,

Mae

Doodle message group MMAM(FTP), April 29, 2024:

Patrick Bright

They don't like one single thing about the installation.

Jonathan Danners

We shouldn't act on our initial feelings. This is just a step on the road to making our client happy.

Patrick Bright

Have we even got time to repaint what we've already done?

Ludya Parak

Typical first notes from a new client. I once worked on an advertorial for L'Oréal that had over forty redesigns. No shit. We stopped counting at forty. It was only a page for a trade magazine.

Cameron Wesley

An honor and a privilege, she says? Shits, giggles, and a happy tax accountant!

Patrick Bright

Hope you're OK, Jem. I'm sorry your binaural project is on hold, after they seemed to love the idea in our pitch meeting. You'll come up with a world-beating soundscape, I know.

Alyson Lang

Client privilege. They pay to change their mind. Also, that many peeps are going to have that much feedback. We'll redesign, simple.

Jonathan Danners

Remember this course is all about adapting our skills to the workplace and the commercial world. We can demonstrate how versatile and flexible we are. We'll sleep on these notes and tomorrow morning meet up in the studio. I'll bring pastries.

Ludya Parak

Gluten-free and vegan.

Alyson Lang

Can't make it.

Cameron Wesley

Ditto.

Doodle message group [Private] Patrick and Jem, April 29, 2024:

Patrick Bright

The client has no clue what works aesthetically. All they want is to feed their guests a dose of promotional patter with their canapés.

Patrick Bright

We'll soon rework the installation. I bet we can switch it up in much smaller ways than they suggest and they won't even notice it's not entirely what they asked for.

Patrick Bright

Jem, please reply. I can see you've read my messages.

Jem Badhuri

They should respect the fact that my ideas have greater artistic merit than anything they have in mind.

Patrick Bright

I know. Criticism of a passion project is difficult to hear, but we'll pull together and get through it.

Jem Badhuri

Pull together? Cameron has left. Alyson has stopped coming in. Gela is pretending they're still here, for the sake of the course. Ludya is only motivated to work when there's money involved, and Jonathan is a liar.

Patrick Bright
Jem, you're just starting out. As the years go by, you'll realize life is not so simple. Things happen, situations arise that you'd never imagine yourself getting into, but suddenly there you are. You have to put one foot in front of the other, rinse and repeat.

Patrick Bright
Alyson is working on a big new commission. That's confidential.

Jem Badhuri
I've written to Mae with my thoughts, and now I'm going to bed.

To: Mae Blackwell, RD8 Systems Ltd.
From: Jemisha Badhuri
Date: April 29, 2024
Subject: A few points

Dear Mae,
There are things you should know about our course group. Two members have left. Cameron is apparently unwell and is only contributing the odd Doodle message (Doodle is Royal Hastings' intranet) while Alyson Lang has got a mysterious art commission and is no longer coming in. Jonathan and Gela are creating the impression she's here, when she isn't. It's just me, Pat, Ludya, and Jonathan working on your installation.

In light of these circumstances, I think you'll understand our reluctance to implement the majority of your suggestions which, if we did them all, would mean a complete redesign of the whole project. There is simply not the time, the personnel, or the budget to do so.

It is therefore my polite suggestion that you allow us to complete the final project to the best of our abilities. Some of your suggestions—such as making the tunnel a wall frieze, and diluting the impact of the soundscape to ambient Muzak—can all be seen as counterintuitive to a fully inclusive experience for your guests.

Yours,
Jem Badhuri

Doodle message group [Private] Jem and Alyson, April 29, 2024:

Jem Badhuri
Congratulations on your commission. I don't suppose you can say what it is.

Alyson Lang
Thanks. You're right. Client in the Middle East.

Jem Badhuri
I found out recently Jonathan is married to a girl called Suzie that he met on a university course he claims not to have done. Wondered if you knew.

Alyson Lang
Yes, I know. Thanks, Jem.

Jem Badhuri
Why would he lie about things like that?

Doodle message group [Private] Jem and Cameron, April 29, 2024:

Jem Badhuri
Hi Cam. How are you?

Cameron Wesley
Been better. You?

Jem Badhuri
A bit down about the RD8 feedback.

Cameron Wesley
Chin up. Do what the client wants and smile.

Jem Badhuri
Even when you know it's not the right thing?

Cameron Wesley
Especially then.

To: Gela Nathaniel
From: Mae Blackwell, RD8 Systems Ltd.
Date: April 30, 2024
Subject: A worrying matter

Dear Gela,

I've had an email from Jemisha, explaining why your group shouldn't implement our suggested changes. She claims Cameron has left your MA course. Is that correct? If so, where is he? Without being alarmist, he still has something of ours. I need it back and he's being obtuse.

Mae

To: Mae Blackwell, RD8 Systems Ltd.
From: Gela Nathaniel
Date: April 30, 2024
Subject: Re: A worrying matter

Dear Mae,

I'm in close contact with Cameron. He's working on another project and is most likely abroad. I know what he has of yours is safe, because he told me it is, and I trust him.

Thanks to you and your team for such comprehensive feedback on the installation. It's given the group a taste of real life—I look forward to watching them get over this psychological hurdle and pull together again. They've organized a coffee-and-cake-fueled postmortem for tomorrow. Jem is struggling to adapt to that aspect of the work, but the rest are very good with her. She's a strong, positive individual with a fierce intelligence, talent, and insight. She'll come around.

Best,
Gela

Message group: 2024 Examiners, May 30, 2024

Ben Sketcher
I'm parked outside RD8. It's so quiet.

Karen Carpenter
The do doesn't start till six. I've got a copy of the invite in my file.

Ben Sketcher
Could you forward that to me, please, Karen? I'd like to see what the evening entails.

Karen Carpenter
You fancy a rager, do you, Ben? Ha-ha! Here it is . . .

RD8 Manufacturing are pleased to invite you to the launch of

ICES Integrated Cloud Exchange System
6 p.m. Champagne reception in the Atmosphere
Room, followed by an exclusive unveiling of the
long-anticipated ICES project, which will usher in a
new era in secure cloud-based payment systems

Invitations are strictly nontransferable

Tilda Ricci
You won't try to get in, will you, Ben? If you embarrass us, they won't support the university again.

Ben Sketcher
If a student is missing, as I suspect, then that student won't be at the event. I just need to set eyes on them all. After that I'll be happy.

Karen Carpenter
You want to count them all in, and count them all out, Ben! Yes, SIR!

Tilda Ricci
Please, be discreet.

Karen Carpenter

If they're not there, they may simply have a cold. I've had a head cold for three weeks.

Ben Sketcher

I can see the Atmosphere Room from here. It's an event space near the front gate, decorated with branding. Visitors don't have to go far into the complex. Catering staff are moving to and from the kitchen.

Karen Carpenter

How will you know who is who?

Ben Sketcher

I have everyone's photograph—the ones taken for their ID cards at the start of the course.

Tilda Ricci

How did you get those? You don't have access to internal records.

Ben Sketcher

I'm in touch with Hannah, the course administrator. She thought I should see them.

To: MMAM(FTP); cc: Gela Nathaniel
From: Jonathan Danners
Date: April 30, 2024
Subject: Next steps

Dear Team,

So, we've had a night to digest the notes, and a morning discussing them over coffee and cake. I'm pleased to say we've got all the weeping, wailing, and hand-wringing out of our systems and are ready to see the installation in the light of all the changes we must make to it. The upside is that we now have an extra £500 to buy new materials, and possibly more, seeing as we no longer need to hire headphones or binaural equipment.

Jem will present a report into the state of our finances ASAP. In the meantime, I suggest we focus on taking the brightly colored components off the tunnel fabric. RD8 are happy to keep the head sculpture, as they felt it represented humanity in an otherwise technological presentation. However, perhaps we should give it more features, so it looks less like an android? Jem recently enjoyed a textured sculpture and has been inspired to rethink the head with a similar makeover. We also need to start work on the multimedia film of the company's history. Ludya and Patrick will focus on that.

Meanwhile Jem, Alyson, Patrick, and I will continue making components to a larger scale and with colorways indicated by the client.

Despite the client's rejection of her binaural experience, Jem will rise to the challenge of rethinking her ambient soundscape to reflect the values RD8 spoke about. She is the master of sound and we know she can do this. Thank you, everyone, for getting through what could have been the most unsettling stage of the final project.

Jonathan

Doodle message group [Private] Gela and Jonathan, April 30, 2024:

Gela Nathaniel
Good work today. Everything gone to plan?

Jonathan Danners
Why do you ask?

Gela Nathaniel
You weren't yourself at the postmortem.

Jonathan Danners
Everyone is down. Even Jem and Patrick.

Gela Nathaniel
It's the stage you're at. You've broken all the eggs, but haven't made the omelette yet.

Jonathan Danners
Gela, don't talk to me like one of your students, please. We'll finish the course and get A's—or whatever you give us. At least the whole thing is nearly over.

Gela Nathaniel
There's one more assignment: you have to finish the final project, write your long essay, and set up the installation for RD8's event. That's it. Thank you again for this.

Jonathan Danners
What? We have yet another assignment??? This is ridiculous.

Gela Nathaniel
Yes, there are six assignments, as well as the final project and tutor assessment. It's a coursework degree.

Jonathan Danners' Doodle Diary, April 30, 2024:

This is bigger than anything RD8 have ever developed. Is it their technology or someone else's they've acquired over the years? Either way, I'm not surprised they've kept it to themselves. Edison and Tesla worked on technology to breach the barrier between life and death. Both were working post–First World War, when so many people lost loved ones, leading to a resurgence in the popularity of spiritualism. Engineers are need-led. People need comfort. They need reassurance and to feel a connection to their dead sons and husbands. If either had succeeded, it would've been the discovery of the century, an eternal question answered and a commercial opportunity: everyone would want a Spiritfinder in their home. Received wisdom has it that neither did. But what if they had and the result was . . . horrifying? Not a comfort to the bereaved at all. But the opposite.

They would "need" to bury the tech, get rid of it. But who destroys something they've created? Frankenstein couldn't kill the monster. Artists don't destroy their art. Nor do engineers. Eventually RD8 found it, took it, and kept it. Then so did we.

Doodle message group [Private] Jem and Gela, April 30, 2024:

Jem Badhuri
Is Alyson coming in before the event?

Gela Nathaniel
She has professional commitments to fulfill and can't participate as fully as she'd like, but she's very much on board still.

Jem Badhuri
When did you last speak to her—face-to-face or over the phone?

Gela Nathaniel
A few days ago. We message or she leaves notes in my pigeonhole when she's been in overnight.

Jem Badhuri
Did you tell her we're another person short, precisely when we've got to redesign the installation?

Gela Nathaniel
Jem, in the real world people must work to tight and moving schedules, colleagues leave or are absent, there are unforeseen problems and the team is understaffed to solve them. And exactly like in the real world,

your value will be determined NOT by how you behave when things go right, but by how you respond when things go WRONG.

Jem Badhuri
Thanks, Gela. I feel a lot better.

Gela Nathaniel
That's the spirit! Work on being a conscientious team member who goes with the flow. You can say all you want in your long essay about how the process unfolded.

Jem Badhuri
Thinking about Mae's feedback, I'm sure we can come up with a new design that will blow RD8 away.

Royal Hastings, University of London
Multimedia Art MA
Final Project

Candidate name: Jemisha Badhuri
Candidate number: 0883479

Teamwork vs help:

I've never had "good team player" on my CV. I don't like relying on other people any more than I have to. If I can do something myself, then I go right ahead and do it. Which is fine. Art in its purest form isn't something that benefits from teamwork, so working with others on a collective project is a new concept for me. And that's why I'm here after all.

Help, on the other hand, is something I often find myself on the receiving end of, whether I want it or not. Dad says I must always be grateful for help, because if I'm grumpy and send a person packing, they may not help someone else in future, when that someone might really need a hand. He's probably right, in that annoying way parents are.

One thing this course has taught me is that I too can help people, even if I risk them being grumpy and ungrateful, just as I've been many times in the past.

A good team player is an obedient member of the pack. A people-pleaser. But I'm a good team *leader*, because I know what's right and wrong and I'm decisive. I can make decisions over and above the consensus of the majority. Which is why I found working with this group of personalities so frustrating.

What do you do if you know the team leader has made the wrong decision? Escalate your concerns. What if you do that and nothing happens because the "line manager"—or, in our case, the tutor—is as deluded as the others? You see, the notion of teamwork can be exploited in all sorts of ways. The team will carry lazy members who don't want to work. A poor leader will delegate tasks they don't like to weak members. People take credit for things they had no hand in—and crush those who did. So why do organizations value teamwork so much? If you ask me, it only serves the domineering bully who can't achieve anything on their own.

I spoke up, I asked questions, and I escalated my concerns on numerous occasions, but when all was said and done, I investigated Alyson's disappearance all by myself.

To: MMAM(FTP)
From: Gela Nathaniel
Date: May 1, 2024
Subject: Assignment Six

Dear all,

As the final project swings into its next phase, it's time for your sixth and final coursework assignment, and it's something you can take forward into the workplace when the course has ended.

You are not the person who started this course. Design a new CV, web page, or social-media profile that sells you as an employee or a freelance creative. Look back at Assignment Two from last year. How are you different from that person? How have you grown and matured? Your page or profile MUST include a 2D work or soundscape that illustrates the transformation that you, personally, have undergone. Deadline: May 17, 2024.

Your deadline coincides with a time when the installation for RD8 should be almost complete.

Best wishes,

Gela

Doodle message group MMAM(FTP), May 1, 2024:

Jem Badhuri

How can Gela expect us to do *another* assignment when we're behind on the final project?

Patrick Bright

It'll be a toughie.

Jonathan Danners

We're not behind on the project. We've had to redesign, but the client's request for larger components on the tunnel wall will serve our timings well. We can cover the area faster.

Jem Badhuri

I have to redesign my head centerpiece. That's a lot of work for me.

Patrick Bright
But won't your soundscape be less intensive, seeing as it's ambient and not binaural? Not that I know a lot about it.

Jonathan Danners
I'm happy to help you with the head, Jem. I can join you on that this week. We'll work together.

Ludya Parak
I can help with the head. I bet Patrick can too.

Ludya Parak
Patrick.

Patrick Bright
If I'm needed, then yes, of course I'll help you, Jem.

Jonathan Danners
Jem? Do you need help with the head?

Jem Badhuri
I'd rather do it on my own.

Jonathan Danners
There we go. We can all concentrate on our manufacturing tasks, to make sure the tunnel does NOT become the wall frieze the client might still request the next time we show it to them.

Patrick Bright
I thought you convinced them, Jonathan?

Ludya Parak
He did, but clients . . .

Doodle message group [Private] Jonathan and Jem, May 1, 2024:

Jonathan Danners
Thank you for adapting your soundscape and clay head. Much appreciated.

Jem Badhuri
I'm a conscientious team member going with the flow.

Jonathan Danners
What's the balance, now that we've had RD8's extra £500?

Jem Badhuri
There's £137.65 left.

Jonathan Danners
There must be more than that. What've we spent it on?

Jem Badhuri
Resin and hardener. Gela says Griff put his foot down and locked away all the department supplies. According to Patrick, we now need even *more* resin for the larger components.

Jonathan Danners
He should know.

Jem Badhuri
If it's any consolation, he gets trade prices *and* a discount through his retailer card.

Jonathan Danners
Ludya wants to subscribe to a music thing for the multimedia display. She'll be tapping you for payment at some point soon.

Jem Badhuri
How's Suzie?

Jem Badhuri
Duh! I mean Alyson. This voice function has a shocking autocorrect.

Jonathan Danners
Alyson's fine, as far as I know.

Doodle message group [Private] Gela and Cameron, May 4, 2024:

Gela Nathaniel
Please submit something—anything—for Assignment Six and I'll make sure it gets a grade.

Cameron Wesley
Bit tricky. Might be going deeper into this job than I thought. Submit something for me.

Gela Nathaniel
You can come up with a basic web page and image. Do something on your phone and send it to me. I'll jazz it up in FlowHand. Where are you, and why haven't you returned kiss-kiss to Mae yet?

Cameron Wesley
You've spoken to Mae?

Gela Nathaniel
She's pissed off, and rightly so. If you tell me where it is, I can get it and give it back. Not much to ask, is it?

Cameron Wesley
Did she tell you what kiss-kiss is?

Gela Nathaniel
It's new tech they don't want in the wrong hands.

Cameron Wesley
Not new. It's old, old, old tech.

Gela Nathaniel
Whatever, it belongs to RD8 and they want it back. Why would you risk your reputation for an old radio?

Patrick Bright's Doodle Diary, May 4, 2024:

Went around to Jonathan's. We sat staring at each other for God knows how long. Probably five minutes, but time means nothing when you walk through that door. We both saw it in each other's eyes: total mental and physical exhaustion. He must be broken, surely? Or did losing his mother and sister make him steely-strong?

I feel like we could work out how we got here by going back, plotting a route, but I don't want to notice other paths we should've taken and didn't. Too late to go back. Didn't see Alyson. Could've popped my head around the door, but . . . couldn't bring myself to, even though she's still in there.

Jonathan finally says, "It's nearly time for the voice. Come on." Couldn't say no, even if it was an option. We went upstairs. The unit has its own room now, which was a bedroom until, well, recently. We don't say a word, he switches it on, and then we wait. Harsh white noise bounces off the walls. The sky is crystal-clear outside, yet the atmospherics are pure raging up there. We hear them over the airwaves. And then, like a thing you dread but know is inevitable, the white noise stops. First the silence. Then the voice.

"It's dark. I'm trapped. Can't move. Please help me. It's killing me. Have you killed me?"

At least I think it asks that at the end, but the white noise kicks back in. Jonathan has scribbled everything down in a notebook. He does this every day, each broadcast copied down and dated. Only, when the voice says, "Have you killed me?" he stops dead.

"This is the first time it's asked that," he says, although he flicks through the book to make sure. "Interesting. It's coming to a realization, I think." When did we switch to using the impersonal pronoun?

"That it's dead?" I ask.

"Yes. It's possible this unit tunes in to a place of transition where the consciousness transmutes after death. The voice says they can't see, hear, or move. That's been the basis of the broadcasts from the start. Well, they are all physical sensations of being. Of being in a corporeal body. If you are suddenly taken out of your body, those are the feelings you'd miss. They are coming to terms with a different state of being."

It's a rational evaluation on the one hand, and on the other it's totally bonkers. But I can't argue. Jonathan needs to believe this.

"What are you going to do?"

"I want to communicate with it," he says, "but the only one of us who knows anything about radio is Jem."

I freak out. "We cannot involve Jem. She's too young, and after all's said and done, it's not her fault."

"It *is* Jem's fault. Partly, anyway. If she hadn't booked us into one room, this would never have happened."

I can see his point, but if we get her involved it will be the beginning of the end, and I say so. It occurs to me that's what he wants: a way to end this that takes the decision out of his hands . . .

"What about you, Patrick? You wired the unit up and got it working. You can make it a two-way thing. Ask radio experts on message boards and YouTube. You can do it."

I can't. I just can't.

"I don't *want* to speak to it. If you want my opinion, then the way we solve this problem is to switch that thing off and dump it. Send it back to RD8 even. It's not ours, we never should've had it, and I wish—wish *to God*—I'd never helped Jem open it up and tinker with it. It distracted her from everything else, but if I'd known . . ."

"Patrick, you have to contribute. You know what the rest of us are doing don't you?"

I have to nod.

"Well, you can do *this*. You can do it. Because if you don't, someone will remember whose fault this *really* is."

Doodle message group [Private] Hannah and Gela, May 6, 2024:

Hannah O'Donnell
When can I expect MMAM(FTP) grades for Assignment Six?

Gela Nathaniel
They had a setback on their final project, so I've only just handed it out.

Hannah O'Donnell
Is Cameron planning to submit?

Gela Nathaniel
Definitely. He's working on something now.

Hannah O'Donnell
I'm sending you an email about the final grades.

To: Gela Nathaniel
From: Hannah O'Donnell
Date: May 6, 2024
Subject: Final grades

Dear Gela,

I'm preparing guidelines for how the final project is graded and those grades reviewed. There's a draft document entitled "Notes for examiners" attached. It's the first thing they read before diving into the students' coursework. I think it's clear and to the point. In addition, please read the points below and come back with any comments and amendments.

- You will grade the students in the first instance. An external examiner will access those grades and other course materials to evaluate both coursework and the final project, and to confirm—or query—the given grades. As we know, the external examiner very much holds the balance of power, and I don't want this course to flounder at such a late stage after everyone has worked so hard. Not least you, Gela! We all want this course to fly.
- As I understand it, the group *won't* be able to assemble the installation here *before* the materials are transported to RD8 and assembled for real, so to speak. As the event takes place outside the college on private property, the onus is on you to document the process for the external examiner.
- Can we have a portfolio of photographs that show the installation before the materials leave the studio, then in situ at RD8, before the event? If you are able to photograph people at the event—or film them experiencing the installation, that would work well.

The deadline appears to be the day before the actual event: can you confirm? Please let me know any ideas you have that will enable the examiner to evaluate the final project and do justice to all the hard work you and your MA group have put in over the last year.

All the best,
Hannah

To: MMAM(FTP)
From: Gela Nathaniel
Date: May 6, 2024
Subject: The long essay

Dear all,

Do not run screaming at the subject line of this email. It's time to start pulling together your long essays. By "long" we mean 5,000–6,000 words.

Of course as you've all been keeping copious diaries of your work on the final project, these will be a cinch. They are basically your chance to evaluate the whole project, start to finish, from your point of view. Imagine you are giving your line manager an idea of what went right and wrong, and in particular what learnings can be taken from the experience, so that the next project will be better still. This form of postmortem is how we all ensure we move on from past mistakes toward a bigger, brighter future!

We'll discuss potential formats and headings, etc. at our next meetup in the studio. The format is flexible, so long as you clearly communicate:

- Who you are as an artist
- A project overview
- What went right
- What went wrong
- Learnings going forward

How you format and structure the essay is up to you.
Best,
Gela

Doodle message group MMAM(FTP), May 6, 2024:

Jem Badhuri
OMG, I can't believe we have to start the long essay before we've finished the installation. I've been keeping a Doodle diary, so hope to get it over with quickly. What's everyone else doing?

Patrick Bright

Feels like two minutes ago we were getting our welcome packs and registering for the print room. I've been keeping a diary too, but don't think it'll be very useful.

Jem Badhuri

The diaries are chronological, so we can do a chronological account, right?

Patrick Bright

That would be the logical thing.

Ludya Parak

It's our opportunity to throw shit around, folks. Point fingers. Lay blame. The worse you can make everyone else look, the less you'll come under the gaze of the man. Tips from the front lines of corporate survival.

Jonathan Danners

If the final project is a success—which it will be—there won't be any blame to throw around.

Patrick Bright

That's right, Jonathan. We'll all be singing each other's praises, that's for sure.

Jem Badhuri

Any failings will be attributed to the project leader. Glad it's not me. Will Alyson and Cameron be doing long essays?

Alyson Lang

We have to submit an essay to graduate. I'll be positive about the project leader. He was the best thing about it.

Cameron Wesley

Why call it "the long essay" for God's sake? Puts everyone off. Call it "the main essay" or "the course essay." "The LONG essay" gives it an air of dread and gloom. That's going in my introduction.

To: Mae Blackwell
From: Gela Nathaniel
Date: May 6, 2024
Subject: Royal Hastings MA installation

Dear Mae,

My course admin is making plans for the MA examination, of which your installation is the pièce de résistance. Please may I check you're happy for us to photograph the tunnel and the centerpiece once it's in place at your headquarters? Only we can't fully assemble it here.

In addition, it would be fabulous to have a short film of guests interacting with the installation. I can make this film myself. In fact I can also film the group as they build the piece, which would work very well—especially as I'm supposed to help them as little as possible! Once the structure is in place, I'm going to suggest the students make themselves available around the piece, to answer questions from your guests, perhaps explain how RD8's history inspired them, etc.

Would you, or one of your colleagues, be happy to be interviewed on camera about how valuable to a corporation a collaboration such as this is? I'm thinking beyond this year now, as next year, hopefully, I'll be seeking another private enterprise to sponsor a real-world artwork.

Please let me know your thoughts as soon as possible.

Very best wishes,

Gela

To: Gela Nathaniel
From: Mae Blackwell
Date: May 6, 2024
Subject: Re: Royal Hastings MA installation

Dear Gela,

I am afraid there is no possibility of you speaking to our employees. As for filming our guests, that is absolutely out of the question. The invitations clearly state that photography is not permitted on RD8 property.

We have not yet discussed the role your students will play on the day of the event. We would prefer that they assemble their artwork an hour or two prior to our first guests arriving, then vacate the premises.

However, as the installation hasn't been built to the health-and-safety standards required by a freestanding structure, I feel they should be present to ensure it doesn't collapse or items fall off it.

While our presentation takes place, they may move to the kitchen with the catering staff. Once the guests have gone, around 9 p.m., they will have until 11 p.m. to break the installation down and remove it. Alternatively I can arrange for it to be destroyed in our incinerator. Let me know.

I hope this isn't too much of a problem.

Mae

Doodle message group [Private] Gela and Hannah, May 6, 2024:

Gela Nathaniel

Hannah, I am apoplectic and have only you to sound off to. Mae won't let us document the event! I appreciate they have sensitive commercial concerns, but it's hardly in the spirit of the collaboration.

Hannah O'Donnell

No photographs or film?

Gela Nathaniel

Mae says "no possibility," but I might be able to sneak some shots between setup and the moment we have to clear off to the *kitchen* (yes, with the staff). Unless we need to stand by to ward off a collapse! That's how much faith she has—in case "items fall off it"!

Hannah O'Donnell

Oh dear! Can they set it up in the studio and take pictures there?

Gela Nathaniel

Surely she can't object to a few basic visuals, if there's nothing sensitive in the shot? They took us to the place, Hannah. It's a plain old 1960s function room on the outskirts of an HQ, not Menwith Hill!

Hannah O'Donnell

No problem. Look, the examiner will understand, I'm sure.

Gela Nathaniel

Mae even said they'd incinerate it for us afterward. Thanks very much. Why not cut out the middleman and take it straight there!

Hannah O'Donnell

Can the material be set up here at the college afterward? I'm thinking that we have spaces it might work in. You can photograph it and film people from the college "experiencing" it.

Gela Nathaniel

You're right, Hannah. That's a great idea. I'm simmering down now. Right, time to think positively and productively, like I'm always telling my students.

To: Mae Blackwell
From: Gela Nathaniel
Date: May 6, 2024
Subject: Re: Royal Hastings MA installation

Dear Mae,

That's rather disappointing as I felt this collaboration would enable the MA group to see their work in a real-world situation, being enjoyed by corporate guests and appreciated by their client. However, of course we will adhere to your in-house guidelines and would never think of doing otherwise.

Regarding the fate of the installation post-event: please do not incinerate the students' hard work! We will take the materials back to Royal Hastings, with a view to assembling the piece again for our department and the wider college world to enjoy. This will work as some additional promotion for RD8 and its exciting new technology.

Many thanks again for supporting the college and its grateful students.

Gela Nathaniel

To: MMAM(FTP)
From: Gela Nathaniel
Date: May 6, 2024
Subject: Logistics

Dear all,

Me again! While you're busy with Assignment Six and the final project, I'm thinking ahead to the event. Mae and her team are *very* excited at the prospect of seeing the installation in situ and have been making plans for how it will get there and what will happen to it afterward.

A corporate organization with health, safety, and security concerns will have certain rules that must be adhered to by outside contractors— that's us. Jonathan, could you liaise with Mae's PA, so we're across everything? I suspect we will have to obtain access passes beforehand and register whatever vehicle and company we hire to transport the materials to the location.

Difficult as it is to think beyond the event right now, we also need to decide what happens to our materials afterward. We'll have to dismantle it that night (Mae has set aside a two-hour time slot) and I suggest bringing it back to RH in the first instance.

Plenty to think about, talk over, and plan for. Good luck!
Gela

Doodle message group MMAM(FTP), May 6, 2024:

Jem Badhuri
I thought RD8 would want it in their foyer permanently.

Gela Nathaniel
They'd love to. Only they don't have room and our installation, as good as it most certainly will be, does not conform to their strict health-and-safety responsibilities.

Ludya Parak
If they've paid for something and want to kick it literally straight in the bin, then it's up to them.

Jem Badhuri
They won't bin it.

Ludya Parak
By the time it's been "experienced" by RD8's drunken guests it's going to look pretty smashed up.

Jonathan Danners
Ludya's right. We want people to interact with the piece. If it's unfit for human consumption by the end of the night, then our job is done.

Gela Nathaniel
I'd love to set it up at Royal Hastings, but logistics may dictate otherwise.

Alyson Lang
Controversial suggestion coming up: shall WE bin it? RD8 have a ginormous incinerator.

Jem Badhuri
No! Apart from all the hard work some of us have put in, think of all that wasted material. It wouldn't be eco-friendly.

Patrick Bright
Is burning it safe? We have a lot of resin components.

Alyson Lang
Let's make a ritual bonfire and dance naked around it, in celebration of the monster's demise!

Jem Badhuri
Those of us who've worked day and night don't consider it a monster.

Ludya Parak
I can take some resin components home for the kids to play with in the garden.

Alyson Lang
BIN THE BEAST.

Jem Badhuri
I'll keep it. All of it. No one take anything off it.

Patrick Bright

Are you sure, Jem? Where would you put something that huge and unwieldy?

Gela Nathaniel

Let's finish the piece before we decide its fate.

Jem Badhuri

Dad can clear a space in the garage and park his car on the drive.

Doodle message group [Private] Jonathan, Ludya, and Jem, May 8, 2024:

Jonathan Danners

Logistics for the day. I've booked a van from a local company. If we do all the loading ourselves, we'll only have to pay for a van and driver. Royal Hastings to RD8. Invoice attached, Jem.

Jem Badhuri

How do we get there?

Jonathan Danners

Luds, will you take us and any additional bits and pieces?

Ludya Parak

OK. But get permits for both vehicles. Remember the attitude on the front gate last year.

Jonathan Danners

Jem, set aside some budget for Ludya's charge receipt, post-event.

Ludya Parak

Have you told the van to wait and return?

Jonathan Danners

No. He'll drop the stuff and leave.

Jem Badhuri

I'll pay for him to wait, then drop it back at my place after.

Ludya Parak
We haven't decided what we're doing with it, right, Jonathan?

Jonathan Danners
It might be that we *have* to get rid of it, Jem. Once the event's over, it's just a length of damaged fabric covered in paper, glue, paint, and resin. I'm sure your parents don't have room.

Jem Badhuri
I'm keeping the clay head.

To: Central St. Martins College of Art
From: Jemisha Badhuri
Date: May 9, 2024
Subject: Employer inquiry re: a former student

Dear Sir/Madam,
I am a gallery owner considering hiring the services of an artist who claims to have studied at your institution. I wonder if you could confirm her claims are true and that the grade she states on her CV is indeed the grade she achieved.

Her name is Alyson Lang and she is forty-four years old, which would make her year of graduation around twenty-two years ago. As Lang may be her married name, perhaps search for someone who spells Alyson with a y?

I would very much appreciate your soonest response.
Best,
Jemisha Badhuri

Doodle message group [Private] Patrick and Jem, May 9, 2024:

Patrick Bright
How are you getting along, Jem? We haven't spoken so much recently. It's all gone a bit dark, has it not?

Jem Badhuri
What do you mean by "dark"?

Patrick Bright

I mean, we're all in our personal hell. I'm making resin bits and papier-mâché. Trying to work on a sketch for Assignment Six, but there's that much dried glue and paper fibers, hardener, and all sorts of rubbish stuck to my fingers. Can barely hold a pencil.

Jem Badhuri

I'm not in hell. Finished the RD8 soundscape ages ago. The head is almost done. Enjoying Assignment Six.

Patrick Bright

Good for you. The head looks awesome, by the way. Perfect reminder of humanity for guests who've come through the technocentric tunnel unscathed.

Jem Badhuri

What do you think we should do with the installation afterward? You didn't say.

Patrick Bright

Best incinerate it. There's a guy in Schull makes sand art on the beach. The tide comes in, washes it away. The next day he's back making another piece. Something authentic about ephemeral art.

Jem Badhuri

Whatever they do with the tunnel, I'm keeping the head.

Patrick Bright

Don't, Jem. Finish the course and leave it behind. You've got your whole life ahead of you.

Jem Badhuri

The head is mine. I'll decide what happens to it.

Doodle message group [Private] Gela and Cameron, May 9, 2024:

Gela Nathaniel

Would be good if you showed your face at the studio in the next couple of weeks. Even better if you help set up for the event.

Cameron Wesley
No can do, either way.

Gela Nathaniel
I need the technicians and admin to see you making the effort to attend. Just once. That way, they'll back up what I put on your special-consideration form.

Cameron Wesley
I'm not even in the country. Sorry, Gela.

Doodle message group [Private] Gela, Jonathan, Alyson, and Ludya, May 10, 2024:

Gela Nathaniel
Everything OK?

Jonathan Danners
Nothing for you to worry about.

Gela Nathaniel
Alyson, can you come into the studio at some point in the next couple of weeks? I take it you'll be at the event for the grand finale. The others need to see you're still involved.

Alyson Lang
Ludya's covering for me in the studio. I might be there on the night—will let you know nearer the time.

Gela Nathaniel
Cameron's coming, and it's only fair to the other students that we have a full team for the final-project unveiling.

Jonathan Danners
Cameron's coming? Has he confirmed?

Gela Nathaniel
Yes. He's feeling much better. I've kept my part of the deal. This is the most important part of yours: the examination.

Alyson Lang
I'll do my best.

To: Jemisha Badhuri
From: Central St. Martins College of Art
Date: May 10, 2024
Subject: Re: Employer inquiry re: a former student

Dear Ms. Badhuri,
Thank you for your email. I have checked our records and I'm delighted to confirm that, yes, Alyson Lang graduated in 2006 from our Bachelor of Arts course with a First-Class Honors degree in Fine Art.
Yours sincerely,
Uzma Mira

Doodle message group MMAM(FTP), May 14, 2024:

Jem Badhuri
How is everyone getting along with Assignment Six?

Ludya Parak
Too busy with the multimedia presentation. I'll get an extension. She can't expect us to focus on the final project *and* these shitty assignments.

Jem Badhuri
In the real world we'll have to juggle different projects with clashing deadlines. Professional creatives often don't have the luxury of time. Life is all about managing expectations. Your own and others'.

Ludya Parak
Thanks for the lecture—seeing as you don't live in the real world and know fuck-all about life.

Jem Badhuri
I know a lot about life actually.

Ludya Parak
Yeah, the view from your ivory tower.

Ludya Parak

Sorry. But until you've been awake all night while two kids vomit their guts up, then done your paid work from 4 a.m. until 2 p.m., when you have to start your UNPAID coursework, all while making food and screaming at the fuckers to keep quiet, when you know they're only rowdy because you haven't had time to take them out all day, while your mom, who doesn't speak much English, is vague about the results of her scan, all while trying to find another apartment because the landlord wants to sell your home. Then you can tell me about life.

Alyson Lang

Sorry, Luds. Hope your mom's OK.

Patrick Bright

Thinking of you, Ludya. Hope the boys are better soon too.

Jonathan Danners

Sorry to hear about your mom, Luds. We're all tired and stressed out. Let's chill.

Doodle message group MMAM(FTP), May 16, 2024:

Jem Badhuri

Is no one coming into the studio anymore? I've been the only one here all this week.

Patrick Bright

I haven't felt like speaking to anyone. Been taking my stuff to the BA studio and working there.

Jonathan Danners

Snap. Can't stand that place. Went to the Aviator to work on my essay. Thing is, we're nearly done with the components. The end IS in sight.

Jem Badhuri

Thanks to those of us who ramped up production after RD8's feedback.

Alyson Lang

I'm working from home and will continue to do so.

Jem Badhuri

I haven't spoken to you in person since Somerset, Alyson. Exactly four months to the day.

Alyson Lang

I won't make the event. My client is hosting a dinner in London and expects me there.

Doodle message group [Private] Jem and Patrick, May 16, 2024:

Jem Badhuri

What do you think about Alyson not coming? Not even to help set up.

Patrick Bright

Concentrate on your long essay, Jem. Let's just get this course over with.

Jem Badhuri

I looked her up at St. Martins. She really did graduate with a First, in 2006. She'd have been twenty-six then. A mature student. I'm sure all the articles say she was twenty-two.

Patrick Bright

Pass your MA, then begin your life. You're right at the start of it. Don't get bogged down with other people and their problems. Look after number one.

Jem Badhuri

Alyson has gone, Pat. She's not been in since you all went to Somerset. If you think she has, then you've been tricked, like the rest of us. Someone—I suspect Jonathan—is using her account on Doodle.

Patrick Bright

Saw her myself when I went around to Jonathan's. She was there. Large as life and quite well.

Jem Badhuri
When?

Patrick Bright
Couple of weeks ago.

Jem Badhuri
You didn't, Pat. You didn't see her. I'm not saying you're lying, I'm saying you were fooled. Because she wasn't there. You didn't *see* her or speak to her, face-to-face, did you?

Patrick Bright
No.

Jem Badhuri
Why did you go around?

Patrick Bright
To deliver materials, so they could make components over the weekend. He said Alyson was there.

Jem Badhuri
Has she left her husband?

Patrick Bright
I understand it's complicated. But I'm absolutely certain she was there.

Jem Badhuri's Doodle Diary, May 16, 2024:

Ever since I found out Jonathan is married, I've been googling Suzie Danners using every variation of spelling I can think of. Been searching for Jonathan too. The lady called Barbara at his father's gallery said he did "something ecological." I have to bear in mind that she might not have been told the truth herself.

All this time there's been one thing that didn't occur to me. I need Dad to take me somewhere.

MMAM(FTP)
Coursework Module: Assignment Six
Tutor's Report, May 17, 2024

Brief: Design a new CV, web page, or social-media profile that sells you as an employee or a freelance creative. It will represent you and your work going forward.

Overview: For their final coursework assignment I want the group to think beyond the walls of Royal Hastings. Any graduate of this MA will take their skills learned into the corporate world, fully prepared for a new career as a creative professional. This assignment is designed to refer them back to the start of the course and reflect on how far they have come. I am delighted to say that each and every student—despite being busy with their final project and essay—completed the assignment in good time and with impressive flair and commitment.

Jemisha Badhuri

Jem intends to start a business making soundscapes for public spaces. For this assignment she created a web page laying out her skills, accompanied very cleverly by a soundscape to illustrate her progress on this course. It's a bright, airy, experimental work that gently slides into a darker, more mysterious and intriguing experience. I found myself shivering as it played, as if an insect were crawling down my neck. Jem's key qualities are her ambition and determination, which together ensure she overcomes any obstacle in her way. She maintains a forward-thinking and optimistic outlook—reflected in the "About me" page she created for this project, on which she states: "I gained a Distinction in my MA in Multimedia Art at Royal Hastings." Grade: A

Patrick Bright

Patrick has discovered resin art and especially the joys and challenges of preserving organic matter. He drew a picture of the web page he hopes to create for a new business preserving flowers as paperweights. At this stage I would have liked to see the actual page, but Patrick has not yet mastered FlowHand 11. His CV was similarly sparse and doesn't even include his name! I'm afraid Patrick is drained by his work on the final project, so his grade is based on his previous work. Grade: C

Jonathan Danners

Jonathan chose to make a PowerPoint sales presentation featuring his photography, which for me indicates that his role as leader of the final project is taking its toll. My theory was borne out by the subject matter he chose: funeral photography, a business he has no intention of starting. His images depict graves, churches, coffins, and hearses. I asked how these represented his MA journey and he said, "They don't. Sights don't exist that would ever illustrate that." When I explained I'd have to mark him down and suggested that he resubmit, he made no effort to do so. Instead he said funerals will be a thing of the past one day and his work will be considered a historical document. Grade: C

Alyson Lang

Busy with the final project and her own high-profile commissions, Alyson proved unable to submit anything for Assignment Six. However, I hope to receive a special-consideration form to this effect and have marked her based on previous work. Grade: A

Ludya Parak

Ludya created a social-media campaign for her existing design business. I would have liked her to venture out of her comfort zone, but she chose only to update her existing website with a few images from the work she's produced on this course. Her submission was accompanied by a special-consideration form that requested I take into account her childcare issues and matters of a personal nature that she didn't wish to divulge. Without the form, I would have marked her assignment with a D. Grade: C

Cameron Wesley

Despite ongoing ill health, Cameron managed to submit a new CV and an oil-on-canvas piece depicting a seed germinating, unfurling, growing, and budding. A very beautiful image to illustrate how the course has reconnected him to the important things in life. His progress on this course has been exponential and he is by far the most-improved student, demonstrating the value of this MA for corporate professionals hoping to build on their skills, expand their awareness, and connect with the mental-health benefits of exploring their creativity. Grade: A

Jem Badhuri's Doodle Diary, May 18, 2024:

So at some point I'll turn my diary entries into a long essay, but first: document what happened today. According to Google, Alyson works in a flexible studio space in Guildford. It's called ReMerge because it's on the site of an old industrial building. Finding that out was easy; my main task was to convince Dad to take me there, so I approached it with the angle that this new space for creative professionals is *the* thing to see right now. Going there to experience it for myself will improve my result by, oh, at least a grade. He could always stop off at restaurants in the area and scout for clients.

So this morning we set off. Dad refuses to use the M25 and took the scenic route. For other people that might mean passing landmarks, but for Dad it means pointing out all the restaurants that don't have a genuine tandoor oven. Or at least that's how it seems.

I try to prepare Dad for me visiting ReMerge alone, but it ends in complete embarrassment. I say, casually, "You wait in the car, Dad. It's best I go in. That way I can get talking to other young people without a Boomer in tow." He goes silent and I can tell he's not happy. "Is it a boy, Jem? Because if you have to chase a boy to Guildford, he's not worth it." I hesitate for a sec, in case that might be a better lie to tell, but explain that I'm looking for the workspace a fellow MA student uses—a girl. I'm here to look for a girl. I don't think Dad knows lesbians exist, because this reassures him immediately. "You're special to me and you need someone extra-special, Jem. I don't want you to get hurt." We drive the rest of the way in silence. OMG, how embarrassing. However, eventually we arrive.

So ReMerge is a large, echoey space with clean air and people who seem to be wandering about in bare feet. Dad stays in the car, but I know he parks so that he can see me inside. They have no front desk. I walk in and stop, but no one asks what I'm doing there. Finally a young man breezes past and I stop him with an "Excuse me, can someone help?" It makes me cringe. I hate that word.

There's a flurry of activity as I'm passed from one resident artist to the next. Typically, they all cite someone else as a better person to help, but finally I'm taken to Alyson Lang's "space."

There's no security here at all. What if I was here to steal her corporate clients? Damage her work? Anyway I'm shown to a chair, and the vague girl with rattling bracelets who has brought me the final distance says she "thinks" Alyson is in, and if she can find her, she will tell her I'm here. She doesn't even ask my name.

Ding a text from Dad to see if I'm OK. I go to reply, but there are footsteps behind me. Unfamiliar footsteps.

"Hello, I'm Alyson Lang. Can I help?" An unfamiliar voice, or is she just on her best behavior?

"Alyson? It's me, Jem. I was passing with my dad and thought I'd drop in to say hi."

"Sorry, do I know you?"

It was her all right. Alyson Lang, professional artist and rising star of 2013. Only it wasn't the mouthy golden girl with the flexible approach to marriage who I've been on a course with for the last eight months.

Doodle message group [Private] Jem and Gela, May 20, 2024:

Jem Badhuri
There's something I need to talk to you about.

Gela Nathaniel
I'll be in the studio all day tomorrow.

Jem Badhuri
I'd rather do it over Doodle, so there's a record of our conversation. Just in case.

Gela Nathaniel
Fire away.

Jem Badhuri
I don't believe Alyson is working on a big-bucks commission. It's my calculated guess that something happened to her in Somerset.

Gela Nathaniel
Jem, that's an awful thought. What makes you say that?

Jem Badhuri

You haven't seen her, not in four months, have you? Have you even spoken to her on the phone?

Gela Nathaniel

I have. I'm sure I have. I must have.

Jem Badhuri

Jonathan knows. Patrick knows. The others, I'm not so sure. But there was something about that trip—that old radio they brought back.

Gela Nathaniel

An old radio came here by accident and was returned almost immediately. Look, Jem, the final project is at a crucial stage. You're doing well and—between you and me—you're on course for a Distinction if you knuckle down and focus. I'll look into Alyson's whereabouts and confirm she's well, but I'm sure it's nothing for you to worry about.

Jem Badhuri

I've already looked for Alyson Lang and found her in a studio in Guildford. It's her older sister's whereabouts we need to look into. Suzie Lang. Or, as she's been known for the last ten years, Suzie Danners.

Jem Badhuri's Doodle Diary, May 20, 2024:

I don't have a sister, but if I did, I wonder if she'd be as different from me as Suzie is from Alyson? The real Alyson is lovely. I perched on her saggy old settee and sipped scalding tea from a chipped mug covered in textured paint smears. She was so nice I forgot my cover story and blurted out exactly why I was there.

"Do you realize someone on an MA course at Royal Hastings is using your identity?"

There was a long silence. The real Alyson exhaled. She said yes, she did know, but that she didn't mind. Her sister desperately wanted to do the course and didn't think she'd get a place otherwise. I might have believed her, if it weren't for her voice. I can't even describe it, but when people lie, it changes the strength of their voice. I wondered what to say next, but Alyson spoke first, and in an urgent whisper.

"Do you know where Suzie is?"

This is the first time I've heard someone else admit that "Alyson" is missing.

"She hasn't been in the studio for ages," I said, and wondered if I should tell her the others pretend that she's there when she's not.

"She stopped taking my calls months ago," the real Alyson tells me. "I went around to their apartment, but they'd moved out. I've messaged, but the responses aren't like her at all. You must understand something about Suzie and me. We're more than close. Nothing can break our bond, but the last time I spoke to Jonathan, he said not to contact them anymore—that they're working on something that could change the world.

"My sister is the strongest person I know. She wouldn't let anyone speak for her, not even him. But they're both so . . . I don't know where either of them would ever draw the line." She stopped herself saying anymore, but I could tell there were tears in her eyes.

As I left the studio and was about to make my way back through the noisy, chaotic building, Alyson stopped me and said, "Did Suzie ever mention AetherGen to you?"

AetherGen? The climate-change group who block roads and damage buildings. When I said as much, Alyson dropped her voice to a whisper.

"They have a new leader who's committed to rather more than that, and I'm afraid Suzie might be under his spell."

"Alyson—I mean Suzie—isn't under anyone's spell; if anything, everyone seems to be under hers."

"I hope I'm wrong," Alyson sighed, but all the way back to the car five of her words rang in my ears. "Nothing can break our bond."

Royal Hastings, University of London
Special Consideration Form

This form should be used <u>only</u> to communicate mitigating circumstances if you feel you have faced sudden and insurmountable barriers to achievement in your final dissertation, coursework, or exams. It is not a guarantee that your final grade will be higher than that awarded by the examiner.

Name:	Alyson Lang
Department:	Media Arts
Date:	May 20, 2024
Course:	Multimedia Art, MA
Exam:	We call it the "long essay." A thesis that explains the final-module art project, its background, inspiration, etc.

In the space below, please give as much detail as possible regarding the mitigating circumstances you feel will affect your ability to achieve your full potential in this exam or submitted work.

I am well aware this form should be completed by Alyson herself. I am her tutor. I've made the decision to submit what there is of Alyson's long essay, which I found in her drafts folder on Doodle. I expected her to revise the content before her final deadline, but that hasn't happened. Alyson threw herself into this project, but at some point—I don't recall exactly when—she became distracted and her attendance declined.

Please believe me when I say this student is outstanding. She worked so hard, for so long. I would hate for that to go unrewarded. You'll see how intriguing and insightful her long essay is, even the little of it we have. She deserves to graduate with not just a pass, but a Distinction (I am also well aware I cannot influence the external examiner here, and this is not an attempt to do so).

If you have any questions at all about why this student deserves special consideration, I am happy to clarify. Thank you for your understanding in this <u>most</u> exceptional case.

Gela Nathaniel.

PS I am hoping against hope she will return to help create the installation, as planned, for the event. GN

Royal Hastings, University of London
Multimedia Art MA
Final Project

Candidate name: Alyson Lang
Candidate number: 0883484

Introduction:
I found a circuit board on the trash heap that was our home in Guangxi Zhuang, my sister and I. It's my earliest memory, that circuit board. A flat, green landscape embedded with tiny colorful shapes made of glass and Bakelite. Set part-haphazard, part-regimented along straight, intersecting lines. I stared and stared at it. I'd wanted a doll's house, like I'd seen on a page torn from a magazine, but this was more than I could dream of. I imagined people small enough to populate these miniature buildings and parks. I was their creator.

Since then I've been captivated by circuitry, old and new. Some boards are like plans for a new town, residential developments, schools, shops, community hubs set along tightly packed streets. Others are industrial. Gas holders, water tanks, cylinders linked by networks of pipes and cables. Each is different. Each a three-dimensional map of a tiny futuristic world.

As I got older, I discovered what these mysterious shapes and lines are: resistors, capacitors, crystals, oscillators, diodes, transistors, fuses. What they *do*. How they *work*. When I stopped seeing them simply as an aesthetic to be admired, I could appreciate the scope they represent, the universe of possibilities in those tiny worlds . . . There and then I knew exactly what I wanted to be when I grew up: an engineer.

Jem Badhuri's Doodle Diary, May 20, 2024:

They say if a woman is killed, she most likely knows her murderer. So likely, in fact, that any police investigation will start with the men closest to her and work outward from there, eliminating suspects as they go. They must know a thing or two about it, so I'll do the same.

Ever since that first inkling I had that Alyson was missing, nothing has happened to disprove my suspicion. Some people on this course have tried to convince me nothing is wrong. Are they party to certain information, or have they been convinced by someone else?

The further I get into my investigation, the fewer people I feel I can trust. Still, I have to bear one thing in mind: the two men closest to Alyson are her husband and Jonathan. Well, now I know they are one and the same.

Message group: 2024 Examiners, May 30, 2024

Karen Carpenter
AetherGen? The hippies who want us to stop driving and eat lentils? I thought they'd glued themselves to one too many buildings. Ha-ha!

Ben Sketcher
According to an article I read, they're under new leadership and the old-style protests have stopped. A change in strategy, apparently.

Tilda Ricci
Our students are intelligent and freethinking. It's only to be expected that some engage in political activism. However, the fact that "Alyson" is really her sister Suzie—Jonathan's wife—is rather curious.

Ben Sketcher
The "affair" was acknowledged only when Patrick spotted them behaving as if they were "together." They only ever meant to appear as fellow students.

Tilda Ricci
Why does Gela not notice the Lang woman who arrives in the studio on day one isn't the artist she's so in awe of? There are pictures of Alyson online. I fear she may have been duped.

Ben Sketcher
Gela is in on whatever scam the Danners are pulling.

Karen Carpenter
I've spotted something! When they first meet, Patrick compliments Alyson on losing weight. She's slimmer than the Alyson Lang whose pictures he finds online.

Tilda Ricci
You're right, Karen. But surely the others google Alyson too? Jem would notice that.

Ben Sketcher
Is Jonathan key to this? Is he so controlling that he makes his wife

impersonate her sister, just so he can take the same art course and keep an eye on her all day?

Tilda Ricci
The real Alyson seems party to the deception, at first. According to Jem, she too becomes worried about Suzie's whereabouts.

Ben Sketcher
For Assignment Five, when the group document lost things, Jonathan submits images that reflect the loss of a partner. By then Jem is convinced Alyson—or Suzie, his wife—is missing.

Karen Carpenter
Yet when Jem asks about Alyson, both Jonathan and Patrick say they've seen her. Gela too.

Ben Sketcher
Gela is in denial that her star student has gone. She's already lost Cameron, who isn't a burned-out professional but a private investigator working on a project called kiss-kiss—a project Gela is well aware of.

Tilda Ricci
He talks about coming from a high-level marketing job.

Ben Sketcher
That was years before.

Karen Carpenter
Young Jem says the trip to Somerset is key. Patrick hints at something similar. Sounds like there was an almighty blowup and Suzie flounced off. Ditched the hubby and went. For their own reasons, neither Jonathan nor Gela want to admit it.

Karen Carpenter
Ben? Are you still there?

Ben Sketcher
I've met Jem. She's here in the car with me, outside RD8. This is getting more worrying by the minute. I need to ask Hannah something.

WhatsApp chat between Ben Sketcher and Hannah O'Donnell, May 30, 2024:

Ben
That time you overheard the voice. You were outside, about to show Jem's dad into the studio, am I right?

Hannah
That's right, yes.

Ben
Please, think very carefully. Was Alyson Lang there?

Hannah
She wasn't there.

Ben
Are you sure? Jem says she was missing, but the rest of the group all say she was there and heard the voice.

Hannah
I'm sure, because I had to tell her the keycode had changed but couldn't because she wasn't there.

Doodle message group [Private] Gela, Jonathan, and Alyson, May 20, 2024:

Gela Nathaniel
I had to call Jem and assure her I know about the Alyson/Suzie thing and that it's under investigation. I hope to God that stops her meddling.

Jonathan Danners
Good work.

Gela Nathaniel
What about Patrick?

Jonathan Danners
Don't worry about him.

Gela Nathaniel
She and Patrick are so close—what if she's shared her suspicions with him?

Jonathan Danners
He won't say anything.

Gela Nathaniel
Where IS Suzie?

Jonathan Danners
She's with me.

Alyson Lang
I'm here, Gela. Don't keep trying to call us. We're not picking up.

Gela Nathaniel
You're not sticking to your side of the bargain.

Alyson Lang
We finished the course. That's our part of the deal.

Gela Nathaniel
The course isn't finished by a long way! There's the final essay and the installation. You can't leave it to the others at this stage.

Jonathan Danners

We'll be there to set up and make sure everything finds its way to the incinerator afterward. Anything else, just pay someone.

Gela Nathaniel

I want to keep the installation, and I can't "just pay someone." This is a respectable college, there are standards, protocols, and best practice. Every process is documented and totally transparent.

Jonathan Danners

You've still got Ludya—then there's Patrick and Jem. You'll think of something. We're too busy here, and anyway, we've already got what we wanted.

Doodle message group [Private] Gela and Cameron, May 20, 2024:

Gela Nathaniel

Suzie and Jonathan say they got what they wanted. How can they have? Thanks to you, they failed. Didn't they?

Cameron Wesley

Failed at what they meant to do. In the process, they found something else.

Royal Hastings, University of London
Multimedia Art MA
Final Project

Candidate name: Ludya Parak
Candidate number: 0883481

Later stages:

The project slid from regular failure to full-on disaster long before the later stages. When RD8 came to the studio, all 200 of them, and sent us pages of feedback, it was yet another turning point downward. Everyone split off into their own hell.

This stage is always a headache. The client can literally turn around and say, "Don't like it, start again." It wasn't that bad but, for Jem, changing the design felt like the end of the world. For the rest of us, the world had already ended and this was just some weird twilight existence. OK, I'm being dramatic, but it *is* dramatic.

At the same time it started to hit us that we actually had to do the installation. People were expecting a tunnel and a giant head sculpture, accompanied by a multimedia showcase of the company's history. I could feel the pressure crowd in on me. Why do I put myself through this? I didn't choose to be here. I was chosen because I'm a jobbing designer. Like that would make me any better at passing for an art student.

So Jonathan holes himself up in the house with the voice, and that's where he and Suzie stay. He's obsessed. When I go around to find out exactly where I stand, he keeps me at the door. But I need to know what I should say. If he doesn't tell me what to say, I'll have to tell the truth—when I'm asked. I end up shouting, and Jonathan hisses at me to keep my mouth shut, this is nothing to do with AetherGen now.

"Gela deserves us to graduate, though, right? She's put her career on the line; we owe her that."

He looked at me like we don't owe anyone anything. This is way above my pay grade. All I can do is make the components, work on the tunnel, finish the multimedia presentation, and deal with the inevitable when it comes.

Doodle message group [Private] Jem and Patrick, May 21, 2024:

Jem Badhuri
Hi Pat, long time no see. The tunnel's nearly finished, isn't it?

Patrick Bright
It's getting there, but everyone's slacked off. Ludya's working on the screen presentation, you're on the sculpture. I haven't seen Jonathan for over a week. Alyson's flitting in and out. Cameron's a distant memory. Even Gela seems preoccupied with other things.

Jem Badhuri
Well, the head is stunning and the soundscape will be brilliant.

Patrick Bright
Could you make some more components, please? You did well with them before and you've always been ace at papier-mâché. These ones are much bigger and less fiddly. I can leave all the stuff on your table. Please?

Doodle message group MMAM(FTP), May 21, 2024:

Jem Badhuri
Why should I do more work just because everyone else wants to do less?

Jem Badhuri
Where are you all? No one's on Doodle anymore and the studio's deserted. I've been making conversation with Griff every day.

Jem Badhuri's Doodle Diary, May 21, 2024:

The head is finished! I'm not troubled by doubt much, but *when* to stop work on a piece is something I have to think long and hard about. I enjoy the process so much. The head in particular has been a great experience. From making the wire frame with Gela the day they all went to Somerset up until now, the moment I realized "This is it!" It's a giant human head textured with unfired clay and inset with the tiniest components we had, plus ball bearings to give the surface texture and nuance. If you run your fingers over it, the steel of the ball bearings sends shivers down your spine. Now it's finished, I've been thinking about that old radio. It came back from Somerset when Alyson—or Suzie—didn't.

To: Polly Johnson, Mae Blackwell's Office
From: Jonathan Danners
Date: May 27, 2024
Subject: ICES launch

Dear Polly,

I'm project leader for Royal Hastings' installation at your ICES launch on Thursday. Can we firm up your requirements for our arrival and setup? We have one van and a minivan. There will be five of us, a driver who won't stay, and our tutor, Gela, who will arrive separately and won't be involved in the construction.

I need to check we can dispose of our packaging material and other refuse in your incinerator. Ideally we'll get rid of the entire installation immediately after the event. I need to check what access we'll need for that.

Jonathan Danners
Project Manager

To: Jonathan Danners
From: Polly Johnson, Mae Blackwell's Office
Date: May 27, 2024
Subject: Re: ICES launch

Hi John,

I'll need both vehicle registrations, and make sure everyone brings a passport or other photo ID. You'll be issued Level B access passes, so you can go in and out of the gate multiple times while setting up. Please forward ASAP. Our incinerators are switched on once or twice a week, but you can leave your rubbish in any of the big bins—you can't miss them.

Cheers,
Pol

To: Polly Johnson, Mae Blackwell's Office
From: Jonathan Danners
Date: May 27, 2024
Subject: Re: ICES launch

Hi Pol,
The thing is, our installation contains volatile materials, such as resin, varnish, and other solutions. I'd feel much happier if I could see it go into the flames myself. Can you find out when the incinerators will be working that week?
Jonathan

To: Jonathan Danners
From: Polly Johnson, Mae Blackwell's Office
Date: May 27, 2024
Subject: Re: ICES launch

It's switched on only when there's enough material to burn. Our site management team are super-thorough. They check through all our rubbish, sort out any recyclable material, and dispose of everything in the most efficient and eco-friendly manner. They know all about volatile materials. We even have a filtration system on our chimney to minimize air pollutants.
Pol

To: Polly Johnson, Mae Blackwell's Office
From: Jonathan Danners
Date: May 27, 2024
Subject: Re: ICES launch

Cheers, Pol, that's good to know. I saw the chimney when we last visited the site. At least it isn't far from the event location. Thanks for your help—I'll make sure you get everything you need in good time.
Jonathan

Doodle message group MMAM(FTP), May 27, 2024:

Jonathan Danners
Everyone remember to bring your passports to the event. Ludya, your vehicle reg, please.

Patrick Bright
I don't have a passport. Help! What shall I do?

Jonathan Danners
Any photo ID, driver's license, etc.

Doodle message group MMAM(FTP), May 27, 2024:

Ludya Parak
OK, so the screen presentation is almost done. Would appreciate everyone taking a look and telling me what's shit about it. For the love of dogs, someone check my spelling on the subtitles. I discharge all responsibility.

Gela Nathaniel
Thank you, Ludya. I'll send a link to Mae.

Jonathan Danners
Good work, Luds. Should we have a voiceover as well as subtitles? Just thinking about accessibility for the visually impaired.

Ludya Parak
I shitting didn't think of that! Fuck! Who's got the clearest voice? Pat, can you record the voiceover tomorrow?

Patrick Bright
If you think my voice is good enough. What time do you want me?

Jem Badhuri
We can't have a voiceover blasting out over my soundscape.

Jonathan Danners
We promised RD8 the installation would be accessible.

Jem Badhuri
We're not having a sign-language interpreter, are we? If RD8 really wanted full accessibility, they shouldn't have thrown out my plans for headphone ports. That would've solved the problem.

Patrick Bright
Perhaps we could ask Mae if any of their guests are visually impaired?

Jem Badhuri
No one is interested in the history of RD8—least of all the visually impaired. If there are any on the guest list, which I doubt, they'll be too busy appreciating my soundscape to bother about the multimedia display. But if, by some chance, a partially sighted visitor wants to experience the installation, I'll take them around it myself.

Ludya Parak
So shall I record Patrick's voiceover tomorrow?

Jonathan Danners
Yes, please.

Jem Badhuri
NO!

Ludya Parak
Sorted then. Thanks.

To: MMAM(FTP)
From: Gela Nathaniel
Date: May 28, 2024
Subject: The final project

Dear all,
I am beyond delighted to declare the final project finished! Well, artistically. We've still to work out the final logistics of the night itself, which I note is shockingly close . . . but something else is closer: the deadline for your long essays. Please submit your essay to me, in person, at the admin office, 12 p.m. tomorrow. I very much look forward to reading them all.

Once that's done, I suggest you experiment with packing the installation, ready for transportation, so that you iron out any potential hitches in advance and everything goes smoothly on the night. You must take any equipment for setting up. Our client will not be in a position to supply scissors, glue, string, or anything else. Remember, you may need to repair any damage that happens in transit, so be prepared.

I'll see you all tomorrow!

Gela

Doodle message group [Private] Gela and Jonathan, May 28, 2024:

Gela Nathaniel

I'm contacting everyone privately to check they're happy about both the long essay and the installation.

Jonathan Danners

This has been the worst year of my life.

Gela Nathaniel

Not because of the course, though? You're happy with the course?

Jonathan Danners

I'm happy it's nearly over.

Doodle message group [Private] Gela and Jem, May 28, 2024:

Gela Nathaniel

I'm contacting everyone privately to check they're happy about both the long essay and the installation.

Jem Badhuri

My essay is brilliant, my work for the installation outstanding. I know my coursework grades add up to a Distinction. Unfortunately, my soundscape—which is genuinely groundbreaking—will be obliterated by Patrick droning about RD8's radar technology in the Second World War. All because I threw a piece of clay at Ludya six months ago. Petty.

Gela Nathaniel

In the pitch meeting last year you assured RD8 the installation would be accessible.

Jem Badhuri

So hordes of nonexistent visually impaired guests won't get the historical context. My bad.

Doodle message group [Private] Gela and Patrick, May 28, 2024:

Gela Nathaniel

I'm contacting everyone privately to check they're happy about both the long essay and the installation.

Patrick Bright

Grand, Gela, thank you. My essay is almost done, the installation looks amazing. Everyone's a bit short with each other, but that's because we all want the event to go well. I'm sure it will.

Gela Nathaniel

Thank you, Patrick. I need that injection of positivity right now!

Patrick Bright

Oh, easy being positive when the nightmare's nearly over.

Doodle message group [Private] Gela and Ludya, May 28, 2024:

Gela Nathaniel

I'm contacting everyone privately to check they're happy about both the long essay and the installation.

Ludya Parak

Happy? You know shit didn't go to plan.

Gela Nathaniel

I gather that. But like I've said from the start, that's not my concern. I need 100% engagement with this course. If "shit didn't go to plan," you still have to complete it to the best of your abilities.

Ludya Parak

You don't know how hard that is.

Doodle message group [Private] Gela and Cameron, May 28, 2024:

Gela Nathaniel

I'm contacting everyone privately to check they're happy about both the long essay and the installation.

Cameron Wesley

Can't do either. Kiss-kiss.

Doodle message group [Private] Gela and Alyson, May 28, 2024:

Gela Nathaniel

I'm contacting everyone privately to check they're happy about both the long essay and the installation.

Alyson Lang

For the long essay, you can have a draft I started months ago.

Gela Nathaniel

Where are you? Please tell me.

Alyson Lang

I'm not far away.

Gela Nathaniel

Is this Suzie or Jonathan?

Gela Nathaniel

For God's sake, Jem thinks you're missing or . . . I don't know what, but she's on to you, and all I can say is she'd better not be right.

Gela Nathaniel

What happened in Somerset?

Doodle message group [Private] Jem and Hannah, May 28, 2024:

Jem Badhuri

Hi Hannah. How will our installation at RD8 be graded?

Hannah O'Donnell

Gela awards grades in the first instance. Then an external examiner oversees the entire course's grading.

Jem Badhuri

Who is the external examiner?

Hannah O'Donnell

A trusted academic appointed by Central admin to ensure the final grades are a fair and transparent representation of the work submitted.

Jem Badhuri

How do I get in touch with the external examiner?

Hannah O'Donnell

You don't. That's the whole point. The external examiner has no connection to the candidates whatsoever.

Doodle message group [Private] Hannah and Gela, May 28, 2024:

Hannah O'Donnell

Just a heads-up, Jem was asking how to get in touch with the external examiner.

Gela Nathaniel

Holy smoke! The girl is desperate for a Distinction. It makes me wonder if this is how she got a First from West Mids.

Hannah O'Donnell

Her grades are in the top percentile. She's on course for the maximum grade. I didn't tell her that of course, but it's easy to work out.

Gela Nathaniel

I have to ask—there's no way she can get hold of the external examiner, is there?

Hannah O'Donnell

If she does, I'd like to know how. The system is impenetrable, even for those of us with the right links and passwords! Thought I'd warn you, that's all.

Doodle message group [Private] Jem and Jonathan, May 29, 2024:

Jem Badhuri

Now that we've finished the installation and there's only the event itself to go, can you tell me if Alyson is OK? Only she never came back from Somerset. An old radio did instead. Now both seem to be missing.

Jonathan Danners

Concentrate on your own work, Jem.

Jem Badhuri

That's the problem. This course is supposed to develop teamwork skills. I don't want someone who abandoned the course halfway through to benefit from my consistent hard work. I'm contacting the external examiner, so he's aware of the issues.

Jonathan Danners

You want a Distinction. You should be working day and night, like any good student at this stage in their course.

Jem Badhuri

When the event is over, I might ask Mae if they'll let me visit the Somerset museum with Dad. He'll drive me anywhere.

Jonathan Danners

Even to a tiny art gallery in Gloucester. Barbara said a girl came in with her father and asked probing questions about me.

Jem Badhuri

Just wanted to see the gallery I'd heard so much about. It's very nice. Could do with a soundscape or two, but we can chat about that when I'm ready to start my business. Why did you tell us your mom and sister died ten years ago, when it was two? Why lie about being married to Alyson, whose name is Suzie?

Jonathan Danners

You, of all people, should know how important self-ID is.

Jem Badhuri

But if you tell people the wrong facts, that's lying. Isn't it?

Jonathan Danners

Ethics is hardly my area of expertise, but it's my understanding that we can each present ourselves however we like. The only person on this course who needs to know the truth is Gela, and she does. It's no one else's business.

Jem Badhuri

What *is* your area of expertise?

Jonathan Danners

Climate science.

Doodle message group [Private] Gela and Jonathan, May 29, 2024:

Gela Nathaniel

Your essays!

Jonathan Danners

We all submitted on time, didn't we?

Gela Nathaniel

But you've all said too much, surely? Even Suzie and Ludya give too much away.

Jonathan Danners

There's something cathartic about writing everything down. It won't matter after tomorrow night.

Gela Nathaniel

I only hope the external examiner doesn't download them before I can rewrite them, and with the event tomorrow, I don't know when I'll have time.

Jonathan Danners

Thanks, Gela, but you won't have to worry about that.

Royal Hastings, University of London
Multimedia Art MA
Final Project

Candidate name: Jonathan Danners
Candidate number: 0883482

The final event:
The voice stopped. I tried everything to tune in again. Nothing.
If only it hadn't stopped immediately after I'd attempted a break
in the circuit. We've lost the wavelength or something. But we
couldn't go on like that—the voice talking, us listening. Communication is, by definition, interactive. I can't believe anyone, let alone
the likes of Edison or Tesla, would develop a machine of this nature and not ensure it was two-way.

What did Jem and Patrick do to the unit when they tinkered
with it? Earlier I wondered if they'd unwittingly opened the door
to its secrets, but now I think they severed a delicate link and disabled a vital component. I kept thinking back to the way RD8
stored the unit. In its own room, a controlled environment. Had
we let it get too warm or too cold? Was humidity to blame? Dust?

We finished the installation a day or so before the event.
After RD8's feedback, panic helped us make up the time we
lost—so the tunnel and the centerpiece were ready early. On another level, time is running out. The event is our chance to move
on. Sell this technology to someone with the expertise, vision,
and resources to do what, in all the years they could have tried,
RD8 clearly never did.

To: MMAM(FTP); cc: Gela Nathaniel
From: Jonathan Danners
Date: May 30, 2024
Subject: Logistics

So the final event is here. We pack up the installation, transport it to RD8, rebuild it in their event space, and introduce their guests to the experiential tunnel. The company will deliver their own presentation, and once everything is over, we'll break up the materials and carry them to the incinerator.

Ludya and Jem will liaise with the tech team on-site to set up the screen presentation and soundscape. I'll be there to oversee lighting. Patrick and I will help load the installation and are responsible for repairs and reassembly, assisted by Jem and Ludya once our tech is sorted.

This is it!

Jonathan

Doodle message group [Private] Gela and Jonathan, May 30, 2024:

Gela Nathaniel

Why are you so keen to destroy the work?

Jonathan Danners

Because it's over. We incinerate everything. That's an order.

WhatsApp chat between Jem Badhuri and an unknown number, May 30, 2024:

Unknown number

Is this Jemisha Badhuri?

Jem

Who is this?

Unknown number

I'm the external examiner for Royal Hastings' Multimedia Art MA. I've just been handed all the coursework, plus your student profiles. I understand you wanted to contact me.

Jem

Did Hannah give you my number?

Unknown number

That's right.

Jem

Well, I got a First in my BA and I want a Distinction at MA. With art being subjective, I don't want the unconscious bias of my tutor (who has always favored another student) resulting in my grade being negotiated down. I'm a lot younger than the other students and I'm very aware their maturity could, potentially, make my work seem juvenile.

Unknown number

I'm confident your final grade will be an accurate reflection of the work you put in and of the progress achieved on the course.

Jem

I hope that's true. If there's even a slight chance I might not get a Distinction, then I *will* be asking for a regrade and won't hesitate to continue that challenge to whatever level it takes.

Unknown number

I'm sure that won't be necessary.

Jem

Good. Because let me tell you, the things that've happened behind the scenes on this course would make your toes curl.

Unknown number

What exactly has been going on behind the scenes?

Jem

One of the other students, Alyson Lang, hasn't been seen since the sourcing team went to Somerset back in January, and the rest are covering it up. By the rest, I mean Gela too. When I looked into Alyson's disappearance, I discovered she's actually called Suzie Danners and is on this course using her sister's name. She's married to Jonathan Danners, another student. He told us he couldn't take a first degree because his mother and sister died ten years ago. I then found out he did a bachelor's at Imperial, works as a climate scientist, and that his mother and sister died *two* years ago. They must have a very good reason to tell such odd lies. But that's not all. Gela had favorites from the beginning. When Alyson and Jonathan stole a radio from RD8, Gela hushed it up to save face. You can request all our Doodle comms from Royal Hastings. But now we're in touch, let me invite you to our final-project event. The installation features an amazing centerpiece, a spine-tingling soundscape, and an experiential tunnel, all made to a strict client brief. The client has zero idea about art, by the way.

Unknown number
I've accessed the Doodle cache already and have secured an invitation to the event tonight. I'm on my way.

Jem
Really? That's amazing! The others will be stoked!

Unknown number
Thank you, Jem, but don't tell them. Let's make it our surprise. In the meantime, if you have any private emails or WhatsApp messages that might give me an insight into the course and its students, please send them to me.

Jem
I'll do that as soon as I can. By the way, what's your name?

Unknown number
Ben Sketcher.

Doodle message group [Private] Hannah and Gela, May 30, 2024:

Hannah O'Donnell
Diversity forms. This is literally the last day before I need to submit the data.

Gela Nathaniel
Yes, yes! Here they are. Attached. Sorry, Hannah. It's this RD8 event. Sorry, sorry.

Jem Badhuri's Doodle Diary, May 30, 2024:

Today's the day! I'm here now in the studio, with the head. Everyone says how amazing it looks. Griff, Rita, Tony, Gela—everyone who's been supportive of me. The other MA students? Well, they're all in their own worlds and there they can stay.

I've just given the head a great big hug. I feel excited but sad. It's like saying goodbye. Before long it'll be out in the world being poked, prodded, and criticized by strangers. I'm not complaining, but the head is mine. My idea, and I did most of the work on it. If I have any regret at all, it's that it's not a permanent piece. The materials will degrade. Should I have devised a sculpture we could fire, that would last forever? Yes, but if I'd fired it I wouldn't have achieved this masterstroke of touch. The cold steel and warm clay is a deliciously conflicting sensation. We can't simply destroy it. I'll make sure, one way or another, that it escapes the RD8 incinerator. Dad can lower the backseats in the car, and once we get it home, he'll make room for it somewhere.

Doodle message group [Private] Gela and Jem, May 30, 2024:

Gela Nathaniel
Hannah called me about your diversity form. You ticked "no" where you should have ticked "yes."

Jem Badhuri
I don't think so.

Gela Nathaniel

It's important for the department that this form is accurate.

Jem Badhuri

Which question?

Gela Nathaniel

"Do you consider yourself to have a disability?"

Jem Badhuri

I don't consider myself to have a disability.

Gela Nathaniel

I realize that, but others—who don't know you—may, and this form is purely to aid the department in its program of inclusivity.

Jem Badhuri

The question says: do you consider yourself disabled?—and I don't, so I ticked "no."

Gela Nathaniel

But it would help us if you ticked "yes," because the department has worked hard to make the course and the studio accessible for students who *do* consider themselves to have additional needs.

Jem Badhuri

So, because I'm blind, I'm disabled? I disagree. I identify as able. That's very important to me.

Gela Nathaniel

And we respect that. But future visually impaired students might feel differently. We want them to know that others have been accommodated and excelled, as you have. You'll be an inspiration to them.

Jem Badhuri

Well, OK then. I'll get Dad to print the form out again and tick the other box. But remember how accommodating I've been when you mark my long essay.

Gela Nathaniel

I will, Jem. Thank you! You know you're on track for a Distinction. You only need to convince the external examiner.

Doodle message group [Private] Jem and Hannah, May 30, 2024:

Jem Badhuri

I'll resubmit my diversity form.

Hannah O'Donnell

Thanks, Jem. I know how important it is to pursue the things you want in life. You've approached this course with energy and enthusiasm and never once logged a special-consideration form. Unlike some of the others.

Jem Badhuri

I don't intend to for the final essay, either. I don't mention it unless I really have to, and I appreciate when others do the same.

Hannah O'Donnell

You know, if you find yourself needing help at any time, it really isn't a problem to ask. There are some things intelligence, ambition, energy, and attitude can't compensate for.

Message group: 2024 Examiners, May 30, 2024

Tilda Ricci
Jemisha Badhuri is visually impaired?

Ben Sketcher
She's blind. Yes.

Karen Carpenter
Does everyone know that? Gela, Jonathan . . . the whole MA group?

Ben Sketcher
Of course. How could they not?

Karen Carpenter
Because no one mentions it in these documents.

Tilda Ricci
I'm shocked. How can we have read this far and not realized something like that?

Ben Sketcher
We have to ask ourselves if it matters—whether or not we knew.

Karen Carpenter
I'd have felt sorry for her if I'd known.

Ben Sketcher
Perhaps that's why she doesn't mention it. For her, it's of no consequence to anyone else.

Tilda Ricci
But it is to us, if we're considering the possibility that another student on the course was in danger and then disappeared. I'm left wondering what happened that Jem couldn't possibly have known about.

Doodle message group [Private] Gela and Cameron, May 30, 2024:

Gela Nathaniel
Who is Lisa Hough and why does she have my phone number?

Cameron Wesley
My lovely ex-wife. She studied at Royal Hastings, so probably knew who to ask. She hasn't got my number, thank God.

Gela Nathaniel
She says you were supposed to be at your son's school sports day, which you never miss. She hasn't heard from you.

Cameron Wesley
Haven't got her number, so couldn't let her know. Tell her I'm stuck on a job overseas. Cheers.

Gela Nathaniel
You share a child and don't have each other's numbers?

Cameron Wesley
Long story.

Gela Nathaniel
Here's her number—you can tell her the long story yourself. I'm leaving now for the RD8 event that you should be at.

Cameron Wesley
I'm there in spirit.

Doodle message group [Private] Gela and Jem, May 30, 2024:

Gela Nathaniel
Jem! I'm in the studio, and *drum roll,* Alyson just walked in! I am delighted to see her again and know you will be too. It means we're almost a full team for the event.

Jem
It's definitely her?

Gela Nathaniel
It's definitely her.

WhatsApp chat between Ben Sketcher and Jem Badhuri, May 30, 2024:

Jem
Hey Ben. Guess what? "Alyson" is here in the studio. She hasn't disappeared, and I feel a bit silly causing such a fuss now.

Ben
The student you told me was missing? Suzie Danners?

Jem
Yes! It's definitely her. It's her voice, her footsteps, and her brand of cigarettes. Her voice has changed, the way my dad's voice changed when my grandad died last August. As if the energy is gone. In Dad's case, it was grief. Anyway, she's here, so false alarm!

Ben
Well, that's good news, but I'm already on my way to RD8. I might as well see the installation now, if I can. It will help me grade everyone properly. I should arrive just before it starts.

Jem
We're all packing up and bickering because we're nervous about the whole thing. The centerpiece is ready for loading in the van. According to the others, it needs rebalancing, so they've weighted it from the inside. They assure me it doesn't affect the way it looks or feels. I'll meet you outside, as planned.

Ben
See you there, Jem.

Royal Hastings, University of London
Multimedia Art MA
Final Project

Candidate name: Patrick Bright
Candidate number: 0883480

What I learned from the experience:
I learned that if you can possibly avoid it, don't get into a situation where someone else is responsible for your sense of security. It gives them far too much power.

I still don't know if I can trust Jonathan or the others. I live from one moment to the next and have for months now. Will they grab me from behind when I least expect it? Then the sudden darkness of a bag over the head as I'm dragged backward into oblivion? In my mind the scene cuts off there, like a film. Cuts straight to the aftermath—a funeral—although I fear that's not what'll happen.

If only I didn't keep hearing whispers about the RD8 incinerator. Biggest, best, hottest. Clean green technology.

In hindsight, if the voice hadn't come through, things would have been different. Better or worse, who knows? It sent Jonathan into a frenzy that infected everyone. It wasn't my fault, but they recoiled from me. Then they blamed me for the voice, said I helped Jem get the unit working, that she couldn't have done it on her own, but Jem knew her way around that circuit board. She read it like braille. The girl's a wonder.

What I could have done differently:
Should have stayed at home that day. I had a cold starting and it was only Jem who convinced me to go. She was so keen to get the gossip, and I felt sorry for her. In my darkest moments I've thrown some blame in her direction for that stunt she pulled with the room. It should be something we're laughing about now. If she hadn't done that, if I'd stayed home, if they'd gone by themselves, who knows what we'd be doing right now. Chances are we'd all be alive at least.

Message group: 2024 Examiners, May 30, 2024

Karen Carpenter
Phew! False alarm! Alyson is back and everything's fine after all, Ben.

Ben Sketcher
I wouldn't be so sure. I'm here now and still not convinced all the students are safe and well.

Tilda Ricci
But how could the death of a student be covered up?

Ben Sketcher
If they all worked together to convince Jem and Gela.

Karen Carpenter
Wooo! A dead body could have been in that studio and Jem wouldn't have known.

Ben Sketcher
Somerset is the key.

Karen Carpenter
What happened there? A row in the museum that's quickly smoothed over. A boozy dinner. At the motel they find they're all booked into one room, so they sober up and drive back to London in the middle of the night, dropping the bags of salvage at the studio on the way.

Ben Sketcher
The next day Griff finds the fabric they'd bought for the installation covered in something that reminded him of pig's blood.

Tilda Ricci
And Jem discovers a strange radio apparently taken from the museum, which she and Patrick experiment with. It's tuned to an obscure wavelength and all it broadcasts is a voice pleading to be rescued from a dark, lonely place.

Ben Sketcher
Jonathan, who hid his scientific background, thinks it's an old machine

developed in the 1920s to contact the dead. He becomes convinced, to the point of obsession.

Tilda Ricci
Meanwhile Cameron is "off sick" while other students pretend Alyson—or rather Suzie—is coming in on at least a weekly basis.

Ben Sketcher
Except Alyson Lang—or Suzie Danners—hasn't disappeared. She's helping the MA group set up the installation right now. I've just seen her with my own eyes. Whoever's dead, it isn't "Alyson."

Karen Carpenter
Oooh! This is better than TV! If it turns out to be a performance-art piece, where this intrigue is all part of their work, I'll personally suggest the entire class get Distinctions.

Doodle message group MMAM(FTP), May 30, 2024:

Jem Badhuri

You'll never guess who I've got outside with me now.

Jonathan Danners

We could do with a hand in here, Jem.

Jem Badhuri

The head and my soundscape are all set up and ready to go. The RD8 tech team is ace.

Jonathan Danners

We need to get the tunnel right—it's what leads the guests to the head. If we can't set it up, they'll suggest we hang it on the wall and the whole installation will be ruined.

Jem Badhuri

The external examiner is here! I did some digging and he contacted me to say he'd love to see the installation. He's going to chat with RD8 at the gate and see if he can come in.

Gela Nathaniel

All the more reason to get this tunnel constructed.

Patrick Bright

I'll come out, see if I can sweet-talk security.

Doodle message group [Private] Jonathan and Patrick, May 30, 2024:

Jonathan Danners

Whatever you do, make sure he stays out there.

Patrick Bright

If we get it past him, we're in the clear. More insurance that nothing's wrong?

Jonathan Danners

DON'T LET THE EXAMINER IN HERE.

Doodle message group [Private] Patrick and Jem, May 30, 2024:

Patrick Bright
You come inside, Jem. The guy on security is from Cork and let me through with no photo ID. I might be able to get the examiner in.

Jem Badhuri
That would be brilliant, Pat. Thanks. Meet us at the gate?

Patrick Bright
On my way, wait there.

Message group: 2024 Examiners, May 30, 2024

Ben Sketcher

There's been a development. Patrick Bright just dashed out of RD8, sent Jem back inside, and asked for my phone number. He said there are things I should read before I come in.

Tilda Ricci

Sounds fishy to me. Karen may be right. This intrigue is all part of their creative installation.

Ben Sketcher

I don't think so. He looks like a ghost and is shaking like a leaf. I'll forward the files he sent me. Let's see what they say.

Documents sent to me by Patrick Bright while I waited outside RD8. He was visibly upset and told me they explain "why he didn't get out sooner." These go all the way back to last year, before the course even started.

To: Patrick Bright
From: Gela Nathaniel
Date: May 18, 2023
Subject: MA course

Dear Patrick,

It was lovely to speak to you properly over coffee today and to hear about your retirement plans. Thank you for showing me your work. I appreciate it's not easy, but let me tell you, in that portfolio of sketches I saw a solid talent—one that deserves to be nurtured.

Attached is an application form for the new MA course I'm running from this September to May next year. It's designed to bridge the gap between creative work and the commercial world. I aim to create a safe space for students to develop unfamiliar skills and practice those they already possess. As you said, artists are notoriously shy when it comes to selling themselves. I promise to bring you out of your shell! Wherever and however you decide to spend your retirement, MMAM(FTP) will help you navigate the demands of a small creative business.

Think about it, and if you have any further questions please don't hesitate to ask.

Best wishes,
Gela

To: Gela Nathaniel
From: Patrick Bright
Date: May 19, 2023
Subject: Re: MA course

Dear Gela,

Thank you for your email. I feel flattered you've considered me for your new course. I thought you had to get a BA before you did an MA, but according to the girls in the shop, what you said is right—these days that's not the case. I've blown hot and cold over the whole thing. It's a lot of time and money to commit. What if I don't enjoy it? What if I'm so far behind the others, I hold them back, let you down, and embarrass myself? I'm honored you think I'd be a good candidate, but I'm going to say no, thank you. You've given me something to think about maybe, for the future, but not this time.

Patrick

To: Patrick Bright
From: Gela Nathaniel
Date: May 19, 2023
Subject: Re: MA course

Dear Patrick,

Your sketches are way above the standard of your average MA student. The group will come from many different backgrounds and specialties—from fine art to 3D to computer animation. I can GUARANTEE you will stand out, not as inadequate, but as excellent.

Now, Patrick, over the years you would not believe the number of people who, when they hear I teach art, confess they would love to pursue it themselves, especially in retirement. There's always a reason not to, and they don't. The result is they go to their graves unfulfilled—and the world is denied the wonderful art they would have created. If time is a problem, remember this course is only three days a week during term time. If money is a problem, I can tap Royal Hastings' discretionary fund for you.

Please, Patrick, reconsider.

Gela

To: Gela Nathaniel
From: Patrick Bright
Date: May 22, 2023
Subject: Re: MA course

Dear Gela,

I've had a think over the weekend and a chat with the girls in the shop and they agree with you. They say they'll work any extra hours needed—I'll have to pay them of course, so, if you could look into the funding, that would be very handy. I can't believe I'm going to be an art

student. I've had people in the shop debating whether to get themselves a watercolor kit or a set of oils—and I've given them the talk you just gave me. I'm taking your advice and my own. I'll see you in September!
Patrick

To: Patrick Bright
From: Gela Nathaniel
Date: May 22, 2023
Subject: Re: MA course

Dear Patrick,
Wonderful news! Thank you. Please be assured the other students will all pull together to support you—and each other. That's the beauty of the small-group MA. We become one big family, and I expect this to be a positive, productive, collaborative experience for everyone.
Gela

To: Gela Nathaniel
From: Patrick Bright
Date: October 9, 2023
Subject: Re: MA course

Dear Gela,
I feel I have to contact you. I've given it a couple of weeks, hoping things would improve, but it's no better. We're all so different and I have nothing in common with any of them. Don't get me wrong, Jonathan seems a pleasant enough fellow and young Jem a delight, but Alyson and Ludya are both nightmares, and don't get me started on Cameron, I might never stop!
The technicians are surly and seem to resent me being there. I've tried to gel with people, but I'm wondering if this course is really for me.
Patrick

To: Patrick Bright
From: Gela Nathaniel
Date: October 9, 2023
Subject: Re: MA course

Patrick,

The course has been running less than two weeks. Everyone feels jittery at the start of anything new, but you'll bond with the others soon enough, especially when we start working on the assignments and the final project. You were given a grant from discretionary funds. Think of all the people who wanted to apply for this course, but had no financial help so couldn't. They'd love to be in your shoes right now. MMAM(FTP) is a fantastic opportunity that will allow you to retire to Ireland as you've always wanted. You can't leave now, you just can't.

Gela

To: Gela Nathaniel
From: Patrick Bright
Date: October 9, 2023
Subject: Re: MA course

I hear what you're saying, Gela, and I would love to throw myself into this, as I wanted to back in the summer when we spoke. But the reality is, the people alongside you make or break an experience like this and I'm not feeling the love. Even Jem, who is the only one I've really got along with, is so ambitious that if she had to push me under a train to get her MA, I think she would, I genuinely do. Who should I speak to about withdrawing from the course, you or Hannah?

Patrick

To: Patrick Bright
From: Gela Nathaniel
Date: October 9, 2023
Subject: Re: MA course

Patrick, you are withdrawing from this course over my dead body. If you DO, then you can rest assured Modern Art's long-term commitment to VAT evasion will come under intense scrutiny from HMRC, and there's no point in escaping to Ireland—you'll just be extradited. All you have to do is complete this course. It's over at the end of May. That's barely six months, it's not much to ask, is it? Now, you've got Assignment One to be getting on with. I look forward to seeing your submission.

Gela

Message group: 2024 Examiners, May 30, 2024

Tilda Ricci

Why would Gela be so desperate for Patrick to continue with the course?

Karen Carpenter

If he's been fiddling his tax, then he shouldn't need a sub from the discretionary fund.

Tilda Ricci

Indeed—how does Gela know that about Patrick's business? She's an art teacher, not a private investigator.

Ben Sketcher

Cameron. His company specializes in financial fraud. Gela and Cameron had some sort of relationship before the course started.

Karen Carpenter

All that kiss-kiss. It's not the first time a tutor has cooked admissions to get their latest squeeze in the class. Naughty-naughty!

Tilda Ricci

Gela wouldn't do that, Karen. She's dedicated to her art and her teaching, with a reputation to uphold. I can't think of anything she would compromise that for.

Ben Sketcher

Kiss-kiss. Patrick is still sending files. Here, more attached.

Documents sent to me by Patrick Bright:

Somerset trip WhatsApp group members Jonathan Danners, Alyson Lang, Cameron Wesley, Patrick Bright, and Ludya Parak, January 17, 2024:

Patrick
You told the shopgirls I'm in the West Country.

Jonathan
Joy messaged you. She would've been suspicious when you didn't reply, so I had to say something. We must use our phones as normal.

Patrick
But you said you took my phone as insurance against ME contacting anyone. Now you've sent all sorts of rubbish to people and pretended it was from me!

Jonathan
Ludya looked at who you chat with regularly and sent them an update about your trip to Somerset. You're having a grand time.

Patrick
Fuck!

Ludya
Don't thank me.

Patrick
That places me right at the scene.

Ludya
This is all to protect you, Patrick. We're pulling together, like coursemates on an MA.

Patrick
We'll go down.

Ludya
We won't. We've got this.

Patrick
Why take my phone and send so many messages, though? You don't even know my code.

Ludya

3265, your birthdate. You really should update to biometric recognition. Far more secure.

Patrick

What the hell are we going to do?

Jonathan

It will help if everyone is equally motivated to move this forward. Pat, you've got your phone back, but please text as you would normally.

Patrick

In the middle of the night?

Ludya

Scroll through Diamond Angels as usual, perhaps message one or two of your favorite ladies?

Patrick

If we all have to text, why isn't Cameron texting? If he's not texting, where is he?

Jonathan

He's driving. Calm down, Pat. We'll all help you. We're doing this for you.

Patrick

But these messages are evidence. We have to delete this thread. Get rid of it forever.

Ludya

Nothing is gone forever. Even when you think you've deleted it, it still exists on the cloud, waiting for you to make a wrong move.

Patrick

Shit! What can we do?

Jonathan

Calm down, Pat. It'll be fine. So long as you *don't* make a wrong move.

Message group: 2024 Examiners, May 30, 2024

Tilda Ricci

This is very worrying. So something *did* happen in Somerset?

Karen Carpenter

Cameron's driving, but they don't say why Alyson isn't messaging.

Ben Sketcher

Any one of these texts could have been sent by someone else. Gela hasn't arrived at RD8 yet. Mae has just sent her an email asking where she is.

Karen Carpenter

How do you know that? Mae isn't part of the college, so she doesn't use Doodle.

Documents sent to me by Gela Nathaniel while I waited in the queue:

To: Gela Nathaniel
From: Mae Blackwell, RD8 Systems Ltd.
Date: May 30, 2024
Subject: Your student group

Dear Gela,

Are you here yet? I've bumped into your student group, hard at work setting up their installation. The clay head covered in metal things is enormous, but very effective. We like the juxtaposition of highly engineered components and this central piece that brings us back to the humanity of technology. I hope the tech team can assemble the tunnel in time. Our guests will be arriving in an hour, and we'd love to lead them through it toward the head.

I understand Jem convinced the tech department to set up the screen farther away, so there wasn't a clash of soundscapes. I expect being blind means she is very sensitive to sound. Shall we meet up for a chat as soon as you're here?

Mae

WhatsApp chat between Mae Blackwell and Gela Nathaniel, May 30, 2024:

Mae
Where are you?

Gela
Jem said they put a weight inside the clay head. I need to see what it is. Don't want anything that will damage your incinerator.

Doodle message group MMAM(FTP), May 30, 2024:

Jem Badhuri
Where's Gela? I want to show her my head before guests arrive and start prodding it. Gela, where are you?

Ludya Parak
Guests are already arriving.

Jonathan Danners
Don't let them in. We haven't secured the tunnel. Tell them to stay outside.

Ludya Parak
I could ask but don't have a lot of sway, seeing as I don't work here.

Patrick Bright
I'm with Gela in the corridor by the toilets. Found her sitting on the floor. She's not well at all.

Alyson Lang
They've had champagne out getting warm for an hour. Gela, did you have some?

Jonathan Danners
No, I told her.

Ludya Parak
Told her what?

Patrick Bright
What the fuck?

Jem Badhuri
What did you tell her to make her ill?

Jonathan Danners
That we had half an hour to get the installation up and chat with guests about it. Don't know why that should make her ill. Like Alyson says, it's probably the champagne.

WhatsApp chat between Mae Blackwell and Gela Nathaniel, May 30, 2024:

Mae
Everything OK, Gela?

Mae

Did you find out what was inside the head?

Mae

Whatever it is, please don't worry about our incinerator. I've been assured it can handle anything!

Mae

My PA said she saw you open the clay head. She said you seemed shocked by what was inside and reeled back, then staggered away, looking most upset. If you're not feeling well, perhaps have a sit-down outside?

WhatsApp chat between Ben Sketcher and Jem Badhuri, May 30, 2024:

Ben
Is everything OK, Jem? Patrick says he'll help me get into the event, but he can't do that until after the guests are let in.

Jem
Awesome! I feel so excited now that the whole class is together again.

Ben
Except Cameron.

Jem
He's still sick and did nothing for the installation. Before you see it, you should know that I'm not happy with what they've done to my head and am not responsible for anything that happens as a result. They've weighted it inside, but Gela and I have been working for *weeks* and we already took its top-heavy alignment into account with a wider plinth— whatever they've done could've destabilized it. Gela was fuming when she heard and said she'd have to take the weight out while I kept an RD8 lady busy in the tunnel. Then Gela screamed. I thought the whole thing had fallen on her! But when the RD8 lady and I ran back through the tunnel, Gela said she just gasped because the head wobbled, but it's fine now. She was shaken up and shouted at me to help her replace the clay on the access hatch, then immediately had to dash off to the toilet. I want you to know, Ben, if there's anything wrong with the head it's not my fault.

Message group: 2024 Examiners, May 30, 2024

Ben Sketcher
I've been Jemmed.

Karen Carpenter
Oooh-er!

Ben Sketcher
As soon as I arrived, the missing student miraculously turned up. Now there's more excitement to keep me guessing. I suspect Jem got me here on false pretenses, so that I see her artwork. Thanks to Patrick, I'm waiting outside to do exactly that. I wonder if the docs he sent were all part of Jem's plan.

Tilda Ricci
Jem always gets what she wants. One must applaud her ingenuity.

Karen Carpenter
I'd give her extra marks for cheek! Now you're there, you might as well enjoy it, Ben. Can I ask how you knew Mae had just emailed Gela?

Ben Sketcher
I received a stream of documents from an unknown number. Correspondence to and from Gela Nathaniel. Either Patrick or Jem must have given her my number. I'll forward them.

Documents sent to me by Gela Nathaniel; they date from April last year:

To: info@alysonLang.co.uk
From: Gela Nathaniel
Date: April 3, 2023
Subject: [Website Message]

Dear Alyson,

I hope you don't mind me contacting you through your website. I was at the rally in Trafalgar Square on Saturday and got talking to your brother-in-law, Jonathan. I teach undergraduate and postgrad art at Royal Hastings and remember visiting your exhibition at the Brewer Gallery years ago.

Royal Hastings is revamping its art courses to better reflect the potential employment opportunities for art graduates. You'll understand that in the current economic climate each course must justify its place in the prospectus. We've had our class sizes reduced already, staff are not being replaced, we lost a studio building to the sciences last year, and the whole department is under scrutiny. In short, if we fail to adapt, then our funding will be cut further and art at Royal Hastings will dwindle to nothing.

So I am planning a new MA tailored to build skills that are useful to commercial companies and corporations. I wonder if you'd be willing to pop in and chat with the class one afternoon? Any time from December to March, depending on your schedule. It should only take an afternoon, and, as I see you're based in Guildford, it shouldn't be too far a journey. I can pay your travel expenses myself.

Yours hopefully,
Gela Nathaniel

To: Gela Nathaniel
From: Suzie Danners
Date: April 4, 2023
Subject: Re: Fwd: [Website Message]

Dear Gela,

Thanks for your email to my sister, Alyson, which she forwarded to me. I understand you were in London on Saturday. I was there with my husband, Jonathan, whom I believe you were talking to on the march from St. James's.

I'm a production engineer currently working in corporate sustainability. Jonathan is a climate scientist affiliated with the pressure group AetherGen. We are both committed to direct action against climate change. I have a proposal that may be of interest to you. Can we meet?

Suzie

To: Matilda Ricci
From: Gela Nathaniel
Date: June 2, 2023
Subject: MMAM(FTP) intake

Dear Tilda,

Just to update you on the inaugural Multimedia Art MA. I have found some excellent candidates, all keen to build on their artistic and/or business skills. I'm confident they will form a creative team that will ensure the first arts-based industry collaboration is a success.

- Alyson Lang is already an artist with a growing profile. She will provide a bedrock of flair and experience for the group.
- Jonathan Danners's family has an art gallery, but he has so far not explored his own artistic side. He will bring his commercial and hands-on management experience to the team.
- Ludya Parak is a working graphic designer. She is looking to gain wider practical skills and grow her business, which has plateaued.
- Patrick Bright runs an art-supplies shop but has always nurtured a passion—and skill—for drawing. His experience running an art-adjacent business will benefit the group.
- Cameron Wesley discovered a latent artistic ability while recovering from corporate burnout. His marketing acumen will be invaluable.
- Jem Badhuri gained a First in her Fine Art BA and brings not only a youthful outlook but also passion and ability in the more unusual mediums of 3D and sound.

This course will help transform Royal Hastings' art department into a powerhouse for commercial art.

Best,

Gela

WhatsApp chat between Gela Nathaniel and Tilda Ricci, June 2, 2023:

Tilda

Thanks, Gela, but we need to observe best practice throughout the admissions process.

Gela

They are fully representative. Ages range from twenty-one to fifty-eight. One has Eastern European heritage, one is from China, one is Bengali and has a disability, one is a mixed-race man with a working-class background, and although we have two white men, one is Irish and the other has suffered two awful bereavements.

Tilda

The panel approves—your inaugural year is a go! I look forward to hearing how successful it's been.

WhatsApp chat between Gela Nathaniel and Ludya Parak, September 4, 2023:

Ludya

Suzie and Jonathan want to know who the other three are.

Gela

Aspiring artists keen to learn new skills. There's no need for them to know any more.

Ludya

Only there kinda is. We gotta make sure they're not gonna get in the way. Compromise things.

Gela

How could three art students who are strangers to each other possibly compromise you?

Ludya

They just want to be sure. We're investing a lot of time in this. We need the others to be good stooges who will say everything was fine.

Gela

I can't predict how people will behave on the course. It's up to you to appear normal.

Ludya

If we pull out because we don't like someone you've chosen, then that'll look bad for you, so best all around if we're across the recruitment process.

Gela

It's not recruitment, it's admissions. A young BA grad from West Mids, the owner of an art shop where I've bought my personal supplies for years, and a man who burned out of his marketing job and discovered art in rehab.

Ludya

S&J want to know why a recovering addict is considered "safe"?

Gela

Cameron isn't an addict! He worked too hard on a failing business, his personal life fell apart, and he hit the bottle for a bit. He's not a dyed-in-the-wool soak!

Ludya

The guy in the shop, what's his story?

Gela

Patrick is the nicest, gentlest guy you can hope to meet. Too nice. They had a horrible robbery last year. It shook him up and he's talked about retiring to Ireland with a small business ever since.

Ludya

The young BA? Is she safe?

Gela

Jem is the safest of them all.

Ludya

Really? A Gen Z with nothing better to do—eyes everywhere?

Gela

She's blind from birth. A visually impaired artist who majored in sculpture and studied sound in her own time. She's bright and ambitious, with strong family support. She'll be an active member of the group, but she literally won't see a thing.

Ludya

We need all three to be compliant.

Gela

And I need you three to be my students. You attend class three or four days a week, complete all the assignments on time, and throw yourselves into the final project to the best of your abilities. You're enthusiastic and engaged from the first day to graduation. This won't work if you're not.

Ludya

I'm a graphic designer since my kids' dad left and I had to earn actual money. Jonathan's dad has an art gallery, and either Suzie's sister or I will do her assignments for her. No one will think we're anything other than regular people trying to better ourselves.

Gela

And the money?

Ludya

We've paid our fees.

Gela

The money you promised me.

Ludya

You'll get half soon. The rest at the end of the course, but ONLY if we locate the unit and get the evidence we need. That's the deal.

Gela

I find it difficult to believe your organization has that level of available funds.

Ludya

They don't, but Jonathan and Suzie can sweet-talk wealthy benefactors like you wouldn't believe.

Gela

And you'll be exemplary students?

Ludya

Shit, no! We'll play our characters. Us, but students again. Nervous, wide-eyed, overconfident, disruptive, lazy, chill. As diverse in approach as anyone would expect a class to be. Personally, I'm looking forward to playing around with clay and paint. Seeing if I've still got it.

Gela

I suggest Suzie and Jonathan don't tell the others they're married. It'll look strange.

Ludya

Sure, well, you want her to be Alyson. He's not married to "Alyson," is he?

Gela

I'm not sure about that now. If one of the others google . . . Alyson and Suzie may be sisters, but they're quite different.

Ludya

She'll say she's lost weight. Been ill. Changed her hair. They're old pics. Whatever. Suzie can walk, talk, and bullshit her way out of anything, and Alyson will make sure she doesn't appear online for the year of the course. Not difficult—she hasn't had any press for the best part of ten years.

Gela

OK. Well, you're all strangers who meet for the first time on the first day. If we keep our nerve, no one should suspect a thing.

WhatsApp chat between Gela Nathaniel and Cameron Wesley, September 4, 2024:

Gela

I've been speaking to a Ludya Parak. The Danners want her on the course because she's their techie. I only know she's a single mother and really does work as a freelance graphic designer.

Cameron

Makes sense. They'll need help for what we think they're planning. She's got no criminal record and, from her website, looks like an art student.

Gela

So will you "look like an art student"?

Cameron

Not getting a tattoo! No, I'll look like the washed-up and haggard husk I was when I walked into your art class at the Sanctuary.

Gela

When all the time you'll be watching them.

Cameron

Watching, listening, and feeding back to RD8 for Operation Kiss-kiss.

Gela

Kiss-kiss!

RH WhatsApp group, members Ludya Parak, Suzie Danners, Jonathan Danners, and Gela Nathaniel, September 26, 2023:

Gela

I need you all to put your phones in the tray for the first few weeks at least.

Ludya

Like I said on Doodle, I've got kids. Phone stays with me.

Suzie

If we want to risk our phones it's up to us.

Gela

But the other three are putting their phones in the tray religiously. Everyone knows the rule is flouted after the first few weeks, but that's all the college needs for their insurance. If an accident happens and Royal Hastings is slapped with a claim, they can say, "Phones went in the tray for the first few weeks and then the student decided to take the risk." A few weeks. That's all.

Jonathan

Don't students rebel anymore?

Gela

They don't kick off in their first week—not about phones, and not about keypads on doors or access to the studio!

Suzie

I don't want Gruff Griff, Rambling Rita, or Tony Slowhand looking over my shoulder.

Gela

You don't want the others guessing you're not proper students.

Ludya

I'm doing this assignment. I'm a proper student.

Jonathan

We need to bring in Alyson's artwork via the parking lot. There's no security out the back. Unbelievable, but useful.

Gela

Does your sister know what you're doing?

Suzie

She knows enough and has a cover story to reel off, if anyone asks. She treats the artwork as a regular commission.

Gela

Could she let slip something about it, deliberately or accidentally?

Suzie

It's not in her interests to, is it?

Jonathan

She's doing most of the work and she'll get a degree certificate in her name for her wall. It's just not her in the studio. Or working with RD8.

Gela

Suzie should talk more about her weight-loss journey. Your sister is . . . well, I don't believe in body-shaming, but Patrick has already done an image search.

Suzie

I'll try and remember, but if you've chosen the other three well enough, they won't suspect anything.

Gela

A professional of Alyson's caliber risking her reputation—why would she do that?

Ludya

You tell us.

Jonathan

Belief in the cause.

Suzie

She's doing it for me.

RH WhatsApp group members Ludya Parak, Suzie Danners, Jonathan Danners, and Gela Nathaniel, October 5, 2023:

Suzie

Shit! Fucking Griff crept up behind me this morning. I have sensitive shit on my laptop. I looked up and there he was. I hit the ceiling.

Jonathan

Did he see anything?

Suzie

I don't *think* so, but it freaked me out. I yelled at him, and heads up, he might complain, Gela. But WTF, he should get noisier shoes or something.

Ludya

Gela, can you find out what he might have seen? Shit, that's all we need.

Gela

I've just spoken to Griff. He's very upset, and I'm not surprised. What I am surprised about is that, in Suzie's position, she is drawing attention to herself in a way that could threaten her place on this course.

Jonathan

She cannot be kicked off this course. Gela, you MUST smooth this over. I mean that.

Gela

Luckily for you, I managed to calm Griff down. Told him you had delicate mental health. He agreed not to escalate his complaint if you apologize to him in private. I must then establish on Doodle, without mentioning names, that such behavior toward studio staff is unacceptable.

Jonathan

Good. Did Griff see the screen?

Gela

I think being called a "creepy prick" and told to "fuck off back to his hole" distracted him from whatever might have been on the screen.

Ludya

Jeez, Suze, that's harsh. Griff is pretty cool. You know the sculptures along the corridor are his?

Gela

He certainly does not deserve to be verbally assaulted for being in the studio, where it is his job to attend those who work in it. The sculptures are resin, and yes, he's excellent in 3D media.

Ludya

You'll apologize, won't you, Suze? I mean, we gotta have the staff onside, right?

RH WhatsApp group members Ludya Parak, Suzie Danners, Jonathan Danners, and Gela Nathaniel, October 16, 2023:

Gela

Suzie, are you taking things from the art studio?

Suzie

Why do you ask?

Gela

Jem and Patrick have presented me with a spreadsheet and time line detailing missing items. Canvas, paint, resin, plaster.

Ludya

WTF? Loads of people use the studio and the storeroom.

Gela

They've logged Suzie's arrival at, and estimated departures from, the studio on all given days.

Jonathan

Jem can't know what's missing and what isn't. She's blind.

Ludya

Patrick must have done that bit. Jeez, the gruesome twosome.

Gela

It's not Patrick, it's Jem. She knows that storeroom inside out. She wants to be as independent as possible, so she familiarizes herself with her environment. Patrick helped with the spreadsheet and the trade prices of the items.

Jonathan

Trade prices?

Gela

Apparently Suzie has acquired £125.81 worth of art supplies.

Suzie

Is this acceptable? For students to spy on other students?

Gela

That depends if they're right or not. Have you taken anything from the cupboard that hasn't been used for a class assignment?

Suzie

Alyson is desperate to get a new exhibition off the ground, and apart from this commission she's got no money coming in. I said I'd help out and get her a few essentials, that's all. We've been shipping it through the rear doors. It's the least we can do, considering the risks she's taking for us.

RH WhatsApp group members Ludya Parak, Alyson Lang, Jonathan Danners, and Gela Nathaniel, October 24, 2023:

Gela

WHAT THE FUCK WAS THAT ABOUT? IT WAS STUPID, RECKLESS, AND DANGEROUS. YOU DO NOT SET FIRE TO ANYTHING IN MY STUDIO. I CAN'T THINK STRAIGHT, I'M SO ANGRY.

Suzie

Cameron's phone has a security feature that claims to alert the police when someone it doesn't recognize looks at it. He works in marketing for financial services. Why that level of security?

Gela

What has that got to do with you setting fire to Jonathan's assignment?

Suzie

I was passing the tray and spotted Cameron's phone. It was off, but I switched it on, out of curiosity. The fucking thing shrieked and the police warning flashed up.

Jonathan

How much do you know about him, Gela? You said he was in the art class you taught at a rehab center. He could be anyone.

Gela

So Cameron has the latest tech on his phone. Why set fire to the whole studio block?

Suzie

I WAS CREATING A DIVERSION.

Ludya

It backfired. Scuse the pun.

Jonathan

It didn't backfire, it worked. Everyone is talking about what a crazy bitch Alyson is.

Gela

Were the police called? That's the last thing I need when my only MA course is hanging by a thread.

Ludya

Cameron flew out and deactivated the phone, so no cops, but why would a marketing exec have such high-grade security? If he shows someone a cat video, the police turn up?

Jonathan

A scare tactic to make robbers drop the phone?

Gela

Whatever phone Cameron has, whatever happened to it, you should NOT have lit a match in the art studio. For heaven's sake!

Suzie

I panicked. I've just burned the rest of our printouts in the bin under the sink. Sorry, but we can't risk being discovered.

Ludya

You burned everything? Well, how will we know the codes when we access the facility?

Suzie

We have backups.

Ludya

We do? Where do I access the backups? Jonathan?

Jonathan

Look, Gela, we're sorry about the fire. It won't happen again. We'll discuss the backups between us and get on with the second assignment.

WhatsApp chat between Gela Nathaniel and Cameron Wesley, October 24, 2023:

Gela

She was creating a diversion because your phone alarm shrieked when she switched it on.

Cameron

So she DID switch it on. Fuck! She set fire to J's assignment to pull focus. Classic. So they're on to me.

Gela

I smoothed it over. Does your phone really dial 999 when it sees a face it doesn't recognize?

Cameron

It has added secure features. Perks of the job.

Gela

So if you show someone a cat video, it switches off and dials 999?

Cameron

Ha! Luckily, I hate cats.

RH WhatsApp group members Ludya Parak, Suzie Danners, Jonathan Danners, and Gela Nathaniel, October 15, 2023:

Gela

Did you let anyone else into the studio this morning?

Suzie

Why?

Gela

Jem just asked me if Griff has become an alcoholic in the last two weeks. Long story short, she's convinced someone who smelled of alcohol was in the studio early this morning, and she suspects you were covering for them when you said you'd been speaking to the department head about the keypad.

Suzie

How can she possibly know that? She didn't get to the studio until after they'd gone.

Gela

We didn't agree you could have strangers on college property. That wasn't the deal. Who was it?

Suzie

We've had to access more codes and liaise with a dodgy character or two. I didn't smell alcohol on the person who came, but she likes a drink for sure. Anyway, how does Jem know it wasn't me, reeking of beer after a big night?

Gela

Apparently you smell of cigarettes. Please can you assure me no more strangers will be let onto college property again?

RH WhatsApp group members Ludya Parak, Suzie Danners, Jonathan Danners, and Gela Nathaniel, October 26, 2023:

Ludya

Switching between Doodle and WhatsApp is doing my head in.

Gela

We should keep our communications course-related and fully visible on Doodle—stop messaging on WhatsApp unless it's absolutely necessary.

Suzie

Jem is in the studio so early. I need to work on our plans before everyone gets in. Can you tell her to arrive at the usual time, Gela?

Gela

It takes her longer to do certain things, so she compensates by arriving early. The course is fully accessible, and if she wants extra time, then I'm not going to stop her taking it.

Gela

The best I can do is mention it to Hannah next week, see if there's a health-and-safety reason we can use to keep her out of the studio before nine thirty.

Suzie

Patrick calls women "dear." He actually asked me to make him a cup of tea today.

Ludya
When you told him to make it himself, he waited till you'd gone and asked me!

Gela
The girls in his shop adore him. I don't think he's ever had to operate a kettle in his life.

Suzie
Cameron is trying to recruit me for his company. Like a professional artist would ever give that up, to be a corporate slave.

Gela
Remember this course is real for them. They're all looking to develop something in themselves. It would help if you all give that impression too.

Ludya
I'm rocking the student life. Especially the discount card. But when do we get to Thorney Coffin?

Gela
There's two more assignments before we get anywhere near RD8. I've got a Zoom meeting this week with Mae to discuss the collaboration.

Jonathan
This is what we came to you for, Gela. We MUST access the radio museum—it's the only room with a data breach in its access code.

Gela
I know. And you will.

WhatsApp chat between Jonathan Danners and Gela Nathaniel, November 14, 2023:

Jonathan
Look, I'm sorry things got heated, but we just haven't got time for these things.

Gela
The deal is that you immerse yourselves in the course. I ask you to take an industry guest for lunch and you act as if I'm being unreasonable. He's

a commercial gallery owner who talks to all our students, and we need to make him feel welcome.

Jonathan
He's a dinosaur! A crashing bore! A lunch with him is the last thing we need right now. You don't know everything we're doing. It's bad enough dealing with Patrick, Jem, and Cameron and the whole coursework thing. I'm sorry we overreacted, but pretending you're something you're not is damned hard.

Gela
I didn't suggest this. You did.

Jonathan
But you agreed. At least now we've cleared the air. You've had your say. I'll make every effort to be present for the course and will make sure industry guests are looked after in future. Ludya will do her best, her family situation permitting. But Suzie has the expertise for this project and she MUST concentrate on it.

Gela
What *is* your project?

Gela
Only I read in the *Guardian* that your mysterious new leader is committed to direct action.

Jonathan
I'm afraid that's classified.

RH WhatsApp group members Ludya Parak, Suzie Danners, Jonathan Danners, and Gela Nathaniel, November 14, 2023:

Suzie
Forgot to take my folder home, thought it would be safe under the desk, got in this morning, and MY FILES HAVE GONE.

Jonathan
What exactly was in it?

Suzie
The codes and binary variations we'll need at Thorney Coffin.

Ludya

We can't access them again. Seriously, this is it.

Suzie

Posted on Doodle. GELA, I NEED THAT FUCKING PORTFOLIO BACK.

Jonathan

Calm down, everyone. Whoever's got it won't know what the codes are for. You can say the printouts are for an art project. You'll think of something. But we need it back.

WhatsApp chat between Gela Nathaniel and Cameron Wesley, November 14, 2023:

Gela

I've got Suzie Danners's portfolio of "codes and binary variations." She left it behind on Friday and I spotted it this morning. Useful to you?

Cameron

Photograph every page, so it can be clearly seen, put everything back as you found it, and return the folder; say it was left in your room by whoever.

Gela

With my phone camera? They're old-fashioned dot-matrix sheets. The ink is very pale.

Cameron

Second thoughts, I'll come around and photograph them. Return it as if nothing out of the ordinary.

RH WhatsApp group members Ludya Parak, Suzie Danners, Jonathan Danners, and Gela Nathaniel, November 14, 2023:

Gela

Suzie's portfolio was shoved into my section of the cupboard with a Post-it saying "Left in studio." No idea who found it, probably a BA student.

Suzie
Thank God! No one looked in it?

Gela
You'll have to check it yourself.

RH WhatsApp group members Ludya Parak, Suzie Danners, Jonathan Danners, and Gela Nathaniel, November 16, 2023:

Gela
Griff saw you with a woman in the studio this morning.

Jonathan
Presumably you're asking Suzie that? Probably Alyson delivering things to make S's workstation look busy.

Ludya
Nothing for you to worry about, Gela.

Gela
If Griff has seen a stranger in the studio who slips away by the back door—before he has to clear away empty wine bottles—it's something for me to worry about. You can't get sloppy about following studio protocols, you just can't.

Jonathan
I'll make sure no one else comes in. It was probably nothing.

Gela
Where is Suzie anyway?

Jonathan
London. Just for the day. She has fires to put out.

Gela
Makes a change from starting them. I'll have to mention the stranger to her on Doodle to cover my back, if Griff escalates it.

RH WhatsApp group members Ludya Parak, Suzie Danners, Jonathan Danners, and Gela Nathaniel, November 17, 2023:

Gela
Ludya, Jonathan tells me you're accepting a payment from Jem for doing her Assignment Three project. Is that true?

Ludya
What the fuck, J? What's the problem if I have a side hustle?

Jonathan
You're pocketing a bribe to do someone else's college work. I've noticed and—if I was on this course for real—I'd say something like a shot.

Ludya
You'd snitch.

Gela
We need to have a discussion about it on Doodle.

Jonathan
It's not in the spirit of the MA.

Ludya
Snitching on me is not in the spirit of our actual working relationship.

Gela
Messaged you on Doodle, Ludya. Make your response sound spontaneous and defensive.

Suzie
It's not like Jem can do the 2D herself. If I was her, I'd ask for special consideration to skip it altogether.

Ludya
I'm a good graphic designer. Gela wants all her MA students to do well, and if Jem submits an amazing 2D project, I don't see what the problem is.

Jonathan
I'm not saying it's not up to Gela to decide. This course is a means to an end. You're being PAID to focus on the real task, not work a "side hustle."

Gela

The message is up on Doodle now.

Ludya

If the "real task" paid me enough to cover rent and support my family, I wouldn't have to take on extra work. If Jem won't ask for a more appropriate project, then I'm happy to help her overcome her limitations.

Gela

She's determined not to submit a special-consideration form for the entirety of the course. She doesn't identify as having a disability, and we have to respect that. Please respond to the message on Doodle, Ludya.

Jonathan

But it's OK for her to pay someone to complete a project on her behalf? Fraud. Unbelievable. Make your Doodle answers sound angry, Luds.

Ludya

I've responded to the fucking message and I AM angry, FFS!

Gela

Thank you. As a student with a registered disability, Jem is within her rights to request additional help with her coursework. I see her enlisting Ludya to do so as perfectly reasonable—in essence. But thank you, Jonathan, for flagging this on Doodle.

Ludya

Yeah, thanks, comrade.

WhatsApp chat between Gela Nathaniel and Cameron Wesley, November 21, 2023:

Gela

This is your second ungraded assignment. Your work isn't worthy of even a discretionary pass—what's wrong?

Cameron

Lots on. Other work. I only need to go with them to Somerset, then I can relax.

Gela

You can't! We agreed you'd do the whole course and write me a testimonial for the corporate side.

Cameron

You write it and say it's from me.

Gela

They agreed to stay on the course whatever happens. If they can, you can.

Cameron

Can't make any promises. It depends.

Gela

On what? You'll stop them doing whatever they're planning, won't you?

Cameron

It's complicated. Not necessarily a case of stopping these people. Sometimes it means just watching them. Getting a feel for their capabilities and power structure. We often let them get away with things because it leads to something bigger and better. You can lose the battle if it means you win the war.

Gela

I don't understand that, but I know I have four—including you—students who have agreed to complete my course WHATEVER. For that, I need you chatting with them about your work on Doodle, sleeves-up in the studio, and engaged. You don't have to be good. In fact be bad, but BE THERE.

RH WhatsApp group members Ludya Parak, Suzie Danners, Jonathan Danners, and Gela Nathaniel, November 30, 2023:

Ludya

That Doodle group is a festering pit of jealousy and resentment.

Gela

I'm shocked you weren't more careful.

Jonathan

We thought we were alone at the sink. Pat must've been skulking. It was only a peck on the cheek.

Ludya

But after the fire, it looks kinda weird. Like J's a masochist or something.

Suzie

If they think we're having an affair, it'll distract them from thinking anything else. *Especially* if there's something weird about it.

Gela

There's a difference between creating a distraction and causing such a stir that you become the entertainment people want to watch.

Ludya

Hard agree.

Suzie

It's no big deal.

Jonathan

We'll have a brief affair that fizzles out. I'm a troubled soul and Suzie's a free spirit, so it's not out of our characters, is it?

Suzie

People must have flings on these courses all the time.

Gela

Well, yes, they do, but Jem and Patrick seem particularly indignant that you're already married, Suzie. They don't know it's to Jonathan. We'll get over it, but if you can stop making out and start fizzling out, the course might settle down.

RH WhatsApp group members Ludya Parak, Suzie Danners, Jonathan Danners, and Gela Nathaniel, December 1, 2023:

Jonathan

Gela, can we talk about the final project, how we organize the team and what Mae has agreed?

Gela

I can meet you in the Aviator on Monday.

Suzie

Patrick or Jem might join us. Can you come to the house now?

Gela

Now? What's the address?

Ludya

Hey. It's meant to be a safe house. J, what do you think?

Suzie

Gela's hardly going to tell anyone.

Jonathan

I'll pick her up. She'll have to lie on the backseat.

Gela

I am not lying on any backseat.

Suzie

We've trusted her with other stuff, it doesn't matter if she knows where the house is.

Ludya

Can we take this convo irl?

Jonathan

OK. We've had a private discussion and I'll pick you up from RH on Monday afternoon. The other MMAMs won't be in. You close your eyes when I tell you to. We trust you.

Gela

Thank you.

Jonathan

BUT you can't bring your phone—or anything electronic. Smartwatch, tablet, e-reader.

Gela

Where do I leave them?

Suzie

In the tray outside the studio?

WhatsApp chat between Gela Nathaniel and Cameron Wesley, December 1, 2023:

Gela
They're taking me to their house.

Cameron
I'll give you a chip.

Gela
Not if it's something they could scan me and detect. I'll try to remember landmarks.

Cameron
I've got something they won't have the tech to ID.

WhatsApp chat between Jonathan Danners and Gela Nathaniel, December 1, 2023:

Jonathan
Are you home safely? Not shaken up?

Gela
It would take more than that to shake me up. Whose house is it?

Jonathan
It's rented. Temporary. Forget you were ever there.

Gela
AetherGen must have a lot of resources if they can afford to rent a house. Is it a short-term contract or an Airbnb?

Jonathan
Gela, you're an art teacher, not a secret agent. We're all clear now on Somerset and how the team will be organized. Thank you. All roads lead to Thorney Coffin.

RH WhatsApp group members Ludya Parak, Suzie Danners, Jonathan Danners, and Gela Nathaniel, December 6, 2023:

Suzie
Your face, Luds! Couldn't stop laughing.

Jonathan
You OK, Ludya?

Gela
Are you injured?

Ludya
A fellow student threw a piece of unfired clay the size of a conker at me. I'm not terminally ill.

Suzie
She got you right between the eyes, and to be fair, that's dead impressive when you can't see shit.

Ludya
Yeah, unprovoked violence is hilarious when you're not the victim, Suze.

Gela
She was demonstrating something fascinating. Sound is multidimensional, so she can judge where your forehead is by the sound coming from your mouth. I wonder if her brain balances lack of sight by utilizing a function we've forgotten we ever had, like echolocation? They say the body compensates for deficits in the senses.

Suzie
So in selecting a stooge who can't see, you accidentally got us one with superpowers.

Gela
I didn't say that. In fact it's a problem for me that she doesn't want to acknowledge her disability, because she has additional needs and we all want to accommodate them.

Ludya
It's because you're so "accommodating" that she doesn't learn not to be so . . . Jem.

Gela

This is an open, inclusive course and we should all remember that Jem can't read body language or facial expressions. She doesn't see people's reactions to what she says and does, therefore she's more outspoken than most. The upside is: we always know what she's thinking and doing.

Ludya

I'm going to escalate my complaint to the department. It's only what anyone would do irl.

Jonathan

Absolutely not. It will draw attention to us.

Ludya

You let Suzie complain about the keypad.

Jonathan

Because it meant we could access the studio out of hours. If you kick off about a disabled student, it could jeopardize things. You take one for the team and DO NOT complain about Jem. That's an order.

Gela

She was only demonstrating the importance of sound to the human aesthetic experience.

Ludya

She could have got my eye! How can you talk about teamwork when you find violent bullying so hilarious/interesting?

Gela

She was making a point in her own way.

Jonathan

She is determined to get a binaural ASMR soundscape. She's not concerned with what the client does or doesn't want, and, as project leader, I'm walking a tricky line.

Ludya

Does it matter, either way? Jeez, we're not here to do an art course. Just let her pitch that idea! You're taking the whole thing way too seriously.

Jonathan

We have to get to Thorney Coffin. Jem could totally derail that if she convinces RD8 to have binaural sound—for which we can hire the equipment. There would be no reason for RD8 to invite us down there.

Gela

Mae has intended to invite you down there from the word go. Whatever Jem says in the pitch meeting, you're going. It's part of the course— visiting clients, working with them, etc.

Jonathan

You've not said that before.

Gela

I've had further chats with Mae since then. I don't tell you everything. Regarding Jem, let her speak at the pitch meeting, as I'm sure she will anyway. I can chat with Mae afterward.

Ludya

I don't want her at Thorney Coffin. It's too risky.

Gela

You have to take Cameron and Patrick. That's not negotiable. It's insurance against scrutiny.

Ludya

Fine, but not Jem. Jem does NOT come to Somerset. Full stop.

WhatsApp chat between Gela Nathaniel and Cameron Wesley, December 11, 2023:

Cameron

Mae is primed. Knows enough, anyway. Whatever idea they choose, the team will be invited to the museum.

Gela

Why not arrest them the minute they get there? Or NOW?

Cameron

Have you seen *Minority Report*? They haven't done anything yet. Strategy.

It's not in their interests to run this unit in. They'd rather neutralize their plans but keep them active. What are they like behind the scenes?

Gela
Every bit as infuriating as they are on the course. I can send you our WhatsApps.

Cameron
They communicate on WA? Yes, please send.

Gela
They don't give details, it might just be useful to you, re personality and hierarchy.

Cameron
Got them. Thanks. Don't let their apparent bungling fool you into thinking they aren't dangerous.

RH WhatsApp group members Ludya Parak, Suzie Danners, Jonathan Danners, and Gela Nathaniel, January 2, 2024:

Gela
Happy New Year!

Gela
OK, so you're not online over the holidays. FYI, Mae sent me a New Year's e-card. It means she sees me as more than a mere work acquaintance. Good news.

RH WhatsApp group members Ludya Parak, Suzie Danners, Jonathan Danners, and Gela Nathaniel, January 11, 2024:

Jonathan
How did Jem take the news that she isn't coming to Somerset?

Gela
I've devised a program of treats for the two of us. She'll be fine.

Suzie

We're also ditching Patrick and Cameron.

Gela

What? No! You need stooges, you said. That's why the three of them are on the course!

Suzie

Things change. It's too risky. J will redefine the sourcing team to us three.

Ludya

Pat and Cam won't be bothered.

Gela

That's not the point. I need Cameron to be there because he hasn't put in the hours yet. Pat has to go—he's in charge of sourcing. Surely you want them there to testify that nothing untoward happened?

Ludya

You don't know what we're planning to do, though, Gela.

Suzie

We could be planning to blow the place up, in which case we're saving the innocents by leaving them at home.

Ludya

Suze, stay vague, FFS.

Gela

It wouldn't be anything like that.

Suzie

If you don't know what we're planning to do, why are you so sure of what we're NOT going to do?

Jonathan

Let's keep focused. Gela, you're working to our old plans, but things have changed. I'll tell them, in my role as project manager.

WhatsApp chat between Gela Nathaniel and Cameron Wesley, January 11, 2024:

Gela

Bad news. You and Pat are bumped from the sourcing trip. They're going to Thorney Coffin on their own. Sorry, I tried, but they were beginning to sound suspicious.

Cameron

Don't compromise yourself by protesting too much. I'll speak to the boss, see if there's a way she can insist more of us go.

RH WhatsApp group members Ludya Parak, Suzie Danners, Jonathan Danners, and Gela Nathaniel, January 15, 2024:

Gela

You're still talking to the group as if everyone's going to Somerset except Jem. When will you tell Pat and Cam they aren't invited?

Jonathan

Changed our minds again. It'll be better to have a couple of them there.

Ludya

To be fair, Cameron probably won't come, and Patrick's been so down these last few days he could cry off too. You might have to come instead, Gela.

Gela

I'm Jem-sitting, remember. Pat is uncomfortable with Suzie and Jonathan flaunting their relationship. He's a sensitive soul.

Suzie

Cool. He's focused on that. Seems I just can't keep my hands off my honey.

WhatsApp chat between Gela Nathaniel and Cameron Wesley, January 15, 2024:

Gela
When will this nightmare be over? They want you and Patrick on the trip to Somerset now. Don't know why they changed their minds, but they have.

Cameron
Probably a test.

Gela
Of what?

Cameron
Of you. To see if you've really chosen three innocent stooges to cover their tracks, or whether you've turned double agent and betrayed them to a corporate PI. Looks like you passed.

Gela
How can you tell?

Cameron
You're still messaging me.

Message group: 2024 Examiners, May 30, 2024

Ben Sketcher
That trip to Somerset was planned all along.

Karen Carpenter
What's happening there, Ben?

Ben Sketcher
I'm still reading the stuff Gela sent me.

Karen Carpenter
Has the event started?

Ben Sketcher
People are joining the line. Suited people RD8 want to impress with free wine and nibbles.

Karen Carpenter
And here I am, watching a pasta bake spin around in the microwave. We're in the wrong jobs, Ben!

Ben Sketcher
The final essays all point to something happening at Thorney Coffin that changes the dynamics of the course. Jem thought Alyson—really Suzie—didn't come back, and the rest covered, but we know now that's not what happened.

Karen Carpenter
Who have you seen so far?

Ben Sketcher
Jem and Patrick. Patrick said Gela "opened the head and found it," so he'll send me his real essay. Not the one he submitted, or "the one they made him write for Cameron."

Ben Sketcher
He handed me something and said it would give me access to the staff entrance. It's a small transparent resin cube. In this light, I can't quite work out what's inside it.

Karen Carpenter

A paperweight? Be careful. You don't want the powers that be thinking you accepted a gift from a student!

Karen Carpenter

Everything OK? I only meant they might think it was a bribe, that's all.

Ben Sketcher

There's something horrible inside it.

Karen Carpenter

A dead scorpion again? They're bad enough alive, but something about the way they curl up—ew, they're even worse dead.

Ben Sketcher

It's a human finger.

Royal Hastings, University of London
Multimedia Art MA
Final Project

Candidate name: Patrick Bright
Candidate number: 0883480

What I could have done differently:
I said how badly the burglary shook me up. It took me all the way back to Schull and the reason I left, back in '88. My man Finn and I, we were twenty and drifting. Our friends had gone off to uni or were working, but neither of us had found our thing yet. We'd pick up casual work and hang out. Anyway we were drinking by the harbor one night and got talking with a chap, the way you do. Schull attracts outsiders. A stranger in town is no big deal. We all have a joke and a laugh. This fella says he's just been paid and stands every round.

Heaven knows how we get on the subject. I think we said how we always end up talking about getting away, making big plans, but in the morning we simply don't wake up in time. At some point he says if we take a suitcase over the water for his friend, we'll get a big pay-out. We're young, but we know better than to agree to something like that. Except this chap has a way about him. Between that and the drink, we find ourselves saying, "Yeah, we'll do it," even though something isn't right. Soon as we agree, the chap nips off to use the payphone and I take Finn aside.

"Finny, let's go home, we don't know him."

Finn says, "Don't worry, Seany, we're not stupid. We'll not turn up to do the job."

But the chap hurries back, drains his pint, and says, "Right you are, lads, let's go" and that was it, he expected us to leave with him.

I said, "No, no, my ma and da will wonder where I'm at."

"Not to worry," he says. "I'll take you home, you explain you're going to England for a couple of days."

There's suddenly another fellow with us and we're put in the back of a two-door car. I'd only ever left Cork for family weddings, but suddenly I had to convince my folks I was setting off for England. Finn had to do the same with his da. As he came out of the cottage, his face was white. Mine probably the same. We'd just gone to the harbor for a pint, and now what?

As they drove us away from town I tried to catch Finn's eye, but he was staring out the window. He may have been crying. I know I watched the lights shrink in the rearview mirror and wondered whether I'd seen them for the last time.

In the middle of the night we arrive at an empty cottage, who knows where. We walk in and there's a whole room full of scary fellows who watch as Finn and I are searched. Pockets, sleeves, trousers, as if we might be carrying weapons. The guy who got talking to us and his friend had melted away. Never saw them again.

That's when it occurs to me that we don't have passports or any other ID. How can we get to England? I don't feel much better, because of course these guys must know that. Sure enough, a fellow with his hood up and a scarf around his face barks questions: name, address. Doesn't write anything down.

"Sean and Finbar. Couldn't make it up, eh." His accent sets my heart thumping. Those distinctive tones of the North. Then he stares Finn and me in the eyes, one after the other.

"Ah, you're the handsome one, sure enough!" he says to me, and they all laugh. "Hope there's a match for you in this gallery of rogues."

He takes out a stack of folded cardboard documents, official-looking and worn, shuffles through them like so many playing cards, holds a couple up to my face until one hits the spot.

"Good to meet you, Patrick Bright." He moves to Finny, does the same. "So you're the lucky one! We have a Finbar O'Leary. You get to keep your first name." With that, he pushes the documents into our shaking hands.

"Temporary passports," he says and I study the face in the picture. It's not me, but in low light and with a seal stamped half across it, perhaps it could be.

"You might not even need them," he purrs, "but if anyone asks for ID, you shrug and slip these out your pockets like you're not

bothered to be asked. Now you can do that for us, lads, can't yers."
It wasn't a question.

I see Finn open his passport. His hands are shaking.

We're herded back outside, as cases are loaded into an old Ford
Escort. All the time they're hissing instructions to us, and I hope to
God Finn's listening because I hear nothing over the blood roaring
in my ears. A thread of hope occurs to me . . .

"We's been drinking. We don't want no accident in your car."

One of the guys chuckles. "You'll soon sober up on the road."

Finn is in the driving seat and I'm passenger. They hand us tickets for the 7 a.m. crossing and shove car documents into the glove
compartment. "Put your foot down," someone says. "It won't wait
for yers."

"How do we get to the ferry from here?" I don't recognize Finn's
voice, or was it mine?

"You follow us."

So we trail after a big old Granada and behind us was another car
that stuck to our bumper like glue, right up to the ferry port at Rosslare. That was the longest drive of my life, but it was over all too soon.
Whenever I drive in the dark now, it reminds me of that night.

We pass through the barrier and hand our documents over with
the tickets. I pray the inspector notices something wrong and says,
"Wait, this passport's a fake—these men shouldn't leave the country," but he doesn't. He glances at them, then shoves them back
at us. This could be our last chance to escape. I see the two cars,
parked up, watching and waiting. One on each side, so whatever
way we try to make a break for it, we can't. The scary chaps have
done this before.

Finn whispers, "Seany, if we're searched when we land and there's
guns or Semtex in those cases, we're finished . . ."

"We'll chuck the cases overboard halfway across."

"What do we say to the fellows waiting on us?"

"That someone must've done it while we were up on deck."

"It won't wash. They might be shadowing us on board too."

"We leave the car on the ferry and make a run for it on foot on
the other side."

"We've got no money, Sean. The fellows took every penny when they searched us and said we'd get paid once their friends pick up the cases."

He was right. We didn't have enough for a cup of tea on the boat.

"You think they'll pay us? What's to stop them taking the cases and . . ."

"They wouldn't do that. Why would they do that?"

"Is the car bugged? Are they listening to us now?"

We're silent for a long time. The car rolls forward, dips, and clatters as it drives up the ramp and we literally leave the beautiful, blessed Irish soil behind.

"What time is our return ticket, Finny?"

"Do you have a return ticket, Seany? Because I don't have a return ticket."

I didn't have a return ticket. Perhaps that, for me, is the moment all this started.

Documents sent to me by Gela Nathaniel:

RH WhatsApp group members Jonathan Danners, Suzie Danners, Ludya Parak, and Gela Nathaniel, January 16, 2024:

Gela

How's the trip going? Weather nice?

Gela

Would be handy to have an update. Jem says hi.

Gela

Did RD8 have the old components for you?

WhatsApp chat between Gela Nathaniel and Cameron Wesley, January 16, 2024:

Gela

Sourcing trip going as planned?

Gela

Hope you're enjoying yourselves while Jem and I are hard at work.

Gela

Send an update as soon as you can. Kiss-kiss.

WhatsApp chat between Cameron Wesley and Gela Nathaniel, January 16, 2024:

Cameron

Museum visited. Bags of junk collected. Having din-dins at Spoons next to motel.

Gela

All go to plan?

Cameron

Mission accomplished. Badly need to crash. Dog-tired.

Gela

Kiss-kiss.

Cameron

Kiss-kiss.

Royal Hastings, University of London
Multimedia Art MA
Final Project

Candidate name: Alyson Lang
Candidate number: 0883484

What went right:
Thorney Coffin isn't just a museum. The old radios are a diversion. They give staff something to do when the whole point of the place is to do absolutely nothing. I doubt everyone who works there knows the truth. They probably bring visitors to look around from time to time. It helps to have people who can say, "Well, I was there and it was nothing out of the ordinary."

We wanted to expose them. Shame them in front of the world. But plans change. What went right was that we got in and found the room. All thanks to our inside woman, whose alcoholism made her easy to manipulate. She got us the maps and codes we needed. It was easy. Way too easy.

What went wrong:
We'd been planning this for so long that, when I saw it there, tiny and innocent-looking, I couldn't help myself. It suddenly felt pointless to take photographs, so I took the whole thing. A moment's impulse. Why do I act like that? Always have. Was that the start, or had the chain of events already begun? Because we'd all been focused on the same thing, then that night in Somerset we spun off in different directions. Until the RD8 event, when we'll come together again. But by the time you read this, Gela, we'll be long gone.

Documents sent to me by Gela Nathaniel:

WhatsApp chat between Gela Nathaniel and Cameron Wesley, January 16, 2024:

Cameron

Jem, the little minx, has booked us all in one room!

Gela

I've asked and she says it's a big room with six beds.

Cameron

A double and four bunks.

Gela

Oh no! Well, mistakes in online bookings are easily made, even if you're not visually impaired.

Cameron

Mistake? Look, we'll sort something out. It'll be fine.

Royal Hastings, University of London
Multimedia Art MA
Final Project

Candidate name: Patrick Bright
Candidate number: 0883480

Finn and I spend the trip from Rosslare to Fishguard too scared to even feel seasick. What can we do? We assume every soul on board is there to spy on us, make sure we do the job. Are we being watched?

Finn says his da will be getting up for work now. He'd been surprised when Finn told him he was going to England, out of the blue like that, but when Finn said he was going with me, his da relaxed. Said, "OK, you do it, lads. Now or never. While you can." The last thing he said was, "Don't get in trouble. Look after each other over there."

I stand on the deck and watch the port get closer and closer with a fearsome nagging dread in my heart. When Finn's shaking hand points to a row of police cars along the dock-front, my blood runs icy cold. Lined up. Like they're waiting for a pair of soft fools to land their car full of weapons and explosives on British soil.

"What you gonna do, Seany?" Finn has lost the quiver in his voice.

"Act like nothing's wrong. What else can we do?"

"Call 999. Or jus' walk up to one of them there. Say your friend Finn got you a passport and ticket and now you're lost."

"Why'd I need to say that? You'll be there. Anyways, we could tell the truth."

The ferry gets nearer the dock. That row of white, red, and yellow cars. Dark uniforms pacing about, waiting for us.

"The truth? Are you out of it? If they there don't hammer you, the fellas back home will. Don't tell the truth, Seany. Promise, now. Here . . ." and he slips something into my pocket. When I look, it's his fake passport. Why give that to me?

A horn blows, deafening above us. A distant announcement to

get back to our cars. One of the police officers on the shore catches my eye and leaps out of his skin, drops the file he's carrying, wavers on his feet. Same time my heart sinks. The guy shouts to his fellows and points right at me.

"Oh no, Finny. Look, they *are* waiting on us. We're done."

I turn, but Finn's gone. Where'd he go?

The police in Fishguard were very nice. Even back then, in 1988, when you'd think things would be rougher. No, they sat me in the station with a cup of tea, food, a blanket, and the very same fellow I'd seen drop his file on the dock.

He was shook up, they said, and chatting with me helped. It was him who told me when they recovered Finn's body. I was at the station all day. Silent with real shock most of the time, except later to answer questions. Thing is, the chap said how the police cars are always there that time of day. The officers have their tea break and chat about their mornings. There was no need for Finn to have done that to himself. I was devastated.

Finally, they said, "OK, you can go on your way." I said "How?" But they'd only brought the car off the ferry for me. It was waiting outside. My hands shook as I unlocked it, climbed in. Dead inside. Where were the suitcases? Where were the guys they said would be waiting for us?

No one stopped me as I drove away, no one waved me down, no car followed me. No one had even once looked at the passports. As I got out of town I turned north, through the rounded hills of Wales, across the border and on to Glasgow, where there was a distant cousin of my ma's sister-in-law. A terrible call home told me the news about Finny had arrived in town and shook it up. It meant everyone was eager to help. Ma called the distant cousin. I got to a housing estate and parked in their drive. It wasn't until nightfall I dared look inside the suitcases.

No guns, no Semtex. Just two battered bricks of heroin wrapped in second-hand clothes. It didn't look like the work of a multimillion-dollar organization, or even a small but smooth operation. The police on the dock, Finn's accident, the furor afterward scared them away. Finn surely hoped that would happen.

Jonathan and Ludya had created a diversion in the museum while Alyson slipped away through a door hidden in the panelled walls. I should have known. I knew all about diversions, after Fishguard.

What was that radio she took? Jem examined it. She'd done a course in electronics, and because she's used to reading braille, she knows her way around a circuit board. While she was focused on that, she didn't ask what happened in Somerset. Didn't ask where Alyson was, not until much later.

Documents sent to me by Gela Nathaniel:

WhatsApp chat between Mae Blackwell and Gela Nathaniel, May 30, 2024:

Mae
We're starting the presentation soon. I was hoping you could round up your group and make your way to the kitchen.

Gela
Sorry. Not well.

Mae
Oh no. Could you ask Jonathan to get everyone together? I can't. I'm backstage with the speakers.

Gela
Does it matter if we hear the presentation? It can't be that secret.

Mae
ICES isn't secret, not once we launch it. But it looks better if staff aren't standing around, don't you think? I can see a crowd gathered around the head. They'll have time to experience it afterward. Could you ask Jonathan to usher people through to the function room?

Gela
No, Mae, I won't.

WhatsApp chat between Jem Badhuri and Ben Sketcher, May 30, 2024:

Jem
Is Patrick with you, Ben? People are moving into the auditorium and we can't find him.

Ben
He was here a few minutes ago. I saw him go back past security. What's wrong with him?

Jem
You mean, why is he so sad and low? I've no idea. You'd think, with Alyson having turned up, he'd be happy.

Ben
You mean Suzie Danners—the student you've known as Alyson Lang.

Jem
Yes, but Jonathan said she self-IDs on this course as Alyson and that her real name is none of my business. I can't really argue with that.

Ben
Is she there now?

Jem
Yes, but if I'm honest, she doesn't seem herself.

Ben
Could it be her sister, the real Alyson?

Jem
No. Her voice is her voice, if you know what I mean. But she sounds exhausted. As if she hasn't slept in ages, and smells as if she hasn't had a bath for just as long. I also overheard a man's voice say, "Look at the state of her" and another replied, "Must be one of the art students." Rude.

Ben
How's Jonathan?

Jem
All fired up for the event, same as Ludya and me. Patrick and Alyson have done hardly any meeting and greeting.

Ben

OK, well, it looks as if they're getting ready for the presentation.

Jem

Good. The catering staff have saved some canapés for us. I've been looking forward to them all evening. Are you sure you can't come in and see the installation?

Ben

I'll wait out here until the time is right. Thanks, Jem.

Metropolitan Police digital evidence log/Case no. 4617655/24/files retrieved September 5, 2024

WhatsApp chat between Ludya Parak and Jonathan Danners, January 17, 2024:

Ludya
It's in the store cupboard, behind some boxes underneath the bottom shelf. No one will find it there. What did you do with the body?

Jonathan
There was a roll of fabric propped up in the corridor. Wrapped it in that and dragged it to the bins.

Ludya
That's material for the tunnel. Gela and Jem will be looking for it—if Griff and Rita don't first.

Jonathan
It's got blood and dirt on it now. Shit!

Ludya
Unwrap it, screw it up, and chuck it by the bins. Make it look vandalized and thank fuck the art department is so underfunded there's no CCTV.

Jonathan
This fucking phone.

Ludya
Dump it in the bins with the body.

Jonathan
We can't leave it for a second. It has tech I've never seen before. You're our techie, you need to see this.

Ludya
Look under Settings. There must be a way to change the level of security.

Jonathan

We're trying but haven't found it yet. Shit, shit. It'll be light soon. We'll have to take the body back to the house.

Ludya

I'll come around the side, leave the door unlocked.

Royal Hastings, University of London
Multimedia Art MA
Final Project

Candidate name: Patrick Bright
Candidate number: 0883480

I lay low in Glasgow for weeks. I wore the secondhand clothes I found in the suitcase and told the family at home I didn't want anyone coming looking for me, and to say I was in Manchester. Didn't even go to Finny's funeral. Ma's cousins left me alone in their annex, and I got by selling little bags of heroin to fellows on the streets.

I was no big-shot dealer. Whenever I ran short of cash, I went out to the car and chopped a bit off the block to sell. I had no idea how much it was worth and probably sold short, but it was just to get by.

After a while the local dealers got wise to me, and I told the cousins I was going to Newcastle. I drove straight to King's Lynn instead. Saw it on a road sign and liked the name. Turned out King's Lynn had a heroin problem too. I stayed in B&Bs and did the same, to pay the rent and buy food. It was survival. I was dead inside the whole time. I drove from city to city, town to town. Never staying anywhere longer than a couple of months. It got that I could turn up anywhere and know where the junkies would be. Could spot them even when they weren't huddled in doorways, under piers, or in parking lots. I went in, did my business, and hopped out before the regular chaps got territorial. And that's how I lived for the best part of a year and a half. But eventually the second block started to run down. I finally turned the car toward London.

How I got the job at Modern Art is a miracle, or luck, or Finny was looking down on me and pulling strings. I was parked up in a backstreet as the sun came up one morning. You could drive right into London in those days, with no ANPR and no Congestion Charge. I'd just sold the last of my brick to the junkies behind Leicester Square and was wondering where I could go from there. Saw an old man struggling to carry a box into the back of a shop and jumped out to give him a hand. It was an art shop, and we got talking about Schull and the artists who lived there. I showed him my little sketchbook.

By sunset I had a job in the shop, a room in the back where I kept an eye on the stock overnight, and even a parking space down the alley. Got rid of the dodgy Escort with its Irish number plates as soon as I could, settled in with a proper job contract and tenancy agreement. And there I stayed. Too scared to go home. Not even for Ma's and Da's funerals. Too scared to go anywhere.

Those were different times and the temporary passport served me well. That and the old boy's lack of attention to detail in his paperwork. Patrick Bright got a bank account, then another. Enough to get by and yet not enough to get back. Even now, there's nothing I want more than to return. I simply don't know if I can.

When the masked men crashed through the back door, my blood ran as cold as if I'd died. Was this it? The scary chaps finally tracked me down to make me pay for stealing their goods? Or simply my payback for not saving Finn, not reaching out to stop him jumping over the rail. Not being there in that split second he needed me.

I saw something in them, despite the masks. Junkies desperate for cash and chemicals. Thought an art shop would have both. When they didn't find either, they smashed the place up, scared the girls. Police said we were lucky and told us to get CCTV "for next time."

All our regular customers got to hear what happened. Some sent flowers and cakes. After a bit, Gela mentioned her new MA. The girls were all for it, said I needed something to take my mind off things. How did they know what my mind was on? The guy that Finn and I spoke to at the harbor, the men who drove us, Ma and Da looking at me, their sad, worried faces in the glow from the TV. Finn's da through the cottage window as we sat trapped in the back of the two-door car. His eyes.

I didn't know what had gone on at the radio museum and didn't care. If Jonathan had got himself tangled up with a woman who treated him like she treated his Assignment One model, it was his call. I'd had a drink and wanted to get my head down. Then we found out about the super family room. I said I'd sleep in the minivan and suggested Cameron come too, but he was on his phone and didn't reply. I went to the bathroom to take a leak and to throw water on my face. The pipes were noisy. It wasn't until I switched the tap off that I heard raised voices next door. Cameron. Ludya. Alyson. Jonathan.

Message group: 2024 Examiners, May 30, 2024

Karen Carpenter
A human finger? You're having me on!

Ben Sketcher
Set in a block of clear resin. It's been dried.

Karen Carpenter
No! It'll be something else. Who'd want a dried finger as an ornament?

Ben Sketcher
Someone who needs the fingerprint to activate a biometric device.

Karen Carpenter
That's impossible.

Ben Sketcher
Not at all. You pour a layer of clear resin into a mold and allow it to set. Then place the dried finger on top and press or weight it, so the fingerprint is fully visible. Then pour the remaining resin on top to seal it.

Karen Carpenter
Do people do that? I've gone all cold.

Ben Sketcher
They probably drained the finger of blood, then cauterized the stump with a soldering iron. The fingerprint is very clear. I know it can bypass biometric security software because it fooled the technology at RD8 just now.

Karen Carpenter
Why did Patrick have a finger in resin? He sounds like such a nice man.

Tilda Ricci
Sorry, folks. I've been at a formal dinner and unable to check messages. I see you two have been busy. Have I missed anything?

Karen Carpenter

Scroll back ONLY if you've finished eating, Tilda. Ben will fill you in on the MMAM's event!

Karen Carpenter

Looks like he's gone offline. Don't blame him. Feel a bit queasy myself.

WhatsApp chat between Mae Blackwell and Gela Nathaniel, May 30, 2024:

Mae

There's a gentleman in the foyer who introduced himself as the examiner for your course. We didn't agree an examiner could come, did we? I've no idea how he got past security without an invite.

Gela

No, but I think Jem may have invited him through Central. She said something loaded about how great it would be if the external examiner could see the installation.

Mae

And it's very hard to say no to Jem, I understand. Well, I'm not sure how he managed to get in, but he can wait in the kitchen area and "examine" everything after our presentation. We're about to start.

Metropolitan Police digital evidence log/Case no. 4617655/24/files retrieved September 5, 2024

WhatsApp chat between Patrick Bright and Jonathan Danners, January 17, 2024:

Patrick
What should I do?

Jonathan
Go home. Go to bed.

Patrick
What about Cameron's family? He had a wife.

Jonathan
He told us he had an ex-wife. We don't know if anything he said was true. He wasn't a burned-out city suit, he was a PI. We've only just started going through his phone and already we can see he worked for the government, security agencies, and big financial institutions.

Patrick
Is it too late to call the police?

Jonathan
After all we've done to cover for you? Patrick—do not go to the police. These WhatsApp messages will be picked over, for a start.

Patrick
Didn't mean it to happen. Thought he was going for Ludya. Simply wanted to stop him.

Jonathan
That's not even self-defense. You'll get life. Anyway it's too late now to chew over what should or shouldn't have happened. It's done and we move forward.

Patrick
What do I say to people?

Jonathan
We discovered we were all booked in one room. It caused a row over who

had which bed. We decided to sober up, got a Breathalyzer test from the petrol station, and when one of us tested negative at midnight, we drove home. The last bits are true anyway—except you say it was Cameron who drove, not me.

Patrick

But what happens next?

Jonathan

There's a straightforward, logical solution. We just have to put our heads together.

Patrick

Can't thank you enough for all you're doing to help me.

Jonathan

Don't thank us. You're one of the team. And it's your responsibility too. Think of a solution to this problem. In the meantime, go into Royal Hastings and keep Jem occupied.

Patrick

Why was Cam going to hit Ludya? What happened while I was in the bathroom?

Jonathan

Patrick, focus on what you have to do.

Doodle message group MMAM(FTP), May 30, 2024:

Jem Badhuri
THE EXAMINER IS HERE! I didn't want to say anything earlier, but I invited the external examiner and he's come!

Ludya Parak
How did he get through the gate? They wouldn't even let our driver in.

Jem Badhuri
I don't know, but he's excited to meet the whole MA group.

Jonathan Danners
Not everyone is here, though, are they?

Jem Badhuri
I know you're here, Jonathan, and Patrick and Ludya. I didn't think Alyson would come, but she's here after all. That just leaves Cameron.

Patrick Bright
Cameron is here. He's been here the whole time.

Ludya Parak
Cameron is sick.

Jonathan Danners
He's on another job somewhere. He left the course. Gela just didn't want to say.

Gela Nathaniel
Cameron is dead, Jem.

Jem Badhuri
What? No! He didn't even see the installation. I'm gutted. I had no idea he was that ill.

Gela Nathaniel
He wasn't that ill. He wasn't ill at all. I see now.

Gela Nathaniel
Why he was suddenly on another job. Why he missed his son's sports day.

Gela Nathaniel

Why, in the paperweight Patrick made for Cameron, the scorpion is dead.

Gela Nathaniel

But who did Patrick give the killer scorpion to? The one poised to strike?

Gela Nathaniel

It happened when you went to Somerset, didn't it, Jonathan, Suzie, Ludya?

Royal Hastings, University of London
Multimedia Art MA
Final Project

Candidate name: Patrick Bright
Candidate number: 0883480

As I come out the bathroom door I see Cameron. His back is toward me and his arm raised to hit Ludya. He has a hold of her other arm, and she's shouting and crying. Alyson is on the floor as if she's already been thrown there. Jonathan is on the phone, shouting for someone. I see red. I don't think. I grab the iron and smash Cameron over the back of his head. He falls to the floor. Ludya scrambles away and I see what Cameron was after. An old radio. Didn't know it then, but I'd end up helping Jem tinker with it. It kept her occupied, stopped her asking questions about what happened on the trip.

We're standing around Cameron's body, and in the silence I remember: "Oh no, Finny. Look, they *are* waiting on us. We're done." They all look at each other: Jonathan, Alyson, and Ludya. They look at each other and at Cameron on the floor, not at me. The only eyes on me are Cameron's. They're frozen, so wide open his lids have disappeared into his forehead. Jonathan takes a breath to speak, but his voice is drowned out—by something I'd heard once before.

It sounds like a thousand fingernails down a thousand blackboards. The same alarm that cut through the studio during our first assessment meeting, when Alyson burned Jonathan's assignment. Back when we were all still putting our phones in the tray.

Ludya grabs it from Cameron's pocket, her sleeve over her hands. The sleek, shiny screen flashes a warning. I glimpse the word "police." Ludya squints sideways at it, like it's the head of Medusa and she could very well turn to stone. I'd soon find out why.

"Military-grade security," she shouts over the din, and she has a confidence that says she knows all about it. Doesn't mean he is military, but it *does* mean he has access. "It needs to see *his* face! No one else's!" The sound is unbearable in my ears.

There's a short tussle between Jonathan and Ludya as they try to switch the alarm off. Jonathan is adamant: "Cameron switched it off because Suzie switched it on that day in the studio." Suzie? In the fog of shock, I can't get past this new name. "Suzie who?" But they ignore me.

Ludya cries as she fumbles with the phone. Jonathan paces, covers his ears . . . I can only repeat the question, "Suzie who?"

It's then that Alyson picks herself up off the floor, her face fixed in an expression I've never seen before, on anyone. She grabs the phone from Ludya and holds it in front of Cameron's poor, dead face. Silence. A tiny click as the home screen lights up: a missed call from Angela Nathaniel and a timer in the top-right corner, shaped like a human face: five minutes and counting.

Metropolitan Police digital evidence log/Case no. 4617655/24/files retrieved September 5, 2024

AetherGen WhatsApp group members Ludya Parak, Suzie Danners, and Jonathan Danners, January 17, 2024:

Ludya

It's called "eco-cloth always-wipe" or something—look in the glove box. IT DOESN'T SWITCH OFF.

Jonathan

Cameron must've turned it off at night, he wasn't looking at it every five minutes. And he put it in the tray at RH. It was switched off then.

Ludya

He knew how to switch it off. *WE* DON'T KNOW HOW TO SWITCH IT OFF.

Jonathan

Fingerprint activation?

Ludya

Didn't work.

Jonathan

Let the battery run down.

Ludya

That's what I'm doing. FFS. Until then, it has to see his face every five minutes.

Jonathan

"Eco-clean forever-wipe." Coming back now. Will use rear door. Cameras at the front entrance.

Suzie

I'm going through his messages. You will not fucking believe this. We've been fucking set up. And that's not all—Gela's in on it. She's been liaising with Cameron all along. They say, "Kiss-kiss" all the fucking time!

Jonathan

Gela can't possibly know what it means. It's insider slang.

Suzie
She's being paid £60,000, and she'll get the same again when the course ends. He was on the course to spy on us!

Jonathan
She's getting £50,000 from us! She won't need her job at RH. With £170,000, that's her retirement right there.

Ludya
We shouldn't be having this convo on WhatsApp, FFS.

Suzie
I've replied to Gela as Cameron. Fucking RD8! They KNEW who we were. They let us in.

Suzie
Cameron calls Mae "the boss."

Jonathan
They must be able to track the phone. There's no way he's off-radar.

Ludya
Location services are switched off. He must've done that before he died.

Suzie
Can they still track it?

Ludya
We'll soon find out.

Doodle message group [Private] Jem and Gela, May 30, 2024:

Jem Badhuri

I'm so upset about Cameron. It's ruined the evening for me. I've texted my dad to pick me up early.

Gela Nathaniel

I'm upset too, Jem. We need to call the police, but not until after the presentation. Our client deserves their event to go well.

Jem Badhuri

If Cameron died in Somerset, why did Alyson disappear?

Gela Nathaniel

I really don't know.

Jem Badhuri

Who told you he was dead? How did you find out?

Gela Nathaniel

Where are you?

Jem Badhuri

In the kitchen with the staff. A lovely waiter has given me a plate of canapés. He thought I was crying because I couldn't find my way to the buffet. I'm stuffing my face, I'm so upset.

Gela Nathaniel

It's safest if you stay where there are other people. When I can stand without feeling nauseous, I'll come to you. But, Jem, promise me you won't look inside the head.

Jem Badhuri

Why not?

Gela Nathaniel

They—the others—put something in it.

Jem Badhuri

Well, they're determined to incinerate the head as soon as they can after the event, so whatever they put inside it will be destroyed too. What is it?

Gela Nathaniel

It's nothing. Really. Just the old radio from Thorney Coffin. But don't worry. I'll call 999 as soon as my hands stop shaking.

Jem Badhuri

They've had it all this time and never told me? Well, they'll burn it over my dead body!

Gela Nathaniel

JEM, STAY AWAY FROM THE HEAD.

Royal Hastings, University of London
Multimedia Art MA
Final Project

Candidate name: Patrick Bright
Candidate number: 0883480

Jonathan told me Alyson's real name is Suzie and they've been married for years. If he mentioned why they pretended otherwise, then I didn't take it in. Time froze before that. Something else I discovered was that Jonathan's ma and sister died recently, not when he was a student. "If people think it happened ten years ago, they'll assume I've moved on," he explained. "They won't suspect it's driving me now."

Here's how innocent I was: I thought they were doing it all for me. That they'd seen me only trying to protect Ludya and didn't want me to go down for it. In return, I was that grateful I did whatever they told me. Over the weeks the truth came out. They belonged to an action group, agitators . . . They had a boss who gave them orders from afar, didn't get his own hands dirty. They weren't saving me, they were saving themselves.

Later I found out Cameron blew up at Ludya because she wouldn't give him the radio from RD8. Suzie wasn't meant to steal it at all, just take photographs as evidence—so they could expose some toxic technology. Only Suzie couldn't help being Suzie and went that step too far.

At last I acted. I did something in time. That's what I learned on this course. I didn't do it on the ferry with Finn. I didn't do it when the robbers tied up the girls and hit them. But I took action in that motel room. That's what this course taught me.

Knowing that made the rest of it better over the following weeks. They encouraged me to keep Jem occupied, so she didn't notice Cameron and Suzie had gone. Staying happy and cheerful for Gela and the technicians, letting them think all I cared about was getting that installation made. Telling the girls in the shop how much I was enjoying the course. Visiting Jonathan and Suzie at the house. Seeing the rot set in. I don't mean the obvious. The rot that it did to them.

Suzie sat there in the back room, and every few minutes she showed the phone what it needed to see. Jonathan stayed in the front room with the radio, tuning in to the voice every day at the same time, hearing it say it was trapped, it needed help. It was Cameron's voice. We could all hear that. The unit somehow tuned in to his spirit, stuck in limbo. Is that what happens? You're trapped in your body when you die? Or only when you're killed unexpectedly? Jonathan believed that and he was our leader, so maybe because he was so convinced, so were we.

He stopped talking to the leader of their group. He focused on the unit, on trying to communicate with Cameron. I thought he was doing it so that I could apologize, explain. But there was no way to speak with that poor, sad voice.

Jonathan and I took it in turns to let Suzie get some sleep. Ludya refused, and I don't blame her. We dreaded it. Sitting in that ice-cold room, the hum of the freezer in the dark. The light as you opened the door. The little brush to dust ice particles off Cameron's eyes and a type of clear oil now and then to give them the appearance of life. That's what the phone recognizes, Ludya says: the eyes and structure of the facial bones. Cameron's phone, tethered to its charger.

We couldn't carry on like that, so it was only right that, when the time came, I took the next step for them.

Metropolitan Police digital evidence log/Case no. 4617655/24/files retrieved September 5, 2024

AetherGen WhatsApp group members Ludya Parak, Suzie Danners, and Jonathan Danners, January 17, 2024:

Ludya

So that didn't work. The phone is programmed to dial a number when the battery drops below 5%. We can't let it run out of charge and die.

Jonathan

OK. So what's the logical solution? Spell it out.

Ludya

Someone has to stay with the phone and the body. Make sure it can see his face, eyes open, every four to five minutes. The phone must be charged regularly, and emails, texts, and messages responded to.

Jonathan

Covert tracking?

Ludya

We'll only know when there's a knock on the door. Even in the absence of CT, they can trace the phone's whereabouts via triangulation.

Jonathan

So what we MUST do is stop Cameron's family, friends, clients, and colleagues suspecting he's missing and calling the police.

Ludya

Yep. Answering texts and messages is crucial. We must tell everyone exactly what they need to hear, so they don't wonder why Cameron hasn't showed.

Jonathan

And make sure the phone sees his face every five minutes. Good. Thanks, Ludya.

Ludya

It's logical—that's all.

Suzie

Just till we find a better solution.

Jonathan

And we'll think of it. Until then, we'll have to stop him rotting or the phone won't recognize his face. Patrick will help me put him in the freezer.

Suzie

Should we involve Patrick? He could crack any second.

Ludya

It's all his fault, so yep, we should.

Suzie

If you'd given Cameron the unit, he wouldn't have lunged for it, and Patrick wouldn't have thought he was about to hit you. It's your fault, Luds.

Ludya

If you'd just photographed the unit and not STOLEN it, Cameron wouldn't have tried to get it back and none of us would be here now.

Suzie

People needed to see the tech to believe it. Anything else wouldn't be enough.

Ludya

NOTHING IS EVER ENOUGH FOR YOU!!

Jonathan

What's done is done. We need to deal with THIS situation.

Ludya

NO WAY. That unit is NOT the atmospheric defense tech. It's all here on Cam's phone. They planted a DECOY for us to find. When we went public with the pics, they were going to reveal it as only a piece of junk. Discredit AetherGen completely.

Suzie

No. It was where she told me it would be, in the middle of its own room. All the right security around it. If it's a dud, then why did Cameron try so hard to get it back? You're right, it's not what we went there to find. But it's important tech of *some* kind. Has to be.

Jonathan
Look, we're a team and blame is collective. Let's move on. We need Patrick to distract Jem and make sure the MA project stays on track. Once that's over, the three of us can disappear. We just need to keep the phone happy every five minutes. It's only a few months, and I know how we can do it.

Ludya
Disappear? I've got two kids in school, an ex with issues, and my mom's on her own.

Jonathan
We'll think of solutions for them in due course. Our immediate problem is Cameron's phone.

Suzie
I'll do it. It's a human body. Nothing to be afraid of.

AetherGen WhatsApp group members Ludya Parak, Suzie Danners, and Jonathan Danners, February 9, 2024:

Suzie
What are you telling everyone about why I'm not there?

Ludya
Gela thinks you're working in the studio some nights but are busy doing other work. We're all telling Jem we've seen you and you're coming in regularly.

Jonathan
Jem loves tinkering with the decoy unit and thinks it's a radio—which it probably was once. Patrick's helping and keeping an eye on her. Everything's fine.

Ludya
Everything's fine? WTF?

AetherGen WhatsApp group members Ludya Parak, Suzie Danners, and Jonathan Danners, February 14, 2024:

Jonathan
WTF is that voice? The unit is a DECOY, a DUD. All Cameron's messages say so.

Ludya
It's massively freaky, Suze. Whatever Jem and Patrick did has activated it.

Suzie
I've just had a convo with Mae on Cam's phone. She doesn't say why, only that she wants it.

Jonathan
The phone call he took from her, right before it happened, made him break cover and seize it. She must've told him what it was and to get it back—fast.

Suzie
The first message I sent from his phone was to tell her everything's fine and not to worry. She replied, "Tell me you've got it?" and I replied, "I've got it."

Jonathan
That unit—if it's not the atmos defense tech, then what is it?

Ludya
Until Thorney Coffin, Mae's messages to Cameron clearly say it's a neutral piece of equipment to fool us. So why that voice, FFS? Can we ask Mae from Cameron's phone?

Suzie
No, because she told him what it was in that phone call. I can't pretend he doesn't know now without raising suspicion.

Ludya
Suze, what did your mole say about the location of the adt?

Suzie
Turn left along the corridor from the museum. Three doors along.

Ludya

Yet the security network runs clockwise. Based on the codes alone, I'd say the turn was right.

Suzie

She said left, so I turned left. Whatever this unit is, how can Jem or Patrick have got that voice out of it? She's blind, FFS, and has only done a basic electronics course. He needs help charging his phone.

Ludya

Don't underestimate Jem. She made her own testing circuit that emits sound rather than light. After just an introductory class? That's pretty awesome.

Suzie

We need to get the unit off them without winding Jem up. Then we can investigate the voice ourselves. Find out what it is we've got.

Jonathan

This is the plan: Suzie will continue to reassure Mae—as Cameron. She'll message Gela—again, as Cameron—and ask her to leave the unit at the rear doors. One of us can pick it up and bring it back to the house. Done. We get to examine the unit, and everyone is happy.

Ludya

Except Jem.

Jonathan

Gela will think of something to tell her.

Ludya

Until they realize Cameron isn't showing up.

Suzie

He's off-radar on a new job. He's messaging his clients and colleagues all the time. Everyone, including Gela, knows he coordinates a team of investigators, each working on different jobs. He'll assure Mae the unit is safe—and that'll give us time to work out what it is.

WhatsApp chat between Jonathan Danners, Ludya Parak, and Patrick Bright, February 14, 2024:

Jonathan
This is important, Patrick. When you worked on that old radio with Jem, could she have altered the tech?

Ludya
What Jonathan means is: could the voice be a recording, put there deliberately by Jem?

Patrick
I didn't want her touching anything electric so kept her away from the insides. Once I got power to it, we closed the case and played with the tuning dial. That's all.

AetherGen WhatsApp group members Ludya Parak, Suzie Danners, and Jonathan Danners, February 27, 2024:

Jonathan
Trying to fathom the workings of this thing. They're so old and delicate. It wouldn't surprise me if some of these were pure gold. The circuit was deliberately disabled and the case sealed, so it couldn't be plugged in and used. Jem and Patrick opened the case, saw where the cable had been stored, and wired a plug to it.

Ludya
We can't rule out the Jem factor.

Jonathan
There are no obvious modern additions to the old components. When Jem says she and Patrick "got the radio working," she means just that— they plugged it in. The result seems to be an unstable wavelength that's ultrasensitive to atmospheric activity.

Ludya
The voice, though.

Suzie

It's potentially a holding broadcast, like the old numbers stations. A channel they keep open with creepy mysterious shit that only spies can understand. So when they need it, it's there.

Jonathan

Give me some time. I'm going to try something.

* * *

Ludya

Did it work?

* * *

Jonathan

It worked. Shit!

Ludya

What?

Jonathan

The voice is Cameron's.

Ludya

WTF? No, it isn't.

Suzie

It is.

Jonathan

I recorded the broadcast and played it back using the technique Jem showed me when we worked on Assignment Four. It clarified the voice, and believe me, it's Cameron. He says something different every day and hasn't repeated himself yet.

Ludya

This has got to be Jem.

Suzie

Jem talks constantly about whatever she's doing, and she's never worked with Cameron. In fact she's said several times that he barely spoke to her. If he had, we'd know all about it.

Jonathan

It's my theory we're hearing what's left of his consciousness, trapped between life and death. That could be because he died suddenly and traumatically—or because we're keeping his body from decomposing. Then again, perhaps this is what happens to everyone.

Ludya

What the fuck? We need to get a grip. Get rid of the unit and the body.

Jonathan

Edison and Tesla both worked on devices to contact the dead. If either succeeded, then I have no trouble believing RD8 would have that unit in their collection.

Ludya

Suzie, come on. You don't believe this?

Ludya

Suze!

Ludya

Suzie!!

Suzie

I'm here. Had to do it again—only can't just open the door and hold the phone up. The eyes frost over. Have to brush them off and wet them. I don't know anything anymore, Luds.

Jonathan

He says he's trapped in a dark place and can't get out.

Ludya

Yes, the fucking freezer!

Jonathan

Chill out, as Patrick says.

Jonathan

RD8 were on to us from the moment we approached Gela with the idea, then the stuff with Cameron. But this is the solution we've been looking for. If we have a radio that tunes in to the Other Side, it's potentially bigger news than any atmospheric defense technology—and what's better still, this is tech we can SELL. This unit is our way out.

Ludya

The Other Side? Fuck, wherever that voice is, it's not heaven.

Suzie

That's why no one went public with the unit, Luds. It's not what anyone wants to hear, but that's not our problem.

Jonathan

Who knows what Cameron did in his past, right? He might deserve to be in hell. If a good person dies—ideally in a less traumatic manner—then we can test it.

AetherGen WhatsApp group members Ludya Parak, Suzie Danners, and Jonathan Danners, March 30, 2024:

Suzie Danners

There's something wrong. It's defrosting.

Ludya Parak

Fuck no! What? What's happening, J?

Jonathan Danners

The freezer is dying, I noticed the motor roaring last night. It can't cope with being opened so often.

Suzie Danners

We need a new freezer, and fast. Yesterday fast.

Ludya Parak

It's past five on Easter Saturday, FFS! The shops are all closed tomorrow and Monday.

Jonathan Danners

I'll call Patrick. It's about time he was useful.

WhatsApp chat between Patrick Bright and Jonathan Danners, March 30, 2024:

Patrick
Entry point for an upright is nearly £500 but there's a cheap chest for £250. The staff are waiting to close up.

Jonathan
Get the BEST upright (freezer only, not fridge-freezer). Don't worry about price. Buy the one in the shop, so you can bring it here NOW. Use your charm, Pat; the staff will help you load it into the car.

Patrick
It's coming in at £709, after £150 off for light shop-soiling. What shall I do? These guys really want to get home.

Jonathan
Good. They won't ask questions. I'll be at the door when you arrive.

Patrick
Guess I'll put it on my card then.

AetherGen WhatsApp group members Ludya Parak, Suzie Danners, and Jonathan Danners, March 31, 2024:

Ludya
FFS tell me everything went OK.

Suzie
OK. The new freezer was cold enough by eleven last night. Between the three of us, we transferred him, and so far, so good.

WhatsApp chat between Ludya Parak and Jonathan Danners, April 17, 2024:

Ludya
I'm shitting myself. I've got kids, FFS.

Jonathan

Just make the components, do the assignments, and get the course done. Don't raise suspicions. I'm experimenting with this tech, trying to tune it. If it can be tuned, then perhaps I could tune in to Mom and Sophia.

Ludya

You MUST get rid of it.

Jonathan

We can't get rid of it while the voice is still coming through.

Ludya

I mean THE BODY!

Jonathan

But the body being so close could be precisely why it's picking up his voice. I'm spending every night tinkering with the unit and keeping the phone working while Suzie sleeps, so we can all get out of this hell. We'll get there, Luds. We're in this together.

Ludya

J, listen to me. We must DO SOMETHING NOW.

Jonathan

DO THE FUCKING MA COURSE AND KEEP YOUR MOUTH SHUT.

WhatsApp chat between Ludya Parak and Patrick Bright, April 17, 2024:

Ludya

S and J have lost it.

Patrick

How could they lose it? She can't leave it for more than five minutes.

Ludya

THEIR MINDS, FFS.

Ludya

Did you see him when you took the new freezer around?

Patrick

I did, God help me.

Ludya
How can they do it?

Patrick
They're used to it now. Denial is very powerful.

Ludya
Patrick, what can we do? I'm going out of my mind, and all I do is feed the kids and make components for the tunnel and computer graphics and shit for the course, like my life isn't about to end any moment.

Patrick
I have an idea how to get rid of the body and still keep the phone active. I've been studying resin and how to preserve organic things in it. I've been gathering what I need from RH, although after Gela's email yesterday I'll have to source some things myself.

Ludya
You MUST. We can't go on like this.

WhatsApp chat between Ludya Parak and Patrick Bright, April 18, 2024:

Ludya
S and J told me what you want to do. There are no words, Pat.

Patrick
Words are useless, Luds.

WhatsApp chat between Jonathan Danners and Patrick Bright, April 20, 2024:

Jonathan
Have you got everything you need?

Patrick
I have. A saw to cut through the flesh while it's frozen, then a bucket of drying powder for the head. It'll dry as it defrosts—I've practiced on flowers and scorpions.

Jonathan

What do we do between the bucket and the resin? The phone needs to be activated every five minutes.

Patrick

We can sink the head in the powder but leave enough uncovered to activate the phone.

Jonathan

That had better work, Patrick.

Patrick

I hope it will.

Jonathan

You HOPE? We need more than that.

Patrick

It'll work. I'll do the hands too, in case we need his fingerprints. The rest can go.

Royal Hastings, University of London
Multimedia Art MA
Final Project

Candidate name: Patrick Bright
Candidate number: 0883480

I needed to think straight. No one else was. Alyson was trapped with the phone. Jonathan was obsessed with the voice. Ludya and I, we flitted back and forth between the two worlds, the house of darkness and the bright studio; Jem and Gela, the project. It was like moving between two layers of hell.

I had an idea to break the cycle: use epoxy resin to preserve the features that activate the phone. I didn't know if it would work, and even if it did, it was a short-term solution. Organic matter of the density we had to preserve will eventually rot, even inside resin. Jonathan and Alyson were so intent on the unit and keeping Cameron talking to us through it. Their belief that it was him, their insistence we continue with the MA course . . . became normal to Ludya and me. That's something they don't tell you about teamwork. It can normalize the horrific. If you break everyone's role down into their micro-responsibilities, then the horrific thing is only the sum of those parts. No one person feels responsible for the fuckup in its entirety. A 3D version of "I was following orders."

Cameron took a phone call while we were arguing about the room. It was from Mae, and whatever she said, he hung up and made a grab for the radio in Ludya's hands. Ludya could have let go of it, but she didn't feel able to challenge Jonathan's order to keep it safe. Alyson jumped to help Ludya, but Cameron pushed her aside and she slipped on the cheap carpet. That's when I came out of the bathroom and saw him. Was it all my fault? They don't feel responsible for what I did.

I hit Cameron, but what happened next wasn't my idea. Jonathan was project leader of a sleeper unit that wanted to expose RD8's toxic tech. It wasn't his fault Suzie stole it instead. Alyson and her sister, Suzie, lived on a rubbish dump in China until a

British aid worker found and adopted them. The real Alyson became an artist. Suzie became an engineer, but she never lost her impulsiveness, or her instinct for survival. Who's fault was that?

And me? I caused the main problem, so I felt I should at least help solve it. End the terrible cycle we were all trapped in. That's another side effect of teamwork. Lack of emotion, absence of empathy—whatever it is that got us that far down the road—is contagious.

Documents sent to me by Patrick Bright:

Somerset trip WhatsApp group members Jonathan Danners, Alyson Lang, Cameron Wesley, Patrick Bright, and Ludya Parak, April 22, 2024:

Jonathan
Luds, is the car charged? We need it overnight.

Ludya
How far are you going? I need it for the school run tomorrow.

Jonathan
Seventy-five miles. We'll have it back by then.

Ludya
I'll take it to the rapid charging point now.

Patrick
Which of us is driving, Jonathan? We'll need to sort out insurance.

Ludya
FFS! Yeah, if you're caught with body parts in the car, you don't want to be done for lack of paperwork.

Jonathan
He's right. The car is registered to a woman. If we're caught on camera and the police see it's being driven by two men, it might ping their radar. We'll both have to get insurance.

Patrick
You're right, they'll stop us for sure. What do we say?

Jonathan
That the owner gave us permission to use her vehicle, and we're going to Birling Gap to take photographs of the sunset for an art project. We remain calm and say WHATEVER to avoid a search.

Ludya
Where will you get rid of it?

Jonathan
A cove near Eastbourne. We'd go on holiday there when I was a kid. It's always deserted and the tide is lethal. A van fell down the cliff once, and in one tide it disappeared.

Ludya
My car had better be back by 6 a.m. with enough charge to reach Earlsfield.

Somerset trip WhatsApp group members Jonathan Danners, Alyson Lang, Cameron Wesley, Patrick Bright, and Ludya Parak, April 23, 2024:

Suzie
It's sinking. The drying powder is like quicksand. Patrick, get more, so we can pack it tighter at the bottom or this isn't going to work long-term.

Jonathan
He's driving. He says it's not long-term, only for a few days. The powder is expensive.

Suzie
I don't care how fucking expensive it is. And days are a long time when you have to do what I'm doing.

Jonathan
Would you rather do what we're doing?

Jonathan
Thought not.

* * *

Jonathan
Luds, the car is on your drive. I'm bringing Pat back to the house to check on the bucket.

Ludya
Did the tide take it?

Jonathan
It's low tide until midday.

Ludya
So, it's lying on a beach somewhere, waiting to be found by tide-pooling kids?

Jonathan
It's not a beach. No one goes down there, and we hid it between some rocks.

Patrick
No one can see it, not even from the cliffs. The path is barely usable. It was hell getting down there.

Jonathan
We're heading into RH to do a day in the studio with Gela and Jem. See you there, Luds.

Alyson Lang
OK, so finally I'll do this . . .

Cameron Wesley *has left the group.*

Somerset trip WhatsApp group members Jonathan Danners, Suzie Danners, Patrick Bright, and Ludya Parak, April 26, 2024:

Patrick
I think we can take the next step. I've sourced a large mold. All the chemicals we need are ready.

Ludya
I won't be there. I've got kids' stuff to do.

Patrick
I keep meaning to ask, Jonathan. Is there any chance I could be reimbursed for the materials? I can't ask Jem for it. We need so much resin I've spent over £384 already, on top of the cost of the freezer, and I still need to get special masks to protect us from the fumes. The stuff is super-hazardous.

Jonathan

Reimbursed by whom? This isn't a commercial operation, Pat. Our financial resources ran out long ago.

Patrick

You said you're going to sell whatever tech there is in the unit.

Jonathan

If it still works after my experiment.

Suzie

You'll get your share when we've sold it.

Patrick

What percentage?

Suzie

A quarter. There's four of us.

Metropolitan Police digital evidence log/Case no. 4617655/24/ files retrieved September 5, 2024

WhatsApp chat between Suzie Danners and Jonathan Danners, April 26, 2024:

Jonathan
What are you saying? We're not cutting either of them in.

Suzie
The promise will keep them onside and QUIET.

Jonathan
Fear of life in prison will keep them Q.

WhatsApp chat between Suzie Danners and Jonathan Danners, April 30, 2024:

Suzie
This between Mae and Cameron just now:

> **Mae**
> You've left the MA course?
>
> **Cameron**
> Like I said. On a new job.
>
> **Mae**
> You've got kiss-kiss and you're AWOL.
>
> **Cameron**
> Not AWOL. Kiss-kiss is safe.
>
> **Mae**
> Where is it? Tell me it's still within touching distance.
>
> **Cameron**
> Everything's fine.

Mae

Because, like I told you, kiss-kiss is highly sensitive and we need it back at any cost.

Jonathan

Interesting. RD8 know exactly what it is.

Documents sent to me by Patrick Bright:

Somerset trip WhatsApp group members Jonathan Danners, Suzie Danners, Patrick Bright, and Ludya Parak, April 30, 2024:

Ludya
I'm in the studio, watching Jem beavering away on the clay head. Has it worked?

Jonathan
Next layer of resin just gone in. This is it. Will it still recognize him?

Ludya
Does it?

Ludya
Well?

Ludya
FFS?

Jonathan
Yes. Yes! It's clicked on. No alarm.

Ludya
Thank God. Now what?

Jonathan
We tune in to the voice again. Whoever is prepared to pay for this unit can witness the phenomenon before they buy.

WhatsApp chat between Jonathan Danners and Patrick Bright, May 4, 2024:

Jonathan
We need you to write a basic CV and make a web page for Cameron's Assignment Six; also, some of his long essay that he can send to Gela. We gave her all he'd written back in March, so merely a few paras about what he's learned on the course since then.

Patrick

What would he have learned? He wasn't here.

Jonathan

ANYTHING. Write what YOU learned. I don't care. Just step up and help.

Patrick

I'll try.

Jonathan

And if you want to apologize to him, be at the house 5 p.m. tonight.

Patrick

You've got through?

Jonathan

I've tried something. It might work and might not.

Patrick

OK.

WhatsApp chat between Patrick Bright and Ludya Parak, May 4, 2024:

Patrick

Jonathan wants me to apologize to Cameron. See if that changes what the voice says. He's trying to set up a two-way broadcast.

Ludya

What do we do? I don't know what to do.

Patrick

I'm going to turn up and apologize. Do what the project manager says.

Ludya

Will that be it, though? How do we end it, Pat?

Patrick

I don't know if we can pull it off, but RD8 have the means to get rid of everything. The radio, the phone, and . . . everything else.

Ludya

The incinerator? I've already suggested taking everything and burning it all somewhere. But Jonathan won't do it, and he's in charge.

Patrick

Then we'll take it out of his hands, literally. RD8 offered us the chance to burn the installation after the event. You and me, we take the unit, the resin block, and the phone to RD8 and incinerate the lot.

Ludya

How do we get it all past them? By "them" I mean J, S, Gela, Jem, RD8, and all the guests?

Patrick

We hide it all inside the head.

Ludya

Who will keep the phone quiet?

Patrick

We're experimenting with taping the phone to the front of the resin block, so it can see the face all the time. The phone's plugged in to a powerbank, but it seems to know when it's not been moved, and the times it needs a shake are inconsistent.

Ludya

Is there room for all that inside the head?

Patrick

Just barely. It's hollow. It has an open section at the bottom, where it was fixed to a stand before the redesign.

Ludya

The head would have to be sealed securely, and it's not that kind of structure. Have you run it past S & J?

Patrick

S & J have lost their minds, and if we keep following their orders, we'll be lost with them. We have to think for ourselves, Luds. Not just think—act. For us.

Ludya

I know, but we're a team. All in this together.

Royal Hastings, University of London
Multimedia Art MA
Final Project

Candidate name: Jonathan Danners
Candidate number: 0883482

The final event continued:

As project manager it's my job to keep the big picture in sight, while everyone else concentrates on their individual tasks. The big picture changed. When we first approached Gela, she was looking for professionals to fill places on a new course. The promise of Alyson Lang's name was the first carrot. Then there was the first payment of sixty grand, and the prospect of another at the end of it, if and when we managed to expose RD8. Someone who fears for their livelihood is an easy target.

My mother was a research scientist at RD8's Gloucestershire laboratories in the early '80s. She worked on active deterrent technology known as the "Dead Hand"—a Cold War dinosaur that refused to become extinct.

This system must be neutralized each and every day to prevent its activation. If it doesn't perceive human interaction, it will suspect a nuclear attack and start a process of attestation. First, it examines its immediate environment for signs of life—then reverts to radio airwaves to elicit a response from survivors. If it gets neither, or that process is blocked, it will initiate the automatic launch of missiles buried deep in the sea and trained on the other side.

Mom would say her specialist subject was "just in case." Just in case the unthinkable happens. Just in case someone fancies destroying half the world. Just in case someone presses that button, they won't live to tell the tale. Kiss . . . kiss.

Documents sent to me by Patrick Bright:

Somerset trip WhatsApp group members Jonathan Danners, Suzie Danners, Patrick Bright, and Ludya Parak, May 18, 2024:

Suzie
Jem visited Alyson's studio today. Don't ask me to reply to Ali's text. No energy.

Ludya
WTF? How did she even know to go there?

Jonathan
No one panic. Think logically. The first thing Jem will do when she realizes the Alyson on the course is in fact her sister . . . is tell Gela.

Ludya
Gela better have something logical to say.

Jonathan
Calling her now with a heads-up.

Royal Hastings, University of London
Multimedia Art MA
Final Project

Candidate name: Ludya Parak
Candidate number: 0883481

What the final project taught me:

I don't keep a diary, because life's about the future, right? When a day's over, it's done with. Having said that, keeping one would've helped me write this essay. It would also have put me away. If I ever have to stand up and defend my actions, then I'll say I was doing it for the kids. Because that's true. I didn't want them—they just happened. I had stars in my eyes, thanks to their dad, who made me think a little life in a little house was what he wanted too. That was the trouble—he wanted two. Another woman on the other side of town. Difference was, she knew all about me. I only found out about her when he left his phone tracker on. He was supposed to be driving to Tring for work, only he was less than a mile away. This is how naïve I was: I raced around to her apartment, ready to confront whoever it was who had stolen his phone . . .

I didn't want kids, because there are too many people in the world and the world is dying. Why add to the pressure on the planet by dumping more on it, for my own selfish reasons? Some call it a "birth strike," but before he came along and changed my mind, it made perfect sense to me.

Once they arrive, nature makes you care for them, and now they mean more to me than anything. Now it's not about changing other people's minds on the climate crisis but literally taking my children's future into my own hands.

I met Jonathan Danners at a conference. He wasn't like the swampies and hippies and geeky activists. I'm not saying they aren't my people, but you can spot them a mile away and that's the trouble. Jonathan wore a suit. He had the accent, the background in science. I told him to his face: he could speak for the organization and people would take him seriously. Only he didn't want that. He'd rather stay in the shadows and DO something than stand in the light and just talk.

I met Suzie later, once the three of us were made a sleeper unit. At first I wondered what it would be like working with a married couple, but they were always professional. My issue was fitting work around childcare, finding the time for everything. Exactly like normal life.

We were all chosen for the RD8 project because we had backgrounds in art and design—kind of. I had no doubts about doing the course, only about fitting it all in. The art was therapeutic, but working in a tiny group day after day was intense. We threw ourselves into it and a whole heap of angst came with that. When we got to Somerset we had work to do: find evidence of RD8's atmospheric defense tech, photograph it, then expose them as environmental terrorists. It felt right. As if everything was going our way. Suzie had a contact in the palm of her hand. I had the tech knowhow, and Jonathan had the organizational skill set.

He and I created the diversion while Suzie got where she had to go, using her contact's codes. Later we discovered they'd set us up, but you know what killed it? The most basic mistake of all. The contact mistook a right turn for a left—so when Suzie took the unit, she stole something else, something RD8 wanted back ASAP and at any cost. That's why, when we got to the motel, this shit finally got real.

Royal Hastings, University of London
Multimedia Art MA
Final Project

Candidate name: Jonathan Danners
Candidate number: 0883482

As project leader I take some responsibility. But throwing blame around never solved anything—when something's done, we have to move forward, neutralize the problem, and get things back on course. In our case, literally get ourselves back on the course.

If I were to blame anyone, it would be Patrick. What was he thinking? Even if he believed Cameron was attacking Ludya, Suzie and I were there; we wouldn't have let him.

Cameron wasn't attacking Ludya. He was trying to get the unit back. We would later realize he was a private investigator shadowing us for RD8. Even Gela knew that much. He got a call when we were in the room, and that call changed everything. We'd later discover it was Mae Blackwell, his boss at RD8. She told him to retrieve the unit immediately. He hung up and said, "OK, game's up, give it back."

When Suzie pulled the old radio from her coat, that was when Ludya and I realized she'd stolen the tech, not just photographed it. Cameron tried to grab it from her, but she threw it to Ludya. I shouted at Luds to keep hold of it. Suzie leapt to help, tripped, and hit the floor instead. Cameron was totally focused on the unit; Ludya looked to me. Her eyes asked if she should let it go. Mine told her to keep it . . . Patrick came out of the bathroom, and before any of us knew it, he'd swung the iron. Cameron staggered to the wall, then slid down it to the floor.

Patrick, Ludya, and I stood there, stunned . . . But Suzie wasn't frozen at all. She jumped up, ran to Cameron, rolled him into the recovery position, sat back, and watched to see if he came around. Patrick staggered backward, dropped the iron, sank down onto the double bed, and began to wail with his head in his hands. Eventually Ludya whispered, "Shall I dial 999?"

"No!" Suzie checked Cameron's pulse, eyes, breathing. She looked at me, and that look told me all I needed to know. He was dead, and there was no way we could have the emergency services here. Ludya reeled away and sat on a bunkbed, turned her back on the whole scene. Patrick joined Suzie on the floor by Cameron's side and tapped his cheek as if to wake him up. Kept saying, "Sorry, Cameron, sorry" over and over. Eventually Pat realized we hadn't called anyone. It could only have been a matter of minutes—four at most—but it felt like an hour. The phone alarm. When it first went off, we all remembered it from that day in the studio. Again it was Suzie who had the presence of mind to act. She grabbed it from Cameron's pocket and held it in front of his face. Silence. And from that moment on, we've had to do the same thing every five minutes, day and night.

As team leader, I must distribute responsibilities according to individual strengths and weaknesses. Well, only Suzie was strong enough for this task. Ludya refused, Patrick tried, but he had to keep Jem busy. So when Suzie has to sleep, it's down to me.

Royal Hastings, University of London
Multimedia Art MA
Final Project

Candidate name: Alyson Lang
Candidate number: 0883484

My earliest memory is of an arm wrapped in a blanket. Three fingers exposed to the sun were burned dark and flaky. At five or six years old, my first instinct was to see if those fingers led to a wrist and a watch or bracelet. I was disappointed. Just a grubby knot of string, which had maybe once held a key, encircled the wrist. I pulled on the hand until the arm emerged from the blanket, severed above the elbow, a blade of shattered white bone jutting from a jagged stump. I don't remember the smell, but I recall my fascination with those two joints: wrist and elbow. The construction of this forelimb, which could twist around independently of the main joint, was mesmerizing. I flipped the hand over and back, over and back. Compared it to my own arm, which was exactly the same and a similar size. I must have shown it to my sister, but she was too young to appreciate the weirdness.

At some point an adult picked their way past us. "Give it!" The arm was snatched away and that was that. Strange how in my memory they said the words in English. Is that because I've forgotten Mandarin? The arm was whisked off into the distance, and my sister and I carried on looking for scraps of metal and food in the rubbish that regular people threw away.

Royal Hastings, University of London
Multimedia Art MA
Final Project

Candidate name: Jonathan Danners
Candidate number: 0883482

There's one problem with the active deterrent system: the other side has a Dead Hand too.

Thanks to my mother and her generation of scientists and engineers at RD8, those missiles planted beneath the sea, trained on the enemy, now belong to a different era.

Instead they developed technology that "drops" a silent, invisible "bomb." It charges the atmosphere with positive ions to devastate towns, cities, countries—whole continents—on a molecular level. You'll never know the attack has happened until, perhaps, everyone around you is dying from cancer or lung disease or suicide. Until you see the polluted rivers, decaying plant life, a dying ecosystem.

These weapons are deployed secretly to weaken a region, nation, or continent. A silent invasion. When the area is devastated enough, ground forces go in and neutralize any existing defense systems. You destroy them, without them destroying you. Kiss . . . goodbye.

When Mom went back to work after I was born, she was exposed to the atmospheric tech at the very start of its evolution, before anyone realized how dangerous it was. As a result, my sister was born with complex disabilities that meant she didn't die but didn't live either. If it weren't for RD8, my mother would be alive today and my sister a perfectly healthy, happy twenty-seven-year-old. You might think the company would take responsibility, but at that level accountability doesn't apply. And you can't sue a department that doesn't officially exist.

AetherGen is committed to disrupting big business that invests in climate destruction. Ludya and Suzie are both passionate activists. Ludya for her kids, and Suzie because despite being rescued from the trash heap where she was born, she will always kick against authority, fighting to survive, like the abandoned child she still is inside. But for me it's always been personal. Whatever happens after tonight, I want it to be known—this was all for Mom and Sophia.

Metropolitan Police digital evidence log/Case no. 4617655/24/ files retrieved September 5, 2024

AetherGen WhatsApp group members Jonathan Danners, Suzie Danners, and Ludya Parak, May 30, 2024:

Jonathan
When the promo film ends, we go into the room and calmly wheel the head away.

Ludya
The event will still be going on. The kitchen is getting ready to serve more canapés.

Suzie
If anyone asks, give them a line. Say we need to protect it from damage and packing it up takes ages. They can explore the tunnel all they like.

Jonathan
Hold your positions while the presentation takes place. I'll be by the entrance doors.

Jonathan
OK, something's come up. Patrick just came over and said Jem's invited the external examiner. He's here, right now.

Suzie
RD8 didn't want our driver inside the grounds, so how did the external examiner get through?

Ludya
He'll simply want to see the installation before we dismantle it. Not an issue, right?

Jonathan
It's an issue. Jem invited the external examiner, but the guy who just walked in is Ben Sketcher.

Ludya
What the FUCK?

Suzie

Shit! We need to go.

Ludya

How the fuck does he know we're here?

Jonathan

Patrick gave him Cameron's finger, so he could gain access to the staff entrance. I'm pulling us out. Get your things and walk calmly to the parking lot. Meet at the minivan.

Ludya

But the head? The phone?

Jonathan

Leave them. That's an order.

WhatsApp chat between Jem Badhuri and Ben Sketcher, May 30, 2024:

Ben
Where are you?

Jem
In the event room, so I have to whisper and keep the volume low on my earphones.

Ben
What are you doing in there?

Jem
They put the old radio inside my head sculpture to weigh it down. They want to destroy both as soon as the event's over, only I want to take them home. If I get the radio out, I might be able to wheel the head to my dad's car.

Ben
Leave it where it is. There's a chance it's very old, very valuable technology that everyone thought was lost forever.

Jem
Really? When I amended the circuit board, I didn't spot anything out of the ordinary.

Ben
You amended the circuit board?

Jem
I was working on Assignment One. Cameron was in the studio early and asked if I needed help. I never react well to that, so I said, "If you insist, you can help with my soundscape."

Ben
Your Ocean Charity soundscape was audio clips of ocean noises. I've got the Tutor's Report here.

Jem
I'd finished that already. Didn't need his help, just wanted him to regret asking! I said, "Imagine you're a tiny sea creature trapped in a plastic bag or discarded bottle. What would you say to humankind?" I pressed Record, and to be fair, Cameron threw himself into it.

433

Ben

Oh my God, Jem.

Jem

He loved the sound of his own voice and said all sorts of funny things about being trapped in the darkness. I didn't stop him, just to see how long he could go on for. It was hilarious! The even funnier thing was that I had no intention of using the recording—until we found that old radio.

Ben

Are you telling me the voice everyone heard over the radio was Cameron's and you put it there? But how?

Jem

I distorted it so that no one—not even Cameron himself—would recognize it, then randomized the playback, set it to start at 5 p.m., and finally hid the new chip in the circuit board.

Ben

Patrick assured everyone you *didn't* do that.

Jem

He's nice, but he's a people-pleaser and I didn't trust him to keep it secret. I'd work on it in the mornings before he arrived.

Ben

Of course. Griff mentions that to Gela.

Jem

I wanted the others to think it was someone stranded on a mountain or at sea. If they escalated their concerns to RD8 or the police, it would be so much funnier!

Ben

Why cause that disruption?

Jem

I tried to explain it to Gela, but she didn't understand. No one did. When you're in a room with people who are older and more confident than you . . . I couldn't get my voice heard. Cameron didn't have that problem, so I used his voice instead. It worked—they all listened.

Ben

But you never thought to tell them the truth, even then?

Jem

They said the radio went back to RD8, so no. Now that Cameron's dead, I'm *really* sorry, but it's all we've got left of him. I want to save the clay head and the radio from the incinerator. Putting my phone away now.

Ben

Jem, this is important. Do not look inside the clay head. The radio wasn't all they put inside it. Stay where you are.

WhatsApp chat between Mae Blackwell and Gela Nathaniel, May 30, 2024:

Mae

Jem has wandered into the room and is talking into her phone at the back. I wonder if she's lost? Our CEO is addressing the guests, and we're about to play the ICES promo film. It's such an important moment for us. I wonder if you could pop in and lead her out?

Gela

I just tried to stand up and can't.

Mae

She's reached the clay head. I wonder if she's checking it? Oh well, the lights have gone down, and the film is starting now.

Gela

She's blind, Mae. The dark won't stop her. Please, get her away from the head.

Gela

She wants to rescue the old radio, but there's something else in there.

WhatsApp chat between Ben Sketcher and Jem Badhuri, May 30, 2024:

Ben

You may remember Cameron had a phone that emitted an alarm if it detected a face other than his. The warning onscreen claimed the police would be dialed automatically, but that wasn't strictly true. It dialed his office. When they received a text from Cameron telling them everything was OK, they were convinced he was safe.

Ben

The Danners thought they'd found RD8's atmospheric defense technology at Thorney Coffin, but they were wrong. A simple change in direction from right to left. A mistake made by their mole was all it took. Ludya's codes worked like a skeleton key and could open any door in that place—I know the company will be grateful to have that weakness exposed. RD8 had planted a decoy for them to find, but Suzie went to the wrong room and, acting on impulse, stole what was there. Not the decoy, something else.

Ben

Mae told Cameron to get it back at all costs. There's only one item at Thorney Coffin that warrants that level of order.

Ben

While the Dead Hand is invisible technology buried deep inside military systems, the radio phase looks, to the untrained eye, exactly like an old wireless. It's kept in carefully controlled conditions, deep in the countryside, covered in stealth technology, and surrounded by an invisible ring of steel. The company contracted to maintain this system will protect such sensitive technology to the death.

Ben

The moment the radio phase is removed from its magnetic plinth, its power is cut. Only, Patrick wired it right back into active mode.

When you added a new chip, you disconnected the original circuit and neutralized it completely. Is it an exaggeration to say you saved the world, Jem, with your instinct to disrupt?

Ben

You certainly threw my sleeper unit into a tailspin. They thought the voice speaking to them over the airwaves was the man they'd seen killed, whose body they still had and whose phone security system made them think they couldn't get rid of it . . . or, at least, his head.

Ben

They encased it in epoxy resin to keep his phone working. But still that was only temporary. The industrial incinerator at RD8 gave them a way out. The fact Suzie Danners showed up here, floating around the installation like a ghost, means they were confident of escaping before anyone asked questions . . . until my arrival panicked them.

Ben

They must be gutted to leave the unit behind. I know it still has value—not as a Spiritfinder, but to RD8. How much will they pay to get it back?

Ben

Jem, do not open the clay head or remove anything from it. Let me take everything. I'll make sure there's no evidence of what AetherGen did. Ironically, that unit will ensure our organization has funds to continue our fight against the destruction of this planet. DO NOT stand in my way.

WhatsApp chat between Gela Nathaniel and Mae Blackwell, May 30, 2024:

Gela

What was that?

Gela

It sounded like a lot of people screaming.

Gela

Is that laughter? It can't be laughter. Are they applauding?

Mae

Gela, I don't recall that being part of the installation. The lights went up after our film and there was Jem, standing in the middle of the room, holding a big glass cube. Inside it was a HORRIBLE model of a preserved head. Like something Damien Hirst might win the Turner Prize for.

Gela

It's resin. Not glass.

Mae

The mobile phone strapped to the outside, as if the head is looking at it, I'm sure there's a deep message there about our dependence on technology, but as pioneers of cloud computing it's not the image we want to promote.

Gela

Where is she now?

Mae

Your examiner led her away. The face in that cube looked familiar. Did they model it on Cameron?

Gela

They've all gone. Jonathan, Suzie, and Ludya. I watched them leave as soon as they saw him arrive. But, Mae, why did everyone laugh?

Mae

Our CEO finished his speech on the line "Wherever cloud computing goes, RD8 will be ahead." The lights came up and there was Jem. Now that the shock is over, I can see how emotive art can be. It's created quite a buzz out here! Seeing as that glass cube made such an impression, is there any chance we could keep it? There might be a display place for it somewhere.

Gela

I need to find her. I need to find Jem.

Mae

She and the examiner wheeled the clay sculpture out. I think your group is intending to incinerate it.

WhatsApp chat between Gela Nathaniel and Jem Badhuri, May 30, 2024:

Jem

Sorry, Gela, couldn't answer your call. I'm outside the incinerator building. It's deafening. I hate not hearing properly.

Gela

Are you OK?

Jem

The examiner confirmed I've got a Distinction, but he's taken everything and left me out here!

Gela

Jem, stay right where you are.

Jem

He says he's going to destroy the sculpture and the block of resin the others put inside it. He wants to sell the radio. Can you have a word with him?

Gela

I'm trying to reach you. Where is the incinerator building?

Jem

Go through the kitchen door. It's not far. My dad just texted that he's at the gate. Perhaps I could cover my ears and try to find him.

Gela

Stay there and let the examiner do what he came here to do.

Gela

Jem? Are you OK?

To: Gela Nathaniel
From: Patrick Bright
Date: May 30, 2024
Subject: Conclusion

Dear Gela,

My long essay lacks a conclusion, so here it is.

Conclusion:

This has happened twice now, and that's enough. I'm going home. What happened with Cameron was an accident, an honest mistake. But what happened with Finn wasn't. As we stood on that deck watching the line of police cars on the shore, I thought my only chance was to create a diversion. They didn't see me grab Finny by his leg and haul him over the side. His struggle to get ahold of something—anything—they saw as his desperate bid to scramble over the rail. I never told anyone. Ended up believing what I told the police. It became another reason not to go home.

The examiner is looking for Jonathan, Suzie, and Ludya. They've been hiding something he wants—he told me. The old radio. He's read our essays and coursework and wants the Spiritfinder himself. Did he really say, "Anyone who stands in my way can go where the head is going?" I'm in here with him now, but he can't see me, and if I'm careful, he never will. If I'm not careful, well, what does it matter anyway?

He's fired it up, and it's so loud I can't hear myself think. One way or the other, this will be the third time.

WhatsApp chat between Gela Nathaniel and Jem Badhuri, May 30, 2024:

Jem
Pat's here! He says he'll stop the examiner. He's gone into the building. I'm trying to find the gate now, but it's all gravel.

Jem
The roar of that incinerator is deafening!

Jem
I'm completely disorientated.

Jem
I need help. Gela, could you help me, please?

Gela
I can see you. I'm nearly there.

Doodle message group MMAM(FTP), May 31, 2024:

Jem Badhuri

I woke up this morning, and it hit me . . . the MA course is over. It all went so quickly. I feel a mixture of sadness and relief—but excitement too, because now I can start my career with an MA Distinction. Jem Badhuri, sculptor and soundscape artist.

Hannah O'Donnell

No one is accessing Doodle anymore. Just a heads-up, Jem. The whole MMAM(FTP) Doodle room will be deleted in eight hours. If you need to save anything, or ask any of the others for personal contact details, etc., do it now.

Jem Badhuri

Thanks, Hannah. I don't need to save anything, and I certainly don't want to contact any of the others again after last night. I've already moved on. Thank you.

Message group: 2024 Examiners, May 31, 2024

Philippa F. Moreton, BA, MA, PhD
I want to download the MA Multimedia Art documents, but it says "retrieval complete." Can anyone help?

Tilda Ricci
Hello, Philippa. Who are you?

Philippa F. Moreton, BA, MA, PhD
I'm your external examiner, based at Central. I understand this is a new course, and as I don't have a background specifically in multimedia art, I'd like to get started.

Karen Carpenter
Examination procedure for that course is almost complete. We're expecting Ben Sketcher's feedback at any moment.

Tilda Ricci
That's why you can't access the files. He's already downloaded them all.

Philippa F. Moreton, BA, MA, PhD
I've double-checked and I am definitely your external examiner. No one here has heard of a Ben Sketcher. Who's in charge of admin? Please unlock the system and allow me access to the documents. Thank you.

Tilda Ricci
Karen and I discussed this course with Ben all day yesterday.

Karen Carpenter
He had a lot of queries. He also asked Hannah O'Donnell for information about the students.

Tilda Ricci
He was concerned for the safety of one in particular, and last night went so far as to attend an event, to check she was there.

Philippa F. Moreton, BA, MA, PhD
My goodness. And was she?

Tilda Ricci

Yes, apparently. I assumed that was why Ben stopped messaging so abruptly. Karen, have you heard from him?

Karen Carpenter

No. And he's not listed as a participant in this group anymore.

Philippa F. Moreton, BA, MA, PhD

Can you unlock the system for me? Thank you, Karen.

Karen Carpenter

Tilda, can you ask Gela what happened?

WhatsApp chat between Tilda Ricci and Gela Nathaniel, May 31, 2024:

Tilda
How did it go last night? I understand Ben Sketcher attended, but now there's a Philippa Moreton claiming she's the examiner.

Tilda
The last we heard was when Patrick gave Ben a severed finger suspended in transparent resin. He then accessed the RD8 building using the fingerprint . . . Karen and I are wondering if your MA group has been playing a practical joke on us all along.

Gela
I wish that was the case. Three of the MA group are members of AetherGen, a climate-change organization. RD8 has defense technology that would have a devastating impact on humanity and the environment if it were ever deployed. The trio intended to gather evidence of the tech and expose it. Only things didn't go to plan.

Tilda
They failed?

Gela
Yes. The company was following them all along.

Tilda
Thank goodness! We can't have a scandal like that, Gela. But who is Ben Sketcher if he's not our examiner?

Gela
The three members of AetherGen gained possession of a different piece of technology and then went AWOL with it. I believe Ben Sketcher is the new leader of their organization, but used his skills as a hacker to pose as the external examiner and track them down. Even he didn't realize there would be such a shocking climax to the company's event.

Tilda
A shocking climax? What happened?

Gela

The activists created a grotesque model of a severed head encased in a resin block, staring at a mobile phone strapped to it. All designed to shock the RD8 people and their corporate guests—a protest about human dependence on technology. Clearly someone is a fan of Damien Hirst and Gunther von Hagens.

Tilda

How did RD8 respond? Could this affect their relationship with our engineering faculty?

Gela

The plan backfired. The audience saw it as a valid artistic statement and applauded. RD8 were speechless at first, but it caused such a chatter around their very dull new communications technology that they had to admit the installation did its job. I've just uploaded my Tutor's Report. As the real external examiner is on board now, there's nothing to concern you.

Tilda

What a relief. In that case I'll tell Karen to send all the documents to Philippa at once. And, Gela, I've had some good news: the MMAM course has been approved! You can start admissions and select the next intake of students. Send Hannah your blurb for the prospectus asap.

Gela

That's great news.

Tilda

Are you sure everything's OK?

Gela

Everything is absolutely fine. Thank you, Tilda.

MMAM(FTP)
Final Project and long essay
Final Grade
Tutor's Report, May 31, 2024

Brief: Create a multimedia installation in the foyer of RD8's headquarters to complement the company's launch event for a new system that blends radio waves with cloud technology for a new generation of mobile payment systems.

Overview: The group had one task left: to move their installation to RD8's event, set it up, and talk to guests during the champagne reception. It was simple—probably the least involved and most enjoyable stage of the whole process. The moment where all they had learned on the course could be put into practice.

Jemisha Badhuri

With her burning ambition, mischievous guile, and ruthless streak, Jem has quietly disrupted this course from the start. Last summer, when I met her at the West Mids degree show, I thought I'd found a student who literally wouldn't see what AetherGen was up to. Jem saw everything, and more. She works hard to overcome any obstacle she encounters. Despite taking some unconventional paths to assert herself, she's an accomplished artist and, more than any other student on this course, has developed her talent into the stratosphere. Final grade: Distinction

Patrick Bright

When I struck up a conversation with Patrick over the counter at Modern Art, it was only to offer my sympathies after the burglary. As he rambled about the break-in and mixed it with yearning memories of his hometown in Ireland, it hit me. This lovely, innocent middle-aged man was the final piece of my puzzle. Someone who, if he saw anything, would see only the good in it. Yet what you see can be deceiving, and he wasn't that innocent after all. Patrick stopped responding to my messages after the event. Wherever he is, I wish him well. Final grade: Merit

Jonathan Danners

I met Jonathan at a climate-change march. I was only there to keep a friend company. We walked beside each other and got talking—it was as simple as that. I mentioned I worked at Royal Hastings, and he said his sister-in-law was Alyson Lang; his wife, her sister, Suzie, was walking way ahead of us, leading the march with a banner and megaphone. Jonathan was lovely, even said he'd help me approach Alyson to visit our undergrads. Later he told me Royal Hastings has strong links to RD8 via the engineering department. Like all bad ideas, I can't remember exactly when we decided I'd be a part of their mission to expose RD8's toxic atmospheric defense tech. But I contacted the company on behalf of the art department. It coincided well with our change in policy: the clause in our mission statement that said all RH art courses must have a clear relevance to industry and commerce. Jonathan is a driven and passionate leader determined to make a faceless organization pay for the deaths of his mother and sister. I hope he finds peace. Final grade: Merit

Alyson Lang

Alyson Lang created the most extraordinary, inventive, and beautiful artwork for this course. But Suzie Danners worked harder and for longer—on a job no one else could do. Suzie and Alyson are sisters, born somewhere in China, but as their earliest memories are of scavenging on a rubbish heap alongside others in similar destitution, who knows what their true background was. They can only have been toddlers when they were adopted by aid worker Sue Lin Lang and her engineer husband, Charlie, and brought to the UK, where they enjoyed a happy and privileged upbringing, in complete contrast to their start in life. Yet something about the horror of those early years meant Suzie was able to do something that drove the other team members to the edge of insanity. Day in, day out, she kept Cameron's phone working and his family, friends, and colleagues in the dark about what had really happened. Final grade: Distinction

Ludya Parak

As a stressed single mother struggling to maintain a freelance career, Ludya was not someone I ever expected to be an outstanding student. But with her background in design, she could bring some weight to my course feedback. So when Jonathan and Suzie wanted Ludya on the course too, I agreed. I see now they needed to balance the power. Three of them against three regular group members. Only in the end, Ludya rejected them. When she drove away from RD8, she kicked Suzie and Jonathan out of the car and told them she was finished with AetherGen. I understand she drove straight to a police station to turn over her laptop and phone. All three discovered the limits of teamwork, and Ludya was central to that learning. Final grade: Pass

Cameron Wesley

Cameron was a remarkable student who, had he not vanished under a cloak of secrecy, I'm sure would have passed his MA and rediscovered the joy of creativity. I hope to name a prize after him, if I can get the paperwork to Hannah on time and the idea is passed by the department committee. It will be awarded to the student who achieved the most, against the odds. I'm sure he'd be pleased to know his time at Royal Hastings is not forgotten. Not by me. Final grade: Discretionary pass

And now that I've got that off my chest, I'll write a Tutor's Report that I can actually submit. One that says how well all the students did and how much I learned from them—knowledge I can take forward to next year's course.

Do you see now what my problem is? After my last exchange with the college admin, I sought out three people connected to this case: Hannah O'Donnell, Gela Nathaniel, and Jemisha Badhuri. They agreed to send me their communications with "Ben Sketcher," so that I could gain a better understanding of events leading up to and beyond that final project. This explains why you can see them here.

I went to the police and gave them all the documents I had, along with every contact detail. They thanked me and said they'd be in touch.

I didn't hear any more.

Weeks later I noticed a small news item about three climate-change activists who were charged with trespass, cyber-fraud, and criminal damage. They belonged to a small underground group called AetherGen, which effectively dissolved when its leader disappeared, around the time of their arrest. They all pleaded guilty, so there was no trial. Two were given sentences of ten years each; the third a suspended sentence, because she had provided evidence that led to the other convictions—her lawyers pleaded that she was a single parent whose mother was unwell. Apparently the trio had broken into a high-security building to damage expensive technology, and the judge was determined that sentencing would be robust—to deter others.

Any investigation into what happened to Cameron, Patrick, or the mysterious Ben Sketcher would shine a spotlight on technology that RD8 and their clients want to keep shrouded in mystery. So officially nothing unusual happened on the inaugural Master's Degree in Multimedia Art (Full-Time Program).

I approved Gela Nathaniel's grades and finally clicked "retrieval complete" on the Doodle files.

The police must surely have additional evidence gathered from the devices of the conspirators and witnesses. If these ever come to light, then you will have a far clearer understanding of this strange case than I ever will.

Yours,

Philippa F. Moreton, BA, MA, PhD
The Examiner

To: Gela Nathaniel
From: Mae Blackwell
Date: May 31, 2024
Subject: Postmortem

Dear Gela,

I appreciate you had nothing to do with what happened last night, but Marketing is holding a postmortem, and I know Royal Hastings will not emerge in the best light. This is a terrible shame, as I understand our research-and-development division enjoys a close relationship with your engineering faculty. The future of that link is in severe jeopardy.

Did you know your group contained AetherGen activists? The only saving grace is that our guests, having explored the experiential and immersive installation, thought Jem's retrieval of the head statue from the sculpture was performance art to round off our presentation. Many took it as a satirical comment on the 24/7 mobile-phone "habit" that most people seem to have these days. If it were not for that, we would be turning this whole episode over to our lawyers as a case of trespass and sabotage.

Please know that RD8 are fully committed to reversing the effects of climate change. We have switched to 100% electric vehicles and maintain a company-wide policy to reuse and recycle. Our aim is to be carbon-neutral by 2030.

On another matter, your student Patrick Bright signed in, but didn't sign out yesterday. We need his ID pass returned ASAP. I see Cameron Wesley signed in and out via our biometric gate, but I didn't see him at all, did you? If you see him, please ask him to contact me ASAP.

Mae

To: Mae Blackwell
From: Gela Nathaniel
Date: May 31, 2024
Subject: Re: Postmortem

Dear Mae,

Thank you for your strategic letter. I would apologize for last night, but that would be inappropriate, given that you not only knew very well the AetherGen unit was taking this course, but also paid me to admit Cameron too. You wanted him to watch them, and intended them to find a dummy unit—one they thought was integral to RD8's atmospheric defense technology, which killed Jonathan's mother and sister. When they "exposed" this innocent tech, you wanted to humiliate their organization.

Only they turned the wrong way and stole something else. A Dead Hand unit that held the power to destroy the world. Jem disabled it when she planted a tiny chip that generated randomized statements in Cameron's voice. A trick designed to punish her fellow students. How lucky that she did. The group never knew what they had really stolen.

Hearing that voice changed the group. Cameron's murder meant it wasn't dismissed as a trivial curiosity, but was given shape, form, and meaning. Call it mass hysteria in the wake of severe trauma. Scientists suddenly believed in the afterlife. Good, kind people found themselves on a pathway to the unthinkable, where every step led them further from their moral core. Those who claimed to hate capitalism considered selling the tech to aid their own escape. For a while they had to live in the moment instead of thinking about the future of the planet. I wonder if they learned anything from that . . .

You know Cameron's dead, Mae. He died working for you. Trying to recover the radio phase of the Dead Hand system that at one time might have launched a thousand nuclear weapons. All to keep your new atmospheric technology secret. And is that really because you don't want the enemy to find out, or because if ordinary people knew, they wouldn't want such destructive potential to exist?

A lot of ex-army men end up in the City. Cameron went from Iraq to Canary Wharf, but couldn't handle the change in atmosphere, in the quality of risk. He called it burnout, but it wasn't quite that. He longed for the danger of his former life. I wonder how his death will be covered up.

We're not as secretive in academia as you are in business. Low-grade hacker and AetherGen's puppet-master, Ben Sketcher, found it all too easy to pose as the external examiner and access course essays and event details. He knew exactly where his errant sleeper group would be. Patrick thought the external examiner would call the police and end the trap he found himself in—he gave Ben access to RD8. That's why you think Cameron signed in and out.

Your incinerator was the group's ticket to freedom. Finally a way to destroy the final piece of Cameron's body and his phone, giving whoever had the unit a chance to escape. Of course the success of any new start depended on that unit being the long-lost Spiritfinder. A scientific endeavor to answer the ultimate question of life . . . and death. But of course it wasn't, was it?

Mae, if you hadn't wanted to discredit AetherGen, then none of this would've happened, because the Danners would never have got near the Dead Hand unit otherwise, far less steal and reactivate its devastating capabilities. It was your luck that a twenty-one-year-old art student had confidence, talent, and cheek enough to save the world.

I learned a lot from this MA course. I underestimated Jem and Patrick, but Patrick the most. He decided to act—to stop what he thought he saw: Cameron attacking Ludya. How did something so simple become so tangled and awful? Because it seems Patrick paid for that mistake with his own life. I saw him enter the incinerator block with Ben. Then I led Jem safely to her dad's car. I didn't look back.

Which of them walked away? Patrick's shop workers say he might have gone back to Ireland, but I can tell how worried they are. Now you say that he didn't sign out, so I fear the worst.

All the time my group was coming into the art studio, working on their assignments and the final project, each of them had their own agenda, which changed shape as we went along. It's all very poetic and beautiful in its own way, Mae.

When the police ask me, I'll tell them everything. But you and I both know nothing will happen.

Gela

To: Gela Nathaniel
From: Lisa Hough
Date: June 4, 2024
Subject: Cameron Wesley

Dear Ms. Nathaniel,

You may remember we communicated a few months back, when I was trying to locate my former husband, Cameron Wesley. The last I heard of him was that he'd enrolled in an art course at Royal Hastings, so of course you were the first person I contacted when he missed our son's sports day.

I am very sorry to inform you that Cameron sadly passed away on a covert operation. They never tell you the details, so when and where this happened we'll never know, but I see now that he must have left your art course to go on that final job. I'm sorry to contact you with such terrible news.

Your sincerely,

Lisa

To: Lisa Hough
From: Gela Nathaniel
Date: June 4, 2024
Subject: Re: Cameron Wesley

Dear Lisa,

Thank you for your email. I am so sorry to hear that sad news about Cameron. He was a lovely man, with genuine creative talent. I first met him at the Sanctuary when I was introducing everyone there to the therapeutic potential of art. We built up a close bond over that time. I will never forget him. Thank you for letting me know the sad news.

All my love,

Gela

To: The Danners Gallery
From: Jem Badhuri
Date: September 4, 2024
Subject: New soundscape artist

Dear Barbara,

I visited the Danners Gallery with my father a few months ago, and you very kindly showed us around the exhibition. At the time I was studying for an MA in Multimedia Art at Royal Hastings, and I'm delighted to say that, after a year of dedication and commitment, I gained a well-deserved Distinction for my work in clay and sound.

While at your gallery I couldn't help but notice something missing—and that vital element was a soundscape. My Royal Hastings tutor described me as "the master of sound," and I agree. Sound is a vital element of the human sensory experience, and I can create an auditory journey to enhance your visitors' uptake of any exhibition or event. I would like to offer my services as a soundscape artist.

As you will be one of my first-ever clients I am happy to negotiate a "friends' rates" fee on the basis that your boss's son, Jonathan, took the same course. I helped him create a project in clay for one of our assignments, so he should give me a good reference. The positive thing about his prison sentence is that at least you know where to find him.

I am happy to visit again and discuss the benefits my services can bring to your business. My dad can drive me to Gloucester at any time. However, due to the fact that I am sight-impaired, I will require some additional assistance to allow me full access to the task, but please rest assured that when I need help, I will ask for it.

Thank you, Barbara. I look forward to hearing from you via the contact details below,

Jem Badhuri, BA, MA

**WhatsApp chat between Jem Badhuri and a withheld number,
September 5, 2024:**

Withheld number
Hello there, young Jem, BA, MA, how are you?

Jem
Gasp! Is this Pat from MMAM?

Withheld number
Are you OK after that crazy night?

Jem
OK? I'm on top of the world! Got my first soundscape commission from a restaurant around the corner. Signed up for an advanced course in sound electronics, tax-deductible. Dad's looking at quotes to soundproof the loft, and he's coming around to the idea of knocking a doorway through to the second bedroom, so I can have a clay studio too. Oh, and do you remember a lovely waiter called Mikael from the RD8 event? We're going to Paris for the weekend, and he's teaching me the guitar. Even my dad likes him.

Withheld number
That's all grand. I'm very glad.

Jem
Don't the police want to speak to you about what happened?

Withheld number
Maybe one day someone will, but too many want to keep RD8's secrets for that to be official.

Jem
The real examiner asked to see all my messages, and the police took my phone. It was very exciting! When they told me what was inside that resin block, I finally realized why everyone had screamed. It barely registered at the time, I was so intent on saving the clay sculpture.

Withheld number
I'm afraid it went into the incinerator with everything else. I'm sorry.

Jem

Oh, I'm glad now—imagine having that big old thing in the house! What was I thinking?

Withheld number

I hope you're OK after everything, Jem.

Jem

When Gela told me what was in the resin, for the first time ever I felt glad I couldn't see. You know me, Pat, I'm a bright-side sort of person, but I don't always feel it, deep down. I look back on how I behaved during the MA and wonder if not identifying as disabled was a kind of denial.

Jem

Now I know there's beauty in everything.

Withheld number

Well, I guess we all learned a lot on our MA, whether it was part of the course or not.

Jem

True! I've been thinking about visiting Jonathan and Suzie in prison, but they're so far away and I'm busy.

Withheld number

Some prisons run art classes, so perhaps they're creating new work themselves.

Jem

Gela will be delighted when she hears you're OK.

Withheld number

Now, Jem, please keep this to yourself.

Jem

She says you signed in to RD8, but never signed out, though someone used Cameron's fingerprint to sign in and out—was that you? She said the old radio was incinerated along with the clay head and the resin cube I found inside it. And that when the incinerator finally cooled down, they discovered fragments of human bone.

Withheld number

I've no idea who that could've been.

Jem

Gela says she told the police everything she knows and that it's up to them now. That we should enjoy our lives, because that's what Cameron would've wanted.

Withheld number

It's good advice.

Jem

You'll never guess where I keep the scorpion paperweight you made! Right beside me on my desk. Did you keep one yourself?

Withheld number

I did. And it's right beside me too. On top of an old radio, which I listen to at the same time every day. As the voice speaks, I look at the scorpion, its sting ready to strike. Neither will let me forget.

Withheld number

Jem?

Withheld number

Jem, please say you're still talking to me.

Jem

Are you back home?

Withheld number

I'm closer. Put it that way.

Jem

Painting and sketching?

Withheld number

I am. And it's all I ever dreamed it would be. But we can't stay in touch. Good luck, Jem. May you achieve everything you've ever wanted in life, and more.

Royal Hastings, University of London 2025 Prospectus
Multimedia Art MA (Full-Time Program)
New Course

Tutor: Angela Nathaniel, BA, MA
Evaluation: Coursework, final project, and long essay
Designed to bridge the gap between arts education and the workplace, this course will nurture each individual's artistic talent and resourcefulness, within a process that places teamwork front and center. Participants will learn to think creatively and develop those ideas collectively as they aim to advance their expertise in the type of logical problem-solving skills demanded by the corporate sector. On this course you can expect to work closely and at length with a diverse group of other students, sharing responsibility for the inception and execution of a real-world project.

It will be the experience of your life.

Click here to apply.

Acknowledgments

Are you reading these acknowledgments before you've read the book? Stop! There are huge spoilers below. Believe me, you don't want to know in advance what *The Examiner* is about. Please return to the beginning and come back when you've read the final page.

Now those of you who know why I asked them to leave can find out what inspired this story. But first I would like to thank my wonderful UK agents at Sheil Land Associates: my book agent, Gaia Banks; and my screen-rights and scriptwriting agent, Lucy Fawcett. They have been my guiding lights for more years than I care to remember. David Taylor, Rebecca Lyon, and Natalie Barracliffe deliver unshrinking assistance, while Lauren Coleman takes care of foreign rights to ensure this book reaches an international audience.

My representatives in the US, Markus Hoffmann at Regal Hoffmann & Associates for books (and Will Watkins at CAA for screen rights) are vital pieces of the international puzzle, not least because I have a dream team in the Atria offices.

The Examiner would not be the book it is without the exceptional talent of my wonderful editor at Atria, Kaitlin Olson, whose skill, insight, and dedication are second to none. Her lovely editorial assistant, Ife Anyoku, is eternally helpful and efficient, but they are just the tip of the production iceberg that is the publishing process. Other vital components include senior production editor Sonja Singleton, managing editor Paige Lytle, managing editorial coordinator Shelby Pumphrey, and managing editorial assistant Lacee Burr. Copyeditor Lisa Nicholas and proofreader Cecilia Molinari were brilliant at spotting my mistakes, while publicist Megan Rudloff and marketer Maudee Genao are no doubt working tirelessly, as you read this, to bring the book to its widest possible audience. I thank them all.

My UK team at Viper in London are helmed by fiercely talented publishing director Miranda Jewess, who is assisted by Charlotte

Greenwood, with head of managing editorial, Georgina Difford, and senior publicity manager, Drew Jerrison, as the tip of this book's UK publishing iceberg.

The Examiner began its germination when I read *Spy Schools* by Daniel Golden, which explores how the open and freethinking world of academia has unwittingly played host to nefarious characters and organizations with their sights on industrial or international espionage.

I wanted to explore the dynamics of small-group educational courses, of which I've taken so many, from the MA degree that changed my life to the professional-development courses that sapped my will to live. I've had brilliant tutors and some who were not so great. I've left with top marks and as bottom of the class. I've been the golden girl and the outcast, sometimes simultaneously. They all strived to create a safe space for learning, and in many instances succeeded, but some impressed me more for their choking claustrophobia, unhealthy competition, and potential for festering toxicity.

What has emerged here is a dark, satirical story that holds a black mirror to the concept of teamwork, at whose outer reaches we find some of the worst atrocities known to humanity.

An expert in security talked to me about the biometrics of facial and fingerprint recognition, voice manipulation, and iris scanning, so that my characters could replicate and exploit them. The subject is fascinating, and they opened my eyes to the complexity of present-day and near-future security technology. Even the most advanced software can have weak spots capable of being sidestepped, if you know how.

I've long been interested in the debate about the value of creative-arts education and the pressure on universities to make nonvocational courses relevant to the job market—or lose them altogether. Recently this argument has widened to the humanities: degrees that were once considered stalwarts of any prospectus. As the graduate of a BA in English Literature and Language, I left University College London in 1990, qualified for no career in particular. However, I had an insight into the power of words and language. I valued and respected creativity as a means to process experience, preserve the lessons learned, and make everyone's world a better place. Through literature, I studied history, geography, philosophy, theology, psychology, world cultures, classics, and the influence of other languages on the words we speak today.

My degree led nowhere in terms of a job, but it opened a window into times and places other than my own, across hundreds of years and thousands of miles, simply by giving me the opportunity and space to study the words written in those times and places. I can't think of a better start to any career.

The artist and motivational speaker Aishwarya Pillai, whose tactile art, TEDx talks, and awareness-raising work are truly inspirational, was a reference for the character of Jem (although Jem's cheek, mischief, and guile are my invention). I also immersed myself in the art of those who face similar challenges and yet have triumphed through creativity. From painters and sculptors to photographers and digital artists, there were so many whose work is stunning and inspiring: Pranav Lal, Pete Eckert, Evgen Bavcar, Rosita McKenzie, John Bramblitt, Eşref Armağan, Terry Hopwood-Jackson, Hal Lasko, and Josée Andrei, to name but a few.

Likewise, British photographer Ian Treherne proved an inspiration for other aspects of Jem's character. His amazing work is well worth checking out at www.iantreherne.co.uk.

The exhibition "Weird Sensation Feels Good: The World of ASMR" was resident at the Design Museum in London between May 2022 and April 2023. Curated in collaboration with ArkDes, the Swedish Centre for Architecture and Design, this interactive world of tactile and sound-based installations gave me a chance to experience binaural sound and its creation, so that Jem could rave about it with the authority and knowledge I certainly didn't have before my visit.

My research into female sound-art pioneers led me to the book *Re-Sisters* by Cosey Fanni Tutti—the book Jem reads over the Christmas holidays—and the documentaries *Sisters with Transistors* (directed by Lisa Rovner) and *Delia Derbyshire: The Myths and the Legendary Tapes* (directed by Caroline Catz).

The inspiration for Suzie and Alyson's backstory comes from a feature by Sophie Williams, published in the *Daily Mail* in 2016. One of the photographs has never left me. It shows a very young child, barely old enough to walk, holding a baby—presumably a sibling—on the rubbish pile they called home, amid the toxic waste discarded by a consumer society . . . the very same commercial machine that deems artistic expression unworthy of study. The rest of their story, of two sisters who take equally creative paths—into engineering and fine art—is entirely my imagination.

For Royal Hastings, I pictured the breathtaking architecture of Royal Holloway in Egham, Surrey, where in 2006, at the age of thirty-seven, I studied for an MA in Screenwriting. It helped me change the direction of my life and led, eventually, to this book. I loved every minute of that course and can only recommend returning to education later in life to anyone considering doing so. Everyone there was a talented creative, none more so than its tutor, film director and activist Sue Clayton. I can't thank her enough for selecting me; nor Ross Olivey, Heather Wallis, Stephen Roberts, Amanda Smith, Adam Rolston, Anna Thomson, Dean Pollitt, Jonny Laker, and Alex Gabbay for being my wonderful, supportive coursemates, who were nothing whatsoever like the characters in this book.

The Examiner is dedicated to Samantha Thomson and Alison Horn, but not just because they are my friends of almost fifty years. Both are inspirational art teachers, who continue to wave the flag for art education in the face of its critics. Thanks to them for their insight into that world and especially the process, scope, and limitations of epoxy resin.

Thanks also to Ellie Horn, who brought me up to speed with what it's like to be a BA student of fine art in the twenty-first century.

My writing world is made so much better by my fellow Viper authors: Tina Baker, Guy Morpuss, Kate Griffin, Kate Simants, Leonora Nattrass, David Jackson, Dan Malakin, James Mylet, Joanna Wallace, Catriona Ward, Oskar Jensen, and Tariq Ashkanani.

My friends are all I could ever wish for. They have cheered me on in this wild publication journey from day one and continue to do so wherever I am in the world. Sharon Exelby, Carol Livingstone, and Wendy Mulhall are my coven of former Raglan Players whose backstage support I wouldn't be without. Felicity Cox, Keith Baker, and Terry and Rose Russell have also been key players in my life, onstage and off.

Lastly, Ann Saffery is without doubt my leading lady: we are approaching a half-century of friendship, which seems impossible when we feel barely out of our thirties. But the person I always reserve my final word of thanks for is Gary Stringer. In January 1984 he was cast as my other half in a Raglan Players' production of Alan Ayckbourn's *Confusions*. He's played that role with the same quiet strength and commitment ever since.

About the Author

Janice Hallett is a former magazine editor, award-winning journalist, and government communications writer. She wrote articles and speeches for, among others, the Cabinet Office, Home Office, and Department for International Development. Her enthusiasm for travel has taken her around the world several times, from Madagascar to the Galapagos, Guatemala to Zimbabwe, Japan, Russia, and South Korea. A playwright and screenwriter, she penned the feminist Shakespearean stage comedy *NetherBard* and cowrote the feature film *Retreat*. She lives in London and is the author of *The Examiner*, *The Mysterious Case of the Alperton Angels*, *The Appeal*, *The Christmas Appeal*, and *The Twyford Code*.